FAUN & GAMES

PIERS ANTHONY

FAUN
&
GAMES

TOR®

A TOM DOHERTY ASSOCIATES BOOK

NEW YORK

This is a work of fiction. All the characters and events portrayed in this novel are either
fictitious or are used fictitiously.

FAUN & GAMES

105737

This book is printed on acid-free paper.

A Tor Book
Published by Tom Doherty Associates, Inc.
175 Fifth Avenue
New York, NY 10010

Tor Books on the World Wide Web:
http://www.tor.com

Tor® is a registered trademark of Tom Doherty Associates, Inc.

Library of Congress Cataloging-in-Publication Data

Anthony, Piers.
    Faun and games / Piers Anthony.—1st ed.
        p.   cm.
    "A Tom Doherty Associates book."
    ISBN 0-312-86162-1 (acid-free)
    I. Title.
    PS3551.N73F38   1997   97-19362
    813'.54—dc21   CIP

First Edition: October 1997

Printed in the United States of America

0 9 8 7 6 5 4 3 2 1

Contents

1
FORREST

H ey, Faun, how about some fun?''
Forrest Faun rubbed what remained of his night's
sleep out of his eyes and looked down to the base of
his tree. There stood a fetching nymph with all the usual nymphly
features: pretty face, flowing hair, perfect figure, and no clothing. But
there was something amiss.

"What do you mean?" he asked as he sat up in a fork, still getting
his bearings.

"What do you think I mean, Faun? Come down and chase me, the
way fauns always do to nymphs."

Then he had it. "You're no nymph."

"Oh, pooh!" she swore, pouting. She dissolved into smoke and
reformed as a luscious clothed demoness. "I am D. Mentia, out seeking routine entertainment or mischief while my better half waxes
disgustingly motherly. What gave me away?"

"If I tell you, will you go somewhere else?" It was usually possible to get rid of demons if one made a suitable deal with them.

"Yes, if you want me to." Her bright yellow dress fuzzed, showing
the vague outline of her body beneath, with almost a suggestion of a
forbidden panty line.

So there was a catch. "Why wouldn't I want you to?"

"Because I have dreadful information that will puzzle and alarm
you and perhaps change your whole outlook."

That seemed like adequate reason. Forrest, now fully awake, jumped down to the ground, landing neatly on his hoofs. "What gave you away was your manner. You were not acting like a nymph. You were way too forward and intelligent. Much of a nymph's appeal is in her seeming reticence and lack of intellect. Now what's this dreadful information?"

"Follow me." Mentia whirled in place, so that her body twisted into a tight spiral before untwisting facing the opposite direction, and walked away. Her skirt shrank so as to show her legs as far up as was feasible without running out of limb. But of course Forrest didn't notice, because nothing a demoness showed was very real.

She led him across the glade to a tree on the far side. "See."

Forrest stared with dismay at the clog tree. It was wilting, and its clogs were falling to the ground. That could mean only one thing: it had lost its spirit.

As it happened, the clog tree's spirit was Forrest's friend: Branch Faun. They had known each other for almost two centuries, because their two trees were in sight of each other. Almost every day Forrest would drop out of his sandalwood tree, and join Branch in the glade between them to dance a jig or two. With luck, their jigging would attract the fleeting attention of a nymph or three, who would join in, jiggling. With further luck, jig and jiggle would lead to a pleasant chase and celebration.

But this morning Branch's tree was in a sad state. It wouldn't fade so soon if its faun were merely absent; fauns and nymphs shared an awareness with their trees that alerted them instantly if harm came to either. Let a human forester even come near such a tree with an axe, and its faun would have a fit. Let a faun split a hoof, and his tree would shudder. Such reactions were independent of distance; a faun could run far away from his tree, and still be closely attuned to it. They felt each other's pain.

"Are you trying to ignore me?" Mentia asked warningly. Demonesses could handle almost anything except that.

"No. You're right. I am puzzled and alarmed by this dreadful scene. Do you know anything about it?"

"No. I just happened to note it in passing, so I looked for the closest creature who might be tormented by it."

He glanced at her. "You're one crazy organism."

"Thank you," she said, flushing red with candy stripes. The color extended to her clothing and hair, and traces of it radiated into the air around her.

The clog tree's distress meant that Branch was in serious trouble, if not dead. What could have happened? Branch had been fine yesterday. In fact he had encountered a nymph from a lady slipper tree whose slippers gave her special fleetness, just as the sandals from Forrest's sandalwood tree gave him excellent footing, and the clogs from Branch's tree protected his hoofs. They had had quite a merry chase. Because that was what fauns and nymphs did; they chased each other until they came together, and then they celebrated in a manner that children were not supposed to see. Because it did tend to get dull just sitting in one's tree all the time.

In fact, Forrest now remembered, the nymph, clad only in her slippers, had led Branch a chase right out of sight. Meanwhile her friend from an oak tree, named Kara Oke, had done some very nice singing to background music of wind through trees, so Forrest had had his own distraction. Naturally he had chased her, and naturally she had fled, but not too swiftly, because she was still singing her oak song. So he had caught her, and they had celebrated in the usual fashion, while she continued singing. That had been interesting, because she had sung of every detail of the experience they were sharing, making it a work of musical art. Then she had returned to her tree, satisfied that her song worked. There weren't any other nymphs around at the moment, so Forrest had returned to his own tree and settled down for the night. And now his friend was gone.

"So what are you going to do about it?" Mentia inquired.

Do? She was right; he probably should be doing something. But what? "What do you think?"

"I think you will follow their footprints, so you can find out what happened to them."

"Now that's really sensible," he agreed.

The demoness turned smoky black. "Darn!"

He set off in search of them. He had no trouble following their tracks: her slipper prints, which were hourglass shaped, in the manner of the nymph herself, and his clog prints, which were forceful and furred. They looped around other trees, as she made cute dodges and diversions. It was the chase that counted; fauns and nymphs loved to run almost as much as they loved to dance. The better the chase, the better the celebration at the end. Forrest remembered a nymph once who had been in a bad mood, because her tree was suffering a fungus infestation, and had simply stood there. This was of course a complete turn-off, and no faun had touched her. Any nymph who wanted nothing to do with any particular faun had only to refuse to move, and he would leave her alone. Sometimes a nymph teased a faun, pretending disinterest, then leaping into pursuit the moment he turned his back. If she caught him, it was her advantage, and he had to do whatever she wanted. Of course that was exactly the same as what he wanted, but other fauns would taunt him unmercifully for getting caught.

Mentia, floating along beside him, was getting bored. "Are you ready for me to depart?"

"Yes," he agreed absently.

"Good." She remained where she was. He realized that he should have urged her to stay; then she would have been sure that he was up to nothing interesting.

The tracks veered toward the Void. That was the nearby region of no return. Of course every faun and nymph knew better than to enter it, because there was no way out of it. Anything that crossed the boundary was doomed. Only special creatures, like the night mares, could escape it, because they weren't real in the way ordinary folk were. They had very little substance.

"Don't float too near the Void," Forrest warned the demoness.

She changed course to approach the boundary, then paused. "Say, you are a cunning one!" she said with admiration. "You knew I'd automatically do the opposite. It almost worked, too. But I'm only a little crazy. You have to be a lot crazy to venture into the Void."

"Maybe next time," he muttered.

The nymph was clearly teasing Branch, by passing flirtingly close to the fringe of the Void. Her prints almost touched the boundary, then moved away, then came close again. The menace of that dread region added to the thrill of the chase. Forrest had done it too, and knew exactly the steps to take to be sure of never straying across the line.

Then his sandals balked. He stopped, perplexed; what was the matter? His sandals were magic, and protected his hoofs from harm, and if he were about to step somewhere harmful, they stopped him. Yet he saw nothing ahead to be concerned about.

"So what's with you?" Mentia asked. "Tired of walking?"

"I didn't stop," he explained. "My sandals did."

"Say, I'm getting to like you. You're almost as weird as I am."

"That's impossible."

"Thank you." This time her flush of pleasure was purple with green polka dots, and it extended down her legs and out across the ground around her. "So why did your sandals stop?"

"I'm not sure. Maybe it was a false alarm."

Still, his sandals had never yet been wrong. So he dropped to his furry knees and examined the ground before him. It was ordinary. There were a few smiling gladiolas, the happiest of flowers, and beyond them some horse radishes were flicking off flies with their tails. He thought of asking the nearest horse if it knew of anything harmful here, but he didn't understand plant language very well, and in any event all it would say would be "neigh." So finally he got up and made a detour around the place.

"Oh, well," the demoness said, disappointed.

But now he couldn't find the trail. Both sets of tracks were gone. So he turned back—and that was when he saw it. A splinter of reverse wood on the ground. He was sure of its identity, because the gladiola closest to it was drooping sadly. And right across it was a lady slipper print. The nymph had inadvertently stepped on the splinter. It hadn't hurt her directly, because it was lying flat. But it must have affected the fleet magic of her slipper, so that she had lost her sure footing.

"You see something," D. Mentia remarked astutely.

Now he saw the clog-print next to it, and realized the awful truth. The nymph had lost her balance, because of the reversal of her slipper magic, and teetered on the edge of the boundary of the Void. Branch had collided with her, caught by surprise by her sudden stop. And the two had sprawled into the Void.

"Yes. They are gone."

It was a freak accident, the kind that would happen hardly once in a century. The reverse wood splinter might have been blown there recently by an errant gust of wind. It would have been harmless, except when it came into contact with something magical. Then that abrupt reversal—

Branch and the nymph were lost. They would never get out of the Void. And their trees would suffer, for without its spirit a magical tree slowly lost its magic and became, O dreadful destiny, virtually mundane. It was a fate, many believed, worse than extinction.

"I'm sorry," the demoness said. "That means that you won't be entertaining me any more."

Forrest had no idea where the nymph's tree was, but knew it was suffering similarly. He hoped there would be another nymph free to join it and save it. Meanwhile, he did know where Branch's tree was. But what could he do? He could not care for two trees; the relationship didn't work that way. He was bound to his sandalwood tree. He knew of no fauns looking for trees. There were more trees than amenable fauns and nymphs, so that some trees that might have flourished magically became ordinary. It was sad, because the right trees had much to offer their companion spirits, but true.

Then he thought of something. It was a vanishingly tiny chance, but marginally better than nothing. "You're a spirit," he said to the demoness. "How would you like to adopt a tree?"

"You mean, become a tree dryad, so that I would live almost forever and always protect it?"

"Yes. It's a worthy occupation. It doesn't have to be a nymph. Any caring spirit will do, if the commitment is there. And the clogs would protect your feet."

"Commitment. Protected feet." She tried to look serious, but smoke started puffing out her ears, and finally she exploded into a hilarious fireball. "Ho ho ho!"

Then again, maybe the notion had been worse than nothing. Demons had no souls, because they were the degraded remnants of souls themselves. They cared for nothing and nobody. "Sorry I mentioned it."

"Oh, I'm not! That was my laugh for the day." The smoke coalesced into the extraordinarily feminine female woman distaff luscious shape of girlish persuasion with the slightly translucent dress. "A tree nymph! You are a barrel of laughs." She formed into a brown barrel with brightly colored pancake-shaped laughs overflowing its rim.

Forrest ignored her as well as he could, and headed for his home tree. How could he have been so stupid as to make such a suggestion to a demoness?

She followed. "The oddest thing is that my better half well might have agreed, were she not otherwise occupied. She has half a soul. But also a half mortal child, so she's busy. I'm the half without the soul."

As if he couldn't have guessed. "You could share the soul of the tree."

"The soul of a shoe tree," she exclaimed, her laughter building up another head of steam. "A clog sole. Protecting my feet. Oh, hold me, somebody; I think I'm going to expire of mirth." Her body swelled until it burst and disappeared, leaving only a faint titter behind.

This time, it seemed she really was gone. But Forrest didn't chance it; he walked directly back without looking around.

When he returned and looked at the clog tree, his heart sank into his stomach. The poor thing was so droopy and sad. It was all that remained of his friend Branch. He had to do something to help it.

He walked up and put a hand on the trunk. "Have confidence, clog tree. I will find you another spirit. Just give me time to do it."

The tree must have heard him, because its leaves perked up and became greener. It knew him, because he had been near it many times, and was the friend of its faun. It trusted him to help it.

He had promised, and he would do his best. Some folk thought that fauns and nymphs were empty-headed creatures, incapable of feeling or commitment, but those folk were confusing types. The creatures of the Faun and Nymph Retreat had no memory beyond a day, so every new day was a new adventure. But that was the magic of the retreat; any who left there started to turn real, which meant they aged and had memories. Some preserved their youth by finding useful jobs. Jewel the Nymph had taken on the chore of spreading gems throughout Xanth, so that others would have the delightful challenge of finding them, and later she had married a mortal man and become a grandmother. Many others had adopted magical trees, just as Forrest had. It was a kind of symbiosis, which was a fancy word meaning that the two got along great together and helped each other survive. The trees kept the fauns or nymphs young, because trees lived a long time and their spirits shared that longevity. The fauns or nymphs protected their trees, bringing them water in times of drought and harassing woodsmen who wanted to chop the trees down. Nymphs had very effective ways to distract woodsmen, or to persuade them to spare their trees. Sometimes a nymph would even marry a woodsman, if that was what it took. But her first loyalty was always to her tree. Fauns had other ways, such as setting booby traps or informing large dragons where a nice man sized meal could be had near a certain tree. One way or another, they protected their timber, as well as enhancing the natural magic of the trees.

But the sudden loss of Branch left the clog tree in trouble. Such relationships were not lightly made or broken. A faun who lost his tree died, and a tree who lost its faun turned mundane, an even sadder state. So he had to find a replacement.

"If only I had the faintest notion *how*," he said in anguish.

There was a swirl of smoke. It formed into a large pot labeled SEX. "I should have thought a faun already knew how," it said. "But I suppose I could show you, if—"

He should have known that the demoness hadn't really gone. She was still hoping he might do something entertaining. "How to find a suitable spirit for the clog tree," he clarified. "Naturally you have no better notion than I do."

"Naturally not," the pot agreed, its label changing to KETTLE as it turned black. "I would never think of going to ask the Good Magician Humfrey. The last time I suggested that, I had to guide a stupid gargoyle there, and he wound up saving Xanth from whatever. Actually that adventure did have its points; it certainly was interesting." The kettle formed back into the luscious lady shape. "So there's no point in suggesting it, especially since the Good Magician charges a year's Service for an Answer. So you might as well abandon all hope and just let the stupid tree die."

"I'll go see the Good Magician!" Forrest exclaimed. Then he realized that she had tricked him into reacting, just as he had tried to trick her. He had said it, and the clog tree had heard; its leaves were becoming almost wholesome. Now he had to do it. But a year's Service? "I can't leave my own tree that long," he protested belatedly. "And I don't even know the way there."

"You need a guide," Mentia said. "I need to go bother my better half some more, but I can find a friend to show you the way to Humfrey's castle."

"I don't want any friend of yours!"

"Excellent. You will find her just as lusciously annoying as I am. I'll be right back with her." The demoness popped off.

Again, he had said the wrong thing. But he was now committed to going. How would the trees fare during his absence? He didn't want them to suffer, but there didn't seem to be much of an alternative.

But there might be a way to get some help on that. There was a cave nearby, where a nice cousin of Com Pewter dwelt. She was Com Passion, and she loved everybody, because a love spring flowed in her cave. Her powers were limited, but she would do any favor she could manage for the local folk. Maybe she would be able to help the trees.

Unfortunately, there was a complication about dealing with her, which was why he normally stayed clear. But at the moment he didn't seem to have much choice. He would just have to hope that it would work out all right.

He fetched his knapsack, which he always used when going far from his tree, and ran through field and dale until he came to Passion's cave. Lovely purple flowers grew at its entrance, and the scent of the air was sweet.

Oh, no! He had in his haste forgotten something important. It was usual to bring a little gift to Passion when visiting her. It wasn't exactly to put her in a good mood, because she was always in a good mood. It wasn't just protocol, either. It was that a gift tended to make her feel that she should do something in return—and he really needed that return favor.

What could he find for a gift? Passion's main weakness was that she couldn't do anything physical. She couldn't walk out of her cave and see the sights or pick the flowers. So sometimes folk brought her stories of the things outside, to keep her informed. But he suspected he would need more than that.

Then he remembered something. The chips! Passion loved chips. What she did with them no one knew, but she truly valued them. He knew where some nice chips grew.

He ran to the glade where the chips were. Sure enough, there was a nice new crop of them. Chips of every kind grew in profusion. Which ones would please her most? He pondered briefly, then went for a Potato Chip. The moment he harvested it, he felt the urge to speak, and his words were really salty. He also felt extremely thirsty. He quickly put it into his knapsack and sealed it shut.

Across the glade was a brown region. He went there and harvested a Chocolate Chip. It smelled good enough to eat, but he didn't dare take time for that now. If he ate one, he might get a hunger for more, and be unable to stop. So he popped it quickly into his bag.

One more should do it. He looked around, and saw an old block in the center of the glade. So he went and took a chip off that. It was very stubborn and didn't want to turn loose, but when he touched it he got stubborn too, and finally did pry the chip off the old block.

Now he was as ready as he could be to face Com Passion. That wasn't nearly enough, but it would have to do. He ran back to her abode.

He nerved himself and entered the cave. It was very nice inside. He knew that it was really a rather ordinary cave, but the overflow from the love spring ran through it, and some of the water evaporated and suffused the air. That was part of the complication. He would have tried to breathe through a cloth or something, but that would be impolite, and impoliteness was bad form when one came begging a favor. So he took it in stride, and his stride was good. He reached the center, where reclined a device fashioned of passion wood. He stopped and took a breath.

Before he spoke, a screen lighted. *Who is there?* it inquired in neat cursive script.

"Forrest Faun," he said. "From the nearby sandalwood tree."

Why dear boy, how very nice to see you! the screen said, with a sweet row of hearts across the bottom: ♥♥♥♥♥♥♥♥♥♥♥♥

"Uh, likewise, I'm sure," he said. This wasn't going well. "Uh, I brought you a gift."

The screen glowed brightly. *Why how very thoughtful of you, dear boy!* And the hearts grew larger. ♥ ♥ ♥ ♥ ♥ ♥

Not well at all! "Uh, here they are." He fumbled in his bag and pulled out the Chocolate Chip. "A sweet for the sweet." He found another chip and fumbled it out. "A salt for the salty." Oops; that wasn't right. So he rushed on to the third: "And a chip off the old block for the stubborn." Worse yet!

☺ *Why dear boy, I believe you are flustered* ☺ the screen said, smiling.

"Uh, yes," he confessed. He was two centuries old, but felt like an adolescent elf.

How very sweet. The screen turned Valentine pink. *And what is your request of me, dear boy?*

Forrest launched into his story of the fate of Branch Faun and the need to save his tree. "So I must go ask the Good Magician what to do," he concluded. "But I can't even leave my own tree that long, safely. So I thought maybe you could, well, sort of change reality to make the trees all right, for a while, if you wanted to, until I get back." Suddenly it seemed rather stupid.

So all this is just to help a tree?

"Yes," he confessed, feeling woefully inadequate. The whole notion was ridiculous. He would have to find some other way. "But I guess you have more important things to do. I'm sorry I bothered you."

Dear boy, you have such a generous spirit, I really like you. Of course you must save the tree. I will help you.

"You will?" He was amazed. He had thought it so trivial, as far as anyone else was concerned, but now it seemed important again.

Yes. Of course I have my price.

Dread surged back. What changed reality would she require of him? "Yes."

You know I have a romantic nature, but that I am a machine. I can only dream of love, not actually experience it.

"Yes." This sounded worse.

But I can on occasion approximate love, if I have a cooperative partner.

She could? What was she going to make him do? But he was stuck for it. "Yes."

Kiss my mouse.

"But you don't have a mouth, Com Passion."

Not mouth. Mouse.

"What?"

I have a mouse, she explained patiently. *I want you to kiss it. What term do you not understand?*

"But—a mouse?"

A small living creature, useful for going where I am unable to go. In this case, romance.

She thought it would be romantic for him to kiss her mouse? "I—if I have to—"

Be thankful I managed to exchange the donkey I had recently for the mouse. It was an asinine creature.

He certainly wouldn't have wanted to kiss her asinine creature. "Okay."

Then the cave chamber shimmered, and he knew she was changing reality. It became a lovely glade surrounded by red, green, purple, yellow, and orange trees, with their assorted round fruits of similar colors, and flour plants growing in the center. From the far side came the prettiest nymph he could remember seeing, with thick lustrous brown hair that spread out to form a cloak for her body. But it could not conceal the elegant curves of that graceful form as she walked.

She came up to him as he stood somewhat bemused by the change. He had not expected a reality shift of this magnitude. And what was the nymph doing here?

"I am Terian," she said. "Kiss me."

"But I'm supposed to kiss a—a mouse," he said.

"I am that one. I am the Mouse Terian. I am older than I look."

"You're the mouse?" He stared at her. "But you're beautiful!"

"Thank you. It has been forty millennia since I have had a compliment like that. Others have thought me to be primitive or crude."

"Oh, you are neither of those things! You are the loveliest creature I can imagine."

"Thank you. Now you must kiss me, for I can't kiss you. I don't know how."

"Like this," he said enthusiastically. He folded her lithe and softly yielding body in his arms and kissed her firmly on her luscious lips. At first she was hesitant, but then she got into the feel of it and kissed him back. What had been a halfway experimental effort became a full-fledged delight.

After a wonderfully long time he felt obliged to break it off. For one thing, he had forgotten to breathe. He looked into her deep brown eyes. "Oh, Terian, that was the greatest kiss I ever had!"

"Thank you." Then she turned and walked back across the glade. Astonished, he just watched, not knowing what to make of it.

The scene shimmered, and the cave returned. He was staring at the screen, where the words *Thank you* were scripted.

"I don't understand," he said.

Mouse Terian could not stay. I can alter reality only so much. Perhaps some day someone will go out into the field and harvest me a cereal port so that I can make better use of the mouse. But she did enjoy your kiss. And so did I.

He was slowly and uncertainly recovering his grip on reality. "She—what is she like, really?"

A mouse ran up on top of the wooden frame holding the screen and stood on its hind feet for a moment, facing him. *Here.*

So Terian really was a mouse. He truly had kissed a mouse. Transformed by a temporarily local change of reality, but nevertheless a mouse.

Yet a detail didn't fit. "But she spoke to me! In sound."

I am rather proud of my sound system. As the words appeared on the screen, they came in sound too. *I was the one speaking.*

So it could all be explained. It had been crafted from sound and temporary reality. It hadn't really been a lovely nymph. Still, it had been impressive. "I think you are getting close to the feeling of romance, Com Passion," he said sincerely.

Thank you. Wait until I complete my next upgrade. Then more than kissing will be feasible.

That was somewhat daunting. "Is—is that all?"

Yes, unfortunately, for now. Take the two disks beside me and set one in each tree. They will alter the trees' reality slightly, so that your absence will seem like only a day. They will not wither or wilt. But you must be back within a month, or the effect will fade, and then they will suffer.

"Thank you," he said gratefully. He picked up the two small wooden disks and tucked them carefully into his knapsack.

Any time, dear boy. It was a pleasure.

He made his way outside. The fresh air cleared his head of the fumes from the love spring. He realized that in that ambiance he had wanted to experience the romance, and that must have helped the effect. What a woman Terian had seemed to be! Some day she would surely make some male mouse excruciatingly happy. And once Com Passion was fully compatible, she might make the notorious Com Pewter happy too.

There was a swirl of smoke before him. Two parts of it descended to the ground and formed into feet. The rest became a smoky nymph figure. "This must be the faun," she said.

"Of course it's me, Mentia," he said. "Who else would it be?"

The dark face frowned. "I am not Mentia."

Oops. Demonesses could be troublesome when annoyed. "I apologize. I thought any creature that lovely had to be Mentia."

"Oh you did, did you? Mentia's crazy. Consider this."

The form shifted and reassembled, becoming so exquisite that it was difficult to look at her without flinching.

"You're right," Forrest said, shielding his eyes with one hand. "That's twice as lovely as she was."

"And only half as lovely as I could be, if I cared to make the effort. Well, come on, faun; I don't have all week."

"Come on? Where?"

"To Humfrey's castle, of course. Where else did you think?"

A dim bulb flickered. "You're Mentia's friend!"

"Hmph. An exaggeration. But yes, I am Demoness Sire, and I did owe her half a favor. So I'll guide you there. But that's all. No round trip; that would require a whole favor. And I'm not going to make you deliriously happy enroute, so forget about that too."

"I wasn't even thinking of it."

She looked disappointed. "You weren't?"

This could be more mischief. "Well, I was trying to suppress the thought of it, with imperfect success. I am a faun, you know. We're related to the satyrs. We have similar urges, but more self control."

She considered. "Suppose I looked like this?" She became somewhat more luscious.

"Please don't, because then I would be thinking of it all the time."

"Suppose I became like this?" The scant clothing on her form shrank, causing parts of her to bulge dangerously.

"Then I would be so overwhelmed I'd be constantly grabbing for you, just like a satyr, unable to help myself."

She nodded, satisfied, and sagged into a lesser form. He was learning how to handle demonesses.

"But first I must see to the trees," he added. "Then I'm all yours— or would be, if I weren't struggling not to think of it."

D. Sire looked even more satisfied. She drifted beside him as he wended his way back to his home glade. "Is it true that nymphs & fauns have very little magic, apart from their longevity, empty-headedness, and insatiable urge to pretend to summon fleets of storks?"

"Flocks of storks," he responded shortly.

"Flocks. So it is true, cute-horns?"

"Not exactly. The magic of nymphs is to become phenomenally attractive to males when they run and bounce, so that any male who spies a running nymph is compelled to pursue her though he knows he can't catch her. The magic of fauns is to run fast enough to catch the nymphs, and to make them desire to celebrate when there is physical contact."

"Fascinating," she said, sounding bored. "Does it work on other females?"

"Why, I hadn't thought of that. I suppose if they removed their clothes and ran—"

"I mean the animal magnetism. Do real women get hot when a faun touches them?"

"Well, we don't chase real women. They know too much, and they aren't as well shaped. In addition, they often regard fauns as misshapen, and are repelled. So there's no way of knowing—"

"So they tend to avoid contact. But if it should happen, what then?'' She dropped to the ground and put her arms around him. Her upper section pressed into his chest in two firm places, and her lower section pressed his fur in one firmer place. ''Is this sufficient contact?'' Then her eyes grew large and dreamy. ''Oh, it's true! Suddenly I want to get much closer to you.'' The three places increased their pressures.

Forrest struggled to disengage. ''You're not a woman, you're a demoness. If I tried to celebrate with you, you would just dissolve into laughing gas.''

''True,'' she agreed, dissolving into puffs of vapor that spelled out HA HA. ''But nevertheless also true that your touch inspires a certain lust. So I shall make sure not to tease you from too close.''

''Thank you.'' It had been all he could do to stop from trying what she had been teasing him to try.

''Unless I change my smoky mind,'' she said, reforming into something luscious.

He went to the two trees, and tucked a disk into the lowest cleft of branches of each. The trees did not seem to change, but he trusted Com Passion. They should be all right. He fetched a spare pair of sandals, just in case, and put them in his knapsack. ''Now I am ready to go. Which way?''

''South. He lives below the Gap Chasm.''

''The what?''

''Don't tell me you don't remember! The forget spell wore off it years ago.''

''It isn't that I don't remember. It's that I never knew.''

''Oh. Well, it's a huge cleft in the ground that is impossible to penetrate unless you know how.'' She pursed her lips as she spoke the words ''cleft'' and ''penetrate,'' as if suggesting something naughty.

Forrest had no idea what nuance she was nuancing, so he ignored it. ''Will you tell me how?''

''Of course not. That's more of a favor than I owe Mentia.''

He had thought as much. Still, limited guidance was better than none. Maybe he would be able to ask along the way.

2
CHALLENGES

Forrest stood at the brink of a monstrous abyss that was yawning despite the fullness of day. So this was the dreaded Gap Chasm! It was indeed impressive.

"So how do you suppose you will get across this impassable abyss?" Demoness Sire inquired.

"I suppose I will have to find a place to climb down into it, cross the bottom, and find a place to climb up the other side. We fauns are good climbers, because of our hoofs."

"Ixnay, faun. The Gap Dragon ranges the depths, eagerly waiting for idiots like you to try just that. He's a six legged steamer, and chomps first and asks questions later."

"Well, maybe I can find a bridge across it. There must be one somewhere."

"Several. One's invisible. Another is one way."

"One way?"

"Whichever way you're going, it's going the other way."

Forrest had encountered a one way path in his day, so he knew how that worked. "Well, I'll keep looking. There must be some way that folk cross it."

"There is."

"And you won't tell me."

"That would be a smidgen over my half favor."

So he walked west along the brink. After an indefinite time, he heard a scrambling in the brush. He turned toward it, holding his sandalwood staff protectively before him. It would kick anything that turned out to be dangerous, giving him time to run to safety.

In two and a half moments he spied an odd animal caught in briers. It looked like a male werewolf, but couldn't be, because that would have changed to human form to pick away the prickly vines. As it was, the poor creature could hardly move, and more briers were reaching for it. They would soon coil completely around and prick it to death so they could feed on its blood.

Forrest didn't like briers much, so he decided to help the animal. "Could you use some assistance?" he called.

The not-werewolf looked at him. "Arf!"

Forrest wasn't sharp on animal languages, but he had a nodding acquaintance. That sounded like canine for "yes." So he used his staff to clear a path through the briers. They whipped around, striking at it, trying to stab it, but couldn't hurt the wood. The staff gave them increasingly hefty kicks in return, until they gave up.

He reached the animal, and carefully pried the briers from its body. Soon it was free. "Now follow me out, and stay close to my staff," he said. The animal nodded.

When they were safely out of the brier patch, Forrest turned to the animal. "If you don't mind my asking, who are you, and what kind of a creature are you? You seem like only half of a werewolf."

"Woof!" the animal replied.

"So your name is Woof."

"Oh, come on, you'll never get it that way," Sire said, appearing beside them. "You are wasting my time."

Forrest hardly spared her a dark glance. "You could save your time by telling me how to cross the Gap Chasm expediently."

She ignored that. "His name is Woofer. He's a Mundane dog."

Forrest was amazed. "A Mundane creature! I thought they were extinct."

"No such luck. There's more than a slew of them north of Xanth." She faded out in disgust.

Forrest looked again at the dog. "Well, Woofer, I've never met a real dog before. So you're Mundane! I suppose that means you are of limited intel—um, that you don't care to talk much. So I'll phrase yes/no questions. One bark for yes, two for no. Okay?''

''Woof!''

''Are you friendly?''

''Woof.''

''Do you have friends?''

''Woof.''

''Are you lost?''

''Woof.''

''Can you find your way back to them on your own?''

''Woof woof.''

''Then I had better help you find them. I'm not making much progress on my own anyway.''

''Disgusting,'' Sire said somewhere in air. ''I'll never get through this chore.''

''You know what you can do about it, demoness.''

''That would be unethical. Half a favor is half a favor, not half a whit more.''

''Where did you last see your friends?'' Forrest asked Woofer.

The dog bounded to the brink of the chasm and pointed upward with its nose.

''Over the pit? Can they fly?''

''Woof.''

''And you couldn't keep up with them, running on the ground. Or maybe you could, until you got into that brier patch. And they didn't realize you were caught, so don't know where you are.''

''Woof.''

''But maybe when they realize that you're gone, they'll fly back the way they came, and find you.''

''Woof!'' Woofer agreed, brightening.

''So let's wait here until they come. Then you'll be all right. Xanth isn't very friendly to a Mundane creature alone.''

''Woof.''

So they waited by the brink, gazing out, watching for flying creatures, while D. Sire faded in and out, her disgust expanding to its farthest boundaries. Forrest took some balm from his knapsack and spread it on Woofer's scratches and punctures, and they started healing.

Then Forrest's sharp eyes spied two things in the air. They might be birds, but they didn't fly like birds. "Maybe that's them," he suggested.

"Woof!" Woofer wagged his tail.

So Forrest waved violently, to attract their attention. The shapes veered toward him. Soon they showed up as two humanoid figures: a young man and a young elfin woman. She had wings, while he flew without wings. Evidently they were a couple.

Woofer bounded across to meet them as they landed on the brink. The young man hugged him, and the young woman kissed his nose. Then they turned to Forrest.

"Hello," he said, feeling abruptly awkward.

"Woof!" Woofer said, returning to him.

"You helped Woofer?" the man asked.

"He was caught in the brier patch."

"Woof."

"But those scratch something awful," the woman said. "He's unscratched."

"Woof woof."

"I used some balm," Forrest said. Then, still feeling awkward: "I'm glad he's safe now. I'll be on my way."

"Woof woof."

"But you *are* safe now, aren't you?" Forrest said to him. "These are your friends."

"I think he means that you helped him, so he wants to help you back," the man said. "Let's introduce ourselves. I'm Sean Mundane."

"I'm Willow Elf," the woman said.

"I'm Forrest Faun."

"And so you won't have to wonder, I really am Mundane," Sean said. "I visited Xanth, and fell in love with Willow. We—well, we ran afoul of a love spring without realizing it at first. She's large for an elf and flies because she associates with a very large winged elm tree. I returned to Mundania with her, and she found it a really weird place. Then when we came back to Xanth, suddenly I could fly. We don't know what happened, but it's great. Now we're just enjoying it. We hope to marry soon.''

Forrest realized that they were as curious about him as he was about them. ''I'm an ordinary tree faun. My neighboring tree lost its faun, so I am in search of a replacement faun for it, so it won't die or become—'' He hesitated.

''Mundane,'' Sean said. ''No affront; I know how awful that seems to Xanthians. Of course you don't want that to happen.''

''So I'm going to ask the Good Magician for advice,'' Forrest continued. ''Though I understand that he charges a year's Service for an answer, and I have to be back with my tree in a month. And I can't even find my way across this crevasse. So I'm not sure exactly what I'm doing.''

Sean and Willow exchanged a Significant Glance. Then she spoke. ''You helped Woofer, and we appreciate that. So maybe we can do you a return favor. I don't know how to solve your dilemma, but I think I know who might be able to help. I'll call her.'' She lifted a whistle she wore around her neck and blew on it.

In barely a moment there was a crashing in the brush as something huge charged through it. ''A dragon!'' Forrest exclaimed. ''You had better fly out over the gulf.''

''A dragon ass,'' she corrected him. ''Friendly.''

Indeed, now he saw that the dragon was striped and had the head of a donkey. It was forging through the brier patch, not even noticing the briers. And on it was a young woman half a shade lovelier than D. Sire in her seduction mode.

''Disgusting!'' the demoness agreed, forming beside him.

The dragon ass came to a stop before them. ''We heard your whistle,'' the beautiful woman said to Willow. ''How may we help?''

''This nice faun helped get Woofer out of trouble,'' Willow explained. ''We'd like to help him in return.''

The woman turned her graceful gaze on Forrest. ''I am Chlorine. My talent is poisoning water. This is my friend Nimby, whom I love more than anything in Xanth, and to whom I owe everything. His talent is making the two of us anything we want to be. We travel around, looking for good deeds to do. Who are you, and why are you worthy of a favor?''

"I am Forrest Faun, and I'm not worthy of any favor."

Chlorine glanced at Willow. "That's not true," the winged elf girl said. "He's trying to find a replacement faun for a tree that will fade or die otherwise. He needs to get across the Gap Chasm so he can go ask the Good Magician's advice. And he doesn't have time to serve a year there, because the tree will last only a month."

The woman's gaze returned to Forrest. "I gather you're not the smartest faun in Xanth, but you mean well."

That summed it up nicely. "Yes."

"So we'll help you," she decided. "Won't we, Nimby?" She leaned forward to hug the dragon's neck. They seemed to be the perfect combination: a beauty and a beast.

Nimby nodded yes. "I love you," Chlorine said, kissing his neck. "You gave me back my tear, and so much more."

Forrest gathered that there was more to that relationship than showed on the surface. Why should such a lovely woman care so much about such an ugly dragon? But that was the same kind of question others asked about fauns and nymphs with trees: why did they bind themselves to such unresponsive plants? There was no point trying to explain the wonders of the relationships to those who lacked any basis for understanding. Maybe Nimby protected Chlorine from other dragons, though he did not look very formidable. Maybe he just had a nice personality. Or maybe it was that great beauty was attracted to great ugliness.

Chlorine straightened up and looked at Forrest again. "Get on behind me," she said. "We'll take you across the Gap."

Forrest looked at the daunting vast void. "But how?"

She smiled, and the local scenery brightened. "You'll see."

So Forrest walked to the side of the dragon, and scrambled up on its back. But his perch seemed insecure. The dragon's small wings were right behind him, and Chlorine's remarkably contoured backside was before him.

"Put your arms around me," Chlorine said. "And hold on tight."

"But—"

She reached back and caught his hands, drawing them forward until his hands touched across her small waist. He clasped his fingers together. His face was almost in her flowing hair, which smelled of new mown hay.

The dragon strode forward, directly toward the brink. His head dropped down into the chasm, disappearing from view. Then the main body crossed the edge, turning at right angles. They were going down into the gap!

The sky seemed to whirl as they changed orientation. Terrified, Forrest clung tightly to Chlorine, expecting to plummet into the awful depths of the chasm.

But it didn't happen. He found himself jammed tight against Chlorine's shapely back, his thighs against her full hips, his face buried in her fragrant hair—and they weren't falling. Instead they were moving down the vertical wall, as if it were level. Chlorine's hair wasn't even out of place.

"Bye," Sean said, waving. He was floating beside them, but angled differently, because to him down was still down.

"It was nice meeting you," Willow said. She was flying similarly, her wings beating with a gentle cadence. Forrest felt the wind from them, and knew it was going down, but it was like a level breeze to him. He was anchored to the wall, and it had become his ground. The experience was weird, but not unpleasant.

"You can relax a little," Chlorine said.

Oh. He loosened the near death grip he had on her body. It really wasn't necessary.

Sean and Willow waved again, then flew away. There was a woof as Woofer followed them, running along the land beyond the chasm.

"Thank you!" Forrest called to them, remembering his manners. "And you," he added to the woman and dragon.

"It's just what we do," Chlorine replied. "Nimby and I have such good fortune that we try to share some of it with others, when the others are deserving."

"But I'm just trying to help a neighboring tree. That's not anything special."

"It's something generous and nice," she said. "The fact that you don't regard it as worthy of comment suggests that you are decent and modest. That's the type of person we like to help."

He was getting quite curious about her and the dragon. "If I may ask—"

"What's with the damsel and dragon ass?" she finished for him. "I'm just a somewhat dull, plain, indifferent girl with not much of a talent. But Nimby makes me beautiful and smart and healthy and nice, and now we live in the Nameless Castle where a full staff of servants takes care of our every whim. Once a month we go out around Xanth, looking for good deeds to do, in this minor way sharing our happiness with others."

"The dragon lives in a castle?"

She laughed, causing his linked hands on her soft but firm belly to shake. "Oh, Nimby changes to handsome princely man form for that, because he wouldn't fit very well in some of the passages in dragon form. And while I love him in any form, when it comes to sharing my bed, I prefer him as a man. More cuddly, you know."

She thought the dragon could become a man? That had to be delusion, because everyone knew that each creature had only one magic talent, and Nimby's was walking along vertical walls as if they were horizontal. So she must have a fond imagination. Her notions about her own body and personality were the opposite: she credited the dragon with making her beautiful, when it was plain that she was stunningly lovely on her own. Still, she and the dragon were doing him a favor, so it would be best not to disparage her notions. "That's nice," he said.

"You don't believe me, do you."

"I didn't say that."

"You didn't have to. But you don't."

"I mean no offense. But yes, I don't quite believe you."

"That's good. I don't want to be believed. Can you believe that Nimby and I are married, and that we spent a month on the far side of the moon, reveling in honey?"

"I do find that similarly hard to believe."

"Wonderful! I could probably tell you anything, and you wouldn't believe it. So I can be completely candid."

"Well, I wouldn't say that."

"If I told you who Nimby really is, you truly wouldn't believe me. So I won't bother."

Maybe that was just as well. The farther they rode, the less sense Chlorine was making.

As they continued down, D. Sire reappeared. "I trust you are having fun?" she inquired, glancing significantly at his hands.

"Yes, this is a remarkable experience," Forrest agreed. "I have never seen such a chasm before."

"I meant hanging on to Miss Water Poison, who looks good enough to drink."

Chlorine glanced at her. "Haven't you got some better errand elsewhere, demoness?"

Sire smirked. "No. I—" Then she looked surprised. "As a matter of fact I do." She faded out.

They reached the bottom of the gulf, for the dragon's big feet made for swift progress. They turned the corner and walked across the level bottom. Forrest looked up, and saw the rim of the chasm impossibly far above, and a couple of gnat sized specks that might be Sean and Willow.

Then he remembered something. "Isn't there supposed to be a Gap Dragon down here, that eats anyone who get caught?"

"He's not in this section at the moment," Chlorine said. "Did you want to meet him?"

"No! I want to avoid him."

"His name is Stanley Steamer, and he eats only folk he doesn't know. I could introduce you."

"Thanks all the same. I'd rather not."

"He has a really cute son named Steven Steamer. All the girls swoon over that baby dragon."

"I'm not a girl."

She laughed again. "Very well. No introduction. But if you should ever meet him, just say that Nimby sent you, and he won't eat you."

"Oh—you mean dragons don't eat the friends of dragons?"

"Something like that. The winged monsters, especially, are very honorable. They protect their own, and the friends of their own. But don't abuse the privilege. They have to make their living, you know."

By eating most folk they encountered. "I won't abuse it," Forrest promised. So was this more fantasy on her part, or was it valid? He hoped he never had occasion to find out.

They reached the far wall of the chasm, which wasn't far off, because the gulf was narrower at the base than at the top. Forrest knew that if he cared to ponder hard on that, he might conclude that this meant that the walls weren't quite vertical. But that intensity of thought wasn't worth the effort, so he didn't reach that conclusion.

The trip up was like the trip down, only now "forward" was toward the distant sky. The dragon seemed to have no trouble walking on the wall, and Forrest did not feel any great pull of gravity holding him back. Just the supple form of Chlorine's body as he kept his hands linked.

"You must be hungry," she said after a bit. "Have a dough nut. They're very filling." She made a quarter turn, and put a big spongy nut to his mouth so he could take it without letting go of her.

He opened his mouth and took it. It tasted very good, rather like fresh pie crust, and was surprisingly filling. "Thank you."

"You are welcome."

Forrest looked ahead and saw a dark cloud approaching. "That looks like Fracto, the worst of clouds," he said. "I hope he doesn't decide to wet on us."

"He wouldn't dare," Chlorine said.

However, the cloud came floating toward them, growing bigger and uglier by the moment. Until Chlorine tapped Nimby on a scale. "Mischief at two o'clock," she murmured.

The dragon lifted his head and glanced at the cloud. The cloud blanched, and then changed course, scudding swiftly away.

Forrest blinked. Surely he hadn't seen that. How could one glance from a comically stupid looking dragon dissuade as mean a cloud as Fracto? It must be an illusion. Maybe the woman's craziness was spreading to him.

They reached the top and bent around it. Things were on the level again.

The dragon stopped. "This is as far as we'll take you," Chlorine said. "There is a magic path right ahead. Follow that, and it will lead you safely to the Good Magician's castle."

"Thank you," Forrest said, sliding down to the ground.

"And don't be concerned about the year's Service," she told him.

"Humfrey won't require it of you. So you will be back with your tree in time."

"I will?" he asked, astonished.

"Yes. And I think happier than you have ever been." She shrugged. "But of course I don't know the future, so I could be wrong."

She seemed so reasonable in her madness! "Thank you," he repeated. "Thank you for everything."

She smiled, lighting up the local scenery again, and waved as Nimby started off into the jungle. He didn't seem to need a path. Forrest turned and followed the magic path.

In a moment he thought of something else, and turned back. A moment wasn't long, so he had plenty of time to catch them and ask his question. But when he returned to the brink of the Gap Chasm, there was no sign of damsel or dragon. He followed Nimby's tracks to the jungle's edge—and there they stopped. It was as if the creature had simply vanished without walking farther. Could he have flown? No, there was nothing in the sky. They were simply gone.

That was one curious pair of creatures! How could he query a vanishing donkey-headed dragon? Oh, well, he had forgotten his question anyway.

"Yes, they are really gone," D. Sire said, fading in.

"What happened to you?"

"I had a sudden urge to busy myself elsewhere. It didn't fade until you got free of Miss Poison. So I never got to see whether any bumps in the terrain caused your hands to bump up to her bumps."

Yet another evidence of the odd woman's power. She had banished a demoness! "Well, I no longer need your guidance, so you can continue your business elsewhere."

She shook her finger at him, and the shaking progressed down her arm and through her body. "Nuh-uh, faun. I have half a favor to complete."

"You have done so. I am now on a magic path leading straight to the Good Magician's castle."

She nodded, and the nodding spread down too. "So you are. But there is a further complication."

"I don't want to hear it."

"Good. The Good Magician always has three preposterous Challenges preventing a querent from entering his castle."

"Preventing a what?"

"A querent. A person who comes to make a query. That's you."

"So how do I handle those Challenges?"

"Sorry, that information is beyond my obligation."

He looked at her, annoyed. Then he realized that that was what she wanted. "Thank you. I appreciate the information. Now I am better prepared to handle the Challenges."

"Curses," she muttered. "Foiled again." She faded out.

He ran along the path, making excellent time. By some process he did not understand, it seemed to be earlier in the day than it had been when he first reached the Gap Chasm, so that he wouldn't need to spend a night halfway there. He wasn't hungry; the dough nut seemed to have fed him for a long time.

Indeed, in the afternoon he reached the Good Magician's castle. This was an appealing edifice, for those who might like that type, with red brick walls, green tiled roofs, and a bright blue moat. In the moat was a peculiar monster. It had the top of a man, and the body of a winged serpent, and it was huge.

There was a drawbridge, and the bridge was in the lowered position, crossing the moat. Somewhat hesitantly, Forrest approached the bridge.

"You'll be sorry," D. Sire murmured behind him.

"Then go away before you enjoy it too much," he said shortly, lengthening his stride.

Immediately the moat monster swam toward the bridge. "Come into my grasp, faun face," he said. "I haven't eaten in days."

Forrest stopped. The human portion looked fully strong enough to grab him and dispatch him, and the serpent portion looked capable of digesting him. There was no way he could avoid those arms, on the narrow bridge. So this must be a Challenge.

He looked around, but the moat seemed to circle the entire castle. He couldn't try to swim, because the monster would catch him that much easier. How was he going to get past?

A nonchalant man of indifferent persuasion came walking around the moat. "Do I perceive a problem?" he inquired.

"I am trying to cross the moat without getting grabbed and gobbled by the monster."

"Now that is a very interesting statement. Why do you wish to do that?"

"Because I need to talk to the Good Magician."

"Indubitably. Why do you wish to talk with him?"

"I need an Answer to a Problem."

The man nodded. "Has it occurred to you that you may be misdirecting your energies? You can't change the circumstance, but you can change yourself. Maybe you can solve your problem yourself, just by developing a better attitude."

Forrest glanced at him. "Who are you?"

"I am the castle psychologist. It is my business to talk to querents and try to enable them to solve their problems the old fashioned way: by themselves."

"If I could solve it myself, I wouldn't be coming here," Forrest said shortly.

"Now are you sure of that? Perhaps all you need is an adjustment of attitude."

Forrest's mood had not been great when he arrived at the castle, and it was deteriorating. "I think all I need is a way across that moat."

"Why do you feel that way?"

Forrest's ire was approaching the blow-off point. "If you're not going to help, I wish you'd go away so I can concentrate."

"I think we need to get at the root of your hostility. Did you have bad parenting as a child?"

"I never had parents!" Forrest snapped. "I'm a faun. We all get delivered to the Faun & Nymph Retreat, where we stay until we go."

"Do you want to talk about it?"

"No!"

The psychologist shook his head. "I'm afraid we have a difficult case here. This may require many fifty minute sessions. Why don't you make yourself comfortable, and we shall proceed."

A bulb flashed over Forrest's head. "You're part of the problem!" he said. "You're another Challenge!"

"By no means. I am a Solution. But you have to be amenable to it. Now I can help you, but you have to really want to change."

"I *don't* want to change! I want to get across that moat!"

"This hostility is doing you no good. I won't be able to help you if you don't develop a better attitude."

Forrest considered. If what the man said was correct, he was a Solution rather than a problem. But how could he help, when he just kept trying to distract Forrest, or to make him give up his quest?

Forrest forced a moderate expression to his face. "Exactly how do you help people?"

"I encourage them to talk about their feelings, in this manner expiating them. In the colloquial sense, I am called a shrink: one who shrinks the head, making it intelligible and less burdensome."

A shrink! Suddenly Forrest saw a possible way. "You know, I have problems. But as you say, they are complicated and will take a long time to shrink. On the other hand, I suspect that the problems of that moat monster are simpler, and can be shrunk in much less time. Why don't you help him first, so that there won't be a backlog?"

"Why that is an appealing idea," the psychologist agreed. He turned to the mer-dragon. "I say there—let's talk."

"What for?" the monster asked.

"I can see that you are troubled. I wish to alleviate your concerns and enable you to feel good about yourself."

"Of course I'm troubled," the monster said. "I'm a monster! Have you any idea how dull it gets being confined to a circular moat?"

"Yes, I can appreciate that. But you can't change the moat, you can only change yourself. Perhaps if you developed a better attitude about it, you would feel less troubled."

"I would?" The monster was interested.

Forrest sat back and watched while the two talked. And as they did, the monster gradually shrank in size. The shrink was doing his job.

"You cunning knave," Sire murmured behind him. "You figured it out."

"Well, I didn't want to get shrunk myself," he agreed, satisfied. "So I thought I'd get the monster shrunk instead."

When the monster was too small to reach the bridge, Forrest walked across to the castle. He was feeling halfway satisfied.

When he arrived at the inner shore, he discovered a set of metal tracks. Beyond them was a blank wall. The tracks and wall continued to either side, with no room around them; they marked the only level ground outside the castle.

So he picked a direction at random, and started walking between the tracks. Something swirled before him. "I wouldn't do that, if I were you," it said. "Fortunately I'm not you."

"Are you still here, D. Sire?" he inquired irritably.

"I have not yet quite fulfilled my half favor," she said, taking luscious shape.

He had to stop walking, lest he collide with her form and get pressed in three places again. "Why wouldn't you walk here, if you had the awful misfortune to be me?"

"Because the locomotive is coming, and there's no way to avoid it."

"Locomotive?" This was a new word to him. "What is that?"

"A great huge enormous giant crazy machine that thunders along these tracks, squishing anything in its path."

"Oh—like a big dragon?"

"No. More like a train of thought."

He looked at her. "You can be pretty irritating."

"It's the flip side of my nature. Those who are most capable of driving a man wild with longing, also are capable of annoying him beyond endurance. I suppose I could demonstrate." Her clothing began to fuzz.

Forrest closed his eyes to avoid being freaked out by the sight of her underclothing. He knew she had no intention of playing nymph & faun with him; she just wanted to drive him mad with desire. That was how demonesses entertained themselves: tormenting ordinary folk. "So what would you do, in my place?"

"I would get quickly back to the landing area. Very quickly."

Forrest heard an ominous rumbling. The tracks were shaking, and giving out sounds of incipient power. He turned, opened his eyes, and saw a bright light in the center of a black blob coming toward him. He ran back toward the bridge as fast as he could.

The blob expanded into a frighteningly large black onrushing machine. Jets of white steam sprouted from it, and big puffs of roiling smoke poured from a chimney at its top. A piercing whistle came from it.

Forrest dived for the bridge. He rolled and got his hoofs out of the way just as the monster engine thundered across, as Sire had predicted. He would have been squished flat, if she had not warned him.

"Thank you, demoness," he said. "You saved me from an uncomfortable experience."

She appeared above him, her skirt threatening to show too much of her legs. "Well, it would have been a waste, to have you squished into oblivion when I was only one and a half challenges away from completing my half favor."

"To be sure," he agreed. He forced his eyes away from her knees, or wherever, and climbed back to his feet. "Now what would you do, if you were in my place?"

"I would board that train before it gets moving again."

He realized that once it had missed him, the locomotive had puffed to a stop not far along the tracks. Behind it were hitched several cars, and the door to one was open right before him. It had many windows, in a row somewhat above the level of his head.

So he put a hand on a rail and stepped up the steps, into the end of the long car.

The whistle blew again, and the crazy engine puffed and resumed motion, struggling to haul the cars along behind it. The steps folded up behind Forrest, sealing him in. He was on his way somewhere.

"Of course I am not in your place," Sire murmured invisibly in his ear. "Mentia might be able to handle this situation, but I doubt I could."

"What do you mean?"

But she had faded out. He was on his own again.

There was only one way to go: on into the main portion of the coach. It was lined with plush seats, all of which were filled with unmoving human figures. They looked like statues, for their eyes never blinked. That made him nervous.

He walked along the center aisle until he found one seat that was empty. The coach was shaking and its floor was heaving as it got up speed, so it was hard for him to keep his feet. So he sat in that one free seat.

He heard a sound beside him. It was a young human woman, sobbing into a hankie.

Forrest had no good notion how to deal with human women, as he had not encountered many. His sandalwood tree was in a part of the forest where humans seldom wandered. But it bothered him to be so close to someone this unhappy. Since there was no other place to sit, he decided that he would have to try to deal with whatever was bothering the woman.

"Hello," he said. "I am Forrest Faun. Is there something I can do for you?"

She turned her head and looked at him with her tear-rimmed reddened eyes. "Eeeeek!" she screamed.

This set him back slightly. "Eeeeek?"

"A satyr! As if I didn't have trouble enough already."

Oh. "I am not a satyr," Forrest said firmly. "I am a faun. We are a related but less aggressive species. We chase after only willing nymphs."

Her eyes began to clear, and her sniffles to snuffle out. "You don't pursue innocent maidens?"

"Definitely not."

"Well, all right then. I am Dot Human, and my talent is making spots on the wall."

"I'm sorry."

"Sorry?"

"That you don't have a decent magic talent. Of course I don't have a talent at all, being only part human." He didn't count his natural faun traits as a talent.

"I have a decent talent."

"But you said—"

"I'll show you." She focused on the back of the seat before her. A picture formed on it.

Forrest stared. "But that's not a spot! It's a picture."

"It's lots of little spots. Dots. All different colors and intensities. So, taken together, they make up the picture."

He looked closely, and saw that it was true. The picture was composed of a multitude of tiny dots, so closely set that the moment he blinked they fuzzed back into the picture. "But that's a good talent. I thought you meant spot-on-the-wall as a euphemism for having a worthless talent."

"No, it's a good talent. But it's not doing me any good."

"Why not?"

"Because I'm stuck here behind the loco-motive, going crazy."

"Crazy?"

"That's what it does to you. Didn't you see all those other folk on this coach?"

"They look like dummies."

"That's because they have gone completely loco. There's no hope for them; they've crashed. But I'm not completely loco yet, so there's hope for me. That's why I'm crying." Her eyes began to brim again.

"I don't understand."

"By the time you understand, it's probably too late. The effect builds gradually. Each lap the locomotive makes around the castle makes it worse. You're still fresh; you're hardly crazy at all. And I guess being close to you makes me less crazy, for a while, until we both are overwhelmed."

Forrest was starting to catch on. "The longer we stay here, the crazier we become? Because of the locomotive?"

"Yes. I was pretty far gone, until you came in. But it won't last."

"Then we must get off the train before it gets us."

"We can't get off. Why do you think I was crying?"

"I wasn't sure. But I hoped to help. Why can't we get off?"

"Because it won't stop. The windows won't open, the doors won't open, and even if they did, look how fast it's going."

He looked out the window, and saw the wall rushing by at blinding velocity. He looked across the aisle to the far windows, and saw the moat passing just as swiftly. "But it stopped for me."

"It stops to let folk on, not to let them off."

"Why didn't you get off when it stopped for me?"

"I couldn't. The seat belt held me."

"What seat belt?" Forrest saw nothing of that kind.

"The automatic seat belt. It clasps you only when the train is stopping."

"So if someone else wants to get on, I'll be belted too?"

"Yes. It belts everyone, so no one will get hurt."

"But that's crazy!"

"Precisely."

"Well, we'll have to get out of our seats while it's moving, then stop it."

"I tried that. The coach is locked up. No way out of it. The locomotive won't stop unless everyone is secured."

A bulb lighted. "The Challenge! It's to make the train stop."

"I guess so," Dot agreed. "But I have no idea how."

"And if I don't figure it out pretty quick, I'll go crazy, and become another crash dummy."

"That's true."

Forrest pondered. He was starting to feel a bit unbalanced already, and he could only have been around the bend once or twice. But there had to be a way to get off the train. He just had to figure it out. Soon.

He saw no way, offhand. The limited scenery zoomed by unabated. Even if he could manage to open a window or door, it wouldn't be safe to jump out. He had to get the train to actually stop, without fastening him down with a seat belt. That seemed impossible.

But there did have to be a way. That was in the big book of rules, or whatever. He hoped. So what was he overlooking?

There hadn't seemed to be much way to cross the moat, either. But he had managed to use the psychologist to change things, so that it became possible. Too bad there wasn't another psychologist, to shrink the locomotive, until it couldn't pull them along so fast.

Then another bulb started to light, but he managed to suppress it before the woman saw it. There was another person, and she was it. She must be the key to escape. She wasn't a fellow trap-ee, she was part of the Challenge.

But her talent was merely spots on a wall. Very good spots, but how could spots stop a train? Unless—

"Dot, can you make a picture outside the train?"

"Well, if there's a surface close enough."

"Can you make a picture of a door through that wall?"

"I suppose. But the wall is moving. It would carry away my dots."

"No, *we're* moving. The wall is still."

"Oh. I suppose that's right." She focused on the wall, and in a moment a picture formed. It was a door. It seemed to be right opposite their window, unmoving.

"Very good," Forrest said. "Now can you make that door open?"

The door slowly opened, revealing a nice garden beyond.

"Now can you make a similar door in our window, and open it?"

The dots quickly formed a door, and it opened.

"Now all we have to do is go through those two doors, and we'll be there," he said with satisfaction.

"It won't work," Dot said sadly.

But he tried it anyway. He reached across her and put one hand through the nearer open door. And banged his knuckle. "Ooooh!" He brought his hand back.

"The window's still there," Dot explained. "So is the brick wall. So is the motion. All I do is pictures, not changes. It just *looks* different." The pictures faded out.

Forrest sighed. The doors were illusion; the window and wall were reality. He should have known. It had been a rather crazy idea.

Crazy. That figured.

He sat back and pondered some more. He didn't want any more crazy ideas, he wanted something that worked. What could he come up with, before his mind lost its common sense?

He still thought it related to Dot, and her talent. How could her talent stop the train? Not with illusion, but reality?

What he really needed was information. Like a manual of instructions, to know how to stop the train. But of course that was another crazy notion, because mere pictures couldn't provide that.

Or could they? Maybe it was worth a try.

"Dot, just how detailed can your pictures be?"

"Infinitely detailed," she said proudly. "I can make dots so small they can't even be seen individually."

"Then let's make a special picture. Of a manual. On the cover it says **LOCOMOTIVE OPERATING INSTRUCTIONS.** Can you do that?"

"Sure. But that doesn't require much detail." The picture appeared in the window, a book with the required words.

"Very good. Now can you open it?"

The cover turned, in much the manner of another door opening, revealing the title page inside.

"Show the contents page."

Another page turned, and CONTENTS showed.

Forrest leaned across to read it. Near the bottom of the page was a listing for Chapter 10: STOPPING. "Turn to page fifty," he said, reading the indicated page number.

The pages flipped across, stopping at 50. But the print was too small to read. "Can you make the page larger?"

The image expanded, until it filled the whole window, and the print was legible. Forrest read it avidly: TO STOP LOCOMOTIVE IN ITS TRACKS, PULL THE CORD ABOVE THE SEAT.

He looked up. There was the cord, that he hadn't noticed before. He reached up and pulled it.

There was a squeal as the train hurtled to a stop. Seat belts jumped out to clasp the two of them, as well as all the dummies in the rest of the coach. Oops—he had forgotten that detail.

"You did it!" Dot cried. "You stopped the train!"

"Can you show the contents page again?"

The pages turned back. He found the chapter for SEAT BELTS, and turned to that page: TO RELEASE SEAT BELT, PUSH BUT-TON THEREON.

Sure enough, there was a button. He pushed it, and the belt un-clasped him and disappeared on either side. Dot did the same. "You figured it out," she said, pleased.

"Let's get off this crazy train before it starts again," he said, stand-ing.

But she shook her head. "Thanks, no. This is your Challenge, not mine. My job is on this train of thought."

He had suspected as much. "Thanks for your help, anyway."

"It was a pleasure. You're a nice person."

He walked along the aisle to the end of the coach, where the door had folded down into steps. He stepped down and off. As soon as he did, the steps folded up again, sealing the train, and it started moving again.

"Well, I guess you got through that one," D. Sire said, fading into view.

"You can go any time, demoness."

He waited while the train rolled out of the way. Beyond the tracks was an open door in the wall just like the one Dot had pictured. He crossed the tracks and put out a cautious hand, just in case the doorway wasn't real. His hand didn't bang. He stepped through. He had won the second Challenge.

Suddenly he was horribly frightened. He reeled, staggering back through the door. His fear abated.

What had happened? He hadn't seen any monster or hurtling locomotive or anything; why had he been so suddenly and awfully afraid?

"I think you have a problem, faun." Sire faded out, satisfied.

He stepped forward again—and was blasted by the fear. He reeled back again, out the doorway. It was this place: he was afraid to enter it. But he had to enter it, because it was the only entrance to the castle he had found.

He stepped close to the entrance, stopping just short of the fear, and peered in. There was a small man, or maybe an elf, or maybe in between. "What's this?" he asked.

"Isn't it obvious? I am LA, the lost angel. I am here to help you enter the castle. But first you must conquer your foolish fear."

So it was the third Challenge. All he had to do was nerve himself and go on through. It seemed simple enough. After all, LA didn't seem to be afraid, so probably there was nothing to fear.

He tried again, and was balked again. There was nothing to fear except fear itself! He couldn't enter that chamber.

He pondered. The chamber itself must be imbued with fear, so that anyone who entered it was terrified. But then why wasn't the lost angel afraid too? Was there some secret way to nullify the fear? No, probably there was a special anti-fear spell on LA, so that he was immune. It wouldn't make sense to have the folk helping the Good Magician be afraid to do their duties.

In each case before there had been a barrier or threat of some kind, and a person of some type, and the person had been the key to the solution. Could this be the case again? He thought it would make more sense to have something entirely different, but he wasn't the Good Magician, and didn't know how the old man thought. So maybe there was a pattern, and the person would have the answer. But not anything obvious.

What would a lost angel have to do with fear? Maybe angels were beyond fear, so that was how he was able to be in that dread chamber. But Forrest was no angel, so he needed something else. Still, maybe he could talk to LA and learn something, as he had with the other two.

He looked in. LA was just sitting there, completely at ease. "I gather that there is a way for me to eliminate my fear, and that you know of it, but won't tell me," he said.

LA nodded. "You seem reasonably smart, for a faun."

"Not everyone considers me so," Forrest said. "I met a damsel and a dragon, and I think the damsel liked me, but thought I was a bit dull."

"Beauty is often in the eye of the beholder."

"She was extremely beautiful, so I must have been dull in contrast." Forrest considered how to proceed. "Do you have a magic talent?"

"Why yes. I can change one kind of wood to another kind of wood. Unfortunately there is no wood here, so I can't show you."

Something nagged at Forrest's mind, but he couldn't place it. So he talked some more, hoping to learn something useful. "You came to ask the Good Magician a Question, and he gave you his Answer, and now you are serving your years's Service for him?"

"Exactly."

"If it is not too personal, what was your Question?"

"It's not personal at all. It wasn't a Question, it was a request. I asked that a significant village be named after me. He told me that one already was, but that it was in Mundania. I suppose that's better than nothing."

"And for this you are glad to serve for a year?"

"It does seem inadequate. But that's what I get for wanting something stupid. I am learning a whole lot during this Service, and will depart here a much wiser creature. If I had known how it would be,

I would have dispensed with the Question, and simply come for the Service.''

That surprised Forrest. "Is it the same with Dot, and the psychologist?''

"Certainly. And for the mer-dragon too. And maybe for you, if you manage to get through.''

"The damsel said he would not require a Service of me.''

Now LA was surprised. "I find that hard to believe. He always requires a Service. It's his way of discouraging folk who aren't serious, just as is this business of three Challenges. Why should you be an exception?''

"I have no idea. Maybe it's not true.''

"Who was this damsel?''

"She called herself Chlorine. She said her talent was poisoning water. She rode a funny looking dragon.''

"Ah, the dragon ass. I have heard of him. They are an odd couple. Well, maybe they know what they are doing. I have heard that good things tend to happen when they are around, as if they somehow reverse the normal perversity of fate.''

Reverse perversity? Then, for no reason, Forrest got a notion. Reverse wood! Could that reverse the fright spell on the chamber? Of course he didn't have any reverse wood, but if LA cared to cooperate, he could get some.

"Will you do me a favor?'' he asked the lost angel.

"Within reason. What do you want?''

"I would like you to change some wood for me.''

"I'd be glad to. But I don't have any wood.''

"But I do.'' Forrest removed one of his sandals. "Will you change this sandalwood to reverse wood?''

LA smiled. "You *are* a clever one! Very well: bring it here.''

Forrest started to walk into the chamber—and was immediately beaten back by utter fear. Oh, no—he couldn't do what he wanted, because of the thing he wanted to eliminate.

But then he found a way. "I will toss it to you.''

He threw the sandal. LA caught it and held it. "Are you sure you want me to do this? There may be consequences.''

"I'll risk them. Change it to reverse wood."

"Very well. Done."

The sandal looked the same, but when Forrest tried to enter the room, he had no trouble. In fact he was drawn into it, delighting in its ambiance. Not only did he feel no fear, he felt absolutely fearless.

"Thank you," he said to the lost angel. "That worked perfectly."

"Did it?"

"Sure. My fear is gone. I'm having absolutely no trouble with this chamber. In fact I could stay here forever."

"That's nice." But LA seemed oddly subdued.

"Well, I must move on into the castle proper. But I'll need my sandal. Please change it back to sandalwood now."

"I can't do that."

"But you changed it before. Why can't you do it again?"

"Because the reverse wood reverses my talent. Now I can't change anything."

Forrest paused. The angel had warned him that there might be consequences. He hadn't paid enough attention.

"Maybe I can use it anyway," he said. "Let me put it on."

"Are you sure you want to do that?"

"I don't have any magical talent. I'm a faun. So it can't reverse it. If I take it away from you, your own talent should revert to normal, so you'll be okay. And who knows—maybe I'll find some future use for reverse wood. So, yes, this seems the best way."

LA gave him the sandal, and he put it on. But he felt suddenly quite odd. His hair seemed longer than usual, and his body felt different. His feet felt oddest of all. What was the matter?

He looked down, and saw his legs and feet. He stared. They were human! They had five toes, and were fleshy, with solid heels.

Then he traced the lines of his legs upward. They were human, with far more flesh than his goat legs ever had had, and got really fleshy near the tops. And above that—

"Oh, my," he breathed, appalled. "I'm a nymph!"

"It seems that the reverse wood reversed your nature," LA said. "You are now a fine looking female."

"But I don't want to be a nymph!" he (she) protested.

"Then take off the sandal."

That made sense. He tore off the sandal, threw it across the room, and felt his body reverting to normal. He was himself again.

"I guess I'll have to do without the sandal," he said. "I'll use my spare pair." He removed the other sandal, put it in his knapsack, drew out the other pair, and put them on.

"You may still have a problem," LA remarked.

"Not if I stay well clear of that reverse wood. I'll just step on into the main castle, leaving it behind." He paused. "Unless it makes things too difficult for you."

"Have no concern about me. I'm here for the duration, regardless. My job is here; I'm a prisoner of this chamber. Your visit has helped relieve the boredom."

"Okay. Then I guess it's farewell, and thank you." Forrest walked to the doorway into the rest of the castle.

But as he passed through it, sudden terror gripped him. He reeled back into the chamber, and the fear faded.

Then he realized what had happened. "The spell is reversed. Now the chamber is fine, but I'm afraid to leave it."

"I know the feeling," LA said.

"But how can I see the Good Magician, if I can't leave the room, and you can't change the reverse wood?"

"It is a question."

A question he had to answer for himself. So he walked around the chamber, pondering hard.

"What, stuck again?" D. Sire inquired mockingly from the doorway leading out to the tracks and moat.

He had had enough. He ran to the reverse wood sandal, picked it up, and hurled it at her. In the course of that action he felt himself changing, and changing back.

The wood passed right through her. "Oooh, that smarts," she cried, flapping her hands to bow the smoke away from a sandal-shaped hole in her mid-section.

The sandal splashed into the water of the moat beyond her. The water shuddered and turned to fire. There was a scream of outrage from the moat monster, who must have had to scramble to land. A little reverse wood in the wrong place could be a lot of mischief.

But Forrest's problem had been solved. The chamber was now normal, and so were his emotions. ''Thanks for your help, demoness,'' he called out one doorway, then walked out the other, into the main castle.

3
IMBRI

A young woman greeted him in the hall. "Hello, Forrest Faun," she said. "I am Wira, the Good Magician's daughter-in-law. He is ready to see you now."

"Just like that?" He was surprised to have such ready acceptance, after the complications of the Challenges.

"He has been most interested in your progress. This way, please."

Magician Humfrey had been following his case? The Challenges had seemed designed to confuse or discourage him.

Forrest followed the woman through dull passages and up a dark stairway. He wondered how she could be so sure-footed, in such poor lighting.

Soon they were at a study so gloomy that "dingy" would be inadequate to describe it. Within it a gnome sat hunched over a huge tome. "Forrest Faun is here, Good Magician," Wira said.

The gnome looked up. "Thank you, dear." It was probably illusion, but there almost seemed to be a nuance of affection when he spoke to her. "Send him in."

Wira turned to Forrest. "Go on in," she said. There was something odd about her gaze, which did not quite meet his own.

Then he realized what it was: she was blind. That was why she was indifferent to darkness.

Embarrassed for no reason he could settle on, he walked on into the Magician's crowded study. "My Question is—"

"Yes, yes, of course," the Magician said impatiently. "Imbri will be here in a moment."

"But how can you Answer, if you don't hear my Question?"

"I am not going to Answer, because I won't charge you a Service. Now stop wasting my time."

Forrest experienced an unusual emotion. After half a pause he recognized it: anger. "You mean I took all this trouble to come here, and to brave your Challenges, for nothing?"

"Not for nothing. For the Solution to your problem. That requires neither Question nor Answer. The mare will clarify it in due course."

"But how can I get a Solution, without—?" He stopped, because he saw that Humfrey was paying him no further attention. The grumpy old Magician was lost in his tome.

Wira reappeared. "Come on downstairs. It will be all right. It always is."

"This isn't what I expected."

"It seldom is."

So he followed her back through the dusky passages.

Hello, Faun. Are you the one I am to guide?

Forrest looked around, startled. No one was there.

You can't see me, the voice said. *I am Mare Imbri, the day mare. I can speak to you only in daydreams.*

"In my dreams?" he asked, surprised.

Wira turned. "Oh, she's arrived? Good. Sit down here and talk with her. I will return when you need me."

Distracted, Forrest entered the room the woman indicated, and sat in a comfortable chair.

I was once a night mare, but I lost my body and became a day mare. I am invisible. Would it help if you could see me?

"Yes."

Then close your eyes and make your mind blank.

Forrest did as asked, bemused. In a moment a horse appeared in his mind, a black mare with white socks on her hind legs. *Or perhaps if I assumed girl form,* her voice said. The horse twisted and changed, becoming a pretty young human woman. "Is this better?" she asked.

"I can hear you!" he exclaimed. "That is, I could before, but now it seems more like speech."

"Yes, it is easier to imagine a human form speaking. It is your own mind doing it; I merely send the thoughts. This is a day dreamlet. You don't need to speak aloud, either; I can hear you if you just imagine yourself speaking. I can use speech balloons, if you prefer."

"Speech balloons?" he said aloud, then caught himself, and resolved to speak silently next time.

A cloud appeared above the young woman's head, with part of it pointing down at the woman image. IN THIS MANNER, the words in the balloon wrote.

"Regular speech will do," he said. Then caught himself again, and added without moving his lips: "But tell me, what is this about guiding me?"

The dreamlet girl frowned prettily. "I must perform a Service for the Good Magician. That Service is to guide you to Ptero, and safely through it."

"I don't know where Tero is."

"Ptero," she said, spelling it in a speech balloon.

"Wherever. In fact I don't know anything about this. I came to ask the Good Magician a Question myself, but he wouldn't even listen to it. I have gone to all this trouble to try to help a tree, and he won't even listen!"

"The ways of the Good Magician are often inscrutable to ordinary folk," she said. "Tell me more of your situation."

So he told her the whole story. She was a very good listener, even making dreamlet scenes to illustrate what he described. That way he knew she understood, because he could see the details, and make corrections when they erred. "So here I am," he concluded. "Ready to ask the Good Magician how to find a companion spirit for the clog tree, and I guess he's mad because for some reason he can't use me for a year's Service, so he won't talk to me at all."

Imbri shook her head. "Humfrey is old and grumpy, but he doesn't waste energy on anger. He always has some obscure reason for what he does. We simply have to figure it out. Obviously he has something in mind for you, because he informed me that my Service is to help you. We just have to understand what you are doing."

"What I want to do is find a spirit for the clog tree, so it won't fade. I have to do it within a month. I don't know anything about this Ptero place. Why should I go there?''

She considered. ''As it happens, I am one of the very few folk in Xanth who do know something about Ptero. Not a lot; nobody knows a lot about it. But some, because on occasion I have delivered daydreams there. It's a very strange place.''

''That explains why you are supposed to be the guide. But what about me?''

''All I can think of is that the spirit you are looking for is there.''

''There are people there?''

She laughed, and little HA HA's went out from her image. When the demoness had made such laughter, it had been derisive; Imbri's laughter was friendly. ''There are more folk there than anyone can count.''

Forrest found this confusing. ''How can there be more? Any person who exists can be counted.''

''That's the thing. Not all of them exist.''

''Now I'm really confused! How can there be people who don't exist?''

''It's hard to explain. Ptero is where all the folk who ever lived in Xanth stay, and all the folk who ever will live in Xanth, and all the folk who ever might live in Xanth. So there are a lot of folk there. But what's really strange is the way they live. They—do you know anything about quantum mechanics?''

''Huh?''

''I guess not. It's a concept I picked up from the mind of a former Mundane scientist. His dreams were really weird! I think Ptero is a quantum world. That is, nothing is certain there; everything exists in all its possible states at once. It's only when the folk there visit regular Xanth that things start making some sort of sense, for a while.''

Forrest shook his head. ''I don't want to go there. I just want to find a faun for the tree.''

''But maybe that faun is there.''

A glimmer began to form. ''A faun for the clog tree?''

''Since all the folk who ever might exist in Xanth are on Ptero, your faun could be there. Then you could bring him to the tree.''

The glimmer expanded. ''I think I am beginning to make some dim sense of the Good Magician's attitude. I don't need his Answer; I just need to go to Ptero and fetch that faun myself.''

"That must be it," she agreed. "And I must guide you there, and through Ptero too, as well as I am able."

"Can you get me through it and back home within a month?"

"I can do whatever you wish. But you must decide how long your search is. I don't know how long it will take to find him. I have delivered daydreams there, but I don't know the actual landscape. I may not be much help, though I will try my best."

Forrest nodded. "I'm sure you will help a lot. At least I won't be blundering there alone." Then he thought of something else. "This is your Service. What was your Question to the Good Magician?"

She smiled wistfully. "I was foaled as a night mare in 897, and became a day mare in 1067. I wasn't the best night mare; I was too tender hearted. It has been better as a day mare, because at least I bring pleasure to dreamers instead of horror, but I'm still not quite satisfied. Now I would like to gallop in some other pasture. The Good Magician will find me that pasture, after I have completed my Service.''

Forrest was impressed. "You are as old as I am! You were foaled the very year I adopted a sandalwood seedling and became a responsible creature. You were a night mare for a hundred and seventy years, and a day mare for thirty years. So you are two hundred years old."

"Yes. I don't mean to complain, but it does get dull after a while. Maybe I'm just a misfit."

"Well, I hope the Good Magician has a good new pasture in mind for you."

"I'm sure he does. Let's find your faun."

"Let's find my faun," he agreed, feeling better. "Where is Ptero?"

"At Castle Roogna."

"This strange land with uncountable folk is at the human capital?"

"In its fashion."

"Oh, you mean that's where the magic is to reach Ptero?"

"That is where the access is. Humfrey will have to give you a spell to cross to Ptero."

"Then I had better wake up and get that spell. I don't want to waste any time."

"I will be with you. Just clear a little place for me in your mind when you want to talk to me."

"I will. Thanks."

He opened his eyes. There was the cell, the same as before, but now it didn't seem so dingy. "Wira?"

In a moment he heard her light footsteps approaching. "Have you finished talking with Imbri?"

"Yes, for now. I need the spell to—"

"Here it is. The Good Magician said to give it to you when you asked for it." She held out a tiny stoppered bottle.

"How do I use it?"

"Imbri knows. Just keep it safe. You may need it to depart Ptero, too."

"I'll keep it safe," he agreed, putting the spell into his knapsack.

"Would you like something to eat?" Wira asked. "I'm sure the Designated Wife will be glad to fix you something before you go."

Designated Wife? Forrest decided not to inquire. "Thank you, no. Chlorine gave me a dough nut, and I haven't been hungry since."

"They do stick to your ribs," Wira agreed. "Then I will show you out."

She led him to the front gate. This was now completely clear; there was no wall and no set of tracks. The drawbridge was down, and the moat was calm, with no sign of fire. It was evident that the Good Magician could change his castle around at will. "Thank you," he told her.

"I wish you good success," Wira replied, with a rather pleasant smile that lacked any trace of the mischief of the demonesses. Then she looked embarrassed. "Oh, I almost forgot: here is your lost sandal." She held it out.

"But that had become reverse wood! How did you—?"

"The Good Magician has ways. It is a good sandal; he thought you would need it."

Not half as much as he needed a good Answer. But he stifled that remark. "Thank you," he said, taking the sandal and putting it in his knapsack. Now he had a complete reserve pair, again.

"And this," she said, holding out a piece of paper.

He took it and looked at it, but it had indecipherable scribblings. "I can't read this."

"The Good Magician scribbled it in his very own handwriting," she said, as if that were a special thing. "I'm sure he had excellent reason. Keep it with you; it may become useful when its time comes."

What could he do? He thanked her, and tucked the paper into his knapsack.

Forrest set out for Castle Roogna. It was not a difficult trek, because he was on a magic path that was supposed to lead right to it. The funny thing was that again it was morning, though there had been no night, so that he should be able to reach it by evening.

He wondered about that, so he tried asking Mare Imbri. He closed his eyes briefly as he walked, making a place for her to appear. "Are you there, Imbri?" he asked silently.

"Always, as long as this Service lasts," she agreed, appearing as the black haired woman. Now he saw that she rather resembled her mare form, in a pleasant way, with white socks on her feet and black gloves on her hands. Her dress was black too.

"I have noticed that it's always morning when I start walking, though I am sure a couple of days should have passed since I left my tree. Is there some magic operating?"

Imbri considered. "Share your recent memories with me. Maybe I can see what is happening."

One hoof tripped, and he had to open his eyes. He lost the image of her. This was awkward, walking with his eyes closed. So he stopped. "First—is it possible to see you without closing my eyes?"

Her voice came in his head. "Yes, if you can concentrate. Reserve a space about five paces ahead of you, and to the side, or wherever you want, so it doesn't interfere with your view of the path. Think of me being there."

He concentrated, and after some effort managed to see a fuzzy region. "That's it," Imbri said. "Just keep working on it as you walk, and I will clarify."

He did, and she did. After a while he was even able to see her as a human sized person walking beside him. "Can anyone else see you?"

"No. Only you."

"It's like seeing a ghost."

"Yes. It just requires the right concentration."

"Now I will review my memories of the day." He thought of his beginning of the trip to the Gap Chasm, guided by the Demoness Sire. Then of the ride through the Gap, on the back of the dragon ass. Then of the walk to the Good Magician's castle.

"You are right," Imbri said. "It's always morning. The first morning may have been the work of Com Passion, because she likes you. She just wanted to give you more time, after you were nice enough to kiss her mouse, so she reset your day. Otherwise it would have been afternoon then. The second morning started when you got off the dragon ass. That's a strange creature; I have no entry into its mind, or Chlorine's. Which is funny, because she used to be an ordinary girl, rather plain and ill tempered, actually, with dreams as foolish as anyone's. Now, suddenly, she is phenomenally lovely and intelligent and nice, and lives in the Nameless Castle with that dragon, and her mind is completely opaque. It's as if she's a different person."

"You mean Chlorine really does live in that castle? I thought she was just pretending."

"She really does live there. The castle sits on a cloud that floats across Xanth, so no one can see that it supports the castle. She lives like a princess, and that dragon assumes the form of a prince, and what they do at night, on those air mattresses that the floating castle has, is beyond any dream I could bring."

"Do you mean, like fauns and nymphs?"

She made an equine snort. "Like fauns and nymphs in much the way Castle Roogna is like a wood cutter's hut. I'm surprised that there hasn't been a flight of storks so big as to darken the sky. They are surely in love. I wish I had been watching when they changed; I'm femalishly curious about what happened. They must have stumbled on fantastic magic. The oddest thing is that they don't make anything much of it. That is, they just trundle around Xanth as a damsel and dragon, doing favors for folk, asking nothing in return. It is very strange."

"Yes. I thought so too. But how could they have made my afternoon become morning?"

"That would require good illusion, or very good magic. Maybe they have a sprig of thyme. At any rate, it does seem to have happened: they gave you more day to do your business. And more day again, when you left the Good Magician's castle. Because the Good Magician would hardly bother to waste such magic so irrelevantly."

"Well, whatever the reason, I appreciate it. It does help me save time, so that maybe I can return to my tree within the month."

By evening they were approaching Castle Roogna. Forrest paused to brush out his hair and make himself presentable. After all, this was the royal human castle, and it deserved some respect.

When he started walking toward it again, Imbri spoke. "This time I caught it! It's morning again."

Startled, Forrest looked around. She was right: the sun was at midmorning level. He also felt fresh and vigorous, as if he had had a good night's rest. "This is nice magic."

"This is very strong magic," Imbri said. "The rest of Xanth doesn't seem to be changing. Just us. We just seem to have more time, without losing what we have done. It is as if we weren't supposed to notice the favor."

"Well, if it's from the damsel and dragon, I will thank them when I see them again. But now I need to find Ptero."

"I will guide you there. Go in and ask to see Princess Ida."

Forrest approached the castle. The moat monster reared up threateningly.

"This one I can take care of," Imbri said. "Soufflé, it's all right. This is Forrest Faun, and he is with me."

The monster nodded, and sank back under the water.

"I thought you said no one else could see you."

"Only those I know well, and show myself to. Soufflé has been around a long time. He baby-sits the royal triplets."

"A moat monster takes care of children?"

"There is no other place like Castle Roogna."

So it seemed. They walked on into the castle.

Two girls, about six years old, ran up to them, colliding before they managed to stop. They wore matching little crowns. "Oh, goody!" the red haired one cried. "Visitors from afar! A faun from north of the Gap!"

"And a day mare," the dark one added.

"Meet the children of Prince Dolph and Princess Electra," Imbri said. "Princess Dawn, who can tell anything about any living thing, so she knows about you, and Princess Eve, who can tell anything about any inanimate things, so she knows about me."

"But you're alive!" Forrest protested.

"No she isn't," Eve said. "She's a spirit. She has half a soul, but no body. She lost that in the Void in 1067."

"They really do know," Forrest said, amazed. "I've never seen such magic."

"That's because no Magicians or Sorceresses ever came to your sandalwood tree," Dawn said.

A woman in blue jeans hurried up. "Girls! Behave!" she exclaimed. The two little princesses immediately stood back and looked angelic. "I'm sorry," the woman said. "They're irrepressible. I am Princess Electra, their mother."

"He's Forrest Faun, here to see Princess Ida," Dawn said.

"And she's Mare Imbri, who has to guide him through Ptero."

"Oh, you are here on business," Electra said. "Girls, tell the Princess she has a visitor."

The two children dashed off. "Uh, thank you," Forrest said. "I didn't mean to make a commotion. I don't know Princess Ida. I'm supposed to go to the land of Ptero."

Electra looked blank. "Go to the land of what?"

"Ptero. Where all the might-be folk stay."

"But Ptero is—" The Princess paused. "Well, I'm not sure exactly what it is. But it's not a place you can go to."

"But we have to go there. Because that's where I'll find my faun."

Electra still looked remarkably doubtful. "I think I'll just have to let Ida explain it."

"I hope someone does. Imbri hasn't."

The Princess nodded. "I can appreciate why. Come this way." She turned and led them down the hall.

The twins came dashing back, their red and black pigtails flying. "Auntie Ida says to go to the Tapestry!" Dawn cried brightly.

"And she'll meet them there," Eve finished, darkly. "She says this could get com-com—"

"Complicated," Electra finished. "I'm sure." She changed course slightly, and led them upstairs. Forrest was much impressed, because this was only the second time he had used stairs, and these were much broader than the ones at the Good Magician's castle.

Soon they arrived at a pleasant chamber with a nice view of the outside moat and orchard. A woman rose to greet them. She was another princess, because she wore a crown. She looked to be about twenty eight, but it was never possible to be quite certain, with women. There was something odd about her head.

"Princess Ida, this is Forrest Faun," Electra said. "Mare Imbri is with him, as his guide and companion."

"Any friend of Imbri is a friend of mine," Ida said graciously. "Please have a seat and tell me your concern."

Forrest took the indicated chair. "I need to find a faun to associate with the neighboring clog tree. The Good Magician told me to look in Ptero. Mare Imbri has been there, so can show me the way."

"Imbri?" the Princess said. It wasn't exactly a question; she was addressing the day mare. Her eyes went halfway blank and she seemed to be listening. After a moment she smiled. Imbri must have given her an explanatory daydream. "Ah, I see; that's interesting."

"So if you can just tell me where—"

Ida raised a hand in gentle negation. "I will, but there are things you must first understand. Consider the Tapestry."

He looked where she indicated and saw a large Tapestry hanging on the wall. It was filled with intricately sewn pictures of Xanthly scenes. They were so realistic that they almost seemed to be moving. In fact they *were* moving! "This is magic," he said.

"It shows all the scenes of Xanth," she explained. "In all times of Xanth, up to the present. Here is your glade."

The scenes changed, and one part expanded to fill the whole Tapestry. It was a picture of his own neighborhood! There was his sandalwood tree, and the nearby clog tree across the glade. He even saw the little disk set in his tree. ''This is as it is right now!'' he said, amazed.

''Here is yesterday,'' she said. The Tapestry became blank. She looked surprised. ''Now that's odd; it has never done that before.''

''Maybe it's because of what Chlorine did with my time.''

''Chlorine is involved in this?''

He explained about the lovely woman and the dragon ass, and how it always seemed to be morning when he traveled. ''I think she had something to do with it.''

Ida nodded. ''That would explain it. Nimby has strange powers. She must have asked him to rerun your mornings, so you could travel better. The Tapestry doesn't know how to account for that.''

''Maybe if you try someone else's yesterday, like maybe my tree's, it would work better.''

She smiled. ''Yes, I'm sure it will.''

The scene shifted. The trees remained, but now there were fauns and a nymph. Soon the nymph ran away, and one faun chased her off the picture. The other faun retired to the sandalwood tree. ''You can see everything!'' he said, twice as amazed.

''Yes, if we know where to look. But it is too complicated to try to watch all Xanth through all time, so we look only when we have reason.'' She turned to face him. ''Ptero is like that, only more so. It would be difficult to explore, and perhaps dangerous.''

''But I have to find that faun, or the tree will fade! It was bad enough losing my friend, without losing his tree too.''

''Yes, of course. I just want you to understand that this is no ordinary mission. It is stranger than anything you may have experienced.''

''Whatever it is, it is better than letting my friend's tree fade.''

''But if you should be lost, then your own tree would fade too.''

That made him pause. ''Do you think that will happen?''

''I don't know. I assume the Good Magician made sure you were capable of handling the situation, to the extent anyone could be.''

''No, he didn't even talk to me,'' Forrest said crossly.

''Did you go through the Challenges?''

"Yes! And then he refused to hear my Question."

"What were the Challenges like?"

He described them to her, as she seemed genuinely interested, though he saw little point in this. Still, it was best not to be impolite to a princess. As he described each scene, it appeared on the Tapestry, just as it had happened.

"So in each case, there was a physical Challenge," she said, "which you surmounted by using the talent of a person who happened to be there."

"Yes, actually. The psychologist, the dot girl, and the wood changing man. I found a way to get them each to help me."

"I think this is the kind of ability that would be required on Ptero," the princess said. "Surely this was the Good Magician's conclusion."

"But he didn't—"

"He always has good reason for his actions, though they are seldom immediately apparent to others. I believe he is trying to help you, in his fashion. He did put you in touch with Mare Imbri, after all."

"Yes. But—"

"Now I think you are ready to see Ptero. It is my moon."

"Your what?"

Then he saw something even more surprising than the Tapestry. A tiny ball was swinging around the Princess' head. It must have been hiding before, because until this time all he had seen was a flicker of something not quite there. It was about the size of a large eyeball. As it came closer to him, it brightened.

"This is Ptero," Ida said. "It orbits my head, and reacts to my moods. But it is more than just a tiny moon. It is an idea."

"It looks pretty solid to me."

"It is, in its fashion. You see, I am a Sorceress, and my talent is the Idea. Ptero is a condensation of all the ideas of Xanth, as they were too numerous and complicated to fit inside my head. So it would appear that the faun you seek is no more than an idea, not yet formulated in Xanth."

"But how can I find a faun who doesn't exist?"

"He does exist. Just not in tangible form. You will have to locate him, and cause him to exist."

She had said this was strange. He was beginning to appreciate how serious she was. "You mean that the idea of him is—is there in that ball?"

"Yes. The idea of everything is there. It seems you will have to go there to find the idea you need."

"But I can't go there!" he protested. "It's tiny!"

"Mare Imbri has a spell to make you small enough, in a manner."

He didn't much like the sound of this. "In a manner?"

"Your body will have to remain behind. Only your soul can go. As you said, Ptero is tiny."

"But suppose something happened to my soul?"

She nodded gravely. "This is the risk you take. I think it will be all right, because the Good Magician evidently thinks so, but there are always risks when the unknown is braved. We don't know what you may find on Ptero. So it might after all be best if—"

"No! I must save that tree."

"Then we shall have to prepare you for your journey. Your body will rest in this room while your soul visits Ptero. I will be going around the castle, but once you and Imbri are there, that will be no problem. I will return every few hours, so that your soul can find your body when it needs to. And of course Imbri will be guiding you. She has visited Ptero before, so has a small notion of its nature. But none of us will be able to help you if you have trouble. In fact we won't even know what you are doing. The Tapestry doesn't orient on Ptero, because it isn't part of Xanth. It's a derivative. So you will truly be on your own."

Forrest swallowed. "And nobody knows exactly what I'll find there? But if Imbri has been there—"

"I went to deliver only brief daydreams," Imbri said, appearing beside him. He realized that she couldn't speak to two people at the same time, because she wasn't physically real. She had to be in the dream of one or the other, so she had disappeared when she talked to Ida. "I had a specific summons. It was like going toward a light. I don't actually know the geography. I caught only glimpses. Enough to know that it's a whole world in itself, bigger than Xanth, and maybe more varied. And that time is strange, there."

"I'm sure Mare Imbri will be a great help," Ida said.

He glanced at her. "How did you know that Imbri had finished speaking to me?"

"I waited for your blank look to pass. It isn't polite to interrupt a daydream."

"She says she doesn't know a whole lot about Ptero, and that time is strange there."

"She will be able to locate friendly folk there, because she is used to entering minds. That may be your most important asset. And she is always good company, because of the nature of her business."

"Yes, of course." But he was being polite. He had expected a competent guide, and it seemed that Imbri was going to be something less than that.

"I'm sorry," Imbri said. "I will do my very best. But it's true; I can't guide you perfectly. I think that I turned out to be the best of a bad lot, as far as the Good Magician was concerned."

There wasn't much he could say to that. It would be dishonest to deny what she said.

"I must ask you again," Princess Ida said. "Do you really wish to make this excursion? Realistically, I think we have to say that your chances of success are no better than half, and if you fail, both trees may fade. This is at best a doubtful endeavor."

He knew she was making sense. But the thought of giving up, of breaking his promise to his friend's clog tree, appalled him. "No. I must do it."

"As you wish. Are there any arrangements you wish to make before you go?"

"No. I just want to get it done, and return to my tree."

"Then lie on this bed, and sniff from the bottle the Good Magician gave you. Its spell will free your soul from your body, so that it can go to Ptero. I will remain close until you arrive there."

"But how will you know?" Now that he had decided, he was finding new things to worry about.

"Imbri will tell me. She will guide you there, then make a quick trip to let me know."

He was already becoming happier to have the day mare with him. The notion of losing his soul halfway between his body and the little moon did not appeal.

He sat on the bed, then removed his knapsack and lay on it. It was very comfortable, but he was unable to relax. This was the weirdest kind of journey he had never before imagined. Still, he had to do it. He reached into the knapsack, which he now had beside him on the bed, and brought out the Good Magician's bottle. He nerved himself, took hold of the stopper, and pulled. It came loose with a pop, and he held the bottle to his nose and sniffed.

Suddenly he felt quite alien. He was half caught in a cloying, clinging swamp, truly bogged down. He fought to haul himself free of it. He needed expansion room.

"Be easy," a voice said. "You don't want to tear off any."

He looked, but his eyes didn't focus. In fact, he didn't seem to have any eyes. He tried to speak, but he didn't seem to have a mouth either.

"Just float," the voice said. "Let your soul coalesce."

His soul? He followed the advice, and found that he didn't have to struggle; he just floated out of the swamp, and as the rest of him came free, it drew in together so that he was a single cloud.

"Now form an eye, so you can see better."

He focused, and the eyeball formed. It focused, and he was able to see a large whitish wall.

"You are looking at the ceiling. Look down."

He rotated his eye, and saw his body lying on the bed, asleep. He tried to exclaim in surprise, but couldn't. So he formed a mouth. "Oh!" For he realized that that was the bog he had just hauled himself out of.

"Now make yourself small."

He willed himself small. That improved his focus. He saw a horse standing beside him. Her hoofs were planted firmly in mid-air. "Mare Imbri!"

"Yes. Follow me to Ptero." She walked away.

He tried to walk, but had no legs, so he just floated in her wake. She was going toward a huge statue. In a moment he realized that it wasn't a statue, but was Princess Ida. They were going toward her head.

"Keep getting smaller," Imbri said. "We have a long way to go."
He realized that he wasn't actually hearing her, for he hadn't formed

an ear; he was simply aware of her thoughts. He saw that she was getting smaller herself, so he did the same.

Ida's head seemed to grow enormous. Then he saw a small object, like a white ball. It was coming toward them, or they were going toward it. It, too, grew, or seemed to, becoming more like a boulder. Then it was like an island. In fact, it was looming like a moon, which was perhaps unsurprising. Finally it seemed more like a whole world, filling his entire view. It was no longer pure white; he saw that the white was in patches, which seemed to be clouds. Their designs were much more interesting from above than clouds usually seemed from below, because they weren't flat, they were mountainous.

Now they were falling toward the planet, and it became ever larger. The spaces between the clouds expanded, and he could see green land and blue sea below. He realized that he and Imbri were still getting smaller, because Ptero was still looking larger. It was amazing how big it seemed, as they plunged toward its varied surface.

"Time to slow," Imbri cautioned him. "We don't want to land too hard."

"But we're just souls, aren't we? We have no solidity."

"That's not true. There is a small amount of substance in a soul, and on a world as small as Ptero, that becomes significant. We will be assuming solid form there."

He thought of the size of Ptero when he had seen it as a tiny moon circling Princess Ida's head. Now it seemed larger than all Xanth. Which meant that they were so small as to be invisible specks. Maybe it was possible for their souls to take physical form on that scale. That was a relief, because he wasn't at all comfortable as a nebulous blob that had to form an eyeball just to see anything.

He tried to slow, but it didn't work. He was plunging faster than ever. "How do I do it?"

"Just form into a wide, flat shape, like a leaf or feather. Then the air will catch you, and you'll drift down."

He tried that, but was still falling uncomfortably fast. "It's not working very well."

"Oh, I forgot: you have a whole soul. It's twice as dense as my half soul. So you are twice as heavy. See if you can form into a parachute."

"What kind of a parrot?"

"Like this." She became a kind of upside-down cup, with strings leading down to a lump of herself below. "It's a Mundane concept. The canopy catches the air, and the blob guides it down."

He emulated her form, and it began to work. His broad cloth-like upper section caught the air, and dragged, and slowed the descent of the compact lower part of him. Even so, they were coming down a good deal faster than he liked. He expanded his mantle, but before it was able to do much good, he plunged into the blue sea near the white coast of the green land.

He descended way down below the surface of the water. He held his breath and spread his hands, trying to swim toward the surface. Then he heard Imbri: "Be a fish!"

Oh. He formed into a fish, and then he had no problem. She formed into a sea horse beside him. "Swim to land. I must tell Ida that we are safely here."

"But—" But she was already gone.

So he strengthened his tail and fins and swam as strongly as he could toward land. He hoped there weren't any sea monsters here, because one of them could gobble him up. Though probably he could change into something else, like a stink horn, and get away.

He saw the sand of the bottom rising beneath him. The water was getting shallow; he was nearing the beach. He was glad; this business of shifting shapes did not come naturally to him, though he supposed it could be fun if he learned it well enough.

The water became too shallow to swim in. Now what should he do? Try to become a flatter fish? But it would keep on getting shallower, until no amount of flatness would work.

Then he laughed at his own stupidity. He was there! He was at the shore. He no longer needed to be a fish. He could assume his own shape.

He did so. In a moment he was standing ankle deep in the surf, complete with his knapsack. His knapsack? How had he managed to bring that along? He reached into it, and found everything there, including the stoppered spell bottle and his spare pair of sandals. Apparently his soul was equipped with whatever his body had. That was reassuring.

Something plunged down to splash in the water behind him. Then the figure of a horse appeared. "I have told her," Mare Imbri said. "Now we are safely on Ptero, and can go about your mission."

"Great," he said. "And exactly how do we do that?"

"I have no idea."

Forrest gazed at the beach ahead of them. This was indeed going to be a challenge.

4
PTERO

T hey waded the rest of the way out of the water and stood on the shore. Forrest splashed, while Imbri's feet moved through the water splashlessly. The beach was a pretty white ribbon of sand, curving around so as to stay between the water and the land with remarkable precision. The air was comfortably warm.

Forrest mulled over what Imbri had said. "If you have no idea what to do, and I have no idea, how are we going to do it?"

"Maybe we can ask someone."

Something was bothering him slightly, and he managed to figure out what it was. "When you talk, your mouth doesn't move."

"That's because mares can't talk well with their mouths. They can only neigh. So I talk in your head, in dreamlets."

"But now I'm using my mouth to talk to you. I can hear the sound."

"That's because you are physical."

"Physical? But only my soul came here."

"The soul has a very small amount of substance. Just enough to make a solid body here, where everything is very small. So you have naturally assumed your regular form, complete with sandals and knapsack."

"And you have assumed yours," he said, catching on. "But you look a bit hazy."

"That's because I have only half a soul, while my mare body is several times as massive as your faun body. So I have less than a tenth of your solidity. If you touch me, your hand will pass through me."

"It will?" He reached out to pat her shoulder—and his hand sank into her body with only faint resistance. He snatched it out. "Sorry."

She shrugged her shoulders, an interesting maneuver. "It doesn't hurt. As long as you can see me and hear me, it's all right."

"I wonder—if you don't mind—could you become all the way solid, here? If you assumed a smaller form? So you could use your mouth to speak?"

"Certainly, if you prefer." She shrank, becoming a small human woman or girl, in a close black dress. "Will this do?" she asked, using her mouth. "I have only about half your mass, so I can't be any larger without diffusing."

"That's fine. You look great." He meant that her form was satisfactory in the solid sense, but actually it was more than satisfactory. She looked just like a rather pretty girl, or a nymph, with lustrous black hair. Except for the slightly equine set of her nose, which was understandable. She was, after all, a type of horse.

Imbri took a step—and tripped, falling on her face. "Neigh!" she exclaimed, chagrined. "I'm not used to being physical."

Forrest realized that that made sense. She had been a half soul, seemingly without substance, for thirty years, and when she had been a night mare before that, she had had four feet. She wasn't used to handling a real human body. "My fault," he said. "Maybe you had better return to mare form."

"But I don't want to make you feel awkward because I don't talk with my mouth," she said. "I'm sure I can learn to handle this form, if I concentrate."

But she had a scratch on her cheek, from a shell on the beach. That made him feel guilty. "I would rather feel awkward, than have you falling and scratching your face."

She looked alarmed. "Oh! Did I do that?"

He dug into his knapsack and pulled out a mirror. He gave it to her, and she held it up so she could see her face. "I did! Oh, that's embarrassing.'' She brushed her fingers across the scratch, wiping it out, so that her face was smooth again. That surprised him, but he realized that since she had shaped the body to begin with, she could readily re-shape it to eliminate an imperfection. Like most females, she was sensitive about her appearance, even in a form that was unnatural for her.

She returned the mirror, and he put it back into the knapsack. It banged into something, and he realized that it was his spare pair of sandals. That gave him an idea. ''You can wear my other sandals! They'll protect you from tripping!'' He dug them out and offered them to her.

''They will?'' She looked dubious.

''Yes. They are magic. They protect the feet. They won't let you misstep.''

''But those are faun sandals. I'm having enough trouble balancing on these human feet; I don't think I could do it at all with hoofs. Of course I'm used to hoofs, but only when I have four of them.''

''Sandals from my tree fit anyone. That's their nature. Try them.''

So she sat down and lifted her knees so she could reach her feet. In the process she showed a very nymphly pair of legs almost up to the panty line, in much the way the Demoness Sire would have done on purpose. He wondered if he should mention that, because it was clear that Imbri was not accustomed to the ways of a physical human body. Then she got the sandals on, discovering that they did indeed fit her human feet—and the position of her legs shifted so that much less showed. He realized that the sandals were now protecting her feet from harming the rest of her legs by undue exposure. Because the legs connected to the feet, and missteps were not merely of the ground. So he didn't have to say anything.

She stood. ''Oh, I feel far more secure! These sandals are helping even now.''

He had already come to that conclusion. ''I'm glad.'' Actually he could have lived with the exposure of her legs, but there didn't seem to be much point in saying that.

She looked around. ''I'm supposed to guide you, and I haven't done a good job. Maybe we can ask someone.''

That seemed like a fair idea. ''All right. Is there anyone to ask?''

''There are countless slews of folk here. I'm sure one of them must be close by. Let's walk along the beach and see.''

So they walked along. After a time Forrest noticed that there was something odd about the air. It smelled all right, but it had colors. It seemed to be green ahead, and blue to their right. But there didn't seem to be any source.

He paused, turning around. ''Do you see colors?'' he asked.

''Yes,'' Imbri said, surprised. ''It is yellow behind us, and red over the sea.''

''Do you think it means anything?''

''It must. But I don't know what.''

''And there just doesn't seem to be anyone to ask,'' he said, frustrated. ''If there are so many folk here, where are they all?''

Imbri pondered, then brightened. ''I think I remember, from one of the dreamers: folk have to be requested. Otherwise they stay away. If they are courteous. So that no one gets crowded.''

''But how do we request someone, when there's no one to ask?''

''I think you just do it.''

He shrugged. ''Okay.'' He stood straight. ''I hereby request the company of someone.''

There was a sound, and in a moment a large figure appeared, flying over the trees. It came to a solid landing on the sand before him. ''Yes?'' It was a winged unicorn.

Taken aback, Forrest looked at Imbri. She looked as baffled as he. So he turned to the unicorn. ''Hello. I was just wondering—''

''With no introduction?'' the unicorn asked. He spoke without moving his mouth.

''Uh, I am Forrest Faun.''

''I am Kero Unicorn.''

''I was just wondering—''

''What service do you have to trade?''

''What?''

''You are impaired of hearing?''

''No. I just don't understand. What service?''

''Precisely.''

"I don't understand."

The unicorn looked more closely at him. "You are impaired of intellect?"

Forrest was getting frustrated. "I am just new to this region. I don't know what you mean."

"Oh. You must have traveled far, to be so out of touch."

"Very far," Forrest agreed.

"I suppose I can explain that much without violating protocol. In this region we trade services. So if you want to know something I can tell you, you must trade me a service for my service in abating your ignorance. What service do you offer?"

This was new to him. "What service do you want?"

"I have no idea. You summoned me, so I assumed you had something in mind."

"I had a question in mind."

"That's not a service. My answer is a service. What other service will you trade for it?"

This wasn't getting anywhere very rapidly, so he tried something silly. "An entertaining jig."

"Done. What is your question?"

"What do the colors of the air mean?"

"They indicate direction, since we have no sun or moon or stars to mark it. Blue is north, because it is cold; red is south, because it is hot; green is To; and yellow is From."

Forrest waited, but that appeared to be the extent of the answer. So he brought his panpipe from his knapsack, played a lively melody, and proceeded to dance his jig. Fauns were good at jigs, so he knew it was competent. The unicorn watched with seeming interest.

When he thought he had jigged enough, he stopped. Kero nodded, satisfied, then spread his wings and flew back over the forest.

"I guess we learned something," Forrest said, watching the creature disappear.

"Yes," Imbri agreed. "We learned two things: that colors indicate directions, and that it is necessary to trade services on Ptero. So we got the better bargain."

"Maybe so. But what is this To and From business?"

"I suppose we could trade for that information. But maybe we'll figure it out for ourselves, soon. Let me see if I can trade for useful information."

Forrest shrugged. "I hope you can."

Imbri faced the air. "I request someone to trade with."

A dark creature faded into view. It was a black centaur mare. "Yes?" What startled Forrest was that she spoke both physically and mentally.

Imbri's delicate jaw dropped. "You're a night mare!"

"Not exactly. Are you curious about my derivation?"

"Yes!" Forrest and Imbri said together.

"I am Chemare. It all started when my sire, who was horribly prejudiced against zombies, was scheduled to have a bad dream in which he and a really rotten female zombie drank from a love spring. But somehow the night mare who was carrying the dream got confused, or maybe she had a secret thing for the centaur, who was rather handsome for his kind, and she fell into the dream herself and drank from the spring instead. The elixir overwhelmed them both, and they promptly indulged in an encounter of love that heated the spring so much it almost evaporated. Then the mare departed and the dream dissipated, leaving the centaur considerably more satisfied than the authentic dream would have left him. In due course the mare bore a foal with half a soul, black as night but with the form of a centaur. That was me. But because I derive from an illicit dream, I came not to Xanth proper, but to Ptero, where I bring bad dreams to those residents who deserve them. It's not the best existence, but it will do."

"Oh, Chemare!" Imbri exclaimed. "How well I understand. I was a night mare for many decades."

"I thought you looked somehow familiar. But you're in human form."

"Yes, so I can be substantial for my companion, Forrest Faun, whom I am trying to help. Would you like to exchange a service?"

"I would love to. But I'm not sure what we could do for each other."

"Is there anything you need?" Forrest asked.

"No. I came only because I was closest when the call went out.

So I truly regret this, because it's so rare to encounter someone with experience nightmaring, but I must go." She faded out.

"Wait!" Forrest cried, too late. She was gone.

"We are slow on the uptake," Imbri remarked. "We had better be prepared to render some service before the next one disappears."

"Yes. They don't seem to wait around long without reason."

There was the sound of running hoofs. A centaur came galloping from the green direction, followed by two centaur foals. She had a white mane and white body, but blue eyes. Forrest tried not to stare at her rippling bare chest, knowing that centaurs paid no attention to certain effects, but he was impressed.

She came to a stop before Imbri. "Hello, mare in human form. I am Ilura Centaur, and these are my foals. We apologize for our tardiness."

"Tardiness?"

"We were some distance when we heard your call, and the foals couldn't move at adult speed."

Forrest realized that more than one creature had answered Imbri's call. But Imbri was already handling it.

"I am Mare Imbri, and this is my companion."

"What have you to trade?"

"A pleasant daydream."

"What do you wish in return?"

"Information on the person on Ptero who can best help us to find what we seek."

"What do you seek?"

"A faun for a vacant tree."

"That would be Cathryn Centaur. She is the one who best knows where to find fauns."

There was a pause. Then Imbri, realizing that she had her answer, looked directly at Ilura. The centaur's eyes went blank in a manner Forrest recognized. She was having a daydream.

He looked at the two foals. One was a dark furred male, the other a light furred female. The male was stoic, while the female was impatiently stamping her feet. "Hello, foals. I'm Forrest Faun. You must be dissimilar twins."

The female looked quickly at him. "I'm in a hurry," she replied.

The male looked slowly at him. "I'm in no hurry," he said.

"Well, I'm sure your dam will be finished here soon."

The female reacted rapidly. She used a forefoot to scratch letters in the sand. THE HURRY TWINS: IMINA AND IMINO.

Oh. "My apology for misunderstanding," Forrest said.

"Don't be," Imina said quickly. "It happens all the time."

"We're used to it," Imino added slowly. "It's probably a good thing we don't exist."

"But how can I be talking to you, if you don't exist?"

"We're might-be's," Imina replied rapidly. "It would take a freakish set of circumstances to make us real. For one thing, our dam isn't real either."

"Only our sire, Hurry Centaur, is real," Imino said tardily.

Forrest was starting to catch on. "Your sire lives in Xanth proper, and the rest of you don't."

"That's it exactly," Imina agreed swiftly. "We can only come to exist if our dam gets real, and encounters our sire, and performs a certain ritual that makes human folk uncomfortable to contemplate. All that seems extremely unlikely."

"I'm sorry."

"It doesn't really matter," Imino said deliberately. "There are far too many might-be's for Xanth to accommodate."

Ilura had completed her daydream. "Come foals; we must be off."

"Already?" Imino asked.

"About time!" Imina said.

"I had a very nice dream of your sire," Ilura said. "I think he may be almost ready to consider something."

They galloped off into the yellow color. Forrest and Imbri watched them go. "Those were might-be's," he said.

"Yes. It's a shame they aren't real."

"How do we find Cathryn Centaur?"

"I think we just ask for her."

"Can we just ask for the faun I need?"

She turned to him, startled. "We could certainly try."

He faced nothing. "I want to trade with the faun I need."

Nothing happened.

"I suspect he isn't close enough to hear," Imbri said. "Have you noticed that all the creatures we have encountered here are equine crossbreeds?''

''I hadn't noticed,'' he said, surprised. ''Could it be coincidence?''

''It could be. But I think there must be sections of Ptero for different types of creatures, and this happens to be the equine section. That would explain why we landed here: I'm equine, so was drawn here. So there would be no fauns close by. Cathryn Centaur must know where they are.''

''That makes sense to me. Very well, let's trade with Cathryn.''

Imbri stood facing nowhere. ''I would like to trade with Cathryn Centaur.''

Another lady centaur appeared, emerging from the forest. She was brown of mane and fur, with large white wings. ''Why hello, mare,'' she said. ''I never expected to be summoned.''

''Why not?'' Imbri asked.

''Because there is no service anyone can do me, so I can't trade. Didn't you know that?''

''I am from far away. I know very little about this region.''

''But the conventions are similar throughout our world. You don't mean to say—'' She broke off, looking startled.

''Yes, we are from Xanth,'' Imbri said.

''That is extremely unusual, as there is virtually no physical contact between Xanth and Ptero.''

''But considerable emotional contact.''

Cathryn nodded agreement. ''All we might-be's long to achieve Xanth proper. But so few of us ever do. Now I suppose if you offer me some way to go there, then we can indeed deal. But as it is impossible to travel there physically, I suspect that your mission is of some other nature.''

''Yes. We need to locate a suitable faun to become the spirit of a vacant tree.''

''Ah. That's why you summoned me: because I know the best route to the faunhold.''

''Yes.''

''I am really sorry that we can't exchange services, because I can certainly start you on your way there.''

''Start us? You can't direct us all the way there?''

"Correct: I can't. It is beyond my range."

"Range?"

"Oh, I see," Cathryn said sympathetically. "You are from afar, and don't understand our system."

"Yes, I don't. But I am willing to trade, if it's a matter of that."

"I'm afraid it is. We are unable to interact significantly without the exchange of equivalent services."

Forrest stepped into the dialogue. "There must be some service you need or desire, that we might do."

Cathryn glanced at him. "I doubt it. I am really quite satisfied, apart from my natural longing to become real. This is a pleasant enough realm, and far better than utter nonexistence. I would gladly show you around it, if—"

"If we could do you some service in exchange," he finished.

"Exactly. But as it is, I see no cause for further association. So if you will excuse me, I shall take off." She spread her wings.

"Wait!" Imbri cried. "There must be something!"

Cathryn paused. "I would be pleased if there were, for you seem like interesting folk, and I'm sure your need must be extreme, for you to make the great effort to come here. But it would be unkind to pretend there is anything feasible."

"Every creature has some secret deep desire," Imbri said. "I am in a position to know."

The centaur seemed genuinely curious. "How could you be in such a position?"

"I was a night mare for a hundred and seventy years, punishing folk for their darkest desires, and a day mare for thirty years, rewarding their brightest desires. I have never encountered anyone who was wholly satisfied with his lot. Some don't know their deepest desires, but all have them."

"And maybe some demons prey on that," Forrest said, thinking of D. Sire.

"Then I think I must be the exception," Cathryn said, "because I am satisfied, as satisfied as it is possible for a might-be to be."

They seemed to be getting nowhere. But Forrest remembered something. "The Good Magician's list," he said. "Maybe that has the answer." He dug into his knapsack and brought it out.

Now he thought he could almost read the first two words of the Good Magician's illegible scribble. "Dear Horn," he said, squinting. "Does that make any sense?"

"Oh!" Cathryn said, putting a hand to her ample breast.

"You have found your secret desire," Imbri said.

"I suppose I have," the centaur confessed. "I never realized it before."

Forrest put the paper away. "What is the dear horn?"

"It is a special horn that when blown will locate a person's True Love. I have no True Love; I did not realize until you spoke that I missed him."

"Then we must find this horn for you," Imbri said.

"That may be no easy thing. I have no idea where it may be. I understand it tends to get left wherever last used, forgotten. So though you have indeed discovered a service you might render me, I fear it is an impossible service."

Forrest found himself becoming canny. "Suppose we agreed to help you find that horn. Would that be a sufficient service so that we could talk freely while we were doing it?"

"Why yes, I suppose it would be. But you may still be wasting your time, because it may not be possible to find it, and in that case I will not be able to guide you toward the region of the fauns."

Forrest shrugged. "We'll take that chance. Are we agreed?"

"Yes," Cathryn said, smiling.

"Then let's proceed. I'm not much, but Mare Imbri can tune in on dreams, and that may help, as the dear horn is surely an instrument for the fulfillment of dreams."

Both mares looked at him. "You're not as empty headed as the average faun," the centaur remarked.

"It's a luxury I can't afford at the moment. I must save that tree, and return to my own tree." Forrest turned to Imbri. "Can you orient on some person who knows where the dear horn is?"

"I'm not sure. But I suppose the Good Magician wouldn't have asked me to guide you, if he didn't think I had some way to do it. Let me concentrate." She closed her eyes. She looked much like a nymph that way, except that she was clothed. "Yes—I am getting a faint glimmering. It's like the colors of the directions, only it's more like light from a distant flickering candle. I think I will be able to find it. But we will have to go straight to it, because it's very faint, and I may lose it if we delay or deviate.''

"Then let's go!" Forrest said, gratified.

They set off to the north, and slightly to the east. There were numerous tracks, all hoofmarks. That reminded him of the conjecture they had made about regions. They had encountered only equine folk in this region: a unicorn, a centaur, and a winged centaur. That could be coincidence, but he doubted it, because in regular Xanth he had seldom seen such creatures. "Is this equine country?" he inquired.

"Yes," Cathryn answered. "Creatures of a kind tend to congregate, being more comfortable with similar types. There's no rule; it just happens."

"So elsewhere there will be regions of dragons, or of elves, or of human folk?"

"Or of fauns," she agreed. "Actually there may be several regions of each type, because of the time."

"Time?"

"Time is geography, so there are limits."

"I don't understand. Will I have to exchange a service in order to find out what that means?"

She laughed. "No. We are in the process of exchanging our services now. It is to my interest to facilitate your search for the dear horn, and you can surely do that better if you understand our system. I had forgotten for the moment that you are from Outside. Have you noticed something about me?"

He glanced at her. "Only that you somehow seem younger than I took you for. I was probably distracted by your—there are aspects of you that resemble a generously endowed nymph, and—"

She laughed again, making those aspects shake. "I think I might even guess which aspects you mean. But you are not imagining it. I am growing younger. I was foaled only twenty years before we met, so even a small distance to the east makes me noticeably younger."

"How can that be? Is there youth elixir in the air?"

"No. It's the direction. When we travel into the From, we become younger. If the dear horn is very far in this direction, not only will we be in ogre territory, I will be too young to take you there. I would regret that, because then we could not complete our agreement.''

"But how can that be? East is a direction, not a time."

"Perhaps that is true where you come from. Here east is From, or what you might call the Past. It's all the same to us, of course, but I suppose it might seem odd to outsiders."

"Are you saying that if we go one direction, we get younger, and if we go the other direction, we get older?"

"That is exactly what I am saying. So I am able to go twenty years east, from where we meet, and seventy years west. For reasons of vanity I prefer to remain mostly in the early maturity section. Neither extreme youth nor extreme age appeal to me particularly.''

He was amazed. "Does this apply to us too?"

"I should certainly think so. Do you feel yourself getting younger?"

"No. But I wouldn't notice five or ten years, and neither would Imbri. We're both two hundred years old."

"You are that age where?"

He was nonplused. "Why, here, of course."

"But you must be five or six years younger than you were. See, I am becoming a teen, and younger."

He looked at her again. Indeed, now her breasts were smaller, her flanks were less solid, and she had acne on her face. Her mane, which had been loose, was now bound into a pony tail.

He checked himself. "No, I remain much the same faun as ever. But I would be only a hundred and ninety or so, instead of two hundred. I would have to go a long way back to get really young."

"So I gather. How far can you go in To?"

"Into what?"

"The future."

"Why, I don't know. It depends on how long my tree lives. Perhaps four hundred years."

"You are a long-lived species!"

"Well, we draw our vitality from our trees. If my tree should be chopped down, I would fade out right then."

"I see. So you should have a wide range of geography, here on

Ptero. That is surely an advantage, in case your faun is long removed.''

Forrest suffered a revelation. ''The Good Magician must have known! That's why Imbri and I are the same age, and both long lived. So we can search farther, together.''

''That does seem to make sense. Every person's territory is limited by her life span. That is not usually a problem, but I confess that at times I do wonder at what must be beyond my territory.'' She was now smaller, with no chest development, and her mane was in pigtails. ''I hope it isn't much farther.''

Imbri, who had been walking with a removed expression, looked at her. ''Not far now, I think. The glow is stronger. But it is still flickering. I don't want to pause, lest something happen to it.''

''But we may have to pause,'' Cathryn said. ''We are approaching the edge of equine territory.''

There was the sound of hoofs, and two adult centaurs came into sight. The hide of one was dark, with a spiral pattern of spots like thickly clustered stars. The other was the opposite, with a white hide speckled with black dots. Both carried bows. ''Ho, ladies,'' the dark one called. ''Are you aware that you are near the boundary?''

Forrest saw that the land ahead did change. They had been walking through a fairly level open forest, the kind that hoofed creatures preferred, but before them was a tangle of oddities.

''Yes, thank you, Alpha,'' Cathryn said. ''These folk are from Xanth, on a mission to locate the dear horn, which it seems is in the adjacent territory.'' Then she turned to the others. ''This is Alpha Centauri, guardian of the boundary. His name got mangled by a passing galaxy, but he is nevertheless one of us.''

''To be sure,'' Alpha agreed gruffly. ''But this is a bad section to cross out. The puns have completely overgrown it, and are horrible.''

The other centaur spoke. ''You are visitors from Xanth proper? You will be returning there in due course?''

''Yes, within a month,'' Forrest replied.

''I am Vision Centaur. I would like to exchange a service with you.''

''Well, I don't know if we have anything to exchange.''

"Surely we do. I have a message I would like you to deliver to certain parties in Xanth."

"I can do that," Imbri said. "I can visit almost anyone in Xanth, in my capacity as a day mare."

"In return I offer my service in helping to protect you from an incipient attack."

"Attack?" Cathryn asked, concerned.

"I'll make that deal," Imbri said. "What is the message?"

"It is for Jenny Elf and Chief Gwendolyn Goblin. It is that if they will seek out a special type of tick, the gen-e-tic, they can use it to cause their myopic gene to recede, that is, to become recessive. That will render their sight normal, so they will no longer need to use spectacles."

"But this is great news for them!" Imbri said. "They will not be able to perform a return service for it."

"Creatures of Xanth proper are not necessarily bound by our conventions. I merely wish them to have the information."

"I will deliver the message to them," Imbri said.

"Thank you. Now I suggest that you make a detour, because your present course is not wise."

"I don't dare deviate, lest I lose the glow," Imbri said. "I must go straight ahead."

Cathryn sighed. "Then we shall accompany you. We don't have time for a gallop poll on the issue. Perhaps my staff will help." In her hands appeared a long stout pole. "If that is not sufficient, perhaps my talent will avail."

"You have a magic talent?" Forrest asked, surprised.

"Oh, didn't I mention that? My talent is blankets. They can be very useful on occasion."

Forrest did not comment. It was interesting that a winged centaur had a magic talent other than flying, though of course as a might-be she wasn't limited by the conventions of ordinary creatures of her kind. But nice as a blanket could be on a cold night, he doubted it would be much help against horrible puns.

Alpha looked into the sky. "Oh, no! I fear the dragons are staging a border raid."

"Precisely," Vision said. "I saw them from afar."

Cathryn followed his gaze, alarmed. "I'm too young to use my bow effectively."

"Then you and your friends had better flee From or To," Alpha said. "Vision and I will cover your retreat."

Now Forrest heard the beat of a number of heavy wings. "Dragons raid equine territory?"

"Yes," Alpha said tersely. "They have a taste for equine flesh. Of course we just dissolve and reform when eaten, but it's an exceedingly uncomfortable process." He unslung his bow and nocked an arrow. "I will hold them off. Flee—and stay out of the air."

"How can we outrun flying dragons?" Forrest asked Cathryn.

"It's a matter of moving out of their time range," she explained, looking worried. "If they are young dragons, we can move From and force them to become too young to fly well. If they are mature dragons, we flee To, hoping they will become too old to fly well."

"Unfortunately it is a mixed squadron," Alpha said, squinting into the sky as dark shapes appeared. "Some will follow effectively, regardless."

"I will make a security blanket," Cathryn decided.

"You are too young to make a really effective one," Alpha warned her.

"I know. But it must do." She gestured, and something spread out from her hands and floated above them. It slowly settled, covering all of them except Alpha. Forrest realized that her talent was not precisely what he had understood.

"I will defend the outer perimeter of the blanket," Alpha said, aiming his first arrow at the first dragon. "Stay low, and perhaps it will suffice."

"The glow is flickering," Imbri said. "I am going on."

"I recommend against this," Alpha said grimly. "Attila the Pun passed by here recently, and left a disgusting trail. It is simply not safe. I suggest that you fly over this section, or run around it, after the dragons depart. Especially since you are quite young, here, Cathryn, and your friends look inexperienced."

But Imbri was already forging into the pun region. So naturally Forrest and Cathryn had to follow.

"This is very bad judgment," Alpha called after them. Forrest was sure he was correct.

"Well, at least the dragons won't attack us within the pun strip," Cathryn said. "They don't like it any better than we do."

Forrest heard the bow twang behind them. Alpha or Vision was firing at a dragon. Could puns really be worse than dragons?

There was a rustle ahead, and something thumped past them. It looked like a man, except that it had only one arm—and one leg. Then it turned its head toward them, and Forrest saw that it had only half a head, with one eye and half a mouth. "Et ut f y ay!" it screamed in half syllables.

Cathryn raised her staff. "No, you get out of *our* way, half brother," she retorted. Her threat must have been effective, because the thing ran away. Forrest saw as it retreated that it was half-reared, too. Now they passed a sign saying MALL. It was an open section winding through the tangled puns, with shops along the sides. The central strip was clear and firm, so they ran along it rather than across it, making better time.

Then Imbri started pulling at her clothing. Forrest's feet felt confined. He just had to get them out of the sandals.

"Oh, no," Cathryn exclaimed, ripping off her backpack. "A strip mall!"

Forrest realized that that made sense, in a pun strip. He took off his sandals and backpack and felt free. Meanwhile Imbri had stripped to complete nudity, and now looked exactly like a nymph. It wasn't so bad; they held their things and ran on along the strip.

Another truncated figure ran by, going the opposite direction. This one was female: a half sister. But while the half brother had been sliced vertically, so that he had to jump rather than run, this one was halved across the middle. She had two nice legs, and was topless. Forrest wondered how the other half of her got along.

But his brief distraction caused him to misstep. Suddenly his foot was in a fish-shaped blob of jelly. It slid out from under, causing him to fall on his rear. He saw that Imbri had taken a similar fall. They were no longer wearing their magic sandals, so their feet could take bad steps. "We'd better get off the strip and get dressed again," he called. "We need to run safely."

Imbri agreed. They scrambled off the strip and donned their things. He was surprised to note that she put her upper clothing on before her sandals. But of course she wasn't really a nymph, however she might look; she was a mare. When she was in girl form, she evidently adopted the conventions of girls, and didn't like to show her whole body. Yet it was a beautiful body. Human beings had funny attitudes.

But again his distraction caused mischief. Suddenly he was struck a blow on the foot. He looked, and discovered that he had tried to put on a sock instead of his sandal. The sock had punched him. Or rather, socked him. He tossed it away and found his sandal instead.

"We must keep moving," Cathryn said behind him. "We're off the mall strip, but not out of the comic strip. These abysmal puns will ruin us if we don't get clear of them soon."

Forrest massaged his struck foot, agreeing. Then he got up and followed Imbri, his steps more confident now that they were protected by the sandals.

They passed a big turtle. "Hey, watch where you're going!" the creature snapped. It was of course a snapping turtle.

"My apology," Forrest said politely, though they really hadn't gone that close to it.

They passed a big tree with a bee sitting on its lowest branch. Suddenly Forrest felt his eyes watering.

"A bay-bee," Cathryn cried. "It makes you cry." Again, he had already discovered that.

Now he was stumbling despite his sandals, because the ground was getting marshy from the tears of those who had gone before. He lurched past a large plant and almost tripped over one of its square roots. "A polynomial plant," Cathryn said. "Attila really did his worst this time."

Then several creatures charged toward them. Their bodies looked human, but their heads were closed fists. On some the thumbs were on the right, and on others on the left. All of them looked vile.

"Knuckleheads!" Cathryn said. "They're not the smartest creatures, but they're mean. Run!"

They ran toward what looked like a hanging curtain made up of thin slices of wood. "Avoid those!" Cathryn cried. They tried to duck down under it, but as they did, they slid into deeper swamp and got bogged down.

"I can't see!" Forrest cried.

"Those were Venetian blinds," Cathryn said. "They made us—"

"I get it," Forrest said. "How do we get our vision back?"

"I think I saw some see weed. If we can find that—"

They blundered about, making big splashes. "You won't find it that way," a voice came.

"Who are you?" Forrest asked, hoping it wasn't a knucklehead.

"I am the anonymous turtle you passed without notice. I can direct you to the see weeds, though I haven't seen them in days."

"Then how can you do it?" Forrest demanded.

"I have turtle recall."

That did seem to make sense. "What do you want in exchange?"

"Something nice to recall. I'm tired of recalling abysmal puns."

"I'll do it," Imbri said. "I will give you a dream of sweet turtle doves."

"Bear to your left. You were headed for the see-an-enemy, which is more trouble than you would care for at the moment. Keep going. There: the see weed is right before you."

Forrest couldn't see anything, but in a moment he heard a pleased exclamation from Imbri. Then she came to him, and touched him with the see weed, and suddenly he could see again. She touched Cathryn. Then she went to do her service for the turtle.

But more B's were flying by. One stung Cathryn. "Well, you took long enough to get to it," she said crossly. "In fact you didn't do it at all! You just stood there stupidly while your friend fetched the see weed."

"Well, yes, I suppose—"

"Not that you ever were much of a creature," she continued. "I don't know why I'm even bothering to help you in your stupid quest. You—" Then a second B stung her. "Oh, you wonderful friend!" she exclaimed, suddenly hugging him. He would have liked it better if she had been at her mature stage. "You're just so great to have around. I don't know how I ever survived without you."

Then something stung Forrest on the leg. He looked down and saw it was a tic marked TAC. He pulled it off, but it was already having its effect. He was realizing how to manage things better. Those B's were from a Have; their stings made folk B-have differently. One must have been a B-little, and the other a B-friend.

A third B was already stinging Cathryn. She pushed Forrest away. "B-gone!" she exclaimed.

"Tell it to the B's," he told her. "Loudly."

Comprehension crossed her face from upper right to lower left. She turned to face the remaining milling B's. **"Begone!"**

The B's buzzed rapidly away, heeding the voice of authority.

Cathryn turned back to him. "Oh, thank you. I really didn't mean those things I said; it was just that—"

"You got stung," he said. "Fortunately I got bitten by a tac-tic, so I figured out what to do."

Imbri returned. "The turtle is satisfied," she reported. "Now we must move on; the glow is flickering again." She plunged on ahead.

They followed—and suddenly they were out of the comic strip, and the dreadful puns were gone. Ahead of them was a tree twisted into the form of a pretzel. "We are in ogre territory," Cathryn said nervously.

Shapes loomed in the sky. "And the dragons are still hunting us," Forrest added, just as nervously.

5
OGRE

athryn Centaur glanced at the sky. "I'll throw a blanket of fog," she said, raising her hands.

"You can make another kind of blanket?" Forrest asked, surprised. "Not just security?"

"Yes. My talent is blankets, not just one kind. But I'm only about eight years old now, and it won't be very big." From her hands poured patches of mist, which spread out and sank around them. Unfortunately it sank too low, so that their heads poked out, and the dragons spied them. "This is the best I can do," Cathryn said. "We'll have to duck down in order to hide in it."

They ducked down. The blanket of fog closed over their heads, concealing them from the air. Unfortunately it also made it hard for them to see their way.

Then there was a great thudding sound. "An ogre!" Cathryn whispered, frightened. Forrest realized that as a child she was much more fearful of monsters than she would have been as an adult.

He poked his head cautiously up through the top of the cloud blanket and peeked at the sky. The dragons were circling, looking for their prey. They were smaller than he remembered, but he realized that this was because they were now younger. As the ogre approached, huge and awful, the dragons peered down at him.

"Stay here no, dragons go!" the ogre cried, shaking one hamfist.

But the dragons knew he couldn't reach them. They were young and foolish. One of them flew over the ogre and dropped a ball of dung. It splatted close, and some of it flew out to speckle the ogre's hairy hide.

The ogre growled. It wasn't that dirt bothered him, but he was not quite stupid enough not to know he was being insulted. Ogres were justifiably proud of their stupidity, but there were limits. He stooped, picked up a rock, and hurled it at the dragon. The dragon tried to swerve, but the rock clipped it on the tail, knocking it upside down. The dragon gyrated desperately to prevent itself from falling to the ground, then flew quickly away. In a moment the other dragons followed; they didn't care to tangle with an ogre in ogre territory.

Satisfied, the ogre tramped on. He was evidently the border guard. It was just as well, because the cloud blanket was thinning. Soon they would have been exposed, and the ogre wasn't a much better bet than the dragons, as far as their safety went. Cathryn could have spread her wings and flown away, of course, but she was too courteous to do that.

Cathryn stood and recalled her blanket. The wisps of cloud funneled into her hands, and the ground was clear again.

Imbri resumed her determined trek. "It is getting close," she said.

"That's good," Cathryn said, because as they walked she was looking more like seven than eight. It was clear that she would be unable to go beyond her limit.

They crested a hill, and looked down on an enormous castle. It had no moat, and evidently didn't need one, because the bashed and splintered state of the trees around it showed it to be the home of an ogre. What else, here in ogre country?

"It's in there," Imbri said. "The one who knows where the dear horn is."

"I don't think there's anything in there but the ogre," Cathryn said. "I don't think it's a good idea to go in."

"But if he's the one who knows, we'll have to ask him," Forrest said.

"Ogres eat other folk, and crunch their bones," Cathryn reminded him, shivering. As a child she lacked courage.

"But that's temporary, here, isn't it?" Imbri asked. "Because all folk are just spirits, so can't be truly killed or destroyed?"

"Yes. But it's awful getting crunched. It hurts. And if he crunches you, you'll be gone from that region. You can never return to where you died, any more than you can go beyond your regions of delivery or ending."

"You mean folk can die here?" Forrest asked, alarmed.

"Not exactly. We can die, but it is limited."

"How can death be limited?"

"Limited to the region where the death occurs. That means that though a person reconstitutes, he can never return to that spot, or ever come close to it. The limit is about six months on a side, From and To, and equivalent distances north and south."

Both Forrest and Imbri were perplexed. "But why can't a person just go there anyway?" Imbri asked.

"He just can't. It no longer exists for him. He can see the limit, but can't cross it."

"You mean it exists, only he can't go there?" Forrest asked. "Others can go, but not the one who died there?"

"Yes."

They pondered that a moment. Then Forrest had another question: "Suppose I get killed by the ogre, so I can't go back there, but then the ogre comes out here? Beyond the six month range? Could I have at him again?"

"Yes. When two folk fight, and one kills the other, he has to be careful when he leaves that area, because the other may be lurking for him, to kill him back. Sometimes two enemies leave a whole series of holes in each other's existences, making things difficult. So as a general rule, folk try not to kill or be killed, because it's such a nuisance."

"What about dragons or ogres?"

"That's another matter. They are so dull that they don't worry about such complications. Dragons don't kill their own, and don't care about others. If an ogre crunches you once, he'll do it again. It isn't easy to talk to an ogre; they're too stupid. I think maybe this a bad idea."

"But if we don't talk to him, we can't find out where the dear horn is," Forrest said. "Then we won't be able to complete our service to you, and you won't be able to help us find faun country."

"That is true," she agreed sadly.

Forrest pondered. "It occurs to me that this is like one of the Good Magician's Challenges. We just have to figure out the way through."

"But we have no guarantee that there is a way through," Imbri said. "This isn't a carefully crafted test. This is real."

"Still, even real challenges often have solutions." He gazed at the castle. "Maybe animal psychology will help. What is the basic nature of ogres?"

"Everyone knows that," Cathryn said. "They are the strongest, ugliest, and stupidest creatures around."

He nodded. "That's my understanding. I hear they even have contests in those categories. But I also hear that they're not bad folk, when you get to know them."

"Who would want to get to know an ogre?" Cathryn inquired.

"We would," Imbri said. "So we can ask him where the dear horn is."

"Oh, that's right; I forgot. I don't have much memory at this age."

But Forrest was working on his notion. "Ogres have pride, don't they? Suppose we challenged him to an ugly contest?"

"But we couldn't possibly win that," Cathryn said. "None of us is even remotely uglier than the handsomest ogre."

"So we would lose," Forrest said.

"Yes. Instantly. Then he would crunch us."

But Imbri was catching on. "Would he crunch folk he had just bested, and who admitted it? Who maybe even praised his superior ugliness?"

Cathryn stared at her. "What a notion! You mean his ogre pride in victory would make him generous?"

Forrest nodded. "Yes. We could rally make him proud."

Imbri remained doubtful. "But if it doesn't work, we get crunched."

Forrest nodded. "So I guess I'd better go in alone."

Both fillies reacted. "We didn't say that," Imbri protested.

"No, we didn't," Cathryn agreed.

"But it's my idea, and there's no sense in having two or three of us get crunched, when one will do."

The two exchanged a generous glance. "We're not sure this is best," Imbri said.

"Consider it this way: if I get crunched, you will still be here to try it, if you wish to, perhaps with more success. If it works for me, then I can ask the ogre to let the two of you in. So you don't need to take the risk either way, unless you decide to."

"I hate to say it," Cathryn said. "But he's making sense."

"Fauns are more sensible than I thought," Imbri agreed.

"And have more courage than I thought."

"Well, we don't just chase nymphs, you know," Forrest said, embarrassed. "Now, how can I make myself ugly?"

"Why even try?" Imbri asked. "Just challenge him, and lose. He won't know the difference."

He nodded. "I'll do it." He squared himself, and marched on toward the castle.

"Wait!" Imbri called. "If you get crunched, where will you reconstitute?"

He paused. "How far is half a year?"

Cathryn considered. "Back about where we emerged from the comic strip."

"Then I'll form there, just this side of it."

"All right," Imbri said. "But be careful, Forrest."

He laughed. "If I was careful, I wouldn't walk into an ogre's den." He resumed his march.

The castle loomed larger and uglier as he approached it. It was huge and squat, with dull thatch for the roof, and mildew on the stone walls. The big front door was well over twice his own height, made of ironwood.

He came to a stop before the door. Entry was a daunting prospect, but he raised one fist and knocked on the wood iron.

There was no response. So he knocked harder. Still nothing. He realized that the ogre probably couldn't hear him. For one thing, there was a constant rumbling or crashing from within the castle, as if something huge and violent were bashing down walls.

He looked around and saw a big bell. On it was printed the word WEATHER. Beside it was a solid metal bar. So he picked up the bar, hefted it high, and swung it at the bell-weather.

There was a loud gong, followed by a crack of thunder. A storm cloud formed over the bell, shooting out bolts of lightning. The lightning struck the bell, adding to the sound. Then a bucket of rain dropped from the cloud and doused the bell. The sound faded, and the cloud evaporated.

There was a rumbling behind the door. Then it jerked violently inward, so that the suction of the air blew Forrest inside. He stumbled and caught his footing, helped by his magic sandals.

There stood the ogre: twice the height of a man, hairy, and disproportionately muscular. "Who you?" the thing demanded.

"I—I'm Forrest Faun. I come to have an ugly contest."

The ogre thought about that. Forrest knew he was thinking, because the unusual effort was heating his head, and huge fleas were jumping off lest their feet get burned. Then he decided to introduce himself. "See me: Orgy."

So far, so good. "I'm uglier than you."

Orgy Ogre stared down at him. "Ugly faun? 'Tis to yawn."

"I'll prove it. Do you have a mirror?"

Orgy shook his shaggy head. "Mirror lack. Ogre crack."

He meant that his face was so ugly that any mirror that reflected it broke. This was a complication. How could Forrest lose a contest if they couldn't compare their faces? But maybe they could do it with water. "Do you have a pool?"

"Sure, pool. It cool."

"Then let's compare faces in the pool. Then we'll see who is uglier."

Orgy considered, and more fleas jumped off. Then he decided. "Me say okay." He turned and led the way into the castle.

Forrest followed. He noticed that much of the castle was in ruins. The walls had been bashed down, and the stones were scattered across the floor. The ogre simply kicked them out of the way, not even noticing, though some were pretty solid chunks.

They came to an inner courtyard where water had collected. It was dirty, but it would do.

Forrest bent forward so that he could see his reflection. He looked just exactly like a faun. "Ugly," he said.

Orgy Ogre bent over. The water quivered and shrank away. Orgy grimaced. The water made waves as it fled to the edges of the pool. Orgy smiled. The water turned muddy and splashed right out of the pool on the far side.

"I'm impressed," Forrest said. "I was never able to make water do that. You are uglier than I am, by far. You must be a legend among your kind." He was sincere; the ogre had truly impressed him.

"No, I am merely an average ogre," Orgy said sadly. "But thank you for the compliment."

Forrest stared. "You're not rhyming!"

"I never did rhyme. No ogre does. It is merely your perception that changed."

"But you still look like an ogre to me."

"But now you see me as an individual, instead of a monster. You have achieved respect. So you are able to hear me as I am."

"I never realized! Do you mean that all ogres are cultured, instead of being stupid?"

"That depends entirely on your perception."

"I was afraid you were going to crunch me."

"I was, until you showed that you had discovered respect. We ogres crunch only the ignorant."

"This is an education," Forrest said. "I'll never view ogres the same again."

"Excellent. You should have no further fear of us. But why did you come here?"

"I need your help. I'm looking for the dear horn."

"Oho! You wish to trade services."

"Yes. Is there anything I can do for you?"

"I'm afraid not. I am completely satisfied. I am sorry you came here for nothing."

Forrest had been afraid of this. "I came here with two companions. They remained apart, for fear of getting crunched. They might be able to figure out a service that you need. Then we could trade. Would it be all right if they joined me here?"

"That depends on their perspective. If they are ordinary, I'll be obliged to crunch them. Protocol, you know."

"Suppose I explain to them about respect?"

"They may not listen. Most folk are sure they know the nature of ogres."

"But if I can make them understand?"

"Then they will be welcome to the hospitality of the castle."

"Let me go fetch them. Maybe we can do each other some good after all."

"As you wish. Meanwhile, I shall return to my bashing."

As Forrest walked out of the castle, Orgy Ogre waded into the nearest wall, bashing it into rubble with his two hamfists. The whole structure shuddered. Such was the ogre's ferocity that it was a wonder that any of the castle remained standing. Forrest realized that this was the sound he had heard before, when he stood outside the door. No wonder it required the bell-weather to get the ogre's attention.

He went out the door, which remained open. But it swung closed once he was clear; apparently it was set to let visitors out, but not to let them in. So it was a magic door. He departed the bleak castle environs, and walked on across the blasted terrain to where the two mares stood. They looked amazed and relieved to see him.

"You may enter the ogre's den," he said. "But there is a caution."

"That's a severe understatement," Cathryn said. "Are you sure it's safe?"

"It will be safe if you have the right attitude."

Both mares looked at him doubtfully. "How can attitude save a person from being crunched by a monster?" Imbri asked.

"You have to leave your prejudice behind, and have proper respect."

"For an ogre?" Cathryn asked incredulously.

Forrest realized that there was a problem. "He's really a very cultured creature. You just have to see him as such."

The two mares exchanged a Significant Glance. "I suppose even a stink horn has its culture," Imbri remarked to no one in particular.

They were locked into their prejudice. He had to get rid of it, or it would not be safe for them to enter the ogre's den. "Remember how you viewed me, at first? As just another faun looking for a nymph to chase?"

They nodded.

"Do you still view me that way?"

"No," Cathryn said. "You have a lot more character than I originally supposed."

"So can you appreciate that originally you were operating on prejudice?"

"Nonsense! Centaurs aren't prejudiced." Then she reconsidered. "But I'm very young now, so maybe you do have a point."

"So can you appreciate that the ogre may have qualities to be respected, if you viewed him without prejudice?"

"An ogre?" Then she heard herself, and laughed. "You wouldn't be teasing a centaur foal, would you?"

"No. I am serious. It is a matter of life or crunching. The ogre doesn't crunch those who respect him."

Imbri was having her own problem. "Respecting an ogre is an oxymoron, a contradiction in terms. They are sheer brutes."

"Then respect his brutishness. But see him as worthy in his own right."

"Well, I suppose I can make the effort."

"So can I," Cathryn said. "Even if I do get crunched."

They walked back to the castle. They came to a stop before the great door. "Now remember: he's an individual. You will know this by his speech: it doesn't rhyme."

"All ogres speak in stupid rhyming couplets," Cathryn said.

"No. They are merely heard that way by ignorant outsiders. If you hear him rhyming, don't speak, because he'll know you don't respect him."

"This is weird," the centaur said.

Forrest picked up the rod and banged the bell-weather. The fierce little storm formed, and the commotion summoned the ogre to the door. This time all three of them were sucked inward by the swoosh of air. The ogre stood there, as huge and brutish as ever.

"Orgy, these are my friends Mare Imbrium and Cathryn Centaur," Forrest said. "Mares, this is Orgy Ogre, master of this castle."

"Hello, Orgy," Imbri said bravely.

"Likewise," Cathryn said, looking as if she were ready to spread her wings and fly away.

"I am glad to make your acquaintance, fair mares," Orgy said graciously.

Imbri hesitated, then smiled. "And I yours, ugly ogre," she replied.

But Cathryn kept her mouth shut. Forrest knew that was trouble.

Orgy stared down at the centaur. "Please repeat what I just said to you," he requested.

Cathryn took a step back with each hoof, looking twice as nervous as before.

"But all he said was—" Forrest began, but stopped when a severe glance from the ogre cut him off. He realized that this was a test the centaur had to pass on her own.

"You said 'Who cares, she mares?' " she said. Then, after half a pause, she reconsidered. "Wait, that isn't quite it. You said—you said you were glad to make our acquaintance, and you called us fair mares."

Forrest breathed a silent sigh of relief. "Then welcome into my castle," Orgy said grandly, and led the way down the hall.

"You're right," Cathryn murmured as she walked beside Forrest. "He doesn't rhyme, when I listen with an open mind."

Forrest noticed that one of the walls he had thought was in rubble was actually solid. Maybe this was a different passage, though it seemed to be the only one available.

They came to a central hall that had some spare furnishings. "You must be hungry," Orgy said. "Come sit at my magic table."

Actually the rough-hewn tree-trunk timber table was way too big and high for any of them. But the ogre found blocks to put on the seats of the huge chairs, for Forrest and Imbri, and gently lifted them up so that they could sit at the level of the table. Cathryn was able to stand on her chair so that her head was high enough.

Food appeared. Steaming pots emerged from a window in the wall at the end of the table and walked on stout little legs to the center, and a big cocoa pot arrived similarly. Plates and utensils slid along until they took their proper places before each person. Then the pots lifted serving spoons and plopped stew onto each plate, while the cocoa pot siphoned steaming cocoa into each mug.

Orgy dived into his stew with gusto, slurping and splashing. But then Forrest reminded himself about attitude, and looked again, more carefully—and saw that the ogre was using a big spoon in the conventional human manner, and neither slurping nor splashing. His prejudice had tried to reassert itself.

They tried their own portions. Forrest found the substance in his stew to be almost nut-like, and quite good. The mares seemed to be enjoying theirs too.

"If I may inquire," Cathryn said, "what kind of stew is this?"

"Horse dropping stew," Orgy said.

She blinked. The stew was brown and lumpy. Then she smiled, surmounting her prejudice. "Horse chestnuts," she said.

"Yes. The chests and nuts drop from the horse trees, and we collect the chests and the nut droppings too."

"And the cook makes stew from them," Imbri said. "How nice."

Then, as they ate, Forrest got down to business. "We need to find a service we can render Orgy, in return for information about the location of the dear horn. Do either of you have any ideas?"

"Not at the moment," Cathryn said. "But perhaps if we knew more about Orgy and this castle, we would get an idea."

"That is too simple to be interesting," the ogre said.

"Even the most stupid thing becomes interesting, when there is a need," Forrest said.

He had uttered a magic word. "Stupid," Orgy said. "I am as stupid as any ogre. Very well, I will tell you about me and this castle. Two years ago I was just another ogre, happily bashing rocks, tying trees in knots, and teaching young dragons the meaning of fear. I mean, it's what ogres do. Then I happened across an odd looking horn that someone had left lying around. Dimly curious, I picked it up and sniffed it, but it had no particular smell. I bit it, but it didn't taste particularly edible. In short, it didn't seem to be very useful. 'Me scorn this horn,' I said, or words to that effect; after all, there might be someone listening. Then I put it to my mouth and blew."

He paused. "Are you sure you want to hear more? This is so stupid that even I am being bored."

"I don't want to be a spoilsport," Forrest said, "but I find it fascinating. Please do go on."

"Oh," Orgy said. "Well, it gets duller. When I blew the horn, it made a noise like none other I had heard. It was, if you can imagine this, the sound of utter longing. When I heard that, I wanted something so badly that I could think of nothing else. I didn't even know what it was, just that I had to have it. So I blew the horn again, and this time I heard an echo from afar, and my longing focused on that distant response. So I trudged toward it, and when I began to lose my way, I blew it again, and got another echo. Gradually I realized that I was the only one who heard either the horn or the echo; other creatures I passed paid no attention, apart from getting hastily out of my way. They did not realize that I was on a mission; they thought I had come to maraud as usual.

"I continued in this manner for some time, until at last I hove into view of this castle. The echo came from it. It seemed to be unoccupied, so I entered. Naturally I bashed down a wall or two, and found it very bashable, so I continued. It was a real thrill, once again destroying something solid. Eventually, pleasantly exercised, I dropped to the floor and snored valiantly for a few hours. When I woke, there was a table loaded with victuals. So I got up and gobbled them down, then resumed my bashing of the walls.

"So it continued for several days, before I realized that the walls did not stay bashed. They restored themselves overnight, or even sooner. This pleased me immensely, for it meant that I could bash them down again. And indeed, so it has been ever since. Bash, eat, sleep, bash, in a perpetual routine. I love it; it is an ogre's heaven. Since I had no more use for the horn, I threw it out a window. After a time—several months—I realized that this was the purpose of the horn: to lead me to my heart's delight. A perpetually bashable castle. So this is surely the dear horn you seek, and I know exactly where I threw it—memory being inversely proportional to intelligence—and will be glad to tell you, if you can find any equivalent service to trade for the information. But I doubt that you can, as I am completely happy as I am."

"It does seem as if this castle was designed with an ogre in mind," Cathryn remarked. "Perpetual bashing."

"With feasting in between," Imbri agreed. "There doesn't seem to be anything missing."

"Yet I, too, thought I had everything I wanted," the centaur said. "Now I realize that I simply had not thought of my missing desire."

Orgy looked at her. "You have a missing desire?"

"Yes. That's why I seek the dear horn."

"To find your True Love?"

"Yes. A companion to be with, to love and cherish and breed with—" She paused. "Oh, that's it for you!"

Orgy was taken aback. "I don't think I would be a good companion for you."

She laughed. "Surely not. I favor intelligence and wings. I mean that maybe you could use a companion of your own kind. An ogress."

"I'm not sure. She might be uglier than I am. Then the castle might like her better than me."

"Maybe a merely moderately ugly ogress?" Imbri inquired.

"Who would want a merely moderately ugly ogress?"

Forrest saw that this wasn't getting anywhere. But it did suggest a line of investigation. "What about one who is distinctly inferior to you in strength, ugliness, and stupidity, but who really appreciates your ogrish qualities?"

Orgy pondered, and the fleas began jumping. "There is something appealing there."

It fell into place. They had sought to applaud the ogre, letting him win an ugly contest. That had worked, in a manner. An ogress could surely do it much better. "Someone to admire your achievement in continuously bashing down the walls. Where's the fun of a job well done, if nobody notices?"

The fleas jumped higher, as if their feet were getting burned. "Yes, I hadn't thought of that."

"Naturally not," Forrest said triumphantly. "You are too stupid. But we who can't compare to you in that respect were able to think of it, and this must be what we can do for you. We can find you such an ogress."

Orgy nodded, and the few remaining fleas hung on. "For that I would tell you where the dear horn is. Find me that ogress."

"Well, if you tell us where the dear horn is, we can use it to find her."

Orgy shook his head, and the fleas were hurled into the nearest unbroken wall. "I am too stupid to understand why you wouldn't simply use the dear horn for your own quest, once you had it. So I'll wait for you to bring the ogress.''

The three of them exchanged a somewhat stretched glance. Naturally it would not be expedient to question the stupidity of their host. "We'll search for her without the dear horn," Forrest agreed.

"Do you have any notion who would know where such an ogress might be?" Cathryn asked with something less than full stupidity.

"Ogle Ogre might know. He sees everything."

"How can we find Ogle?"

Orgy put his last remaining fleas to flight. "He especially likes to look at esthetic females. Maybe if you stood on a mountain and looked esthetic, he would spy you and come to ogle you."

This time Cathryn and Imbri shared a female type glance, excluding Forrest. Then they shrugged. "Maybe so," one of them agreed.

Thus, in due course, they departed the ogre's castle on a new mission: to discover a suitable ogress. They headed for the nearest barren peak. "I hope we are able to compliment Ogle Ogre before he crunches us," Cathryn muttered.

"If he comes to ogle you, he shouldn't crunch you," Forrest pointed out.

"And that's another thing," Imbri said. "Do you suppose all females exist just to be ogled?"

"Why no, of course not," Forrest said, taken aback. "A number of them exist to be chased and celebrated."

For some obscure impenetrable reason she turned a dark glare on him. "He is a faun," Cathryn reminded her, for some similarly unfathomable motive.

Since they had nothing important on their minds, Forrest shared a concern of his: "If I am the size I am because of the solidified mass of my soul, and Imbri is the size she is because of the mass of her half soul, how is it that creatures like Cathryn and Orgy have so much more mass? Are their souls so much larger?"

"Now that's an intelligent question," Cathryn said. "Just when we thought you had used up your supply of intelligence. No, souls don't vary in size like that. In fact, we of Ptero really don't have souls. They come only when we assume reality. We have inferior substitute filler material that assumes the semblance but not the essence of souls.

Thus we are limited to our life spans, and have no existence beyond them. It is one reason each of us hopes to come into genuine existence. So we amass as much material as we require to fill out our standard forms, and that's it.''

"You mean I could assume larger size, by adding some of that filler substance?" Imbri asked.

"You could. But why would you want to? You are pure soul now; what higher aspiration can there be?''

"To be fully souled. To be fully real. I am only a day mare; I was fully real only briefly, when I had a mission in Xanth, and was king for a moment. Ever since, I have longed to be fully real again. And once I complete my Service to the Good Magician, by enabling Forrest to find his tree spirit, I will be, perhaps.''

"I envy you your chance at reality. All of us here on Ptero hope for it, but most of us know that we will never achieve it.''

"How do you know that any of you achieve it?" Forrest asked. "Could you all be victims of a cruel hoax?''

"No, we do know the chance is real, because some of us are real. We see them, and know it can theoretically happen for others.''

"But didn't you say that none of you actually have souls?''

"I said that all of us hope for genuine existence, and gain souls only when we assume reality. Some of us do achieve it, and the rest of us envy them despite the inconvenience it brings them.''

"Inconvenience?''

"There is a year-wide swath missing from their lives, corresponding to the period they are in Xanth. It is similar to the excluded regions of death, but broader. Because a creature can't be both here and in Xanth at the same time.''

Forrest shook his head. "I don't understand that.''

"Neither do I," Imbri agreed.

"Well, it is rather complicated to appreciate, until you see it," Cathryn said. "Perhaps we shall encounter a living person before we separate.''

Forrest hoped so, because this was one peculiar thing she was describing. Souled folk with missing year-wide bands?

They reached the top of the peak, which really wasn't all that high, but it made up for it in barrenness. As far as they could see, there was nothing except dirt and rocks and stunted weeds that didn't dare grow bold for fear of the ogres. So visibility was good, which was what they wanted.

"Now we shall have to give him something to ogle," Cathryn said distastefully. "I understand males like to look at forbidden female anatomy. But centaurs, being more sensible, have no forbidden anatomy. So it may be up to you, Imbri."

"But I'm a mare," Imbri protested. "I assumed this form only because it's all that my half soul can substantiate, and because it facilitates physical verbal speech. I wear a dress only because otherwise I would be confused for a nymph."

"But nymphs are mindless creatures," Cathryn said. "While you clearly have a mind."

"Not unless I speak."

The centaur nodded. "Point made. From afar, Ogle would take you for a nymph, unless you are clothed. So he would ignore you, because ogling just doesn't work unless the subject is embarrassed. So you wouldn't be of interest, clothed or unclothed."

"Maybe if Cathryn put on clothing," Forrest suggested. "Since centaurs don't normally wear anything, that might make her interesting."

"I doubt it," Cathryn said. "Even straight human beings, who have the worst hang-ups about exposure, don't worry much about children, and I am now seven years old."

He had to admit that was true. A clothed juvenile centaur would not be worth ogling, because even an ogre would know she had nothing to conceal. But he refused to give up on the quest. "We'll just have to establish that Imbri is an adult human female, and then have her remove her clothing."

"But that would be improper," Imbri protested. "A human woman wouldn't."

"Precisely," Cathryn said. "That makes it ogleable."

The logic was impeccable. So, reluctantly, Imbri agreed. She re-formed her dress, which was made of her own soul-stuff, so that it had a number of pieces. Then Forrest and Cathryn stood on either side of the peak, serving as an audience. Imbri, who had experience with male dreams, explained what was required, so that they could make suitable comments that would help attract the ogre's notice. Then Imbri stood on the highest knoll and lifted her arms.

"Behold!" Cathryn said loudly. "A modest human style female woman lady is about to do a naughty strip tease dance, that no decent person should observe."

"Great!" Forrest exclaimed, just as loudly. "As an improper male type faun I can hardly wait."

Then Imbri began her dance. She stepped around, wiggling her bottom. She was pretty good at it; her experience making daydreams must have helped. Then she kicked one foot high, so that her leg showed all the way to the knee. Her sandals were still protecting her from moving her feet incorrectly, so that she managed to show only as much as she meant to.

"Disgusting!" Cathryn pronounced.

"More! More!" Forrest cried.

Imbri whirled, so that her skirt flared out and lifted, showing both knees.

"Stop this vile display at once!" Cathryn said in her best imitation of an adult voice. "Don't you realize that a child might see?"

"Who cares?" Forrest demanded irresponsibly.

There was a faint shudder in the ground. Either the earth itself was disgusted at the display, or an ogre was stirring far away.

Imbri took hold of the kerchief she had formed and drew it from her head. She tossed it into the air, where it fluttered a moment, then dissolved into vapor.

"Indecent exposure!" Cathryn protested.

"Take it off! Take it off!" Forrest insisted wickedly as he sat down on the ground.

The ground rumbled. Something huge was trudging in their direction.

Imbri worked off her blouse and threw it at Forrest, who caught it and sniffed it in as vulgar a manner as he could imagine. Actually it was a very nice blouse, with a faint smell of fresh hay. It was Mare Imbri's natural soul substance. Then it dissolved, because of course she couldn't afford to get fragmented.

"Absolutely revolting," Cathryn proclaimed.

"Divine," he countered sincerely.

Imbri was now dancing in a bright red halter and skirt, and really did look nice. She was small, because of her lack of much soul substance, but well formed, and the tight halter offered a strong hint of even better things to come. Especially when it bounced with the vigor of her motions. Forrest was intrigued despite knowing that this was only an act. There was something about clothing that enhanced interesting aspects into exciting aspects.

Imbri kicked up a leg, and one of her slippers went flying. Then she danced closer and kicked off the other, and such was her position that Forrest saw halfway beyond the knee. That was dangerously close to panty territory! "Awesome!"

But as he sat, half stunned by the prospect, the slipper hit him on the forehead. It didn't hurt him; it felt more like a kiss as it dropped and dissolved.

Then the ogre arrived. "Who she me see?" he demanded.

Startled, Forrest turned to him. "You must be Ogle Ogre," he said. It was a good guess, because the ogre's eyes seemed to bulge halfway out of their sockets. There was something else about him, but Forrest wasn't certain what it was.

"From dawn to dawn, me ogre, you faun," he agreed.

"Oh, come off it, Ogle," Forrest said. "We know you don't really talk in stupid rhymes."

The ogre looked crestfallen. "What gave me away?"

"Nothing. It was Orgy Ogre who let slip the secret. We want to make a deal with you."

"I am not interested in any deal. I came merely to get a closer look at your dancing maiden. She was just about to reveal something interesting."

"No I wasn't," Imbri said as her blouse, kerchief, and shoes reappeared on her body.

"Then I'm out of here," the ogre said crossly. "I can't crunch you because you know my nature, and if I can't ogle you, then any further dalliance here becomes pointless."

"He has a soul," Imbri murmured. "See that faint glow."

That was the oddity Forrest had noted. What an unlikely place to encounter a soul!

Imbri reconsidered. "Suppose I dance while you negotiate with the faun?"

Ogle considered, and his eyeballs heated to a dull red. "Okay," he concluded in due course.

So Imbri resumed her dance, with all her clothing in place. She did not look perfectly pleased, but yielded to necessity. Also, she seemed to enjoy dancing, and might have done it for pleasure, if it were not for the ogling.

"We need to know where to find a suitable ogress to go stay with Orgy in his bashable castle and applaud his heroic efforts," Forrest said.

"That would be Olé Ogress. She's not phenomenally ugly, but she is extremely enthusiastic." The ogre's eyeballs were unwaveringly oriented on Imbri, who was twirling her skirt dangerously high.

Forrest tore his own eyes away, realizing that he could probably make a better deal while Ogle was distracted. "What can we do for you in return for this information?"

Ogle considered again. This time his eyeballs turned white hot. Maybe that was mostly because Imbri was drawing off her blouse again. That might not seem like much, but the ogre probably had forgotten that there was a halter under it, and the centaur was frowning so determinedly that it was obvious that something truly naughty was happening. "Nothing," he concluded. "I don't need anything."

Forrest had a notion, based on what he had recently learned from Cathryn. "You like to see things," he said. "Especially things you're not supposed to see, like human pantomiming," he continued, emphasizing the first syllable of the last word, so that it sounded as if he were about to say the P word. Cathryn's sudden shocked intake of breath aided the effect.

"Yeah, yeah," Ogle agreed, his eyeballs bulging as if he actually had seen the forbidden thing. It was clear that being souled did not change his fundamental nature.

"Well, the one thing you can't see is what is within your blanked out year."

"Yeah. I can see everything on this side, and everything on the far side, but when I try to go into it, I just slide right across and my age changes a year in a single moment. It is exceedingly frustrating.''

Now Imbri's shoes were coming off. Forrest knew that he had to get on with it quickly, lest she be forced to show something really naughty. "Well, we can go there, because we aren't you. We can tell you what is happening in your forbidden section."

That prospect actually brought the ogre's eyes from Imbri, which meant that she was able to dance without removing any more items, giving her more time. "But only souled folk can see souls," he said.

"I am souled," Forrest said. "Don't you see my glow?"

"So I do," Ogle agreed, surprised. He glanced at Imbri. "And hers, too. That makes her even more interesting. A naughty view of a souled creature is much more effective than of an unsouled one. So it seems you can indeed go into my barred region. Very well: if you will tell me what I am doing in there, I will tell you where to find Olé Ogress."

"Agreed! We'll go now." Then Forrest realized that it wasn't quite that simple. "Uh, where is it?"

"Right this way." The ogre led the way east.

As they progressed, Cathryn continued to grow younger. Soon she was dancing along like a yearling foal. Fortunately the ogre stopped before she hit the limit of her range. "Here," he said. "Right now it's when I am twenty four years old, and moving slowly forward. I don't seem to be much changed on either side of it, but I sure am curious about what's in there."

"We will go in and observe carefully," Forrest said. "And when we come out, we'll make a full report."

"I don't think I'd have the patience for that. How about half a report?"

"Half," Forrest agreed amicably. "Or even a quarter, if you prefer."

"Wow! That's great." Then a slow thought percolated through what passed for the ogre's brain. "But what will I do, with nothing to ogle? My attention span is very short."

Cathryn stepped in. "I will tell you a foal's story I know. 'The Ogre and the Three Bares.' At my present age, it's the only one I know, but I think it's a good one."

"I love that story!" Ogle said. "I haven't heard it since I was in my ogret range."

"I will refresh your memory. Once there was an ogre who was lost in the forest. Of course he could simply have bashed all the trees to smithereens, but of course he was too stupid to realize that."

"Of course," Ogle agreed appreciatively.

"So he stumbled about until he saw this odd house. He bashed down the door and went in, and there were three bowls of really icky gruel. So he gulped down the first, but it was too hot. . . ."

Forrest and Imbri quietly departed as the story enraptured the ogre. It seemed that forbidden adventures were almost as compelling as forbidden sights. The story wouldn't last long, so they had to get to the center and see what there was to be seen and get back.

As it happened, there wasn't much. The vegetation was much thicker, because it had had a chance to grow up during the year's absence by the ogre, but since other ogres occasionally passed this way, large patches of damage remained. Forrest could appreciate how Orgy Ogre liked the perpetually bashable walls of the castle, because it was obvious that natural terrain simply could not stand up long to an ogre's presence. The undergrowth gradually thinned as they progressed east, because in that direction it had had less time to recover.

Then Forrest saw a hulking figure ahead. "That looks like an ogre, sort of," he said.

"Sort of," Imbri agreed. "But it's insubstantial."

"Who ever heard of an insubstantial ogre!"

But lo, it was true. The figure was bashing a small mountain into a molehill, and they could see through its outline as well as the mountain's outline. What could this be?

"It's Ogle," Imbri said, surprised. "See those bulging eyeballs."

She was right. The faint image was their ogre. "And that must be a mountain on Xanth, because it's flat here," Forrest said, walking through both ogre and mountain.

They paused to study the figure. Soon the ogre stopped bashing and stepped up on the top of the large molehill he had made. He turned around, looking in all directions. Then his eyes bulged and his jaw went slack. He remained frozen in place.

"He's ogling something," Imbri said.

"I wonder what it is?" Forrest walked around the figure. He discovered that at the right angle, he could see a reflection in one of the eyeballs. It seemed to be a white square, inside of which was pink material, bulging in two places.

Then Forrest freaked out. He found himself lying on the ground with small planets spinning above his head. Imbri was kneeling beside him, trying to help. "Forrest! What happened?"

He tried to speak, but his mouth had not yet recovered from the freakout. Imbri sat on the ground, picked up his head, and cushioned it in her lap. She stroked his forehead, her soft hand passing pleasantly across his horns. "It's all right," she said. "Just relax. You don't seem to be physically hurt."

He finally got his tongue unfreaked. "How could I be, in soul form?" he asked.

"Forrest!" she exclaimed. "You're recovering!" She leaned down and kissed him. It was a surprisingly nice kiss, and the way her soft yet resilient blouse nudged his face enhanced the effect.

"I am getting good care," he said. "I can't remember when I've been so comfortable."

She hugged him, in her fashion, and that bordered on delightful. "I was concerned. You were looking at the ghost ogre, and then you abruptly collapsed. What did you see?"

Then he remembered. "I saw the reflection of what he saw. What he was ogling in Xanth. It was—"

"Yes?"

"A panty. In a window."

Imbri dumped his head on the ground. "You're not supposed to look!"

"I'm sorry," he said, as he waited for another tiny planet to clear away. "I didn't know what it was, until I saw it. And it was just a reflection, not the real thing."

"Well," she said, faintly mollified. "Just don't do it again."

He sat up, then made his way back to his feet. The ogre was still standing like a statue. "I guess now we know why he was bashing down that mountain. It was to make a platform so he could see something better, inside that house. When he saw in the window—"

"He saw a woman changing her clothing," Imbri finished, disapprovingly.

Suddenly the ghost ogre fell off his platform. He lay on his back, and ghost planets spun over his head, just as they had with Forrest. The woman must have moved away from the window, breaking the freakout view.

"We have more than enough to report, I think," Forrest said. "Let's go back, before Cathryn runs out of story."

"Yes," she said tightly. She was becoming more like a woman and less like a mare in attitude as well as appearance. Forrest wasn't sure that was a complete improvement.

They left the ghost ogre to recover on his own, and hurried back west. They emerged just as the centaur foal was finishing:

"And so the ogre bashed his way out of that house, and never went there again. And he never ate icky gruel again, either."

"Yeah, yeah!" Ogle agreed.

"We have returned," Forrest said.

Both centaur and ogre looked at them. "You look as if you are recovering from a freakout," Cathryn said to Forrest.

"And you look as if you are recovering from awful outrage," Ogle said to Imbri.

"Right on both counts," Forrest said grimly. "We saw the image of your Xanthine self."

"Bashing a mountain into a molehill," Imbri continued.

"Until he could look in a window and see a panty," Forrest concluded.

Ogle was amazed. "I ogled a panty?"

"That is correct," Imbri said primly. "It was outrageous. You should be horribly ashamed."

Ogle tried to wipe the amazement, awe, and delight off his puss. "Horribly," he agreed. "No wonder I feel so high near that border." He glanced at Forrest with a women-don't-understand expression. Forrest could only nod slightly hoping the females wouldn't catch it.

"So now you can tell us where Olé Ogress is," Cathryn said. As a foal she did not seem as upset about the report as she might have been, but it plainly set her back somewhat.

"Right this way," Ogle agreed, and began tramping northwest.

They followed, with Cathryn rapidly aging, and with each step her expression became firmer. She was achieving adult female human perspective on the report, unfortunately, even though centaurs normally didn't care about human hang-ups. Forrest knew there would be no point in discussing the matter. The ogre was right: women just didn't understand some things. Maybe that was to prevent them from getting freaked out by their own apparel.

They passed the general vicinity of the knoll where they had met Ogle and went on. They entered a region of tumbled timber trees, and there in a crudely fashioned pig sty was an ogress. She was covered with stinking mud.

"Hey, what are you doing, Olé?" Orgy asked.

"I'm trying to make myself ugly," she responded dolefully. "Using bad smelling mud packs."

"Maybe you don't need to be ugly. These folk have a deal for you." Then Ogle, having fulfilled his part of the exchange, tramped away, looking at everything except the not-ugly-enough ogress.

She noticed Forrest, Imbri, and Cathryn for the first time. "Faun, mares—who cares?" she inquired.

Forrest leaned over the rail of her sty. "How would you like to live in a castle with all the food you want, and an ogre who heeds your every word and doesn't care how you look?"

"Me think me—oh, phooey on the rhymes! I'd love it. What deeply disgusting thing do I have to do to get it?"

"Just make sure your every word is praise for the ogre's accomplishment in knocking down the walls so well."

"But that comes naturally! Normally I have to stifle it, lest I be unogressly nice."

"Come with us, and we'll take you to castle and ogre."

She lurched out of the sty, shedding squishes of manure. "Let's go!"

"You don't even need to wear the mud," Forrest said.

"Excellent." She tramped to a nearby well, hauled out a huge bucket, and doused herself with cold water. In a moment she was wet but clean.

They set off for the castle. "Out of curiosity," Imbri said, "why is it that Ogle stares at attractive human women, and their clothing, but wants an uglier ogress?"

"I have wondered that myself," Olé said. "I think there is something wrong with his vision, so that he thinks human women are somehow uglier than ogresses. It's a sad case."

"Very sad," Imbri agreed, satisfied.

They reached the castle and stood at the closed door. Olé glared at the bell-weather, and it immediately sounded the alarm. In a moment the door opened and Orgy stood there.

"Are you the ogre who so successfully bashes down walls?" the ogress asked.

"Yes." Orgy looked pleased, for an ogre.

"Show me how you perform this great art. I can never see enough of superior wall bashing."

Soon it was apparent that they would get along. Orgy was bashing down walls at twice his prior pace, and Olé was waxing ever more delighted in his accomplishment as she feasted at the well stocked table. The visitors had fulfilled their service.

Orgy paused in his bashing and pointed out through the hole in the wall he had just made. "Fifty three of your paces straight out that way," he said. "Good fortune on your quest."

"Thank you," Forrest replied, and the three of them stepped through the wall and started counting paces. It required three paces to get beyond the castle. Sure enough, just fifty of Forrest's paces out from the wall lay a glowing horn.

Forrest picked it up and gave it to Cathryn. "Now you can show us where the faun territory is," he said.

She considered. "No, I think not. This is merely the means to the end; the exchange will not be satisfied until the end is achieved."

Forrest sighed inwardly. She was right. They would have to complete that aspect before moving on. Still, this was progress.

6
TRUE LOVE

They returned toward Cathryn's adult range, as she was not comfortable as a juvenile. They came to the comic strip. There was nothing to do but plunge on in, hoping to make it through without suffering permanent damage to their dignities.

There was a wall. On it were the words PUNNSYLVANIA PUNITENTIARY: ABANDON SANITY, ALL YE WHO ENTER HERE.

"We have no choice," Cathryn said grimly as she scrambled over. "How I hate the comic section!"

Forrest and Imbri followed her. He was used to puns in Xanth, but here on Ptero they seemed to be festering out of control. But he knew the strip wasn't deep; they would soon be out of it.

They almost crashed into a billbored. It seemed to have been fashioned from unpaid bills that had gotten bored with their inaction, so had clumped together to form a sign saying BORING. "Don't touch that!" Cathryn warned. "You will have to pay any bill you get."

But she was too late. Forrest had already touched a corner, and a bill had stuck to his hand. It formed into a face. "Pay me!" it cried.

"Why should I? I don't even know you."

"Because otherwise I'll turn you over to a collection agency." And it indicated a horrendous hooded ogre shape labeled YOUR MONEY OR YOUR LIFE. It held a huge bone in its paws, which it snapped in half.

Imbri burst out laughing. "It's not funny," Forrest said. "I'm about to get my bones broken."

"I'm not laughing at you," she chortled. "I'm stuck in this article."

He looked. She was indeed caught in a bush whose twigs resembled little R's. They were tickling her unmercifully. It was an R-tickle plant.

"How did that happen?" he asked her.

"I followed that head line." She gestured back, where there was a line of heads on the ground.

He took a step toward her, but stumbled into a plant that looked like a tangle of spaghetti. "Use your noodle!" it exclaimed angrily.

So he did. He reached across and plucked a handful of R's from Imbri's bush. "Here is your pay," he told the bill, rubbing the R's against it.

"Oh, ho ho, hee hee!" it squealed. "That's not—ha ha!—what I meant."

"Then blame it on the R-tickle bush, there; that's where I got this ticklish business."

"Collector—hoo hoo!—take care of it," the bill cried as it slid off his hand.

The hooded ogre tramped to the bush and began pounding it with two hamfists. R's flew all over. Soon the ogre was laughing as it flattened the bush. Imbri escaped, but didn't manage to stop laughing. "I'm not getting—hee hee—tickled any more," she explained. "It's that it serves it so right."

They lurched away from the bushes. Cathryn was trying to work her way past a counter made of packed beans. "I can't get by this bean counter," she complained.

A head formed from the counter. "Of course you can't," it said. "Nothing gets by me."

But Forrest saw something else. It looked like a huge man, bigger than an ogre, but it was standing quite still. His feet seemed to become roots, and his hands sprouted coin sized mints. "What is that?"

The centaur glanced at it. "A Man-Age-Mint, I think," she said. Then she brightened. She plucked a mint from the tree and stuffed it into the mouth of the bean counter's head. "Take that," she said with satisfaction.

The bean counter began to fade. His beans became shriveled. A vile odor of indigestion issued from him. "Help! I'm genuinely aging!" he cried.

"That's because you ate the mint," Cathryn informed him. "Now you will age rapidly into stinking extinction, unless you do whatever the Man-Age-Mint plant demands."

"What does it demand?" the bean counter asked.

"Count its mints," she said.

"But I'm a bean counter. I don't count mints."

"Too bad. I hope you fade out before your odor of spoiled beans permeates the entire neighborhood."

"I suppose I could count some mints," he said dolefully. "One, two, buckle my shoe; three, four . . ."

Then, while the counter was distracted, they squeezed by it and out to decent terrain. They had gotten back through the comic strip without quite going crazy.

"Some day I'm going to gather a posse and stamp out every pun in existence," Cathryn muttered.

They went to the section where they had first met the centaur. It was interesting to see her age as she walked, progressing from foal to gangly juvenile to early filly and finally to fully flushed young female. Her mass changed, but didn't seem to affect her directly; she evidently didn't have to eat to add weight, any more than she had had to eliminate to lose it. He knew that he and Imbri were aging the same amount in years, but it didn't make as much difference to them.

Then Cathryn stopped. "Are we ready for the next adventure?" she inquired. When there was no objection, she lifted the dear horn and blew on it.

There was no sound. Yet the centaur stood as if enraptured. "Marvelous!" she breathed.

"But it didn't work," Forrest protested.

She didn't even waste a glance on him. "You forget that only the one who blows it can hear it. The echo is from that direction." She pointed due east.

They set off east. That was a relief, because it was open range and ordinary trees as far as the eye could see; no pun strip to struggle through.

But Cathryn was getting young again. That was mischief of another nature. Suppose her True Love were beyond her range? That would make him truly inaccessible.

And that was what happened. The centaur grew smaller than either of them, and had to pause. "This is near the limit of my range," she said. "I can go farther, but I won't be able to talk, because I didn't learn until I was two. You will have to go on without me."

"But we can't hear the echo," Forrest protested.

"You won't have to. Just continue in a straight line, and you will encounter him. He hasn't moved in some time, so he may be sleeping. Bring him here, and your service will be complete. I'll wait."

Forrest exchanged a look with Imbri, but since it was the same look, neither gained anything from it. So they walked forward, following the direction.

"Suppose the limit of his range is beyond hers?" Forrest asked Imbri when they were beyond the hearing of the centaur. "So that they can never meet?"

"I don't think the dear horn works that way," she said. "The ideal True Love has to be one you can be with. I hope."

He hoped that was true. But things were so odd here on Ptero that he lacked confidence.

They saw an odd region to the south. It was somewhat foggy, but they could see a number of figures standing there, like statues. "Do you suppose her True Love could be there?" Imbri asked.

"It's not the right direction. But we could ask." He used a hoof to mark a line pointing the right direction, so they could resume travel without going astray, then walked south. They entered the fog somewhat warily, but it seemed to be harmless.

Forrest approached a glowing young woman. "May we talk to you?" he asked her.

"Sure," she replied. "That's what we're here for."

"All the people are here to be talked to?" Imbri asked.

"Yes. This is a section of limbo. We are the characters who aren't even might-be's. I'm Astrid."

"But what kind of existence do you have, then?"

"A very feeble kind," the woman said sadly. "We all long to achieve regular might-be status, but we can't until someone takes an interest in us and recognizes our talents."

Imbri exchanged half a look with Forrest. Characters who weren't even might-be's?

"If we talk to you and identify your talent, will you become a might-be?" Forrest asked.

"Yes! Please do that. I would do anything to become might-be-real. Do you need a girlfriend? I'm rather metallic, but I can be very soft when I want to be, in the manner of my mother's side of the family."

"I don't need a girlfriend. I'm a faun. I just chase nymphs. No relationships last longer than a day, and most are merely minutes. But I'll be glad to help you. How do I recognize your talent?"

"You just talk with me and ask me questions until you are able to figure it out. I can't tell you, because I don't know it, but I can tell you anything else about me."

"How can you know about yourself, if you aren't yet real, or even theoretical?"

"Well, I haven't done anything, of course, because limbo is the place of nothing doing. But every person has an origin, so I have a family history. I can't tell you that on my own, but will do so if you ask."

That seemed straightforward, or at least not too far angled. "Who is your father?"

"Esk Ogre. His father is Smash Ogre, and his mother is Tandy Nymph."

"Oh, you have some nymphly ancestry," Forrest said, becoming more interested.

"Yes. About a quarter. So I'm sure I could run and scream in the nymphly way, and do what nymphs do, if you are interested."

Forrest was interested. "Can you kick your feet cutely, and fling your hair about?" For these were specialties of nymphs, and such actions really delighted fauns.

"I'm sure I can. How's this?" She flung her hair so violently that her feet left the ground, and she kicked her bare legs in a fetching manner.

"Well, perhaps—" But then he saw Imbri frowning, and realized that he was drifting from business. He was just trying to find out about this region, in case it held a clue to the whereabouts of Cathryn's True Love. "Who is your mother?"

"Bria Brassie. That's where I inherit my metallic nature from. She's made wholly of brass, but I'm only half brass. So I can become halfway hard, but that's not my talent. I'm also fairly strong, from my ogre heritage, and not too bright."

Something connected. A bulb flashed over Forrest's head, exactly as in Xanth proper. "I think you're mistaken, Astrid. You *are* bright. Your talent must be shining."

"Oh!" she cried, suddenly glowing more brightly. "Yes that's it! I know it now. Oh, thank you, faun." She grabbed him and kissed him, and she was right: she was surprisingly soft beneath her coppery sheen. "I'm halfway real now!"

"You're welcome," Forrest said.

"Oh, I think I'll kiss you again, and maybe even—"

"There is no need," Imbri said quickly.

Actually Forrest wouldn't have minded, as he hadn't celebrated with a nymph since his arrival on Ptero. But of course Imbri was right: they had to get on with their business.

So Astrid ran off to find her proper territory. Forrest and Imbri returned to the line he had drawn in the dirt, to resume their quest, as there didn't seem to be much help in limbo. How could the folk there know about Cathryn's True Love, when they had no experience as might-be's?

Before long they came to a small forest of normal pines. It would have been better to avoid them, but then they would have lost their direction, so they went straight. Tears ran down their cheeks as they brushed by the trunks of the sad trees. Then they entered a glade— and there was a juvenile centaur.

"Young," Imbri whispered. "Maybe eight years old. So he can go forward and overlap Cathryn's range. Eight years isn't too much of an age difference."

"Yes. The dear horn knew what it was doing." But then he had a bad thought. "If this is the one."

"It has to be. We wouldn't have encountered him otherwise. There's always reason for folk to meet, in Ptero."

That did seem to be the case. So they approached the centaur. He was standing within a circle of fourteen crosses set upright on the ground.

He looked out at them. "Hey, want to play crosses?" he asked.

"Actually, we have come on a more serious matter," Forrest said. "We would prefer to talk."

"Well, I want to play crosses."

Forrest saw that this was in the nature of an exchange of services. "Suppose we talk while we play crosses?"

"Well, okay, I guess." He sounded just like a human boy of that age, which was surprising, because centaurs were generally far more intelligent and adult than humans. How could this be the ideal love for Cathryn, who was a true centaur in attitude?

"Very good," Forrest said, though he was afraid it wasn't. "I am Forrest Faun, and my companion is Mare Imbrium."

"So?"

"So what's your name?"

"Oh. Contrary."

That figured. "Well, Contrary Centaur, let's play the game and talk. You will have to explain the rules to me."

So they played the game while Imbri quietly watched. "It's like this," Contrary said. "We take turns standing inside the circle of crosses. The one outside takes a cross and throws it at the one inside, and he can't dodge or anything."

Forrest was not especially pleased with this. The crosses were small, but what if one hit an eye? It could hurt. "And what then?"

"That's it. Ends when we run out of crosses."

Forrest remained uneasy, but there was nothing for it but to play the game so he could talk. He hoped that he could ascertain whether this was the correct centaur, and he hoped the answer was no. "Who starts in the circle?"

"You do. You're the challenger."

Forrest stepped into the center and stood still. Contrary walked around outside, eyeing Forrest from every angle. Then he pulled a cross out of the ground and threw it at Forrest's face.

If the centaur expected his target to flinch, maybe forfeiting the game, he was disappointed. The cross struck Forrest between the eyes. It didn't hurt; in fact it disappeared. But his eyes felt funny.

He looked around. He saw two images of the surroundings, and a lot of fuzziness. What had happened?

Two young centaurs trotted up. "Okay, your turn."

Forrest knew there was only one centaur. Why did he see two? He made his way out of the circle as much by feel as by sight. He saw two Imbri's sitting just far enough from the pine trees so she wouldn't cry. "What—?"

"You're cross-eyed," she murmured.

Then he caught on. The cross had made him cross-eyed! So he couldn't properly focus on things.

He turned to face the centaurs. He closed one eye, and one image disappeared. It would be harder to aim, but he could do it; tree fauns were good with wood. So now he could throw a cross at Contrary and make him cross-eyed too. Or were there other choices?

He decided to experiment. He pulled up a cross, aimed very carefully, and threw. Contrary did not flinch, and the cross struck him on the back of the head.

Nothing visible happened. Then the centaur spoke, frowning. "What you do that for?" he demanded crossly.

It had worked: now Contrary was really cross. "I want to know something about you," Forrest said, as he came in to exchange places. "Do you ever go west?"

"What's it to you, goat hoof?" the centaur demanded angrily.

"I am merely curious. You must know that you will age as you go, achieving maturity. Why do you remain here in your youth?"

" 'Cause I don't want to grow up!" Contrary snapped. Then he hurled a cross at Forrest's legs. It struck one knee, and suddenly he was crossing his knees, though he was standing. It was awkward, but in a moment he found he was still able to move about, if he did so carefully.

He wobbled his way to the outside, while Contrary stomped crossly inside. He was catching on to the game, but he still didn't have all the information he wanted. "Why don't you want to grow up?" he asked.

" 'Cause there's a stupid filly out there I don't want to meet. Now throw your stupid cross."

That sounded like Cathryn. Forrest threw his cross at the centaur's arms. It struck and disappeared, and Contrary uttered an illegible syllable and crossed his arms. With luck, he wouldn't be able to throw well.

"Why don't you want to meet her?" Forrest asked as they exchanged places again.

" 'Cause I played a game of crosses for stakes with someone from the far west, and he had seen my future, and he told me that this stupid filly would completely change my attitude on everything, and get me to liking mushy stuff, and make me a responsible adult. Yuck! So I'm staying right here, sensibly young. What's it to you?" And he kicked his cross with a foreleg, sending it hurtling into Forrest's torso.

Forrest twisted around so that his head faced the opposite way from his hoofs. His body was crossed. This made it even more awkward to stand. But he was still able to walk, moving his knee-crossed legs backward. He was coming to the conclusion that he didn't really like this game.

At least now he knew the problem. The juvenile centaur didn't want to grow up. So he was able, in the unique environment of Ptero, to avoid adulthood. Because time was geography, and the creatures had freedom of geography. As an adult, in love with a responsible centaur filly, he would become a responsible citizen. Children of any species lacked the experience to appreciate the qualities and satisfactions of maturity. So how could he persuade the errant juvenile to approach his later life?

Meanwhile he was reaching the outside, and Contrary was inside. Where should he throw his next cross? Would the centaur quit playing if struck on the ear? Would that prevent him from hearing? Forrest wasn't sure, but decided to try it. He just wanted to finish this game, so he could recover his faculties and consult with Imbri. Maybe she would have a notion how to get Contrary into his adult territory.

He oriented carefully, and threw his next cross at the centaur's ear.
He scored. But nothing seemed to happen. "How are you doing?"
he asked.

Contrary looked the opposite way. "Where are you?"

So that was the effect: the centaur was cross-eared, and heard things
crossed, so that sounds seemed to come from the opposite direction.
"Look away from my voice," he said.

Contrary turned around. "Oh, yeah," he said crossly. "Crossed
hearing. I should have remembered. Well, get ready, because I'll really get you with the next one."

Forrest didn't like the sound of that, but had to go back into the
circle. They had used up only six of the crosses; this game had a long
way to go, unfortunately.

Contrary hurled his cross. It struck Forrest on the chest, right over
the heart. The feeling was strange, but not bad; it wasn't making his
heart malfunction. So what was the point?

"I crossed your heart," the centaur said with satisfaction. "Now
you have to tell the truth."

"I always tell the truth," Forrest said, annoyed.

"Not this way. Tell me your most embarrassing experience."

"I don't have to do that!"

"Yes you do. Now talk."

And he found that he did have to do it; his crossed heart compelled
him. The thing he hated most to confess. This game had abruptly
gotten worse.

"I was in my tree when a flock of harpies passed," he said. "They
were noxious creatures with the heads and breasts of women and the
bodies of birds, and foul of aspect and language. They liked to soil
the leaves and branches of my tree with their droppings, and snatch
away sandals, for which they had no use; they just dropped them in
the nearest bog. So I did my best to drive them off, throwing sticks
and stones at them. I didn't try to curse them, because no one has a
mouth as fowl as a harpy. They love to indulge in swearing contests,
and can make an ogre blush with a bad series of expletives. They
were just out for mischief, and I just wanted to be rid of them.

"Then I heard a maidenly scream. The dirty birds had gotten hold
of a nymph, and were dragging her away. I leaped from my tree and

ran to her rescue, beating off the clustered harpies. They cursed me so villainously that the nearby foliage wilted and my poor ears turned bright red. But I rescued her, and the harpies flew away, screeching imprecations. 'You'll be sorry!' the last one cried as she flapped skyward.

"Meanwhile the nymph was excruciatingly grateful. 'My hero!' she cried, throwing her fair arms about me and kissing me ardently. Naturally I returned the favors, and proceeded to that celebration for which fauns and nymphs are justly known. She was unusually eager to complete the celebration, and I assumed it was because of her joy at her deliverance from the horrors of capture by the harpies. So it was an even more delightful experience than usual. She kissed me repeatedly, seeming unable to get enough, even after the culmination. But at last she relaxed, and I made ready to return to my tree.

"But then I saw that the harpies had returned and utterly befouled it. Their stinking manure drenched every branch, and the leaves were wilting, and the sandals were rotting. My brief distraction had allowed them free access, and they had taken full advantage of it. I looked back at the nymph, and saw that she was changing form. She was not a true nymph; she had been changed by a spell of illusion, and now was revealing her real nature. She was a harpy herself, one of the filthy flock. 'Hee, heee, heeee!' she screeched as she spread her dirty wings, which had only seemed like arms, and flapped away.

"I was sick. Not only had I failed to protect my tree from befowlment, I had celebrated with a noxious harpy hen. They had tricked me doubly, and made me as squalid as my tree. Of course I went to work cleaning the tree with buckets of water I hauled from a nearby spring; the job took days, and it was weeks before the smell faded. But I couldn't similarly clean myself. And thereafter that harpy hen would flap by and chortle at me, reminding me of my folly. It took me half a century to live down that humiliation, and I hoped no one would ever again hear of it."

Forrest stopped talking. He had done what he had to do, telling his deepest shame. Because of the compulsion of the cross, which would not be denied.

"It wasn't your fault," Imbri said. "They tricked you."

"I'll tell everyone!" Contrary exclaimed. "What a great story!"

There was definitely something about this juvenile centaur that Forrest didn't like. So this time he threw his cross at Contrary's mouth.

It worked. The centaur brat got so tongue twisted that he couldn't speak at all intelligibly. "I think I'm ready to quit this game," Forrest said, getting a reasonably smart notion. "Don't you agree, Contrary?"

"Fftbbabble#ughh."

"That's what I thought. Then we are agreed: this game is done."

At that point his body untwisted, and the missing crosses returned to their places in the circle.

"That's not what I said!" Contrary protested.

"Oh? It sounded like it to me. I suppose we'll have to play another game, then."

"You bet! And this time I'll play to win."

"But not crosses," Forrest said. "I have a better game in mind."

"There is no better game than crosses!"

"Yes there is. Let's have a contest to see who can free more folk in limbo."

"But there aren't any penalties, so that's no fun. They just run off to their territories."

"We can make our own penalties. If you lose, you must come with us west until you reach age thirty."

"But I told you, I don't go into the green. I stay here in the yellow."

"That's why it's a good penalty. You really don't want to do it, because you know that filly might catch you and make you disgustingly adult and responsible."

"Yeah. A horrible fate."

"And of course you might escape it, if you can run back east fast enough. You don't have to do anything there, just go and touch the spot where you are thirty."

"Yeah. Then I can close my eyes and gallop back into the From before the fatal female shows up." Then he glanced cannily at Forrest. "But what's your penalty, if you lose?"

Forrest gulped. "A day of playing crosses with you."

"A year!"

"A week."

"A month."

Forrest yielded to horrible necessity. "A month."

"Done! Let's go play." Then he paused again. "But how will we know who wins?"

"We'll take turns questioning limbo folk. Whoever guesses more talents, so as to free more folk, wins."

"But what if we miss?"

"If one of us misses, he loses a point. Then the other can question that same person, and if he succeeds, he wins a point. A two point advantage wins the contest."

Contrary remained canny, seeking the catch. "How much time to question each? I mean, someone might not be able to guess, so he would just keep asking questions indefinitely."

"Good point. We need a timer."

"There's some baby hourglasses growing nearby. We can harvest one that goes for five minutes."

"Agreed. When its sand runs out, time is done."

"Let's go. I'll really enjoy tromping you at Crosses for a month straight."

"I hope you know what you're doing," Imbri murmured as they went to harvest a minute glass. "If you get stuck for a month, you'll be too late returning to your tree."

"I know. But we have to get him into her range. I'll just have to make sure to win the contest."

They reached the hourglasses, which were actually the fruits of a large thyme plant. They were in all sizes, from two seconds to several days. Contrary plucked one of the smallest. "This should do for three minutes."

"How do you know?"

"See, it's got the number on it." He held up the little timer, and sure enough, there was a 3 on it.

Then they went to the section of limbo, which wasn't far away. "Who goes first?" Forrest asked.

The centaur considered, trying to figure out where the advantage was. The one who went first might win and be ahead—or might lose and be behind. The confidence of youth won. "I'll go first."

"As you wish."

They entered the fog. "How do we decide which one to start with?" Contrary asked.

"Each of you choose the subjects for the other," Imbri suggested.

Both centaur and faun were startled by the notion. Then both agreed. It made a certain sense.

So Forrest got to choose for Contrary. He saw a number of statues; it seemed that they weren't allowed to speak until spoken to. Maybe that was what gave them their first suggestion of potential reality. One was a halfway handsome young man of almost princely mien. Forrest shrugged and indicated that one.

Contrary approached the figure. "Hi, you. What's your name?" As he spoke, Imbri set down the minute glass, and its sand began sifting to the lower section.

The figure came to life. "I am Crescendo."

"Whose son are you?"

"I am the son of Prince Dolph and Princess Electra."

That startled Forrest, because he knew only of the twins, Dawn & Eve. But he realized that a given set of parents could have additional children—and in any event, the folk here were merely might-be's, who might never actually be delivered to Xanth parents. There could be hundreds of such children; there might be no limit.

"What's your talent?" Contrary asked.

It was a clever try, but it didn't work. "I regret I don't know it. If I did, I wouldn't be here."

"Is there anything about your ancestry that would suggest your talent?"

"Yes. All the descendants of Bink, my great grandfather, have Magician caliber talents. So I must be a Magician."

"But that's just a matter of opinion, isn't it? There's no way to be sure how a given talent will be judged."

"True. But mine should be a good one."

Forrest, watching, began to get a notion. That name, Crescendo, sounded like growing force, or something musical. When he played his panpipes, he sometimes crescendoed. Could this person's talent be associated with music?

"Your name sounds like a word," Contrary remarked. "To what does it apply?"

"As a word? I wouldn't know."

"Why wouldn't you know?"

"I don't know."

"Is it because it relates to your talent?"

"I can't say."

"If it doesn't relate to your talent, you ought to know. So it must relate to powerful music."

"Why, I suppose so," the figure said, surprised. Forrest saw that Crescendo had not been able to think of that himself, but could see it now that it had been suggested by an outside party.

"Can you play music?"

"I don't know."

Contrary looked at Forrest. "May I borrow your panpipes?"

Forrest hesitated, but realized that it would not be fair to interfere. He dug out his panpipes and handed them over. As he did so, a piece of paper fluttered away in the breeze; it must have been stuck to the panpipes. Contrary in turn handed the pipes to Crescendo. "Play this."

The pipes began to play beautiful panpipe music. But Crescendo wasn't playing them; he was just holding them. They were playing themselves.

Contrary took the pipes back and returned them to Forrest. Then he picked up a stone. "Play this."

Crescendo took the stone, and it immediately played rock music. Contrary gave him a cup of water, and it made water music. He gave him a handful of air, and it made air music. Crescendo's talent was coming clear. "You have the talent of touching anything and making it make music," Contrary said. "That's must be close to Magician level, considering the beauty and power of the music."

"Yes!" Crescendo exclaimed, and suddenly the very ground around him was playing earth music. "That's it! Oh, thank you! What can I do for you in return for enabling me to become halfway real?"

The centaur considered, but Imbri intervened. "He has done you a service already, by giving you a point."

"Oh, yeah," Contrary agreed, remembering. "Depart, Crescendo; you are free."

The man needed no further urging. He took off at a run for wherever his territory was. Forrest realized that the geography/time effect must be suspended for the limbo folk, until they took their places where they belonged. Bit by bit, he was learning the devious ways of the Idea planet.

But now it was his turn. Contrary walked among the statues, and stopped by one that looked much like the last. "This," he told Forrest.

Imbri turned the minute glass over, and the sand started sifting. Forrest addressed the figure. "Who are you, and what is your lineage?" It was best to be efficient, so as to conserve time for more questions.

"I am Revy, son of Magician Grey and Sorceress Ivy."

Another Magician, then! Powerful magic should be easier to guess, as it was more comprehensive. Still, this wasn't easy. So he borrowed a device the centaur had employed. "Does your name suggest your talent?"

"I can't answer that."

He was getting warm. What could "Revy" mean? Revered? That didn't seem quite like a talent. Revelry? Again, it didn't seem apt. Reverse? Aha! "Could your talent be to reverse things?"

"It could."

That helped. "Can you make hot things cold?"

"No." Interesting; a talent couldn't be confirmed, but it could be denied if wrong. No—it *could* be confirmed; the centaur had done so. It was just necessary to find the right thing to confirm.

"Can you reverse the flow of a river?"

"No."

Hm. This was trickier than anticipated. Revy could probably reverse something, but not ordinary things. How could it be a Magician caliber talent, if it was so limited? Unless—

"Can you reverse magic itself?"

"Yes!" Revy exclaimed with happy realization. "My father can nullify magic, so I can reverse it. He prevents magic from happening; I can send it in the opposite direction."

"Good for you," Forrest said, well satisfied. "Go find your range."

"Thank you!" The man ran off.

"You're welcome," Forrest murmured. He hoped he was getting the hang of this.

But now he had to select another candidate for the centaur. What might be tough enough for Contrary to miss, but easy enough for Forrest to get? He wasn't sure. So he looked for something different—and found a demon child. The figure was male, with small horns, and looked about five years old. Of course apparent age didn't matter much, because of the time/geography factor. Still, this one might do. "This."

Contrary approached the child. "Who are you, and what is your derivation?"

"I am Demos, and I am the son of Prince Demon Vore and Princess Nada Naga, Xanth's most handsome couple. Also the brother of Demonica, who had the undeserved fortune to make it to Xanth instead of me."

"So you are not a descendant of Bink," the centaur remarked.

"Of who?"

"Never mind. Demons generally don't have magic talents, other than their demonly qualities, and neither do the naga folk, because they can already shift from full human to full serpent to their natural combination form. So you may not have an actual talent."

"Oh, but I do! I'm sure of it. I just don't know what it is."

"Curses," the centaur muttered. "Then it could be anything."

"Yes. I hope you can discover it."

The centaur considered, as the sand ran through the minute glass. "Could it relate to the changeability of your parents?"

"Yes."

"Ha! So you can change yourself?"

"Oh, sure. To human or naga or serpent form, or any other, because of my half demon heritage."

"That doesn't count," Contrary muttered, disappointed. "A magic talent isn't quite that way. Can you affect other things with your magic?"

"I wouldn't know."

The centaur pondered again. Forrest saw the sand running low. Unfortunately he couldn't figure this one out either. "Can you take magic away from things?"

"No."

"Then can you give magic to things?"

"Yes."

That meant he was suddenly very close. The centaur oriented on it with greater precision than he had shown thus far. "Can you make a non-magic object in some way magic?"

"Yes."

"Like, for example, a candlestick: could you imbue it with the power to burn without using up its wax?"

"Yes! That's it! I can do that."

Contrary looked surprised, then relieved. Forrest realized that he had been guessing more desperately than was apparent, and had been lucky.

But now it was Forrest's turn to guess. The centaur walked among the statues, and selected a boy with a fish's tail. "This."

Then there was a sound overhead. They all looked up. "Oh no!" Imbri exclaimed. "The dragons are back."

"Dragons?" Contrary asked. "Who stirred them up?"

"I think we did," Forrest said. "When we were headed for ogre country."

"Well, get rid of them, then."

Forrest thought of something. "Imbri, can you diffuse to dream form and plant a thought in their minds?"

"Yes. But what thought would distract them from us?"

"Maybe if you gave them something else to chase, like a wild goose. Dragons like to eat geese."

"Because they don't like getting goosed," she agreed. "So they try to eat the geese first. It's a personal thing. I'll see what I can do." She expanded, fading into mist as her density decreased.

The dragons had been drawing up their formation, about to go into strafing mode. Suddenly they hesitated. Then they winged rapidly away. Imbri had given them a dream of wild geese on the wing.

Soon Imbri reappeared, condensing into her small human form.

"That should hold them a while. But we had better not dally, because I won't be able to distract them that way again."

Forrest approached the figure Contrary had designated, as Imbri set the minute glass again. "Who are you, and what is your derivation?"

"I am Nigel, son of Prince Naldo Naga and Mela Merwoman."

"I don't know of your parents. What are their qualities?"

"My father is a prince of the naga folk, who are a serpent/human crossbreed whose natural form is a serpent with a human head. My mother is a human/fish crossbreed, like a mermaid only better developed in front, and able to turn her tail into legs so she can walk on land. There was some notoriety when she was advised to put on clothing, so she went to a pantree and harvested a panty, and freaked out every male she encountered."

"Oh, that one. News of her did penetrate my corner of the forest. So does your talent relate to either of your parents' natural abilities, such as changing from human to serpent or fish form?"

"No."

"Is it a minor talent, of the spot on the wall variety?"

"No."

Forrest was getting the hang of this. The folk of limbo knew what their talents weren't, so it was the fast way to zero in on what they were. "Is it a major talent, Magician class?"

"No."

"Then it must be a significant talent, neither major nor minor."

"I wouldn't know."

Uh-huh. "Does it relate to yourself?"

"No."

"Does it relate to objects?"

"No."

"Does it relate to other people?"

"I wouldn't know."

Forrest paused. "Does it relate to anything *other* than other people?"

"No."

He was definitely developing technique. But he saw the sand running low in the minute glass. He needed to identify the talent readily. "Does it affect other people?"

"I wouldn't know."

"Does it change their mood?"

"No."

"Does it change their appearance?"

Nigel hesitated. "I'm not sure."

Now that was interesting. A qualified response. But the sand was almost out, and he had to get it in the next couple of questions. "Does it change their nature?"

"Yes."

"Can it heal them?"

"No."

"Hurt them?"

"Maybe."

The last gasp of sand was going. He had only one more chance. What would change appearance without necessarily healing or hurting? So he took a halfway wild guess: "Can it change their age?"

"Yes! I can rejuvenate others."

And there he had it, as the sand ran out. It had been a close call.

"Hey, you cheated!" Contrary protested, looking at the minute glass.

"What are you talking about?"

"You got an extra minute."

Forrest looked at the glass. It now had the number 4 on it. Four minutes. How had that happened?

Imbri had the answer: "We moved west—toward the To. So we got a little older—and so did the minute glass. So it's bigger."

The centaur nodded. "Yeah, I guess so. Maybe I got an extra minute too. Okay."

Forrest looked for another subject. He needed to find one that would stymie the centaur, because otherwise he would be stymied himself all too soon. He found a reasonably pretty young woman. It was a foolish notion, but maybe a woman would be trouble for Contrary, who was trying to avoid meeting a filly centaur. "This."

Contrary approached the woman. "What is your name and heritage?"

"I am Scintilla. My father is Crony and my mother is Vendetta.

They don't get along too well, so I'm not sure they'll ever get around to signaling the stork to deliver me."

"Too bad," the centaur said without sympathy. "Does your talent relate to your name?"

"No."

The centaur continued to question her, establishing that her talent affected herself rather than others, but not in any obvious way. Indeed, it was not obvious to Contrary, who finally ran out of time without establishing her talent.

Unfortunately Forrest was no better. "Does your talent help you or others?"

"Not usually."

"Does it hurt anyone?"

"Sometimes."

"Does it annoy you or anyone else?"

"Sometimes."

"Does it do anything physical?"

"Not really."

"Mental?"

"Possibly."

"Emotional?"

"Perhaps."

These indefinite answers were balking Forrest just as they had balked Contrary. He was unable to center on any particular talent, and time ran out for him too.

The worst of it was, they couldn't even admit defeat and ask for the correct answer, just to satisfy their curiosity. They were left to their infuriating ignorance.

"Whose turn is it to pick the next?" Forrest asked.

"You picked the last; now it's my turn." He scouted around, looking for a winner for him. "This."

It was a rather hairy old man. Forrest wondered about the variation in age among the folk of limbo, as they were all merely potential beings; shouldn't they be ageless? But maybe they could be any age they chose, until they reached their territories, when they could control their age by moving around.

Forrest approached him as Imbri set down the timer. "Who are you and what is your parentage?"

"I am Hugh Mongus, son of Scab and Svelte."

"Does your talent affect others?"

"In a manner."

"Does it affect you?"

"That depends."

This promised to be another frustrating interview. Forrest soon established that the talent didn't affect anything physical, but might affect something mental. "How do others feel about it?"

"That depends."

"Depends on what?"

"On how they feel about it."

Forrest suppressed his annoyance, because he didn't have time for emotion; his glass was sifting sand. But no matter how he tried, he could never pin Mongus down, and finally he ran out of time.

Contrary, aware that he could win the contest by getting this one, did his best, but the subject was just as balky for him. "Does your talent affect inanimate things?"

"That depends."

"Depends on what?" the centaur asked, in much the tone Forrest had found himself using.

"On your definition of inanimate."

"You don't know what the word means?"

"I know what it means."

"Then give me your definition."

"Anything that isn't living or moving."

"Very well. Does your talent affect anything that isn't living or moving?"

"That depends."

"Depends on what?!"

"On how you see it."

"I see it the way you do! Does it affect anything that isn't living?"

Hugh considered. "Yes, I think it does."

"Good! Does it affect any living thing?"

"That depends."

"Confound it! Can't you say anything else?"

"Not if you don't ask a more relevant question."

The centaur seemed about to swell up to adult size, but then his time ran out. This candidate, too, had defeated both of them.

Now it was Forrest's turn to choose, again. He spied a gnome woman. Did gnomes have talents? "This."

Contrary approached her as Imbri set down the timer. "What is your name and ancestry?"

"I am Miss Gnomer, of respectable but anonymous gnome stock."

"Miss No More?"

"No."

"Miss Gnome?"

"No."

The centaur looked a bit nettled, understandably. "Well, whatever your name is, do you have a magic talent?"

"Yes."

"Does it affect you?"

"Yes."

"Does it affect others?"

"Yes."

"Does it affect things?"

"No."

"Does it help anyone?"

"No."

"Does it hurt anyone?"

"No."

Contrary paused. "It is indifferent to the welfare of anyone?"

"Yes."

"Is it under your conscious control?"

"No."

"Is it apparent to others?"

"Sometimes."

"When?"

"I can't answer that."

"Is it like a spot on the wall?"

"No."

The centaur paused again. His time was running out and he was getting nowhere. Forrest was stumped too.

"Does it please anyone?"

"No."

"Does it displease anyone?"

"No."

"Confound it, woman, it has to be one or the other!"

"Does it?"

Contrary scratched his head, trying to think of a definitive question. "Time," Imbri announced, showing the exhausted minute glass.

"Darn!" the centaur swore. He had lost another, giving Forrest another chance to win.

Forrest tackled the subject as Imbri turned over the glass. Since he had no idea how to proceed, he tackled a minor irritation. "Exactly what is your name?"

"Miss Gnomer."

"Miss Nomare?"

"No."

"Can you spell it?"

"No."

Forrest began to get a glimmering. "Does your talent relate to your name?"

"Yes."

"Is it that it is unspellable?"

"No."

"So you can't spell it because that would reveal your talent?"

"Maybe."

"Miss Gnoma," he said, but realized that he had gotten it wrong again. "Miss Gnome." Still not right. Then a light bulb flashed. "Is it that no one gets your name right?"

"Yes!" she cried with realization. "Misnomer."

"That must be very frustrating."

"No, I am used to it. May I go now?"

"Yes, of course."

Then, as the woman departed, Forrest realized that he had gotten two points ahead, and won. All because he had tried to get the name straight, and failed. He looked at Contrary. "You must go to your age thirty."

"Darn," the centaur repeated glumly. "I should have guessed that talent."

"This was a tougher game than I anticipated," Forrest said. "It was just luck that I won."

"It's just luck when any ordinary creature beats a centaur."

"Well, let's head west."

But then the dragons reappeared. There was something about their flight formation that looked angry. "We had better hurry," Imbri said. "I can't fool them again."

So they ran west, trying to find cover under stray boulders or trees. But the dragons weren't fooled. They oriented, and prepared to dive down on their victims.

Contrary unslung his bow. "Run for cover; I'll hold them off."

"You can't stop a whole flight of dragons!" Forrest protested.

"True. But I can delay them. I am older and stronger now. Go!" Indeed, he was now about twelve; they had come several years To. He seemed to have matured somewhat in attitude, too.

Forrest hesitated, not wanting to desert the centaur. But what else could he do? Then he had half a notion. Maybe there would be a hint on the Good Magician's list of words.

He dug into his knapsack, but couldn't find it. Oh, no—that must have been the paper that had fluttered away when he took out his panpipe!

"What's the matter?" Imbri asked. "Aside from the dragons?"

"I lost the Good Magician's list of words."

She looked stricken, but she tried to put a good face on it. "We'll get through without it."

He hoped so. They were really on their own, now.

The centaur fired an arrow upward. It would have been a remarkable shot, for anyone but a centaur. It struck the lead dragon on the snout, pinning it closed. The dragon huffed and puffed, but couldn't dislodge the barb, and wee-wawed out of control. The flight of dragons followed their leader, making a crazy display as they all wee-wawed across the sky, huffing and puffing.

Then another dragon caught on. Flying dragons were not known for their intelligence, because the heat of their fire tended to fry their lightweight brains, but they had some experience with injuries. The other dragon took the end of the arrow between its teeth and hauled it out. That freed the leader, who cauterized its wounds with fire, then resumed the chase.

Meanwhile the fugitives had run farther west, and had a lead. But the dragons quickly caught up again, and there was still no cover. So Forrest took his turn. He brought out his panpipes and played a military melody: reveille.

The dragons were militaristic creatures. They heard the music and immediately fell into formation for review. Then Forrest played a marching tune, and the dragons proceeded to march across the sky, their wing-beats keeping perfect step.

Then the leader, who had been a bit distracted by the fresh holes in its snout, realized what was happening. It roared, drowning out the melody. The dragons milled about, then oriented once again on the targets.

But the desperate fugitives had made further progress west—and caught up to Cathryn Centaur, who had cut south to intercept them. She was about five years old at this point, with cute pigtails and a toy bow and quiver. Her white wings, too small at this age to enable her to fly, were folded, forming a kind of cloak over her body.

Contrary, now thirteen, glanced at her with disdain. "Go away, twirp. I have no interest in you."

She stared at him. "You mean you're the one? My supposed ideal mate? A wingless, landbound creature? What a laugh!"

"For sure, brat. Now get out of the way before you get toasted and gobbled by a dragon."

"Don't quarrel, you two!" Forrest cried. "Can you help, Cathryn?"

"I think so. There's a forest just north of us; run to that for cover." She turned to show the way, her little hoofs galloping swiftly.

"The dragons will follow the sound of our hoofs, and close in on us anyway," Contrary sneered. But he turned to follow her, and Forrest and Imbri ran along behind.

The dragons wheeled in air and looped around to cut them off. But the fugitives had just enough time, and reached the cover of the edge of the forest just ahead of the first blast of fire. They turned west to go into the center of the wood.

Cathryn raised her hands as if throwing something. "What's the matter, twirp?" Contrary demanded. "Giving up already? Don't worry; in a mo—"

His voice cut off. Forrest looked, afraid something had happened, but the centaur was still running and still talking. His mouth was moving, but no sound was emerging. What had happened?

Then a dreamlet voice came in his head. *Cathryn threw a blanket of silence,* Imbri explained. *Now the dragons can't hear us. They can't track us by sound.*

And with the cover of the trees, the dragons couldn't track them by sight, either. Now the four of them could make good their escape. Cathryn's remarkable talent was really helping.

But there were harpies in this forest. The dirty birds came flapping down, intent on mischief. There were so many of them that there was no way to avoid them.

Cathryn, now a size larger at age six, raised her hands, drawing in her blanket. Suddenly the harpies became audible. "We've got you, you $#@&!!'s," one was screeching. "We'll poop your faces!"

"I'd rather face the dragons," Contrary muttered.

"So would I," Forrest agreed. One of the harpies looked a lot like the one who had tricked him, a century ago, though of course she couldn't be the same one.

Cathryn made a motion as of throwing something toward the harpies. It was another blanket, but it was hard to see. It spread out and surrounded them with a fine sparkling net. At that point their cursing was silenced, but it hadn't ceased. They were all screeching worse than ever; it just wasn't getting out.

"I threw a blankety blanket," Cathryn explained. "Now their cussing is reflecting back on themselves and smirching their own feathers."

Indeed, provocative symbols were appearing, of lightning strikes, corkscrews, exploding cherry bombs, asterisks, and stars. They were striking the harpies, who were screeching worse than ever as they felt themselves tagged by their own expletives. This only intensified the problem. Scorch marks were appearing on their tail feathers.

"You can do that to harpies?" Contrary asked, amazed. "That's not bad."

"Gee, thanks," little Cathryn said, blushing.

That reminded Contrary of his objection to her. He shut up, so as not to let slip any other compliment.

The four ran on by, leaving the harpies to their fate. But now the dragons could hear them again, for the blanket of silence was gone. Cathryn could throw only one blanket at a time. Still, she had really helped them to move along.

Imbri ran beside Cathryn. "I'm sure he's much more mature when he's adult. He has already shown some beginning signs of centaur decency."

"But the wings. He has no wings."

"Nevertheless, I think he is the one. Maybe we can verify it with the dear horn."

Cathryn nodded as they ran. She lifted the horn and blew on it. Forrest heard nothing, but the filly nodded again. "It echoes from him."

"It must know," Imbri said.

"I suppose." But the filly seemed anything but certain.

The dragons were reorienting on their sounds. But now Cathryn had to draw in her last blanket, because she couldn't maintain it at a distance, and the harpies were escaping too. They were horrendously furious. "Wait till we catch up with you!" their fowl-mouthed leader cried. "We'll tear you to quivering stinking bits!"

A dragon, swooping down to spy out the fugitives, heard. It roared. It thought she was screeching at the dragons! Soon several more dragons came swooping down, ready to avenge their honor. Dragons and harpies didn't get along too well together at the best of times, and the dragons were in no mood to be insulted. So they shot fire first and saved the questions for later. But the harpies were in no mood to brook interference either, and this was their forest.

Forrest and the others ran on, not staying to watch the developing fray. But they heard the roars and curses as it worked its way into something the forest would probably remember for a long time.

They emerged from the forest. They were at this point a fair distance west, and Contrary was a stallion in his twenties, readily taking the lead. Cathryn followed, now coming into her teens. Her wings had grown, and she was using them to add to her forward velocity. Then came Forrest and Imbri. They had been running for some time, but Forrest didn't feel really tired; apparently soul-bodies didn't fatigue the same way physical ones did. So while the centaurs had to hold back somewhat to keep from leaving the two more human figures behind, it remained a fast pace.

Contrary put on a spurt and came to a line marked 30, stepped across it, and stopped. He was now a fine mature figure of a centaur, muscular and handsome. "There is my mark," he said. "I have crossed it. Now I must flee before I get trapped." He turned as the others were catching up.

Cathryn drew to a halt. They knew this was the turning point in a second way. If the stallion passed her and escaped back to his childhood, she would never see him again. But how could she stop him?

Contrary took a step back. Forrest saw that the centaur's eyes were closed. He was refusing to look at the filly. So that was how he proposed to avoid the dread confrontation! If he never saw her in her mature aspect, he couldn't be impressed by her.

"Look at me," Cathryn cried. "You owe me that much, I think."

"No I don't," Contrary retorted. "I made a deal to cross my thirtieth year. That was all." He took another step.

"What can I do?" the filly asked, defeat looming.

"Kiss him," Imbri said succinctly.

Cathryn smiled. "I'll give him fair warning." Then she called to the stallion: "If you don't open your eyes and look at me, I'll intercept you and kiss you."

Contrary took another step. Cathryn took two steps. She could travel faster with her eyes open than he could do safely with his eyes closed. The stallion heard her hoofbeats, which she was taking pains to make loud. His fine centaur mind processed that information, and he realized that he would have to compromise. "Very well. One look. Then I'm gone, and you can't intercept me."

"Agreed. But I will throw one blanket at you."

He laughed. "A blanket of silence? Do your worst, foal."

Forrest realized that the stallion had not gotten a good look at her since the forest, and retained a mental picture of her as six or seven. That was an understandable but foolish error.

Contrary faced Cathryn and opened his eyes. His jaw dropped slightly. Forrest looked at the filly, to see what the stallion saw. She was now a lovely full-breasted, long-maned, white-winged centaur filly with a deep brown hide and flowing tail. She was panting slightly with her recent exertion. If she had been a nymph, she would have been stunningly attractive. She was surely similar for a centaur.

Then she threw a blanket. Again, Forrest didn't see it directly, but the scintillation of the air indicated that there was something flying toward the stallion. It reached his head.

Contrary blinked. His eyes lost focus. "What's this?" he asked, confused.

"A blanket stare," Cathryn said.

"A blank stare? I don't understand."

"That is its effect. Why are you fleeing me?"

He looked at her again. "I'm drawing a blank on that. Is there some reason?"

"There may be. Why don't you blow this horn?" She stepped forward, offering it to him.

He looked puzzled. "What horn is this?"

"It is the dear horn. It will show you by its sound where your True Love is."

He frowned. "Is that a challenge?"

"Is it?"

He took the horn and blew it hard. There was no sound—but then he stared at Cathryn in a new way. "You are the one," he said in wonder. "You really are the one! I will sacrifice anything for you."

But now it was Cathryn who wasn't sure. "If only you could fly," she said regretfully.

"Who said I can't fly?" And suddenly from his body two massive black wings unfolded. What they had taken for his body color was actually the hue of the flattened wings. "I never had use for them before, for they would only have taken me where I didn't want to go, but now I want to fly with you, you fantastic creature, forsaking my prior childishness."

Now it was Cathryn's jaw that dropped. "The dear horn did know," she breathed. "It really did!"

Contrary dropped the horn. "Come fly with me, my sudden love. We have more than geography to explore."

"Oh, yes! But first I must guide my friends to the territory of the fauns, or as close as I can get to it."

"We will do it together," he said graciously. "And to hurry it up, we had better give them a ride there."

"Yes," Cathryn agreed. Little hearts were forming around her head; she was falling in love.

Forrest picked up the dear horn and put it in his knapsack. Then he climbed onto Contrary, behind the huge wings, and Imbri mounted Cathryn. "It's funny to ride an equine," she said. "I'm equine myself."

"The faun region is To," Cathryn said. "I don't know whether it's within my range, but I'll do my best to give you good directions if it isn't."

The two centaurs galloped west. Then they spread their wings and leaped into the air, surprising Forrest. This was indeed faster; he saw the ground passing rapidly behind. But as they gained elevation, the ground became smaller and passed behind more slowly, as if annoyed at being neglected. The mixed fields and forests gave way to mixed mountains and valleys, and then to mixed ponds and islands. The landscape seemed to be just as varied here as it was on Xanth.

After a time the two centaurs glided back to land. "We're getting a bit old for this," Contrary explained. Then Forrest saw that the creatures' hide had become mottled with age. He was now nearing the old end of his life, and was slowing down. Forrest looked across at Cathryn and saw she had aged too. They had come a long way in a short time.

Then the centaurs stopped. "This appears to be my limit," Contrary said. "I don't want to become so feeble that I fall."

Forrest hastily dismounted, and so did Imbri. They were in rolling country, and ahead, oh dread, was a comic strip.

"The faun territory is farther away than I thought," Cathryn said with regret. "But I can tell you who can take you farther: the human princess twins, Dawn & Eve. Continue straight To until you come to Castle Roogna, and seek them out.''

"But we are already in Castle Roogna," Imbri said. "Ptero is a moon circling Princess Ida's head."

"Perhaps in that larger frame. But it is here, too, and this is the one you need. We have set you due From it, so you can't miss it if you stay on course. And if you return this way, send a signal and we will come to pick you up again."

"Thank you," Forrest said. He realized that Cathryn really had been a big help; they had learned a whole lot about Ptero in her company.

"Oh—one more thing," she said. "You have been more than accommodating in our exchange of services, and I have not been able to complete my exchange service adequately, so I feel I should provide you with something extra. Here is one of my blankets that a passing Magician obligingly canned for me." She held out a small tin can.

"But I thought you had to invoke your spells yourself, and that they fade after a while."

"True. But this canned spell is special, thanks to the preservative properties of the can. You may invoke it at any time simply by saying 'Invoke' while holding it before you. It is a blanket of obscurity."

"Obscurity?" Imbri asked. "What effect does that have?"

"It makes you unlikely to be noticed," the centaur explained. "It wears off after an hour, but you can invoke it again thereafter. It takes the same time to recharge: an hour. So don't try to invoke two blankets at once. I realize that this isn't much, but I have nothing better to give you. Please accept it with my thanks for your assistance to me."

"Of course," Forrest said, moved by her gesture. "I'm sure it will be useful if we have to pass by a monster. Thank you."

"You are most welcome." Cathryn's old eyes were bright. It seemed she had appreciated their association.

Then he and Imbri turned to the west for the next leg of their journey. It was bound to be an adventure of its own.

7
GOOD MAGICIAN

T o either side they could see nice solid land, but straight west was a bog. It was tempting to deviate, but then they might lose the line to Castle Roogna. So they went straight ahead, splashing into the shallow water. Forrest hoped that the puns would not be too bad this time.

Fortunately the land soon rose up, restoring their firm footing. But no sooner had they set foot and hoof on it when two odd birds marched up. "Who are you?" the birds demanded in unison.

"We are visitors from afar, in search of Castle Roogna," Forrest answered. "We are named Forrest and Imbrium."

"We are a pair o' keets," the birds answered. "Peet and Deet. Welcome to Canary Island."

They didn't look much like canaries to Forrest, being more like small parrots, but he didn't comment on that. "Thank you. We hope just to cross it quickly and go on our way."

"Do that. We don't like landbound folk to stay long." With that the two birds marched on.

They came to a tree. It was huge and globular, with feathery leaves, and it was right in their way. The trouble was, it was also astride the only feasible path leading due west. To the south was a section of what looked a lot like slow sand, which would take forever to cross, and to the north was a similar patch of what looked like quick sand, which had risks of its own. "I wish we could just go right through this tree," Forrest said.

"Maybe we can climb over it," Imbri said.

Then the tree opened a huge round eye. That was followed by a second eye, and a beak just below it, that they had taken for a broken off limb. "Hooo!" it hooted.

"It's an owl!" Forrest exclaimed. "A huge owl!"

"An owl tree," Imbri agreed.

Then the owl spread its wings and took off. "Well, this is Canary Island," Forrest said, bemused. "We have to expect birds, even if they aren't all canaries."

Several white birds flew overhead. Their bodies were in the shape of the letter C. "C-gulls," Imbri said, identifying them.

A ball of blackness approached. Forrest paused, not sure whether it was dangerous, but then he saw it was in the shape of a bird of prey. "Oh, it's just a night hawk," he said. He stepped aside to let it pass, then stepped back onto the path when the light returned.

But another bird flew up. "What a weird set of characters," it said, eyeing them. "You are absolutely laughable. Haw haw haw!"

"And a mockingbird," Imbri said. "One of the more obnoxious avians, but harmless."

They ignored the mockingbird, and of course that discomfited it so that it flew away. But another bird flew in to perch before them. "What are you fools doing here?" it demanded harshly. "You don't belong here! Go away! Go away!"

"We are only crossing the island," Forrest explained.

"You are polluting it with your foul presence!" the bird raved. "Get off our land! Go away! Go away!" The bird continued to shout at them, going on and on.

"Now I recognize it," Imbri said. "It's a rave-on."

Then a harpy appeared, dripping wet. She smelled terrible. "You're one of the canaries?" Forrest asked, surprised.

"I'm a waterfoul," she answered.

"I should have known," he said, hurrying by.

They passed a large trunk. A bird was pecking a big hole in it. The moment it spied them, it flew to a branch above them and pecked a shower of sawdust and bits of bark, so that they were dirtied. "Hey, what are you doing?" Forrest demanded, annoyed.

For answer, a smelly bird dropping came down, just missing his head.

"That's a peccadillo," Imbri said. "A bad mannered pecker."

Then there was the melodious cry of a lady bird to the north, and the peccadillo flew off to have something to do with her. "They especially like the ladies," Imbri explained, with what might possibly have been the hint of a smirk.

At last they got off Canary Island, and the edge of the comic strip was there, so that they returned to regular land. "I can see why not many folk care to cross the boundaries," Forrest said. "Those puns don't really hurt you, but they're annoying as anything."

"I understand that some folk like them," Imbri said.

"Who would like anything like that? Mundanes?"

"Maybe. Mundania is a strange, repressed place."

"It must be, to have folk who like such junk."

The new region was hilly, and it was impossible to keep to a straight line west. But they oriented as well as they could, returning to the correct direction and compensating for their deviations, hoping they were close enough to find the castle.

They were rewarded: they crested a ridge, and there in a colorful valley below was a picturesque castle. "There it is," Forrest said, relieved.

Imbri wasn't so sure. "That doesn't look like Castle Roogna."

"Things are different, here on Ptero. Maybe the castles are different too."

"Maybe," she agreed doubtfully.

They trekked on down the slope and reached the bowl-shaped valley where the castle stood. The trees closed in around them, each a distinct color: brown, including the leaves; green, including the trunk; yellow, blue, or white. They were pretty, but so thick that the castle was now hidden, with no clear path.

Then Forrest noticed that one white tree had a brown trunk. It was comparatively normal. He went to that tree, and spied a blue tree with a brown trunk. Between them ran a straight brown path. "This must be the route," he said.

So they followed the path. It turned at right angles, then turned again, refusing to be rounded. But it stayed between the brown trunked trees. So they followed it, despite its constant square turns, and in due course it brought them to the bank of the square moat around the castle.

From this vantage, the castle was much larger than it had seemed from afar. It had massive white stone walls, red roofs, and three squared towers rising above the second story. The drawbridge was up, and the moat was deep. There seemed to be no way in.

"This seems less like Castle Roogna," Forrest admitted. "The landscape is different, and there's no princess in blue jeans to greet us."

"It's the Good Magician's castle!" Imbri exclaimed. "It's always different, and always a Challenge to get into."

"Three Challenges," he agreed, remembering. "So we did go astray, and came to the wrong castle."

"I'm not surprised. The path across Canary Island was somewhat crooked, and there were distractions. Then we had to guess at the direction when we passed the hills."

"I suppose we'll just have to retrace our steps and try to find the right direction."

They turned—but now the magic path was gone. The forest had closed in solidly behind them. Forrest had experience with trees, and could see immediately that these ones had no intention of allowing them to pass back through; brambles, thorns, stickers, nettles, and sharp pointed plants festooned the region between trees.

"It was a one way path," Imbri said. "I should have thought of that. I'm not used to being solid."

"I should have thought of it too," Forrest said ruefully. "I'm supposed to relate well to trees."

"Well, we'll just have to ask the Good Magician the way to Castle Roogna."

Forrest eyed the moat. "Does that mean we'll have to get through three Challenges, and pay a year's Service?"

She nodded. "I'm afraid it does. Unless we can talk him into letting us through without all that."

"Well, he didn't charge me before. I'm still not sure why."

Imbri looked thoughtful, but didn't comment.

So they addressed the Challenge of getting into the castle. There was no sign of a moat monster, but they didn't trust that. So Forrest experimented: he picked up a pebble and flipped it into the smooth water.

Enormous teeth snapped out of the water and caught the pebble before it splashed. Then the water was still again. It had happened so quickly that he wasn't sure he had actually seen it, but he concluded that swimming would not be a good idea.

"We might dissolve into floating souls, and condense again on the other side," Imbri suggested.

"I'm not sure that's in order. I think we should stay with the rules of this realm, while we are in it."

"I suppose so. I suppose dissolving into vapor might count the same as getting crunched by an ogre, and prevent us from returning to within half a year of this spot."

"That, too," he agreed. He had actually been thinking of the ethics of it, assuming there were any. Physically it seemed possible; after all, she had dissolved to send the dragons their distracting dream. But it seemed unwise to tempt the limits.

He couldn't reach the drawbridge from this side, so couldn't cross that way. The moat looked way too deep to fill in, even if he had a shovel, and the bank seemed too solid to dig anyway. But if this was like the castle in Xanth, there would be a way. He simply had to find it.

He looked around. There was a brief cleared area around the moat, before the trees socked in tightly. There was room to walk. So he walked around the larger square, to see what he could see.

Imbri walked with him. "I never had to worry about moats," she said apologetically. "I just trotted across them, being insubstantial." She looked at the nearest tree. "I don't suppose you could cut down a tree to make a bridge or raft?"

"Cut down a tree?" he asked, horrified. "A living tree? I could never do that! I am a tree protector."

"Sorry. I wasn't thinking. But maybe if there is some deadwood?"

"That would be fine. But I don't see any."

"Neither do I. But what's that over there?"

He looked. "An upside-down bush. Someone must have pulled it out. Maybe we can help it."

They went to the bush, which was in an embarrassing predicament: its roots were in the air, and its leaves halfway buried in the ground, though it was a living plant. Forrest lifted it carefully, and set it down the right way up while Imbri used her hands to scrape dirt in around its base.

But the moment Forrest let go, the bush flipped over, spraying dirt, and was upside down again.

They contemplated this phenomenon. "It can't live and grow that way," Forrest said. "It's a regular plant. It needs earth on its roots and sun on its leaves."

"What would make it reverse itself like that?"

"Reverse," he murmured, an idea homing in on him. Then he lifted the plant up again. "Dig down deep: there may be a piece of reverse wood there."

Imbri dug in the earth, and in a moment found it: a fair sized stick. She set it on the ground, and the green grass turned red in its vicinity. Then she dug out a place for the bush, and Forrest set it in. She packed the earth around it, and this time it stayed put.

"I'm sure it will be more comfortable now," Forrest said, satisfied.

"You really do have a feeling for plants," Imbri said.

"Yes. It comes from associating so long with a tree. I don't like to see green growing things abused. That's why I'm on this quest, after all."

"Yes." She looked thoughtful again.

"We'll have to put this reverse wood where it won't do any more mischief," Forrest said. He picked up the wood. It didn't affect him, because he had no magic talent to reverse. Of course reverse wood was funny stuff; sometimes it did reverse things in unexpected ways.

Then another notion hovered around his head. "Imbri—do you suppose there could be any magic in that water?"

"Magic?" she asked blankly.

"Let's find out." He tossed the stick into the water in front of the lifted drawbridge.

Then water quivered, then solidified. It wasn't frozen, just solid.

Forrest set one foot on it, then the other. The water was now like ground. Its natural liquidity had been reversed, in this section.

Imbri joined him. "You solved it!" she exclaimed. "I would never have thought of that."

"I almost didn't," he admitted. "But usually things are as they are for a reason, at least around the Good Magician's castle. I'm glad the reverse wood didn't turn the water into fire."

They reached the inner bank. But the drawbridge remained up, and its planks blocked off the main entrance. So they walked to the left, which had the green haze of To, and rounded the corner of the castle.

There was an odd procession of people garbed in black. Several of them were carrying a large long and evidently heavy box, which was closed.

"What is this?" Forrest asked, perplexed by the scene.

"I think I know," Imbri said. "It's a funeral."

"A funeral? Who died?"

"I don't know. But that looks like a coffin."

"I don't want to get mixed up in death!"

"Then this must not be the right way."

They backed off, and went into the yellow haze of From. They rounded that corner.

There was an amazing assemblage of big white long-legged birds. "Storks!" Imbri exclaimed, identifying them. "What are they doing here?"

"Same thing the funeral is doing here," Forrest suggested. "When we walked around outside the moat I didn't see either. They appeared after we crossed the moat. It's another Challenge."

"It must be a Challenge," she agreed. "But a strange one. What are we supposed to do with either a funeral or a group of storks?"

"I wonder. There must be something. Do you suppose we could question them?"

"I suppose we could try. They will cooperate to exactly the extent they are supposed to."

So they stepped around and hailed the nearest stork. "Will you talk with us?" Forrest inquired.

"Sorry, don't have time. I'm too busy watching the screen for blips."

"Blips?"

"Signals. If I miss one, the supervisor will pull my tail feathers out. One feather for each blip I miss. That hurts."

"Well, could we help watch your screen while we talk?"

The stork considered. "It's highly irregular."

"But not forbidden," Forrest said. "We'll help, and the supervisor can pull out one of our feathers, or whatever, if we miss any."

"Very well," the stork agreed. "Hello: I am Stanley Stork. You are?"

"Forrest Faun and Mare Imbrium."

"Imbri for short," Imbri said.

They joined him at the screen. This was a large square panel with a black background. "What's a blip?" Imbri asked.

"Three little points of light. There's one now." Stanley pointed with the tip of his wing.

Forrest saw them. Three bright specks, like stars, in a row, moving quickly across the screen from left to right. In a moment they were gone; it would have been easy to miss them. "What are they?" he asked.

"A signal. I have to record its exact azimuth and elevation, and relay the information to Central Processing." The stork used the tip of his beak to peck at several numbers on a keypad.

"There's another," Imbri said.

Stanley looked up quickly. "Oh, thanks. I would have missed that while I was recording the other." He punched in more numbers.

"What kind of signals are they?" Forrest asked, still perplexed.

"You know. Orders."

"Orders for what?"

"Babies, of course. That's the only product we carry."

At last it dawned on him. Signaling the stork! This was the receiving end of those signals.

"Do you get many signals?" Imbri asked.

"Just the right number. The problem is the infernal bogies."

"Bogies?"

"The irrelevant signals. There's one now." On the screen was a pattern of two dots. "Only one in ten is valid. The others are spurious. We have to weed them out."

"How does someone send a bogie?" Forrest asked, fearing that he knew the answer.

"By going through the motions at the wrong time, or not completing them," the stork said. "Or when they aren't qualified. Demonesses do that a lot, and nymphs. They think its funny to imitate the procedure, when they aren't on the list for deliveries."

That was what he had feared. All his celebrations with nymphs were just cluttering the stork's screen. He felt guilty.

"The valid ones are bad enough," Stanley said, catching another blip. "If those idiots had any idea how hard we have to work to prepare a delivery, and get it exactly right. I mean, suppose we delivered an ogret to a human female? Think of the notoriety that would cause. But no, they keep signaling merrily away all night, as if it's nothing at all."

"How are babies actually made?" Forrest asked. "I mean, once a valid signal comes."

"Well, it's complicated. We—" Then the stork glanced warily at him. "Are you cleared for restricted information?"

"I guess not."

"Then move on. I'm busy enough as it is."

Stanley seemed to have a case. "Sorry," Forrest said, somewhat lamely.

They moved on. Other storks were busy handling paperwork and sorting and wrapping babies. There was a loading dock where storks hooked their long beaks into the top loop of the slings holding the babies, and with much labor took off on their delivery routes. It was a very busy scene.

They reached the far corner of the castle, and saw the straight and narrow ledge crossing the back side. "There must be some way to get into the castle," Forrest said. "But between the funeral and the storks, I don't see it."

"I don't either," she agreed. "We really don't belong to either the beginning or the end of life; we're in the broad middle section. Should we cross to the other side and check out the funeral again?"

"I'm not sure what good that would do. If only there were something halfway between the extremes!" Then he paused. "Do you think it could be literal?"

"Literal?"

"Halfway between the two sides of the castle."

"That's so stupidly simple it can't be right."

"Right," he agreed, remembering how similarly stupidly simple the solutions to the Challenges of the Good Magician's castle in Xanth had been. Yet none of them had been obvious ahead of time. Magician Humfrey just seemed to have a way of making ordinary folk feel stupid.

They walked down the far side of the castle. There, halfway, was a small door. They tried it, and it opened. They had found the way in, passing the second Challenge.

Inside was a large chamber with a raised stage at the far end. There was painted scenery, and several people before it. A man was directing the exact placement of the scenery, and giving the others admonitions for their performances. It was a rehearsal for a play, and it was just beginning.

"I'm not sure we belong here," Forrest said.

The Director turned. "Be silent and sit down, or I'll throw a curse at you."

"Curse fiends!" Imbri whispered. "Don't annoy them."

Forrest had heard about the curse fiends. They lived in a castle under Lake Ogre Chobee. They all had the same talent, that of throwing curses, and they put on plays. They didn't like interference or competition. Sensible folk stayed well clear of them.

He looked at the door, but it had closed and barred itself. They would get hit by a barrage of curses if they tried to get out, because the door would surely make a lot of noise, disturbing the play. That was the way of such things. So he looked for the nearest chair, and Imbri looked also. They would have to watch the play rehearsal. Maybe they could get away when the intermission came.

There were two empty seats in the audience. Unfortunately they were not together. So Forrest had to sit between two young men, while Imbri sat between two women.

"Hello," the man on the left whispered. "I am Justin Case. My talent is to always have just the thing someone needs."

"Hello," the man on the other side whispered. "I am his twin brother Justin Time. My talent is to have my brother present just when he is needed.''

"I am Forrest Faun. My talent is to care for my tree."

"Well, that is surely a worthy endeavor," Justin Case said in a disparaging tone. "At least it lacks the frustration I experience. I always have what others need, but never what I myself need."

"Our talents don't work on ourselves," Justin Time explained. "I am never in time to do myself any good, and I don't help my brother either."

"I am sorry to hear that," Forrest said. "I can see that it must be very frustrating."

"Yes. We'd give anything to have even one bit of selfish good fortune, like marrying two lovely young women and living happily ever after."

Forrest wished he could help them, and wondered whether he should give them the dear horn to use. But then the stage was called to order, and the play began, so that had to wait.

An old man stepped to the center of the stage. "The Curse Fiends present *Raven,* a play in one act by Sofia Socksorter, the Good Magician's wife." He stepped away.

A young man came on the stage and stood before a painted mountain. "I am called Son," he announced. "I am the unacknowledged son of Magician Grey and Sorceress Ivy." He looked at his feet. "It seems they took too long to marry, so when the stork brought me, they weren't ready. So I was raised in an orphanage, with no proper name. But now I am eighteen, and ready to claim my heritage. But first I must perform some significant service for the King, so that I may earn my recognition. I also want to prove that my talent of the ability to manipulate people's minds is truly Magician caliber, because someone claims that it's not; that my mother Ivy Enhanced it to make it seem greater than it is. So now I will go to Prove Myself and Seek my Fortune." Son marched in the direction marked To, which was his near future.

Meanwhile the light on him faded, and another brightened on another part of the stage, showing a painting of a fancy castle. Inside the castle sat a man on a throne. The man wore a crown. "I am King

Dolph,'' he announced. "I am the human ruler of Xanth. My talent is to assume any form I wish to.'' He suddenly turned into a dragon, then into a male harpy, then into a unicorn. He returned to man form. "But today I am receiving visitors, in case any member of my kingdom has a comment or complaint.'' He glanced to the side. "Queen Electra, who is here?''

A woman wearing blue jeans and a crown appeared. "It's a man who claims to be your real father.''

"This should be interesting. Send him in.''

Electra pushed an electric buzzer. A buzz sounded, and a door opened. A man entered the royal chamber. He looked somewhat scruffy.

"So you claim to be my true father?'' King Dolph inquired. "Don't you know that I am the son of King Emeritus Dor and Queen Emeritus Irene? That was established long ago.''

"No it wasn't,'' the man said. "You were delivered to me, but I was busy cutting magic canes, so I set you under a cabbage leaf in the Castle Roogna garden and went on with my work. Before I could return for you, Queen Irene discovered you, and claimed you for her own. There wasn't much I could do, because I had to deliver my load of canes to the local store immediately or I wouldn't get paid for them. By the time I had done that, I had forgotten all about the matter. But now I have remembered, so I have come to fetch you home and put you to work cutting more canes, so I can retire.''

King Dolph did not look entirely pleased by this news. "It is true that I was found under a cabbage leaf, but that's because the stork was unable to get into the closed castle.''

"No it wasn't,'' the man insisted. "It's because I put you there. My wife was most upset when I mentioned it this morning, and insisted that I set the matter to rights immediately.''

"I will have to ponder this,'' King Dolph said. "Come back next week.''

"My wife won't like the delay.''

"Here is a pretty bead. Give her that to distract her.'' King Dolph plunged his hand into the Royal Treasury and fished out a sparkling bead. He gave it to the man.

"Gee, she'll like that,'' the man said, departing with the bead.

"Next," King Dolph said in a businesslike manner.

"That will be Son," Queen Electra said. "He just arrived." She pressed her buzzer.

Son entered. "And what can I do for you?" King Dolph inquired politely.

"I am your unacknowledged cousin Son. I want you to send me on a significant quest, so I can prove myself and claim my rightful heritage as a member of the royal family and maybe marry a nice princess."

"That's a worthy ambition," King Dolph agreed. "Very well: go find out whether the man with the bead really is my true father."

"Okay. I'll go to Stork Headquarters and check the records."

"Do that."

Son exited. The light faded on the King and followed Son. He walked slowly across the stage, and the scenery moved past him in the opposite direction, showing his progress. But before he got to the Stork Works he encountered a pretty girl. She had long dark hair with a matching dark temper.

"I say," Son inquired, "are you by any chance a princess?" For he had always been intrigued by dark-tempered girls; there was just something about them. His attitude on stage showed this clearly.

"No, I am merely Raven, an ordinary person whose talent is to change the color of my cycs to match my moods." Her eyes brightened as she spoke.

"Too bad," he said with real regret. "For I mean to marry a princess."

"Too bad," she agreed, her eyes darkening moodily. "For you are a handsome man with the look of a Magician about you. I mean to marry a Magician."

"Well, maybe you'll find one. Are you going my way?"

"I believe I am. Shall we travel together until we separate?" Her eyes turned hopeful blue.

"That works for me." So they walked together, and the scenery moved on behind them to show their joint progress.

"Shall I tell you my abbreviated life history as we travel?" Raven inquired as the scrolling scenery threatened to become repetitive, and therefore in need of distraction from.

"I am always interested in the life histories of pretty girls," Son said. "Even if they aren't princesses."

So she told him her story. "My mother wanted me to be a powerful Sorceress. She wasn't much impressed with my eye colors." Her eyes turned motley dull depressive brown. "So she made a deal with a demon. The demon gave me a bottle on a cord around my neck. It enables me to take snatches of other people's talents and store them inside the bottle. Then I can use these samples of magic."

"Oh, I say now—could I use any of those talents? I can think of some that would be really handy."

"No," she said regretfully, her eyes turning a gloomy gray. "There is a spell on it which allows only me to use it. In return for this bottle, which does on occasion give me Sorceress-like powers, my mother agreed to give the demon her other child to be his slave. She believed it to be a good bargain, because she had no other children."

"One can never be certain of such a thing," Son said. "I am the unacknowledged first son of Magician Grey Murphy and Sorceress Ivy, and now I have returned to make my status known. I am on a quest to ascertain whether King Dolph has an unacknowledged father."

"That's fascinating," Raven said, clearly unfascinated. Her eyes turned dishwater dull. "I am now sixteen, and I have a lovely sister named Robin. I am afraid that the demon is going to take Robin away to be his slave, especially if she grows up to be as pretty as I am. She is fifteen, and shows every sign of it. So I am traveling to Castle Roogna to seek help."

"But I just came from Castle Roogna," Son said.

"Why didn't you say so?" Raven demanded angrily, her eyes turning smoldery.

"You didn't ask."

"Oh. Well, I suppose I had better turn around and go the other way."

"But you can't do that!" Son protested.

"Why can't I?"

"Because I have fallen in love with you."

This made her pause. "But I'm not a princess," she protested.

"But you are beautiful."

"True," she said reasonably. "But however persuasive that may be, it still doesn't make me royal, unfortunately."

"Yet if I successfully claim my heritage, and am recognized as a prince, and marry you, then you will become a princess," he pointed out with a certain appealing logic.

Raven's eyes turned speculatively bright. "I suppose if you prove to be a Magician, it would be feasible. You are, after all, a handsome man."

"Good. Let's get on to the storks."

"The storks!" she exclaimed, alarmed. "I wasn't ready to go quite that far, that fast. I think signaling even one stork is a very serious thing, especially before marriage."

He realized the nature of her confusion. "I am going to Stork Headquarters, to check the records of deliveries, to ascertain whether King Dolph was delivered to Dor and Irene, or to an anonymous cane cutter. For some reason, the King wishes to know."

Raven's eyes blushed beet red. "Oh! I'm so embarrassed. I thought you meant—"

"Well, I certainly wouldn't mind summoning the stork with you, so if you prefer to take it that way—"

"No, I think I'll quit while I'm ahead," she decided, her eyes becoming a peaceful green. "Let's go question the storks."

So they continued on to the Stork Works, which were exactly as Forrest and Imbri had seen them. The stork in charge of Records didn't want to show them to unauthorized personnel, but Son used his talent to change its mind and satisfy it that they were authorized. They looked on the page listing Dolph. "Delivered to Ruben and Rowena, cane cutters," it said.

"Oh no!" Son said, somewhat dismayed. "I fear I will have bad news for ex-King Dolph."

"I fear I have even worse news for him," Raven said faintly.

He looked at her in surprise. "What could be worse than suddenly never having been a king?"

"Suddenly being enslaved to a demon."

He stared at her in wild surmise. "You mean?"

"Yes! Ruben and Rowena are my parents. He is my Long-lost brother I never knew I had."

"But how is this possible? Dolph is thirty years older than you are."

Raven's eyes turned a nonplused color. "Why, I never thought of that. They aren't old enough. This whole scene is impossible."

"Cut!" the curse fiend director cried. "This is all wrong. How did that ending get in the play?"

"I'm sure I don't know," Raven said.

"Look, Madame Take, you spoke the line. You—"

"My name is *Miss* Take," the actress said primly.

"Well, this is all your fault, *Miss* Take! You got the line wrong."

"Don't yell at my sister like that!" another curse fiend exclaimed. "You are the one who cast her in that role."

"As a favor to you, Out Take," the Director retorted. "Now we're in a prime picklement. Tomorrow is the show; it's too late to get another actress."

"Well, if you were a better director, you'd have had an understudy."

The director pulled out two handfuls of his hair. "Oh, woe is me! The shame of it! The play won't go on!"

There was a silence. Slowly Forrest realized that this wasn't really a curse fiend play rehearsal, but a Challenge: he was supposed to figure out what to do. That meant that there must be something, if he could just comprehend it.

He was getting half a notion how these things worked. The elements of the Challenge were always in plain view; it was just a matter of understanding their relevance. There usually wasn't much that was extraneous; most of a given setting was pertinent. That meant that the play, the audience, and the chamber all related. But how?

Suddenly he had it. "You can fix the play!" he called.

The Director whirled to face him. "What interference is this?"

"I am Forrest Faun, and I have a notion how you can fix it," Forrest said, standing. "But it may seem unusual."

"No idea is too unusual, if it saves the play. What is it?"

"My neighbor on my left must marry the actress for Raven."

"What are you talking about, you foolish faun?" the Director demanded. "The private lives of the actors and audience have nothing to do with the play!"

"Yes they do," Forrest said. "Your play went wrong because the actress, Miss Take, has a talent that is bound to foul it up. Since it is too late to change the actress, you must change her name, so that it no longer has a bad effect. As it happens, Justin Case here can do that by marrying her, so that her name becomes Mrs. Case."

"But he doesn't want to marry a failed actress."

"Speak for yourself, Director," Justin Case said, standing. "She's a beautiful woman, in or out of the play."

"But she wouldn't want to—"

"I'd do anything to save my role," Miss Take said.

The Director nodded. "Very well, then, but be quick about it. We'll have to stage another partial rehearsal, to be sure it's straight."

"But how can you marry and leave me alone?" Justin Time asked. "After I have so loyally gotten you where you needed to be, at just the right time?"

"That's right," Justin Case agreed. "You deserve a lovely actress too."

Forrest thought quickly. "Is Raven's beautiful sister Robin a character in the play?"

"Yes, of course," the Director said. "She has to be saved from the dread demon."

"Then she can marry Justin Time."

"But Miss Inform wouldn't—"

"Speak for yourself, Director," a lovely young woman said, walking on stage. "Let me get a look at this man."

Justin Time stood. He was a handsome man, appearing almost ageless.

Miss Inform nodded. "He'll do."

"But if you are only fifteen—" Justin Time began doubtfully.

"That is my role age," she replied with a smile. "I am actually slightly older, and a good deal more experienced."

"Good enough!" Justin Time agreed.

"Then let's get this done with," the Director said. "The four of you stand before me."

The two men and two women lined up before him. "By the authority vested in me as Almighty Director, I now pronounce you men and wives. Now get on with the play."

The men quickly kissed their brides and returned to their places in the audience. "Pick it up from Raven's 'Yes' " the Director directed. "Give her the cue, Son."

On the stage, Son stared at Raven in wild surmise. "You mean?"

"Yes!" she replied, striking her dramatic pose. "Ruben and Rowena are my parents. He is my long-lost brother I never knew I had."

"But how is this possible? Dolph is thirty years older than you are."

"That's right. There must be some mistake. Let's look at that record again."

Son peered at the stork records. "Oh, now I see that it is mismarked. There's a note: ERROR: PROPER PARENTS ARE DOR & IRENE OF CASTLE ROOGNA."

"Oh, that's a relief," Son said. "I liked King Dolph. I'll be glad to bring the good news to him." He paused. "But then why did your father say that the baby was his?"

"Obviously he lied, because he wanted a son instead of only daughters."

"That makes sense," Son agreed.

"But what about my sister, whom the demon will now claim as his slave?"

Son looked grim. "I shall have to fight him, so as to keep your family happy."

"But you can't fight a demon!" Raven protested.

"You forget my talent of manipulating men's minds. He's male, so maybe I can change his mind." He struck another pose. "Demon, come here!"

There was a gout of fire and a puff of smoke. When it cleared, there was a horrendous figure of a demon. "Who calls Demon Ize?"

"I do," Son said. "I shall not let you make a slave of this woman's lovely little sister."

"Lovely sister?" the demon asked. "I thought it was a vastly older brother."

"No, that was a clerical error. Raven has no brother, only a sister."

"Hm. What does she look like?"

"Here is her picture," Raven said, holding it forth.

D. Ize peered at it. "That could be airbrushed. She's probably really ugly."

"She is not! Here, I'll conjure her in person, and prove it."

"You can conjure?" Son asked, surprised.

"It's one of the pieces of talents I have saved in my bottle," Raven explained. She brought out her bottle and popped the cork. "Sister Robin, come here," she intoned.

A bird with a red breast flew in. It landed on the floor and became a beautiful young woman. "Yes, sister dear?"

"Demon Ize here thinks you're ugly," Raven said.

"Really?" Robin turned to the demon, inhaling.

"Not really," Ize said quickly. "You are truly lovely."

"And he plans to make you his slave," Raven continued sourly.

"Really!" Robin said, frowning. "Does that mean I won't be able to look for a nice man to marry who will have the talent of changing form and flying with me?"

"I can do that!" Ize cried, changing into a green jay. "Suddenly I don't want to enslave you, to my surprise; I want to marry you, you lovely creature," the bird said.

"Gee—that's nice." Robin changed into her bird form, and the two of them flew away.

"Well, I guess that solved your problem," Son said. "And King Dolph's problem. Let's go back to Castle Roogna so I can gain my recognition as a Magician."

"You changed Ize's mind?" Raven asked, impressed.

"Yes. It really wasn't difficult, when he saw how pretty she is. I hope you don't mind having a demon in the family."

"Well, it does seem better than the alternative. And it does seem like a Magician caliber talent. Let's go to Castle Roogna."

They linked arms and walked off stage.

"That works for me," the Director said. "Be here tomorrow for the official production." The members of the cast scattered, and the two actresses went to join their husbands. Meanwhile the Director's roving eye fell on Forrest. "What are you waiting for, Faun? Go on in to see the Good Magician." And a door opened beyond the stage.

Forrest and Imbri walked up to the door and through it. "You figured it out," Imbri said admiringly. "You're a pretty smart faun."

"No, I just caught on to how these Challenges work. In real life I probably would have flubbed it." But he was pleased with her appreciation.

An old, dull woman approached them in the next chamber. Assorted socks were tucked in her apron pockets. "So you repaired my play!" she said. "Thank you. I am Sofia Socksorter, Designated Wife of the moment."

"Uh, yes," Forrest said. "We came to—"

"Of course. Himself will see you now. Just follow the trail of socks."

They followed the trail of socks. "He always had trouble keeping track of his socks," Imbri murmured. "That's why he married Mundania's best sock sorter. But even she can't keep up on a bad day."

"So I see—and smell."

The trail led up to the Good Magician's cramped study. There was Humfrey, as before, hunched over his monstrous tome. "Uh—" Forrest began.

The gnome-like figure looked up. "Yes, yes, of course. Your Service will be to serve as adviser to the princesses Dawn & Eve, to enable them to save the Human territory from marginalization. The magic path will take you directly to Castle Roogna."

"But I haven't even asked my—"

"You came to ask the way to Castle Roogna," Humfrey said irritably. "I have Answered." He returned to his tome.

They had been summarily dismissed. Again. But it was true: they had only sought the way. And for that they had to pay the equivalent of a year's Service. It didn't seem quite fair.

They went back down the dingy winding stairs. "How can Humfrey be here, the same as ever?" Forrest asked Imbri.

"He sips youth elixir to maintain his age at about one hundred," she reminded him.

"No, I mean shouldn't he be banned from Ptero, since he's a real person in Xanth?"

"Only a year, I think. The rest of his life is unobstructed, as with Ogle Ogre."

"Oh, yes, I suppose so. It's strange, seeing someone I met there, here."

"Yes. But it will be stranger seeing Dawn & Eve."

Sofia gave them lunch, and showed them to the magic path. "Be sure not to stray from it," she warned. "There are dragons out there."

"We will stay on it," Imbri promised.

"Himself does appreciate what you are doing, even if he doesn't show it," Sofia said. "If not for you, those two foolish princesses would be off looking for husbands."

"Isn't that normal, for human beings?" Forrest asked.

"Not when their territory is being marginalized. Save that, and then they can do whatever else they want."

"But I don't even know what the term means."

"I'm sure you will find out. Now off with you; the matter is urgent." She shooed them out the door and toward the magic path.

"This realm is as strange as Xanth," Imbri murmured.

"It's stranger," Sofia called after them.

She was probably right.

8
DAWN & EVE

Tender path brought them safely and conveniently through the forest. But it was a fair distance, just as it was in Xanth, so they stopped at a rest station as night came. They knew that night had nothing to do with the progress of the sun across the sky, because Ptero simply used the light of Xanth. Sometimes when Princess Ida put her head in shadow, the scene dimmed.

Forrest wasn't sure whether he should be tired, but when darkness closed, he found he wanted to sleep, so that was all right. Sleeping was no more unnatural here than eating; it seemed they could take or leave either, depending on the local circumstance.

"What does it feel like, being solid?" he asked Imbri as she settled down beside him. "I mean, I'm used to it, but you aren't."

"Especially not in girl form," she agreed. "But I find I am getting used to it, and at times I rather like it. I am even beginning to feel solid girl emotions."

"Oh? What are they?"

"Appreciation for the beauty of the forest, and the niceness of folk like Cathryn. Even things like eating and sleeping are interesting experiences."

"I suppose so. This world of Ptero seems all right, as I become accustomed to it."

"Yes." Then sleepiness overtook him, and he faded out.

He woke later, feeling a motion near him. He discovered that it was Imbri, putting a conventional blanket on him. "You looked cool," she explained.

He had indeed become cool, but the blanket fixed it. "Thank you."

"You are welcome, Forrest."

He started to drift back to sleep. But then he realized that she had no blanket of her own. "Aren't you cool too?" he asked.

"It does not matter."

"Yes it does. Isn't there another blanket?"

"I found only one. Use it, and sleep in peace."

"But you must be sleepy too. You should have it."

"But then you would be cold."

Forrest pondered briefly. "We could share it."

She hesitated.

He had been afraid of that. "If you are concerned that I view you as a nymph—"

"No, it is clear that you do not. You are a far more responsible faun than I expected."

"Caring for my tree has made me that way. Please do join me, Imbri; we are both warm, and the blanket is large enough for us both."

"Thank you." She dissolved her clothing and joined him.

After an astonished instant, Forrest realized that she did not care to sleep under a blanket in her clothing; it wouldn't feel comfortable. So she had eliminated her dress. It made sense. But in that instant she had indeed looked exactly like a nymph. That had an effect on him that he hoped he could conceal from her. He did not want her to think that he had tried to deceive her.

She settled down beside him. Her body touched his at shoulder and hip. She was soft and smooth and warm. Just like a nymph. But she was not a nymph, he reminded himself forcefully. She was a mare in girl form, and an intelligent and thoughtful creature, not interested in nymphly pursuits. So he faced away from her and did his best to ignore her presence.

It took some time, but at last he did manage to sleep again. But later he drifted awake to discover her nestled against his side, her nymphly attributes very soft. He didn't dare move. But he wasn't quite sure he dared sleep again, lest he dream of chasing and catching a nymph, and do something that would appall her. He wished he had anticipated this situation, and avoided it. Yet at the same time he also liked this unexpected contact with her. He knew that his awareness of her had changed in a way that could not be undone. She was still Imbri, his helpful companion. But now she was also somewhat more than that—in a way he must not allow to show.

Forrest lay awake, struggling to adjust his thoughts, but they would not fit back into their former simplicity. He knew Imbri as a person, not a nymph—but now he wished she could be both. That was of course impossible.

So it was a long night. But in the morning he was not tired or logy; apparently in this state he did not really need sleep. It was just a convenience during darkness.

As the light brightened, Imbri stirred and woke. She stretched, rubbing against him, then sat up. "Oh—of course," she said, glancing at him. "We shared warmth. For a moment I wondered what I was doing under the blanket with you."

"Just sleeping," he said.

"Yes. Thank you." She stood, glanced down at her bare body, and concentrated. Her dress formed from her substance, covering her. "I feel like a Sorceress when I do this," she confessed. "But it's really not magic, just reshaping of my soul material."

"Yes." But how different it was to see that nude body, when he knew she was not a mindless nymph. That awareness should have caused him not to care how she looked, but instead it made him care even more. Last night he had wished she could be both nymph and friend, the two aspects separate, taking turns; now he wished she could be both at once. That was a significant change in concept: the idea of celebrating with a real person, a friend, instead of doing the mindless thing with one, and respecting the other. A human woman could have fit that description, as humans had minds and bodies, but Imbri was not human and she had no body, except in the present rather special situation. So it was pointless to dwell on it.

"You seem rather thoughtful this morning," Imbri remarked. "Did you sleep well?"

What could he say? The truth was not appropriate, but he did not like the notion of deception. So he hesitated.

"Oh, you didn't!" she said, in brief anguish. "I shouldn't have taken part of your blanket! You lacked room to sleep freely. I must have tossed and turned and poked you in the night."

"No, no, that's not it," he protested. "You were perfect."

"I didn't poke you?"

"Not exactly." This struggle to find a compromise between accuracy and discretion was awful. It was not an exercise normally required of tree spirits.

"I don't understand. Did I poke you or didn't I? Did I disturb your sleep or didn't I?"

Forrest decided that evasion was untenable. He would have to be forthright, and take the consequence. "You did poke me, but it didn't hurt. You did disturb my sleep, but not because of any restlessness on your part. You slept quietly."

"But I poked you with my elbow?"

"No."

"My knee?"

"No."

"I don't understand. What did I poke you with?"

"Your—" Still he hesitated.

She looked down at her body. "I don't see how—" Then her human mouth turned round. "My maidenly bosom? I poked you with that?"

Forrest felt himself blushing, a thing he had never done before. Possibly no faun had managed it before.

"Oh, Forrest," she said, chagrined. "I never thought—I look like a nymph, don't I! And you're a faun."

"Yes." Now it was out.

"And you had to hold yourself back from being a faun. All night."

"Yes."

"I would never have—if I had realized—this isn't my natural form—it just never occurred to me that—"

"It doesn't matter," he said, wanting to get off this embarrassing subject.

"Yes it does! I have treated you with discourtesy, and caused you distress. I don't know how I can make up for that. I should have understood—it's so obvious in retrospect—"

"Please. It's not important. Let's just resume our trek."

"I was just so thoughtless! No apology can be enough. But I must do something—" Then a new expression crossed her face. "Forrest, I keep forgetting that I'm solid, here on Ptero. Even when that makes mischief, I forget that it can also abate it. I can be a nymph for you."

"No. I don't want that."

"No, really. It is no affront to me. We animals don't take such things seriously. I can play the game perfectly, if you will just tell me how. Let's see—nymphs run and scream cutely, and kick their feet, and fling their hair about, and pretend to signal the stork." As she spoke, she dissolved her dress, ran around in a little circle, kicked up one foot and then the other, and flung her lengthening hair in a full circle. Then she tried a cute scream: "Eeeeeek!"

"No!" Forrest cried. "Stop it!"

She stopped immediately. "I'm sorry, Forrest. Do I have it wrong?"

"No. I just don't want you as a nymph."

"But you said—in the night—"

"You're not mindless."

"Oh. But I can pretend to be."

"I would know better."

She nodded sadly. "So I can't be a nymph for you. All I can do is frustrate you."

"Yes."

"I truly apologize, Forrest. If there is any other way I can make it up to you—"

"No. We must get on with our mission."

"Yes, of course," she agreed, chastened.

So they resumed their trek. But in his mind he saw her again and again, acting exactly like a nymph. He had wanted so much to play that game with her! But to have her pretend to be mindless, and believe she was satisfying him, when what he truly wanted was—no, he couldn't accept that. Neither would he ask her to do it while *not* pretending to be a nymph, because that would imply some actual commitment on her part, and he had no right to desire that. She was just with him on an assignment, to help him find a faun for a tree. When this quest was done, she would be free to go her own way, her service to the Good Magician fulfilled.

"Forrest, I see you are still depressed," Imbri said as they walked. "I know it's my fault. I wish—"

"No. It's my fault." And he knew that was the truth. He had no right to soil her innocence with his unrealistic desire. "I want to speak no more of it."

"Of course," she agreed, chastened again.

No danger threatened them on the way, because the path was enchanted. The scenery was mountainous, but the path wound around, remaining almost level, so that this was no problem. They could admire the view with impunity. Only when there was no alternative did the path climb to any height.

In due course they came to Castle Roogna, which was in a forest in a valley. The path had climbed over a ridge, and the valley was laid out for their view, like a large picture. But there was something wrong with that picture. "What are all those lines?" Forrest asked, startled. "I don't remember seeing them." For the valley was crisscrossed with long colored lines that extended from hillside to hillside, as if some giant had drawn them with a pencil. Only the area immediately around the castle itself was clear of the lines.

"I'm sure they weren't there in Xanth," Imbri agreed. "But of course this isn't Xanth; it's a smaller replica."

"Still, we haven't seen such lines elsewhere in Ptero. I don't think it can be normal."

"Do you think it could relate to the problem we are supposed to solve?" she asked. "Marginalization?"

"Marginalization," he repeated, pondering. "They do look a bit like margins. As if somebody drew some lines to mark off the valley, then drew some more lines inside those, and more farther inside, leaving less space in the center. It reminds me of a game I used to play as a faun."

She laughed. "You aren't still a faun?"

Actually, he wondered. The fauns of the Faun & Nymph Retreat were shallow creatures, intent on only one thing, and the nymphs provided that. The fauns who left the retreat and sought useful employment became deeper, but not by a whole lot; it was just that they now realized that the pursuit of nymphs was not the only thing, though it did remain the main thing. Those fauns who chose to associate with trees became deeper yet, but still were not by any means really serious people. On this quest Forrest had become far more thoughtful than ever in his life before, and the episodes on Ptero had accelerated that change. Right up until last night, when he had actually held back from doing what was natural, and this morning when he had declined Imbri's offer to play nymph, despite considerable temptation. No faun he had ever heard of would have done that. So he was certainly no longer a normal member of his kind. But that was too complicated to go into right now. "When I was young."

"What was the game?"

"We played it with stone knives. We cleared a patch of dirt, and took turns flipping our knives into it so that they stuck point first. Then we extended the direction of the blade each way, making a line that divided the patch into two sections. Whoever missed the clear patch, or didn't get his knife to stick in the ground, lost his turn. The clear patch kept getting smaller as it got subdivided, until finally it was too small to hit. The last one to get his knife into it was the winner."

"But what was the point?"

"Just to win. We had to have something to divert us when there were no nymphs in sight. That was it."

She glanced sidelong at him. "Your horizons have broadened since then."

If only she knew how far! "Yes. Anyway, a game would look like that valley. It was hard to get the knife to fall just the right way, and it got harder as the game progressed, so that usually just a slice was taken off the edge of the remaining patch. If this is a game, it's about three quarters through."

"What kind of creatures could play such a game with the human territory of Ptero?"

"Invisible giants?"

She nodded. "If it is such a game, what does the winner get?"

"Castle Roogna," he said. "And with it, dominion over all the human beings of Ptero."

She nodded again. "And you have to help Dawn & Eve save the

human territory from marginalization. Now I think we know more about the nature of the threat.''

"Marginalization,'' he repeated. "Pressing in of the margins. Until there is nothing left in the center. That seems like something that needs to be dealt with.''

"Yet the King would be a Magician,'' Imbri said. "How is it that he could not fight this incursion?''

"Something must have happened to him. We had better get down there quickly, before it gets any worse.''

"But won't the giants see us, and stop us from getting there? Especially if they should suspect our mission?''

"Yes. So we'll use Cathryn's blanket of obscurity.'' He reached into his knapsack and brought out the little can.

"You are getting smarter all the time. I wouldn't have thought of that.''

"Please don't compliment me.''

She looked at him, surprised. "Why not, when it's true?''

He would have bitten his tongue, but it was too late for that. So he told the truth. "Because I already care too much for you, in your present shape, and that just makes it worse.''

She stared at him in astonishment. Then she looked thoughtful. "I will try to be more careful.''

He held the can in front of him. "I invoke you.''

Nothing happened. But that was the way it was supposed to be. He put the can away, and they started down the hill.

At the edge of the forest they came to their first line. They halted just short of it. The thing was green, and marked the ground without actually cutting into it, in the manner of a shadow. It crossed rocks and trees the same way. It wasn't visible in the air, but its dark green line showed against the leaves and branches above it, indicating that it was a vertical plane. "Do you think it's safe to cross it?'' Forrest asked.

"With the concealment of the blanket, it should be. But maybe we should move carefully, and not talk much, when we cross.''

"I agree. I'll go first.''

"Why?''

"Because if it is dangerous, I don't want you hurt."

"But the quest is yours. I should be protecting you, not you me."

Her logic was good, but it wasn't enough. The thought of her in danger because of him was not to be suffered. "Please Imbri—let me go first."

"You idiot!" she cried.

That startled him. "What?"

"Did it ever occur to you that I might feel the same way about you?"

He considered. "No."

"I know I'm just a day mare, but I have feelings too. I don't want you to be hurt any more than you want me to be hurt. And what would I do if I didn't see you safely through this quest?"

She was right. "I apologize, Imbri. Suppose we take turns trying the dangerous things?"

"All right. I apologize too. I shouldn't have blamed you for caring for me." She stepped forward and crossed the line.

Nothing happened. Apparently it was dangerous in itself, or the blanket of obscurity was protecting them. Forrest stepped across. There was no sensation. It was just a marking, not an actual barrier.

Forrest breathed a sigh of relief. "I think we'll have to cross several more lines, but it seems to be safe."

Imbri nodded, and they continued toward the castle. They did cross other lines, each a different color, without trouble. He wasn't sure whether this was because of the obscurity spell, or the enchanted path, or because the lines weren't actually dangerous. He didn't like the idea of wasting magic, but he didn't like unnecessary risk either. Until they understood exactly what was happening here, they had to be careful.

The path led through the great orchard, where pie trees and shoe trees and many other types were cultivated. It passed a cemetery with a sign saying BEWARE OF ZOMBIES. It led up to a deep moat where an old moat monster eyed them warily. In short, things were completely ordinary, near the castle. Even the monster was familiar: "Hello, Soufflé!" Imbri called.

"But this monster is too old to be that one," Forrest said.

"You forget we have come far west, into the To," she reminded him. "Folk are older here." She went up to pat the monster on the nose.

But Soufflé shied away, not recognizing her.

"You're in the wrong form," Forrest murmured.

"Oh, yes." She faced the monster. "In my natural form I look like this." She fuzzed out and assumed her mare form. It wasn't dense, but it was clear enough to see.

Soufflé's eyes brightened. Now he recognized the day mare. He lowered his head as she returned to girl form, and this time suffered himself to be patted on the nose. "I have only enough mass to be this form," she explained. "Besides, I'm traveling with Forrest Faun, so it's easier to be two footed. But I'm still Mare Imbri."

They crossed the moat and came to the castle entrance. A woman came to meet them at the gate. Something was orbiting her head. "Princess Ida!" Imbri cried.

"Do we know each other?" the princess inquired politely.

"I'm Mare Imbrium, in human form because that's all the mass I have. This is Forrest Faun. We met a few days ago, in Xanth."

Forrest nodded as he was introduced. But he wondered, because this woman was older than the one they had met before.

"I'm sorry, but I don't remember. About what age was I then?"

"Twenty eight, I think—the same as Princess Ivy."

"That explains it, then; that is in our blanked year. Until that passes, we won't know what happened therein."

"Blanked year?" Forrest asked.

"Remember Ogle Ogre," Imbri murmured.

Now he understood. The year surrounding their "present" existence in Xanth.

"What year is it now?" Imbri asked.

"We are forty now. Twelve years after that."

That explained why she looked older. But there was also something odd about her moon. "When we met you, your moon was round," Forrest said.

Princess Ida smiled. "Of course. My present existence here is a derivative of that reality, so my moon differs." She angled her head so that the moon swung into full view. "This is Pyramid."

Now he saw that the moon was not round, but triangular. Or at least had a triangular outline. It seemed to have four sides, each triangular. It rotated around three, while the fourth faced down, becoming the base of the figure.

Forrest found this a bit hard to assimilate. "Is—is it also a world in its own right? The way Ptero is?"

"Of course. Though we don't know what is on it. No one has been there. But we suspect that the ideas that never were are there."

"That makes sense," Forrest agreed.

"And what brings you folk of Xanth to our realm?" Ida inquired politely. "We seldom if ever have visitors from there."

"Forrest has a quest to find a faun for a neighboring tree," Imbri explained.

"Oh, you will have to go farther To for that; the faun territory is there."

"But meanwhile I'm on a mission for the Good Magician," Forrest said. "I have to advise Princesses Dawn & Eve, to help them save the human territory from marginalization."

"Oh, that's wonderful! We were so afraid that help would not come. Now I'm hopeful that it will be all right."

"But I hardly know what to do."

"The Good Magician would not have sent you unless he were sure you could do the job. Our situation is verging on desperate. There are so few of us left."

"So few?" Imbri asked.

"Come, you must meet King Ivy. She will help explain."

"King who?"

"King Ivy. She had to take over when King Dor was lost. Right this way."

"But what of King Dolph?" Imbri asked.

"Oh, he's not until later. But he's lost too."

"Lost?"

"There are only six of us here now. Ah, here we are."

They had arrived at the throne room. Sure enough, a woman of forty sat on the throne. She rose to come to them as they entered.

"King Ivy, this is Forrest Faun, and Marc Imbrium, from Xanth,"

Princess Ida said. "They are here to enable Dawn & Eve to handle the margins."

"What a relief!" King Ivy said. "Come, we must have a banquet."

"But is this the time for that?" Forrest asked. "I mean, if the situation is serious—"

"We can talk best then," Princess Ida explained. "Everyone gets together for a banquet."

Soon they were at the banquet hall. The other members of the castle arrived and were introduced: Consort Grey, a handsome man just beyond forty, Princess Electra, who was 872 or 38 depending on whether chronological or normal living time was counted, and her daughters Dawn & Eve, who were a buxom eighteen. Dawn had flame-red hair, green eyes, and wore bright clothes. Eve had jet black hair and eyes, and wore dark clothing. Both were startlingly beautiful.

"When I met you two, a few days ago, you were six years old," Forrest said, bemused.

"Yes, that's our blank year," Dawn agreed.

"So we don't remember you," Eve said. "But we're sure you're an interesting person."

"Girls, don't be too forward," their mother Electra warned them.

"Oh, pooh!" Dawn said. "He's a faun."

"It's impossible for us to embarrass him," Eve agreed.

Then they both leaned forward over the table, so that their décolletages fell open, flashing four impressive hemispheres. And for the second time in his life Forrest blushed.

"Girls!" Electra exclaimed indignantly.

"See?" Dawn asked her sister as they straightened up. "I told you it was possible to embarrass a faun."

"You win," Eve agreed. "But we probably couldn't do it again."

"You won't!" Electra cried before they could do it again. "You'll have to excuse my impetuous children."

The two girls shrugged in unison, looking halfway smug. Forrest found himself becoming a trifle nervous about having to advise them. While he was trying to show them what to do, what would they be showing him? It would have been easier to work with the two six year olds, whose naughtiness would have been more limited.

The banquet was good, with slices of buttered breadfruit and chipped potatoes, and pitchers of drink. Forrest spied one whose label seemed to say Boot Rear, so he poured himself a mug of that, as he liked forest products. He took a sip, and it was very good. But Dawn, sitting across from him, looked alarmed. "You're drinking Toot Rear?"

Oops—had he taken the wrong drink? He had seen only the latter part of the label. The last thing he wanted was to embarrass himself at the King's banquet! But then he saw that the pitcher did say Boot, not Toot. Both girls, seeing his face, burst out laughing. They had fooled him.

Electra glared at them, and the two subsided. This was surely going to be a long assignment.

"How can we help you perform your Service?" King Ivy inquired as they proceeded to dessert.

"I admit that I have no idea how I should proceed," Forrest said. "I don't think I have any qualifications."

"Oh, you are surely qualified," Consort Grey said. "The Good Magician always knows. You just have to discover how you are qualified."

"But I don't even know anything about human women, let alone princesses. How can I presume to advise them?"

"Your authority derives from that of the Good Magician," Ivy said. "The twins may pout—" As she spoke, Dawn & Eve pouted prettily. "But they know the mission is quite serious, and will do their best. They know that this is the only way to save their father, Prince Dolph." And at that the twins were abruptly serious.

"Can you tell me just what the situation is? We passed a number of lines as we approached the castle, but don't know what they mean."

The King sighed. "They mean that the human sector of Ptero is being marginalized. Some hostile force is laying siege to us, and has already limited us to the immediate region of the castle, so that we can't range through our lives and become young or old as we choose. This means that I am stuck at age forty, which is definitely not comfortable for a woman, and so is my sister Ida. But that's the least of it. All the human beings of this territory have been lost to the margins, so that only the six of us you see here remain. Soon all of us will be gone, if you are not able to guide the twins successfully."

"All are gone?" Imbri asked, appalled.

"All," Ivy said firmly. "At first we sent folk out to try to deal with it, but none of them returned. Even Magicians and Sorceresses were lost. Our daughters Melody, Harmony, and Rhythm are gone, and my grandparents Magician Trent and Sorceress Iris, and Grey's parents Magician Murphy and Sorceress Vadne. They went out and got caught by the margins."

"The margins," Forrest repeated. "Those are the lines?"

"Yes. They appear suddenly, and whatever is caught within them is lost. Sometimes we can see their forms faintly within their enclosures, but we can't reach them."

"You can't cross the lines?" Forrest asked.

"We can't cross. They are like glass walls, impenetrable."

"But we crossed them without difficulty."

"They seem to be one way walls," Grey explained. "My talent is to nullify magic, but I have not been able to nullify the margins. I think it is because they are merely the effects of some distant magic, which I can't reach. Similarly Eve's talent is to know anything about anything inanimate, but she can't discover anything about the margins. So it may be that they aren't really there, though their effects certainly are. Did you try to cross any margins the other way?"

Forrest exchanged a chagrined glance with Imbri. "No. It didn't occur to us. But still, how can folk be trapped behind the walls, then? Why don't they cross in toward the castle?"

"When the margins are laid down, they seem to exert control over whatever they enclose," Grey said. "The inanimate things remain as they were, but the animate things become ghostly. You are the first folk to pass through them and reach us, since the marginalization began a few weeks ago. On occasion we have seen birds from elsewhere fly in, but soon they drop into a marginalized segment and become ghostly."

"But then that should have happened to us, too," Imbri said.

"We would have thought so," Ivy agreed. "But we are very glad you got through."

"The blanket!" Forrest exclaimed. "It must have helped."

"Blanket?" Princess Ida asked.

"He has a blanket of obscurity that Cathryn Centaur gave us," Imbri said.

"Cathryn!" Eve said, her dark eyes brightening like stars. "Is she all right?"

"Yes, she's fine," Imbri answered. "She's the one who told us to come to you twins. But how do you know her, since you live beyond her limit of old age?"

Eve smiled. "Our From limit comes close to her To limit. We used to explore that way, and we met her. We were so small that we had gotten lost, but she called out to us and directed us back To, so that we were all right."

"So we like her, and feel that we owe her a service," Dawn said. "But we have found no way to render it."

"That must be why she sent us to you," Forrest said. "She knew that you would help us in our search, since she couldn't."

"Search?" Eve asked.

"I am looking for a faun for a tree in Xanth. That is what brought us to Ptero. Everything else constitutes the complications of that search."

"Things do get complicated," King Ivy agreed. "By any chance, did the Good Magician in Xanth send you to Ptero?"

"Yes," Forrest agreed. "And the Good Magician in Ptero sent us—" He paused. "Why, he must have chained himself, I mean, made a chain from himself to himself, to get help to you from Xanth! He sent us to his other self, here, and then—" He paused, momentarily confused by the complication of it.

"It isn't easy to fathom Humfrey's ways," Grey agreed. "But they always make sense at the end. I came to appreciate that during the years when I worked for him."

"But I'm still just a faun," Forrest said. "I can't do any special magic, and I don't know a whole lot. How could I possibly succeed, where Magicians and Sorceresses have failed?"

"If the Good Magician believes you can succeed, then I'm sure it's true," Grey said. Then he looked thoughtful. "Tell me, Forrest: do you happen to know Princess Ida's talent?"

"Yes. It's the Idea."

"Too bad," King Ivy muttered.

"What?" Forrest asked, startled.

Grey raised a hand. "My wife was thinking of something else. Allow me, if you will, to explore this just a bit further. Do you know how Ida's talent actually works?"

"Yes. Her moon is a solidification of all the ideas associated with Xanth. It's where they are stored. That's why we are here: in pursuit of an idea. The idea of a faun who can associate with my neighboring tree."

Ivy looked up, seeming interested.

"And that is the extent of it?" Grey asked. "It's just the moon?"

What was the point of this? "Yes, as far as I know. Am I being stupid about something?"

"By no means," Grey said quickly. "No one can be expected to know what he hasn't seen and hasn't been told."

"I suppose so," Forrest agreed. He glanced at Imbri, but she averted her gaze. That bothered him. He looked at the twin girls, and they averted their gazes too. "There *is* something, isn't there!"

"There is something you don't know, but it is no fault in you," Grey said carefully.

"So why don't you tell me what it is, so I won't be so stupid?"

"You are not stupid, you are merely ignorant of something, as anyone in your situation would be. I shall be glad to tell you, but I would like to establish something first."

This was getting annoying. Forrest didn't like games where everyone else knew what he didn't, and shared a smug superiority because of it. "Establish what?"

"I would like to ascertain whether you agree with my point about the Good Magician."

"That it isn't easy to fathom his ways? Yes, I agree."

"And that since he seems to believe that you can succeed in this mission to Ptero, it must be true."

"Yes, I suppose, though he seems more devious than he has to be."

"So you too believe that you will succeed."

What was with all this circuitous dialogue? "Yes! I don't know *how* I'll succeed, but I probably will."

"I'm sure you will," Ida agreed.

"Thank you, Princess." Forrest turned his attention back to Magician Consort Grey. "So what is it I don't know, aside from how to live up to the Good Magician's expectation?"

"The rest of the nature of Princess Ida's talent. It is true that it is the Idea, but that is not the whole of it. It is that anything she accepts as true, is true, and she is glad to agree with the beliefs of others."

"That's nice," Forrest said, glancing at Ida. "But isn't that true of anybody? I don't accept anything as true that I know is not true, after all."

"But you could be mistaken."

"Yes. Anyone could."

"Princess Ida is never mistaken."

This was odd. "But anyone can be confused, or have wrong information, at some point."

"Not Ida. When she accepts an idea, it is true. That is her talent."

"But—" Forrest looked again at the princess. "No offense, Princess. But so what?"

"Since she agrees that you will succeed in your mission, you will succeed," Grey said. "That is her talent. Her reality becomes our reality."

A pale gleam dawned. "As a Sorceress, she makes things come true," Forrest said. "That really helps. But why didn't she just decide that one of you could overcome this marginalization? Why bring an ignorant faun into it?"

"Because the idea has to come from someone who doesn't know her talent."

Forrest pondered that. All of them obviously knew Princess Ida well. Even Imbri had known the Princess before. Only Forrest himself hadn't known her talent, though he had thought he did. So only his own belief in the success of his mission counted. His ignorance had been his greatest asset. "So now I will succeed," he said slowly. "But what I believe after this won't count, because now I know the true nature of Princess Ida's talent."

"That's it," Grey agreed. "But it is enough. That assurance guarantees not only your personal success, but the salvation of the whole human complement of Ptero. Until this point, we have had to face the prospect of extinction."

Forrest was amazed, and not completely pleased. "So I was sent here because of what I didn't know, so that you could persuade me that I could succeed, so that it would become possible for me to succeed, thanks to Princess Ida, so that you could escape your fate."

"Oh, don't be so poopy about it," Dawn said.

"We'll make it up to you," Eve added. Both of them inhaled.

"You will *not!*" Electra snapped.

They burst into mirth. Even Forrest had to laugh at that. The prospect of working with them was beginning to seem not so bad. At least they were cheerful, and surely their talents were worthwhile.

"So now it seems we all know where we stand," King Ivy said. "We have no better notion than you do how to proceed from here, but we will give you any support you need."

"Thank you," Forrest said. "I suppose I should consult with the girls and see if we can develop any strategy for dealing with the margins."

"Sure, let's go to the bedroom right away," Dawn said brightly.

"I'll turn down the sheets," Eve agreed darkly.

"Girls!" Electra said severely. "When I was your age, at least I had some manners."

"Mom, when you were our age, you were married," Dawn said. "And exploring the Adult Conspiracy."

"And in blue jeans, too," Eve added. "While we wear dresses." She spun about, causing her skirt to rise dangerously. "Now it's our turn, while we're lush and full."

"Of all the ages to be stuck in," Electra moaned. "You're impossible."

"Oh come on Mom," Dawn said. "You enjoyed signaling the stork to order us. Admit it."

"Maybe the Tapestry room," Imbri suggested. "If it's not being used. So you can show us exactly where things are."

"Oh, we can do that without the Tapestry," Dawn said serenely, tugging at her blouse. Eve tugged at her skirt. But this time King Ivy added her glare to that of Electra, and the two decided to behave.

They went to the Tapestry room. Forrest was almost afraid that he would see himself lying on the bed there, but it was empty. The four of them sat on the bed, facing the Tapestry. Forrest found himself flanked by Dawn & Eve, their soft hips touching his. He was uncomfortable, but pretended not to notice. He knew they were having innocent fun with him, and didn't mean what they hinted.

"Can the Tapestry show the margins?" he asked.

"Sure," Dawn said. She was usually the first to speak, and Eve the last. "There they are."

A pattern of lines appeared on the picture. They crisscrossed the valley, forming a giant circle. Castle Roogna was in the center of the portion that remained clear. The lines extended out to the pun strips that bordered the human territory, and stopped there. None seemed to be near the Good Magician's castle, however.

"So the attack is limited to the human region," Forrest said, trying to proceed intelligently despite his continuing awareness of the maidenly hips touching him. He tried to think of the girls as the little ones he had first seen, but it just didn't work; they were big girls now.

"Yes," Eve agreed somberly. "Even the margins can't stand the puns."

"Imbri and I thought the pattern resembles a game played by invisible giants," he said. "Tossing knives."

"Oh, you're so smart!" Dawn exclaimed, nudging him.

He was determined not to be falsely flattered. "Do you have invisible giants here?"

"Sure," Eve agreed soberly. "But they haven't done anything like this before."

"In any event, they wouldn't have magic like this," Imbri pointed out.

"Who would have magic like this?"

"We don't know," Dawn said.

"Maybe an evil Wizard," Eve added.

"Not a Magician or Sorcerer?" he asked.

"We don't think there are any left," Dawn explained. "So it must be something non-human."

Forrest nodded. "That makes sense to me."

Both girls turned their heads to look at him. "You mean you're taking one of our suggestions seriously?" Eve asked.

Forrest was taken aback. "Shouldn't I? You both know more about this situation than I do."

"Nobody ever took us seriously before," Dawn said.

Forrest began to get a glimmer why they tended to misbehave. "I'm supposed to advise you how to handle the marginalization. I can't do that if I don't take you seriously."

The two exchanged a glance, on either side of his face. It brushed his head, feeling like a caress. "You'll actually pay attention to our ideas?" Eve asked.

"Yes, of course. What are they?"

"We think the Wizard must be hiding in the hills somewhere, in an ugly castle, hating human beings because he's not pretty like us," Dawn said.

"And he's casting out margins to hem us in so we can't escape, so he can destroy us all," Eve said.

"Then we should find him and stop him," Forrest said. "But how?"

"You got through the lines," Dawn said. "So maybe you can take us through, so we can sneak up on him."

"But the lines are one way."

"We can't be sure of that," Eve said uncertainly. "Maybe it just seems that way."

"But if even Grey Murphy couldn't dent them—"

"We think maybe the Wizard is watching, and does something to strengthen a margin when one of us approaches it, to make us think we are trapped more solidly than we are," Dawn said eagerly. "Maybe if we could go to a line without being noticed, we could get through it, or do something to it."

"Well, if my blanket of obscurity helps—"

They clapped their hands in perfect unison. "Let's try it!" Eve said. "The worst we can do is fail."

"By all means," Forrest agreed, pleased with the progress they were making. The twins were no longer trying to distract him; they were genuinely interested in the project.

They went downstairs and to the front gate. There Forrest brought out the canned blanket and invoked it. Nothing seemed to happen, but he proceeded with confidence toward the margins.

They stopped before the nearest line, which was red. "When Imbri and I came through, the lines were visible, but we couldn't touch them," he said. "But we didn't try very hard. If your theory is right, we should be very quiet and careful, because the spell of obscurity may not be very strong. I don't know how far out it reaches, so we should remain closely grouped, too."

They clustered in close, the twins touching him on either side, but this time they were not trying to tease him. "It might also be that it's the margins themselves that react when people approach," Dawn said. "So that you got through because they didn't know you were challenging them."

"That makes even more sense to me," Forrest said. "The lines are here all the time, and if they have any awareness—"

"The inanimate does have awareness," Eve said. "I can talk to it, though not the way Grandpa Dor can. I will try to fathom the nature of the margins, if I am able to get close enough to make contact."

"You couldn't touch it, before?" Forrest asked.

"It was just a blank nothing," she said. "I reached out my hand, and it stopped as if meeting a wall, but there was nothing there. I can tell anything about anything inanimate, but this wasn't a thing, it was a force. I couldn't reach its substance, if it has any."

"Let's see if we can cross the line," Forrest suggested. "Then let's explore it from the other side. But if we do succeed in crossing it, don't make any exclamations of joy or victory, because that might attract the attention of whatever brings down those birds who fly in. We don't want to be trapped as they were."

The two girls shuddered together. "We'll be very subdued," Dawn said.

"I'll go first," Forrest decided. "Then you follow me, Dawn. Then Eve, then Imbri."

"But shouldn't someone remain on the other side, in case we are trapped?" Eve asked. "So she can tell the others what happened?"

Forrest nodded. "Good point. Maybe Dawn should be last, so that both of you aren't at risk."

The twins exchanged another glance. Forrest noticed that their glances were identical, except that one was bright and the other dark, and met exactly in the center of the space between them. Then Dawn nodded. "When there is something animate to check, I'll cross first," she said.

Forrest reached across the space over the line. A faint shadow showed on his arm, but there was no resistance. He stepped across, and stood on the other side.

Eve tried it next. She reached to the invisible wall, and found nothing, so she too stepped across. She looked back at her sister. "Can you hear me, Dawn?"

"Yes," Dawn agreed. "So we're doing it."

Imbri crossed. "Now let's see if you can analyze it from this side," she said.

Eve squatted so that she could touch the line on the ground. "It's still not—wait, it's very faint, but I can feel something. It's not the thing, just the energy from it, which piles up at the ground. It—it's because it isn't projecting up from the ground, it's coming down from above."

"Down from above!" Forrest echoed, surprised. "But there's nothing up there!"

Imbri looked up. "Nothing except Xanth. Is this an idea coming from Princess Ida in Xanth?"

"She wouldn't do anything mean like this," Dawn said. "We know her; she's nice."

"Then it must be from somewhere else," Forrest said. "Can you trace it?"

Eve moved her hand. "Maybe. It's energy, but I can feel the slightest tingle. It seems to go straight up from the shadow on the ground."

"If it comes from above, it must come from somewhere," Imbri said. "Ptero is turning, so shouldn't the shadow be moving across the ground?"

The other three looked at her. "It should," Dawn agreed. "So maybe it isn't coming from above."

"But it is," Eve said. "I can tell."

"Maybe not from beyond Ptero," Forrest suggested. "Could it curve or bend?"

"That's it," Eve said. "I can tell now; it turns a corner. I can feel that much from its nature. A corner that way." She closed her eyes and pointed.

"That's toward Castle Roogna!" Imbri said.

"The enemy menace is in Castle Roogna?" Dawn asked, appalled. "But that's us."

"Could you have an enemy in your midst?" Forrest asked, feeling a chill.

"No," Dawn said. "There's only King Ivy and Consort Grey; they would never betray the human territory. After all, they govern it. There's Mom—she'd never do it either. And Aunt Ida is Ivy's twin sister; she'd never do it. It isn't the two of us, either. And there's no one else in the castle, now; we know."

Forrest got a weird notion. "There could be others."

Eve looked at him. "We have explored every cranny of the castle, with our magic. There's no one."

"Have you explored Pyramid?"

Both their mouths dropped open. "Pyramid!" Dawn said. "It's a whole separate world in itself! Anything could be there."

"Including even an evil Wizard," Eve agreed. "We never thought of that."

"It's Forrest's business to think of it," Imbri said. "He must be right. We have seen how much there can be on a seemingly tiny moon. Ptero is such a moon. Pyramid is another, and there could be anything at all there. Including someone who wants to take over Ptero. Your evil Wizard."

"It could be," Dawn breathed. "That would explain everything. But what can we do about it?"

"We can go to Pyramid," Forrest said.

"But can we?" Imbri asked. "You and I came here by leaving our bodies behind, and letting our souls become solid. But our souls wouldn't fit on Pyramid. And what of Dawn & Eve? Their souls are mostly tied up in their living year in Xanth. How could they go?"

Forrest pondered. "Dawn & Eve must have small soul fragments here—maybe about the same amount as we have, relative to Ptero. Enough to animate their bodies on Pyramid.''

"That's true," Dawn said. "Souls are living, so I know. We have just that much. But what of you two, who are all-soul here?"

"We'll just have to leave most of our souls behind," Forrest said. "And use just enough for Ptero. It should be similar to what we did in Xanth, leaving our bodies lying in the Tapestry room."

The other three nodded. "I think we shall have to go to Pyramid," Imbri said. "But first we'll have to tell the others."

"Mom's not going to like this much," Eve said darkly.

"But she'll get used to it," Dawn said brightly. "She always does."

Forrest and Eve stepped back across the margin, and the four of them walked back toward Castle Roogna. Forrest was pleased with the progress they had made, but nervous about what might be in store for them. This mission had just become more complicated than he had expected.

9
PYRAMID

You want to go where?'' Electra demanded, appalled.
"Mother, we already explained," Dawn said, as if the
woman were slow in intellect.

"It's the only way to deal with the marginalization," Eve continued. "The margins are coming from Pyramid, so we have to go there to stop them."

"But it's just a decoration spinning around Princess Ida's head! How could any of you fit there?" But the question was rhetorical, because her next question was "Suppose you don't return?"

"I fear it is a risk they will have to take," King Ivy said. "The alternative is to allow ourselves to be marginalized out of existence. Remember, they are going to succeed."

"Forrest Faun will succeed," Electra said. "That says nothing about my daughters."

"But his mission is to advise them how to accomplish it," Grey said. "So if he succeeds, so do they."

"Yes, I'm sure they will," Ida agreed. "And I confess to being curious about who lives on Pyramid."

Electra seemed to have some continuing misgivings, but she knew that the alternative was just as bad. They went up to the Tapestry room with Ida, and the four of them lay down on beds there. "I will guide Dawn," Imbri said. "And Forrest will guide Eve. It will be somewhat strange at first, but that will settle down once we are on Pyramid.''

"It should be fun," Dawn said bravely, but she looked a smidgen uncertain.

"If nothing goes wrong," Eve agreed, looking two smidgens uncertain.

Forrest was not at all certain that nothing would go wrong, but he didn't care to say that. He hoped that Ida's belief in their success would make it true, but he had not seen her talent in action. So he proceeded with the program. He sat up, dug out his bottle, and took it to Dawn. "Sniff this," he said, hoping that it worked the same way as it did in Xanth. He pulled out the stopper.

Dawn sniffed. A strange look spread across her features. She closed her eyes and stopped breathing.

Forrest brought it to Eve. She sniffed, and faded similarly out. Then he lay back on his own bed, the same one he had used in Xanth, and sniffed it himself.

Soon he was floating, as before. But this time it wasn't his soul leaving his body, exactly; it was a tiny part of his soul detaching itself from the main mass, and carrying his awareness with it.

"This way." It was Imbri's voice, directing Dawn. She had not had to use the elixir, perhaps because she was long accustomed to soul form.

Forrest concentrated, and formed his own eye and ear and mouth. He oriented on Eve, who was lying there with a haze drifting above her. Rather, she was the haze, floating above her unused body. The body was dark and lovely, but looked dead. "Form an eye," he told her. "Pull yourself together."

The mist quivered and coalesced. A bulbous eye developed in its top.

"That's it," he said encouragingly. "Now form a mouth and ear."

Slowly these things formed. "This is weird," the mouth said.

"It will become familiar, once we land on Pyramid," he told her. "See if you can form your own shape as we go. In a moment we'll join Imbri and Dawn, and fly to that world."

She shaped up, getting the hang of it, and became a somewhat tenuous naked woman.

"You can use your substance to make clothing," he told her, realizing that she was now going into what amounted to full-soul status. "Just concentrate on it the same way."

"Oh." A clumsy dress formed around her.

"Now follow me." He made sure her eyeballs were aimed in his direction, and started moving toward Imbri and Dawn.

Dawn had made similar progress. Her form was lighter in color, with an ill-fitting white dress, but her face was recognizably her. When Eve caught up, the two gazed at each other—and burst out laughing.

"Easy," Forrest cautioned them, as they threatened to fragment into cloudlets.

The two managed to stifle their mirth. Actually it was probably a good thing, because it meant they were adapting to their situation.

"This way," Imbri said. She was in her mare form. She started trotting up a steep invisible hill.

They followed, using their legs to run up the same hill. "Make yourselves smaller as you go," Forrest said, doing it himself. "Keep condensing."

Soon Pyramid came into sight above and ahead. It looked like a distant moon with a sharp triangular outline. It expanded as they contracted, until it resembled a close planet. Then it looked like a huge turning world. Each of its faces was a different color: blue, red, green, and the bottom was gray.

"This is wild," Dawn remarked appreciatively.

"And perhaps fun," Eve agreed.

They oriented on the middle of the triangle they were headed for: the blue face. "Forrest, maybe you should use the obscurity spell again," Imbri suggested.

Good idea. He reached back into his knapsack and brought out the can. "Invoke," he said. Nothing happened, but it was probably working. Now no evil wizard would notice their landing, maybe.

"Ooooh, we're falling!" Dawn cried.

"But we can control it," Imbri said. "Just focus on slowing, when you wish to."

They came down onto a land that was surprisingly ragged, considering the evenness of the outline. There were mountains and ravines and tilted plains, with lakes splashed between. But what was most remarkable was the color: it was all in shades of blue. Forrest hadn't marveled about it before, being too distracted by the problem of landing safely. But now he realized that even the clouds they had passed were blue. So this was no special effect, like the blue sky of Xanth; it was the color of the substance of this world on this side.

"I don't think we're on Ptero any more," Dawn murmured. "That isn't the blue of North; it's all over."

"The magic of Pyramid must be different from Ptero, just as Ptero's magic is different from Xanth," Forrest said. "It may take us a while to adapt."

"I'm getting dizzy," Eve said. "The idea of not knowing the direction by color is awful! How will we know From and To?"

"There may not be any," Forrest said. "Age and geography may not be linked, on this world."

"Oooh, ugh!" Dawn said.

"I hope I don't get sick," Eve added.

"You may be feeling blue," Forrest said.

Both girls glanced at him sharply, and he realized that he had said something funny. He had been thinking of the loneliness of leaving one world and trying to adjust to another, but he doubted that they would believe that.

They had landed on a field between mountains. It was covered with blue grass and blue flowers. It was also tilted: when they stood, they were at an angle to the plain. But they were safely down. Imbri retained her mare form; evidently she had enough soul mass to assume her natural mode on this world. She was a glistening blue-black, with a sleek hide and nice mane and tail.

Dawn knelt to check the grass. "This is natural and friendly," she reported. "It will produce seeds for us, if we're hungry."

Dawn got down beside a rock. "This is natural and friendly too," she said. "It will make itself soft if someone wants to sit on it."

So far, so good, Forrest thought. Given a choice, he preferred friendly things.

Then a horde of little creatures came charging across the ground toward them. They were like squirrels, except that they ran on their hind two legs. They were light blue.

"Are they friendly?" Forrest asked, worried.

"The grass says no," Dawn said.

"The rock says yes," Eve said.

Forrest made a quick calculation. "Does that mean that they eat grass and don't eat rocks?"

"Yes," they said together.

Then the creatures were upon them. They formed circles around each of the four visitors, chirping avidly. They all stood perpendicular to the plane, in contrast to the visitors.

"These are lings," Dawn said as she touched one. "A variety of a broad species that appears in many places. There are Earthlings, Xanthlings, Pterolings, and Pyramidlings. They can make the impossible possible. They are widespread on Pyramid. They noticed us because we stand skew and aren't blue."

Forrest was impressed. Her talent went beyond what he had imagined. "Maybe we need to change, so that we aren't immediately obvious to folk we might not want to be obvious to," he said. "Also, I had better renew the spell of obscurity; it must have worn off."

"But if the magic is different here, the spell won't work," Imbri pointed out. She didn't use her mouth; she used a dreamlet. Evidently she was able to do multiple dreamlets here, having more than enough soul to go around, so they could all hear her at once.

"Unless the lings really can do the impossible," he replied. "Can they make us blue?"

"Yes," Dawn said after a moment. "And they can make us tilt with the land, the way they do. But there's a cost."

"There always is," Imbri muttered.

"What cost?" Forrest asked warily.

Dawn touched the lings again, trying to understand. "Whoever gives anything away, on this world, gains equivalently." She looked up. "Does that makes sense? It seems impossible."

"And they are creatures of the impossible," Forrest said. "So it must be true. So maybe we don't want to accept anything until we understand its consequence. If the giver gains, what does the receiver lose?"

Dawn's brow furrowed as she concentrated on the little creatures. "The receiver gets smaller," she said. "The giver gets larger."

"Weird," Eve said.

"How much larger and smaller?" Forrest asked.

"Not a lot. But some. For an individual gift. Those who give a lot can become giants, eventually. But those who accept a lot can get rather small in time, and even disappear."

"Then let's choose carefully," Forrest said. "I think we do need to merge with the natives, and if the obscurity spell doesn't work—" He paused. "Can they fix that? It seems impossible, so—"

"Yes, they can," Dawn said.

"Then let's accept three things from them: the ability to stand at right angles to the terrain, as they do, and blue color, and a working obscurity spell. I don't think we need more. After all, Dawn's & Eve's talents are working, so maybe our direct personal magic isn't lost."

"They'll do it," Dawn said.

The lings closed in around the four, and suddenly they all changed color and tilted to conform to the terrain. The lings looked a size larger—and maybe the four visitors were a size smaller.

Forrest brought out his canned spell and invoked it. Then the lings lost interest, roaming on across the field, nibbling on stalks of grass. So the blanket of obscurity was working again.

The four surveyed each other. Their tilt did not seem odd, because now they matched the lay of the land. But their color was something else. Dawn's red hair was now purple, and her white dress was pale blue. Eve's black hair was midnight blue, and her dark dress was perhaps two hours off midnight, while her skin was light blue. Mare Imbri was also midnight blue. Forrest was medium blue, his furred legs darker than his upper torso, and his hoofs darker yet.

"Actually, we don't look bad," Dawn said, smiling. Her teeth were metallic blue.

"And now we fit in," Eve agreed. "This isn't so bad, so far."

"So far," Forrest agreed. "But we know there are mean folk here, because of what they're doing to Ptero, and we don't know their full powers. That's why I felt it was worth a price to become halfway anonymous."

"So now that we're halfway anonymous, what next?" Imbri asked.

Forrest found decision making awkward, but that was his job now, so he pondered briefly. "We need to find the source of the margins.

I think the blue ones must come from this side of Pyramid. Maybe the center.''

Dawn nodded. ''Makes sense to me. So let's go to the center. Do we know which way that is?''

Eve knelt down and touched the ground with one hand. ''Yes. That way.'' She pointed a direction.

''You can tell direction by feeling the ground?'' Forrest asked.

''I can tell anything about anything inanimate. The ground is inanimate. So I just selected for its orientation. The center of this face is that way.''

''You girls really do have formidable talents,'' he said. ''I didn't realize how useful such magic could be.''

Eve looked at Dawn. ''He appreciates us. Shall I blush, or shall you?''

''It's my turn, I think,'' Dawn said. Whereupon she turned as red as her hair. But since her hair was no longer red, but a shade of blue, her blush was blue too. However, it was a redder shade than the rest of her.

Forrest wasn't sure whether they were teasing him again, and decided not to inquire. They might decide to make *him* blush again. They were being helpful now, but they remained mischievous girls.

They set off for the center of the blue triangle. However, they soon encountered a body of water. It was on the slope, and it sloped the same way, but this no longer seemed odd, because the four of them were oriented at the same angle.

''Oh, good, I'm thirsty,'' Dawn said. ''Is it safe to drink?''

Eve lay down at the edge of the water. She touched its surface with one finger. ''How come you got to be the one to blush?'' she demanded suddenly. ''I'm sure it was my turn.''

Dawn was evidently surprised. ''Well, you can have the next turn. I didn't realize—''

''And how come you rate the bright red hair and green eyes, while I'm dull shades of black?''

''Well, we're both blue now, but—''

''And how come you always get to speak first, and I always have to be second? Ever since we were children—''

''Eve, I don't understand—''

"The water!" Forrest exclaimed. "It did something to her."

Dawn nodded. "Eve, what's with the water?"

Eve concentrated. "This is the jealous sea. It makes anyone who drinks it or touches it jealous." Then she heard herself talking, and was startled. "Oh, no!"

"Oh, yes," Dawn said. "That's why you're suddenly jealous of me, when you never were before. That water's no good."

"Right," Eve agreed. "Still, I don't see why you—" Then she stifled herself, realizing what was happening.

"We had better not drink this water," Forrest decided. "We'll walk around it. There's bound to be other water."

"This way," Imbri said in a dreamlet, and trotted around to the side.

Soon the jealous sea gave way, and they came to another large body of blue water.

"Should I try this first?" Dawn asked.

"Oh, now you're trying to do my work," Eve grumped. She squatted at the edge and touched the water.

Then she stood. "I feel like doing something new," she said. "Forrest, look at this." She pulled off her blue blouse. She dropped it, and it dissolved into soul substance as it left her hand. She was left wearing a blue bra that hardly seemed up to the chore of containing her bosom.

"That must be the Indecen Sea," Imbri said, catching on to the symptom.

"You bet it is," Eve said, pulling off her skirt and letting it dissolve similarly. She wore a blue slip that seemed hardly better than nothing.

Forrest had been slow to react, but now he turned to face away from her. He had had enough trouble when Imbri was in girl form; the last thing he needed was trouble with an indecent princess.

"What, don't you like me?" Eve demanded, coming up behind him. "Let's do something really outrageous."

"Let's go find another sea!" Dawn cried.

"Why? I like this one." Eve put her arms around Forrest from behind. "Hey, I asked you a question, Forrest Faun."

"I think you're beautiful," Forrest said, struggling to free himself. But the more he struggled, the tighter she clung to him, and the more her body flattened against him. She wasn't small, the way Imbri had been on Ptero; she was almost his own height, and almost his mass, but the distribution was way different.

"Let go of him, sister dear, or I'll—" Dawn started, tugging at Eve.

"You'll what, sister dear?" Eve demanded challengingly.

"I'll jump in that water!"

Eve paused. Then she let go. She knew that if Dawn jumped in, she would suddenly be twice as indecent as Eve, and therefore twice the competition. She didn't want that.

Forrest took advantage of his release to move quickly away. Eve's indecent proposal had interested him more than he dared admit. He needed to stay well away from her, until the effect of the water passed.

Imbri approached him. "Maybe you should ride me," she suggested in a dreamlet.

"Thanks." He hopped onto her back. She was big and solid enough now so it was no problem for her, and this would keep him pretty much out of the Princess' reach. That was of course why Imbri had suggested it.

They moved on, leaving the Indecen Sea behind. They hurried, because all of them were getting thirsty, and they didn't want to give Eve any time to think of anything else to do. As it was she remained without her outer clothing, and was trying to catch Forrest's eye. It was obvious that the effect of the water had not yet worn off.

Then they came to a large blue rock. It extended to the edge of the sea, so that they had either to splash through the edge of the sea to get around it, or make a long detour the other way.

They stopped before it, considering. "Maybe we could climb over it," Forrest suggested.

"Maybe you could," Imbri said. "But I would have to change form."

Which would put her back in girl form. He knew she had adopted her natural form so as not to tease him any more. Her shape shifting ability seemed to be pretty much limited to going between her two "natural" forms. He preferred to keep her as a mare. "Maybe we could make a ramp high enough to cross it," he said.

But there was nothing from which to make a ramp. So Eve approached the rock. "I'll find out if there is any good way to get past it," she said. "But first, how about a little kiss, faun?"

That was more mischief. Forrest faced away from her. He didn't want to offend her, but he knew that it was only the water that made her so forward.

"Well, maybe after I get the answer," Eve said. She bent over to touch the rock, after making sure that Forrest was looking. Her slip was becoming shorter as time passed. She was getting smarter about her indecency.

Her hand passed through the rock. She fell into it and disappeared.

"Hey!" she cried. "This isn't real rock. It's sham rock!"

Dawn tittered. "You must be lying, then."

"It's not that kind of sham rock," Eve retorted. "But you can lie if you want to."

"Very well. I don't want to kiss someone all over his fur."

"Neither do I," Eve said. "I really hate the notion."

"Enough lying," Dawn said. Then she walked into the rock to rescue her sister. In a moment they both emerged. "We can walk right through it," Dawn called. "Come on."

Imbri walked cautiously forward, carrying Forrest. The blue darkness of the rock closed about them. In a moment they emerged from the other side.

And there ahead of them was a third body of water. Forrest hoped that this one was good.

Eve walked toward it. "Are you sure you should—?" Dawn asked nervously.

"Better than you risking it," Eve said, flopping indecently down on the ground with her legs spread. Forrest managed to avert his eyes just before disaster.

She touched the surface. A beatific smile crossed her face and drifted some distance beyond. "Oh, I feel so relieved!"

"What is it?" Dawn asked.

"It's a Mer Sea," she said in kindly fashion. "It forgives everything."

"Then we'd better drink it," Imbri said.

Forrest jumped off her back, and they went to drink. As soon as he touched the water, a marvelous feeling of compassion washed through him.

Eve approached him. "Forrest, I apologize for my unfortunate behavior. I really should not have—"

"That's all right," he said quickly. "It was the water."

"Yes. But you still look doubtful."

"It's just that, if you don't mind—"

"Yes?"

"If you would put your clothing back on."

"Oh." It must have been her turn to blush, because she did so to the waist before reforming her outer apparel.

After that they walked more comfortably on toward the center of the triangle. But the blue landscape darkened. Night was coming. That probably meant that Xanth was darkening, and with it Ptero, and with it, Pyramid. It had nothing to do with the spin of this world. So they looked for a suitable place to spend the night.

The darkness wasn't complete. This was awkward, because the blue landscape remained somewhat strange to their eyes, and made relaxation for sleep difficult.

"That looks like a nightshade tree," Imbri said. "That should help."

Sure enough, under the blue tree there was a pool of darkness. It was midnight blue-black, the same as Imbri's hide, and impenetrable. Beside it was a sweetgum tree. So they picked a number of the leaves and twigs, which were made of sweet gum with a slightly woody flavor. This was enough to satisfy their incidental hunger. Their renewed thirst was satisfied by several small local ponds which turned out to be teas: serendipi, sereni, punctuali, joviali, and naugh. They were especially tempted by the last one, but after the experiences of the seas, concluded that discretion was best. Farther along they spied calami, adversi, frail, and pomposi, which were worse, so they gave up on their search for anything better. They drank the sereni-tea and soon relaxed into sleep in the pleasant darkness of the nightshade. Imbri remained in her mare form, needing no blanket, while the girls lay close together and were warm. That left Forrest alone, thinking thoughts that made him feel guilty. It had been bad enough when Imbri was in girl form; now there were two genuine girls.

Next morning they took turns bathing in the pool with punctuali-tea, then promptly got on their way. This was just as well, because the terrain became much rougher. They were no longer walking tilted, relative to the larger landscape, which suggested that they were approaching the center of the blue triangle, and Eve's testing of the ground verified this. But this levelness of the underlying land seemed to encourage the surface features to splurge, and the landscape was like tumbled blue blocks left by a giant. They had to scramble over and under and around, and squeeze through reluctant crevices, so that it took them most of a day to travel what might otherwise have been a two-hour walk.

Then, as they finally cleared the blue blocks, they came to a jungle inhabited by cat people. Fortunately Forrest had remembered to reinvoke the blanket of obscurity, so the cats didn't notice them. That was just as well, because when they changed from cat to people form, and various combinations of the two, they probably wouldn't like being spied on.

"But maybe I can approach one separately, and get her advice on the local situation," Dawn said brightly. "Because there must be something to send out the blue lines, and we had better know what we are looking for before we blunder into it."

The others agreed. But when Dawn located an isolated blue cat woman, and approached her, she had a problem. "Please, miss—can you tell me about this region?"

The woman ignored her, and went about her business of scratching out blue catnip.

"I just want to know what is ahead," Dawn said, trying again. "Is there any special danger?"

The cat walked away.

"It's the blanket of obscurity," Forrest said, catching on. "It makes you unnoticeable."

Dawn sighed. "That's right. And I'm sure it has protected us from much mischief. But how can I talk with this feline?"

"Just touch her and learn all about her, dummy," Eve said.

A dim bulb flickered over Dawn's head. She touched the cat woman's arm. "She is Catrina," she announced. "Of the category of Feline Folk who cater to the catacombs. She had a whole collection of cat combs she has made for the ones who live in maze-like tunnels. On occasion she brings some combs to the Blue Wizard's castle. It's very forbidding, and no one can get in who isn't invited. It's guarded by all manner of monsters."

"You can tell all that from one touch of the cat woman?" Forrest asked.

"Yes. It's part of everything about her. But I can't get beyond her personal experience. She's never actually been inside the castle, and knows nothing about its content. But she's afraid of the Wizard, who has given so much away that he has become enormous."

Forrest took a moment to work that out, remembering that on this world creatures gained size and power by being generous. "But how can he give so much away?" he asked. "I mean, where does he get anything to give away? It must come from somewhere."

"From Ptero," Imbri said in a dreamlet.

"That's right!" Eve agreed. "See if he gives away any talents."

Dawn checked. "Yes, he has given away many talents—and I recognize some from people I know on Ptero. One cat woman got the talent of changing things to strawberry jam, for all that it comes out blue. Another got the talent of Charisma, which becomes purr-suasion; now she is queen of the cat people. Another got the talent of spell-checking."

"Hey, isn't that Com Pewter's talent?" Imbri asked.

"No, his talent is changing local reality to suit himself," Forrest said. "But checking spells—that's a strong one. If that belonged to one of the folk captured by the margins, it is becoming clear where all the magic is going. The Blue Wizard is getting it and giving it away to add to his power."

"Another got the talent of changing the color of the sky," Dawn continued, checking the cat woman. "So she can make it any shade of blue. Another got the talent of throwing his voice with his hand, so he can make it go anywhere."

"So the Wizard is stealing talents from Ptero to give away here," Imbri said indignantly. "How can he get away with that?"

"Apparently Pyramid's rules don't take account of the outside realm," Eve said thoughtfully. "So he has a dandy way to become all-powerful."

"And there must be other Wizards on the other faces of Pyramid," Forrest said. "Doing the same thing."

"And we have to stop them," Dawn said, letting the cat woman go on her way. "Does anyone have any idea how?"

There was a silence that bobbled around from one to another. None of them knew what to do.

Which meant it was up to Forrest. "I suppose we should approach the Blue Wizard's castle and see what we can do," he suggested feebly.

"Now I am just a naïve girl," Eve said. "With barely a notion of the Adult Conspiracy, and no experience." Her sister smirked at that. "But even I know that we'd probably get hauled in and executed without trial."

"I couldn't have said it better, even if you did usurp my turn," Dawn said.

"It wasn't your turn. You spoke last before me."

"But this is a new subject. I always comment first on new things."

"Girls, girls," Forrest said, finding himself shoved into a role their mother had played on Ptero.

Both turned to him, their motions so well coordinated that he knew he had been had. Imbri faced away, letting him handle it in his own fashion. "And what are you going to do about it?" Dawn inquired. "Spank us?"

"Shall we hoist our skirts for it?" Eve continued. "So you can smack our pan—"

"Girls!" he cried in boldface. Then, more quietly: "After this mission is done, and your friends have been saved, and we are no longer in danger of being executed, then you may tease me as much as you want, and maybe even make me blush again. You are both extremely attractive young women, and I am a faun, and I would love to play games with you in my natural fashion. But at present we are in danger, and any mistake we make could cost us not only our lives, but imperil the fate of all the human folk remaining on Ptero. So though you may regard me as unqualified, and perhaps laughable, I hope you will allow me to do the best I can in the role that the Good Magician requires of me. That is to guide you to success in saving your land from marginalization.''

The two exchanged a glance. Then they turned together to look at Forrest. All four of their eyes were bright. ''We apologize most abjectly,'' Dawn said. ''We were indeed forgetting our mission.'' She wiped a tear from her right eye.

''But we ask you to understand that we do take the mission seriously,'' Eve continued. ''We tend to joke around when we are under tension, because it is better than crying.'' She wiped a tear from her left eye.

Forrest was chagrined. ''I didn't realize. I apologize for—''

''We will behave from now on,'' Dawn said. ''Until the mission is done.''

''But thereafter,'' Eve said, ''we may indeed tease you in fun, and play with you in the manner of nymphs.''

''That isn't necessary,'' he said quickly. ''I never meant to suggest—''

''We are of age,'' Dawn said.

''And we are learning respect for you,'' Eve added.

''But—''

''So now we will apologize to you in the manner of the gourd—''

''And leave you with a moderate notion of what we have in mind.''

''But the gourd apologies are excessively—'' he began, alarmed.

But he was cut off by Dawn, who stepped into him, embraced him closely, and kissed him with such passion that his head seemed in danger of floating away. It was as if the sun were rising and blinding him with its warm, delightful light. Then she released him, and Eve hugged him so firmly that he needed no eyes to appreciate her every contour, and kissed him even more passionately. This time it was as if the sun were setting and carrying him into the lovely encompassing night.

Then she let him go, and he stood stunned, with little suns and moons circling his head. Dawn had primed him, and Eve had wiped him out.

From what seemed like a far distance he heard them speaking again. ''We do like you, Forrest,'' Dawn murmured in his left ear.

"And when we do show you our panties, we won't be fooling," Eve murmured in his right ear.

Then they kissed his pointed ears, simultaneously.

Forrest found himself lying on the ground, with little hearts and planets spinning crazily over his face. The girls were fanning him and brushing off his fur. "I guess we overdid it," Dawn said. "He fainted."

"But we'll be more careful from now on," Eve agreed.

"We had better change to blue jeans."

"And not too tight."

"But once this is done—"

"We'll show him everything."

This had gone on more than long enough. Forrest opened his eyes. "I think I'm all right," he said. "I—"

"We double-teamed you," Dawn said. "We apologize."

"No!" he exclaimed desperately.

They both laughed. "Not gourd fashion, silly," Eve said. "We've already done that." Then they helped him up. They were now in baggy blue jeans and blue plaid shirts that cut their feminine appeal in half. Since there were two of them, that was still more than enough.

"We thought you were being gallant," Eve said. "Now we realize that you really do like us, as we like you."

"I'm a faun," he repeated. "I like nymphs. Recently I have been learning to like real folk too. But I'm not used to the emotions."

"So we gather," Dawn said. "You have surely had far more physical experience than we, as delicate maidens, would care to imagine. While we have had more emotional experience than you have been equipped to comprehend. It will be fun merging experiences, in due course."

"But it is true that we face what may be a deadly challenge, here," Eve said.

"So while maybe we shouldn't have teased you," Dawn said, "we do feel that you were being naïve about the approach to the Wizard's castle."

"And while we don't want to interfere with your role as assigned by the Good Magician," Eve said, "we hope you will reconsider."

"I think I had better," he agreed ruefully. "Suppose we approach the castle cautiously, staying out of sight, and see what we can make of it?''

Imbri returned to the dialogue. She had been so still that he had almost forgotten her. ''The girls can explore the castle to a degree without even approaching it.''

''That's better,'' he agreed. ''If we can find someone who goes in and out of the castle, or some object that has been inside—''

''We can watch and see,'' Imbri said.

So they made their way on toward the castle. Forrest refreshed the blanket of obscurity; that was proving to be a big help, because they might otherwise already have been noticed and surrounded by the Wizard's minions, if he had minions.

The castle was a huge, grim structure of mottled blue. There was an odor wafting from it. ''I know that smell,'' Imbri said. ''I have encountered it on the moon. Blue cheese!''

''But isn't that squishy?'' Dawn asked.

''Not when it's old enough. The cheese of the moon ranges from almost liquid brie to rock hard cheddar. Any cheese gets firm when exposed to the sun for a few years.''

''And magic could stiffen it,'' Eve said.

A guard marched around the castle. He didn't see or notice them, thanks to the obscurity and their care in hiding, and passed quite close. ''Look at that!'' Dawn whispered. ''His hand is metal!''

''Silly—that's a hand gun,'' Eve pointed out. ''It makes sense for a guard.''

The man marched on past them, and Forrest saw that his hand really was a gun. He wondered what happened when the man wanted to shake hands with anyone.

A light came on at the side door of the castle. It was a special shade of bright blue. ''Oh, I wouldn't want to smear that Ultra-Violent light bulb,'' Eve said. ''Those are mean when messed with.''

Then the door opened and a man emerged. He was carrying a bag of something. He walked to a pit some distance from the castle, and tossed the bag in. Then he returned and reentered the castle.

''Garbage!'' Dawn said. ''Ugh!''

''But it's been inside the castle,'' Forrest pointed out. ''So—''

''Ugh!'' Eve said.

"Well, maybe it's not a good idea."

Eve sighed. "No, it makes sense. It's just not very romantic."

So they circled the castle at a distance, until they came to the pit. It had every type of refuse, and it stank. But they climbed down into it, looking for the most recent bag.

"Ah, here it is," Eve said, putting her hand on it. "Recently carried by Jan Itor. It contains trash and kitchen leavings collected by the night watchman, A. Lert. They are from all over the castle."

"Just what we need," Dawn said. "I know you'll just love sinking your hands in all that, sister dear."

"With luck, some of it isn't dead yet, sister dear," Eve agreed, wrinkling her nose. "So you will also have the pleasure." She opened the bag and pulled out a tube. "Toothpaste that pastes the mouth closed. No wonder they threw it out."

Dawn spied a large ant struggling to escape the bag. She let it walk on her hand. "This is a de-odor-ant. It can make a person lose the sense of smell. I guess they threw it out because they like the smell of blue cheese."

Eve pulled out an old pen. "This is what is left of an invisible ink pen," she said. "Originally the pen held several large ugly animals, but each animal used up some of the ink, and the pen gradually shrank, until it was too small to be of use."

"What about the layout of the castle?" Forrest asked. "Is there a secret entrance? Where does the Wizard stay?"

In due course, piecing through the thrown away junk, they were able to work out a fair notion of the castle plan. The Wizard lived in the highest chamber, through which the blue lines passed. The lines actually seemed to come from below, however: the dungeon. That was entirely sealed off from outside, and only the Wizard had access from inside. There was no refuse from it; evidently it had its own internal garbage dump. So the riddle of the lines remained.

"We need more information than we can get from outside," Forrest said. "But if even the servants don't know what's in that dungeon, who else will know?"

"Only the Wizard," Imbri said. "And he keeps the secret, so that no one else can steal talents from Ptero and give them away for power.''

"But someone else must know," Forrest said. "Because there are three other Wizards with the secret.''

"And they used it to make themselves supreme in their triangles," Dawn said.

"And they won't tell us either," Eve agreed.

"We need a better idea," Imbri said.

Something flirted with Forrest's attention, and slid away. He pursued it, and managed to nab it before it escaped. It was an idea. "Idea!" he exclaimed. "Ida—her talent is the Idea. Maybe she would have an idea.''

"But Ida's far away," Dawn said.

"That is, her head is—and huge," Eve agreed.

"No—I mean the Ida who must be here. Your world of Ptero orbits Ida of Xanth; this world of Pyramid orbits Ida of Ptero. So there must be an Ida here with another world, and maybe she would know the secrets of the worlds.''

The girls exchanged another glance. "This is weird," Dawn said.

"But maybe true," Eve said.

"And worth a try," Imbri said. "If there's any chance she's here, and she would know—she's a nice person, and surely would help us.''

They climbed out of the pit and walked away from the castle. They found a lake that didn't have any objectionable magic and washed up. The girls simply waded in with their clothing on, and after a startled moment Forrest realized that since their clothing was part of their soul-stuff, it didn't matter.

Then they pondered how to locate Ida. "I can learn much from living folk," Dawn said. "But it's sort of random; finding out whether they know a particular person could take a long time.''

"Same for the inanimate," Eve said. "I could see whether a rock had ever seen a particular person pass, but first I'd have to go through its entire list of people, which could be hundreds. And it might not recognize a particular person anyway; rocks aren't very smart.''

"Grandpa Dor could make them talk," Dawn said. "That made it much easier.''

"Of course we had to watch our skirts when Grandpa Dor was around," Eve said. "Any rock we stepped over would blab about what it saw."

"Unless Grandma Irene was there," Dawn said. "She could glare a rock into silence from far away."

"We miss them," Eve concluded sadly.

"I think we'll have to ask someone," Forrest decided. "That means letting the blanket of obscurity wear off."

"Which in turn is risky," Imbri said.

"I know it. So maybe the three of you should remain protected by it, while I stay apart, so I can become evident alone."

"Maybe you should ride me, so that if there is trouble, I can gallop away with you."

Forrest thought of protesting, but realized that she wanted to take the same risk he did. "Good notion." He looked around. It seemed to be getting late in the day. "Let's find a place to sleep, and in the morning the girls can take the canned blanket spell while we go out."

They looked for a good place to settle. Soon they found a small range of blue mountains. Very small: they were hardly waist high. But the mini-peaks should serve to conceal them from the view of the main path, when they lay down.

But as they approached the range, it got up and walked away. Astonished, they watched it depart. Then Dawn laughed. "A mountain goat!" she said. "I should have recognized it."

They found another place, near blue berry bushes, which made it handy for supper. As they ate, the wind came up, whistling softly through the trees. It made a sad melody. "I always liked the blues," Eve remarked.

But as darkness closed, the temperature dropped. Forrest realized that he hadn't thought to bring a second blanket. So he dug out the one he had and gave it to the girls. "This will do for the two of you," he said.

They looked at him. "I wish this wasn't a serious mission," Dawn said.

"Because then we could share the blanket with you," Eve said.

"I'm sorry too," he said. "But I will join Imbri." For Imbri in mare form was both warm and safe. So things worked out after all.

He lay down beside Imbri. "You really are a nice person," she murmured in a dreamlet for him alone.

"No I'm not. I really wanted to sleep with them."

"I know you did. Right between them. Knowing that they would probably dissolve their clothing under the blanket, just as I did. But you refused to do it. That's what makes you nice, just as you were with me."

"But I should not even be wanting to do such things!"

"You are a faun. It's your nature."

"And what of you?" he demanded. "What do you think, when you see me reacting to those pretty girls?"

"It makes me feel less guilty for what I did to you."

"You didn't do anything to me!"

"Yes I did. And I will make it up to you, when I figure out how."

"You know I can't really do anything with those girls. They're princesses."

"They are of a slightly different culture than the one we encountered in Xanth. Maybe it's all right for them to play with fauns, if they want to."

"I doubt their mother would approve."

"Mothers never do. In the old days I delivered thousands of bad dreams to worried mothers. They think their daughters must be pristine and never do what the mothers did when they were young. So the daughters simply don't tell their mothers." She chuckled, in the dreamlet. "Now that Queen Iris has been rejuvenated to her twenties, she doesn't tell her daughter Irene, who would Not Approve Iris's present activities. Folk seldom approve the fun others have."

"Still—"

"Forrest, those two girls know their own minds, and they know your nature. If they decide to celebrate with you, you should feel free."

"Well, I don't feel free. I mean, I would love it, but I don't think it's proper."

Her dreamlet image shook her head. "Because you have been placed in the role of adviser, which implies parental authority. So you act as a parent would, though you wish you could act as a normal faun would."

"That's it!" he agreed as a bulb flashed over his head. "How well you understand."

"Well, I have had some experience in dreams, and what you feel for the girls is a dream."

"Thank you, Imbri! You have helped me to clarify my mixed feelings."

"Maybe that's what I'm here for." The dreamlet image walked across to the fading bulb and planted a kiss on it. Forrest felt the kiss on his face.

He was startled. "Imbri—"

"I will change to maiden form, if you ask me. I know my own mind too."

Suddenly he was horribly tempted. Imbri was definitely of sufficient age and experience, and she surely did know her own mind. But he had to demur. "I—can't ask you to do that."

"I know, Forrest, I know. You don't feel free to be a faun, or free to make commitments of that nature, so you are caught in a personal limbo. I wish I could free you from it. And I will, if I ever find the way. Meanwhile, I respect your stance, and I respect you."

"Uh, thank you."

"Would it help if I sent you a wish-fulfillment dream?"

"It might. But I think I need to focus on my mission, now, and not waste imagination on anything else."

"Then I will send you a dream of deep sleep."

In his mind's eye he saw a pale blue cloud floating toward him. The words DEEP SLEEP were embossed on its surface. It loomed large, smelling of gentle music, and encompassed him, and he sank into it with relief.

He woke much refreshed. His head was against Imbri's gently heaving side. Dawn & Eve were up and picking blue berries, wearing blue skirts and slippers. In a moment they spied his flickering eyelids and came to join him.

"Have a berry, Forrest," Dawn said, plumping herself down cross-legged beside him.

"Yes, they are very good," Eve said, doing the same. Their firm legs showed well beyond the knees. Were they teasing him again?

He opened his mouth to say, "But I can pick my own berries." But before the first word popped out, Eve leaned dangerously forward and popped a berry in. It was delicious. He chewed it, then opened his mouth to thank her—and she popped in another.

He gave up the unequal struggle, and ate the berries he was given. There was something to be said for being catered to by willing maidens.

But they had a day ahead of them. Forrest dug into his knapsack and brought out the canned blanket. "Don't invoke this until after Imbri and I are out of range," he told them. "And don't do anything too wild; we don't know the limit of the obscurity."

"Yes, Master," they said together, and laughed, their tightly bloused bosoms heaving.

"And get out of those nuisance clothes before something freaks me out."

They glanced down, startled. "Oops, we forgot," Dawn said. Her pale blue blouse rippled and became a heavy blue plaid shirt.

"We just naturally dressed our usual way, when we woke," Eve said. Her blue-black skirt twisted and formed itself into baggy dark blue jeans.

"After just naturally sleeping nude."

"And dreaming of fun with a faun."

Then they stood, together. Dawn's light blue skirt changed to pale blue jeans just a bare instant before it would have shown Too Much, and Eve's dark blouse changed to a dark shirt just a transparent instant after it had shown More Than Enough.

They were definitely teasing him. Apparently they just couldn't help themselves. He would simply have to try to ignore it. He wished himself success. Already he was wondering just how blue their panties might be.

Then he mounted Imbri, and she walked out onto the path. She didn't hurry, because they weren't trying to go anywhere, just to meet someone they could ask directions of. He glanced back, but didn't notice anyone. Good; that meant that the girls had invoked the blanket of obscurity, and unless they did something foolish, like dancing naked and screaming, he wouldn't notice them.

Soon they approached a woman who was walking along the path in the opposite direction. "Hello," Forrest called, hoping that this was the right way to address a Pyramid native.

She looked sharply at him. "Do you want something from me, faun?"

He reminded himself that the folk here always looked for chances to get ahead by giving things away. "Yes, actually."

"Who are you and what do you want?"

This seemed surprisingly easy. "I am Forrest Faun, and I want to locate Princess Ida."

"We don't have any princesses here."

"Maybe she's not a princess here. She has a moon orbiting her head."

The woman shook her head. "Never heard of her. So I can't help you. So I might as well harass you."

"Harass me?"

"I am Polly Morph, and I can change myself into what I can imagine. Today I am irritable, so I shall become a dragon and gobble you and your stupid horse up, hoping you don't taste too bad." Her face stretched out to become a dragon's snout, and her body burst out of its clothes to become serpentine.

"But we haven't done anything to you," Forrest protested.

"Precisely," the dragon said, snapping at them.

Imbri leaped into the air to avoid the teeth. She landed at a full gallop, getting out of there.

Unfortunately Forrest wasn't used to riding, and wasn't ready. When the mare shot forward, Forrest didn't. He landed on his butt in the path.

"Well, now," the dragon said. "You're too small for a dragon, but just right for a griffin." She warped into a griffin.

Forrest scrambled to his feet and ran. But the griffin's beak darted forward and caught his tail. His hoofs were moving, but he wasn't getting anywhere.

Imbri turned and came charging back. "Naaaay!" she neighed. She leaped, her forehoofs aiming for the griffin's body.

"Curses," the griffin muttered, in the process releasing Forrest. Then it twisted into a flying snake and wriggled out of the way.

Imbri landed and galloped on, unable to halt on such short notice. But she had given Forrest the reprieve he needed. He ran after her, hoping to get enough of a lead so that the monster couldn't catch him.

But Polly morphed back into the griffin, and took flight. Forrest heard the wing-beats as she gained on him.

Then, suddenly, he collided with something remarkably soft. He landed in a tangle of limbs. He blinked, and saw what he hadn't noticed before, though she was up against his chest: "Dawn!"

"Hey, I finally got your attention," she said, drawing her face from his ear and fluffing out her red hair.

"But the griffin—"

"Has lost track of you," Eve said.

He looked at his legs, and discovered what else he hadn't noticed: they were tangled up with another girl's legs. "Eve!"

She drew her face from his belly and fluffed out her tangled black tresses. "I really didn't think we would get to this stage until after the mission," she confessed.

"What are you girls doing?"

"We are saving you from getting chomped," Dawn said, prying her flattened bosom from his chest.

"With the help of the blanket of obscurity," Eve said, unwrapping her cramped legs from his thighs.

"Because we really don't want you to be hurt."

"Even if you would simply be launched back to Ptero."

"Because without your guidance, we would not be able to complete our mission."

"And we really do like your company."

By this time they had unstuck the rest of themselves from his body. Both girls were disheveled, but still pretty in a wild sort of way.

"Uh, thank you," Forrest said, realizing that he could indeed have been gobbled and banished from this region for whatever period was required by the framework of Pyramid. They had saved him from that by intervening in the only way they could, considering that he was not aware of their presence: by tackling him and bringing him into the coverage of the blanket.

Dawn gave him a direct green eyed glance, as bright as sunshine. "You are welcome."

Eve gave him a sidelong black eyed glance, as mysterious as night. "It was our pleasure."

Forrest tried once more to get through to them. "You know, your teasing ways are very difficult for me to handle."

Dawn shook her head. "Some of what you take for teasing is merely our natural flair."

Eve frowned. "And in this particular instance, we were not teasing. We really did want to save you, and we really do like you."

Forrest was nonplused. "I mean, you really are two very lovely and provocative young women, and I—"

"We know," Dawn said seriously. "We know our nature, and what kind of reaction is to be expected from a male of any type."

"And we are ready," Eve said, just as seriously, "to make absolutely plain our readiness to accommodate that reaction, in due course."

Every time he tried to reason with them, it just got worse! "But I told you, this mission—"

"We understand," Dawn began.

"But we are falling in love with you," Eve concluded.

Then tears dropped from all four of their eyes.

Forrest's jaw dropped. "But you were just flirting, and I knew that. It wasn't serious. You are princesses, and I'm just a faun."

"We are girls who have never been certain whether any given man's interest in us was because of our royalty," Dawn said.

"Or because of our physical appeal," Eve continued.

"Or our Sorceress caliber magic."

"Or our novelty as morning and evening twins."

"And we cared for none of these kinds of interest, in themselves."

"We wanted to be valued for ourselves."

"But I do know of your royalty, and appreciate your beauty, and your magic, and your novelty," Forrest protested. "I am fascinated by all of them. So I am no better than any of those you have encountered. And I am just a faun of no particular authority or ability. So—"

"So you have no ambition with respect to us," Dawn said.

"Just a healthy desire to celebrate with us in your quaint fashion," Eve said.

"And accomplish your mission."

"And go your way."

"Yes. I can't remain in your world. I must return to my tree. And since I know that true human beings don't believe in dalliance for its own sake, I am trying to avoid it."

"Which is our point," Dawn said. "You know us, and appreciate all our points, yet have no ulterior motive."

"You are the first male outside our family," Eve said, "whom we can truly trust. Therefore we love you."

"But trust is only one element of a meaningful relationship," he protested. "And it is a property of fauns to make the females they touch want to celebrate. So your emotions may not be genuine, or at least not natural."

"But we are young and fickle, and our love will not endure."

"So we hope to indulge it with you during this window of opportunity."

"And then we will go our separate ways," Dawn said.

"And remember each other with a certain wistful fondness," Eve said.

"With delight in the memory of the experience."

"Which was our very first of this type."

"And no regrets."

"And no regrets."

Forrest was overwhelmed. Maybe they were influenced by his faunish effect on females, but they had understanding too. "This—this is not an offer I can decline. But while we are on the mission—"

"It would be an abuse of the trust placed in all of us to play certain fauny games," Dawn said.

"And such faun & games might interfere with our pursuit of the mission," Eve agreed.

"So for now we will pretend that this dialogue has not yet occurred."

"But we will never doubt that it will occur in due course."

"Uh, yes," Forrest agreed. He was deeply touched, but knew that this was no time to be distracted from the mission. "Where's Imbri?"

They looked out at the rest of the region. Polly Morph, in whatever form, was gone. Imbri was walking along the path, looking around as if seeking something she had lost.

Forrest disengaged from the girls and approached the mare, hoping that the spell of obscurity was not actually on him, since he had not been present when it had been invoked. He needed to be visible to Imbri.

"Hey!" he called.

She whirled, orienting on him. "Where were you?" her dreamlet query came.

"The girls hauled me under the obscurity blanket."

"But you were gone for some time."

"We had something we needed to work out."

"Oh?"

"They are in temporary love with me."

"Oh."

"They don't get to meet many males who don't want something from them."

"Don't you want something?"

"Nothing that would diminish them or commit them, it seems."

"And did you get it?"

"Not yet. Right now the mission is more urgent."

Imbri might have inquired further, but at that point another creature appeared on the path. Forrest quickly mounted Imbri so that they could appear as faun and horse, and they walked toward the new arrival. It didn't resemble Polly Morph, fortunately.

In fact, it didn't resemble anything Forrest remembered seeing before, anywhere. It seemed to be a mass of curving projections, some furry, some bare, some pointed, some floppy, and some vaguely like nothing specific.

"Hello!" Forrest called.

The thing cringed away. "Don't yell!" it exclaimed from somewhere within, faintly.

"Sorry," Forrest whispered. "I just wanted to ask—"

"No, no, questions are too loud," it said, sidling away.

"Just what kind of creature are you?" Forrest asked, mildly annoyed.

"I'm all ears," it said, disappearing around a curve.

"That's true," Imbri said in a dreamlet. "Now I recognize the different shapes of ears. It must be very sensitive to sound."

"Maybe we'll have better luck with the next one," Forrest said.

"And here he comes," Imbri said. "Maybe this time I should try addressing him."

"My technique hasn't been getting us far, for sure."

The man looked to be about thirty two, wearing an elegant blue royal robe and a blue crown. He was smiling, and looked friendly.

"Hello," Imbri said in a dreamlet directed to both Forrest and the man.

He looked at her, startled. "Why, it's a night mare!" he exclaimed.

"Former night mare, now a day mare," Imbri's dreamlet figure clarified. "How did you recognize me?"

"Oh, I have had many deliveries! I was originally from an awful place called Mundania. I have my Mundane name to prove it: Todd Loren."

"Mundania! How did you get here?"

"I'm not sure, but I think it was my imagination. I dreamed of a special world, where I was a royal character and could do magic, and suddenly I was here, with my talent of being able to direct wind to blow to particular places. It may not be much, but I enjoy it."

"Do you happen to know a woman called Ida?"

"The one with the moon?"

"That's the one. Can you tell us how to find her?"

"No, but I can direct you to her. Just follow that gust of wind." Todd gestured, and wind stirred up some dust, becoming visible as a fuzzy ball.

"Thank you!" Imbri's dreamlet figure cried as they pursued the wind.

"You are welcome. I'm always glad to gain size."

"That's right," Forrest said as they moved on. "Folk grow and gain power as they give things away. But I don't think I lost any mass."

"I did, because the favor was to me," Imbri said. "But I have plenty of mass, now. If I lose too much, I'll have to resume maiden shape, is all.''

"I hope you get it back, when we leave Pyramid."

"Pyramid is so small that whatever we lose here is surely unmeasurable elsewhere.''

He realized that this was probably the case. This was the moon of a moon, as it were, and its entire mass was much less than that of either of their condensed souls on Ptero.

They followed the wind along the path, glad that it wasn't zooming wildly cross-country the way most winds did. Forrest hoped that Dawn & Eve were keeping up, because the wind didn't pause.

But then it did pause. It hovered in place, barely hanging on to the blue dust that made it visible. It was beside a young woman. Her hair and eyes were a silver shade of blue, and there was even a sprinkling of blue snow on her head. She was pretty, but looked hard.

"That's not Ida," Forrest murmured.

"There must be a reason the wind is waiting," Imbri said in a private dreamlet. "We had better inquire."

"I'll do it." He looked at the woman. "Hello."

She looked coldly at him. "Do I know you?"

"No. And I mean no harm. But we are following a wind, and it is pausing by you, so I wondered whether there is a reason. I am Forrest Faun, and this is Mare Imbri."

The woman turned deep blue eyes on him. "I am the Lady Winter, otherwise known as Winter Lee Cheryl Jacobs. I don't know why I am here, but I don't think it is to dance with the wind."

"That name—are you Mundane?"

"Yes. At least I was, before I came on this trip."

"Maybe that's why the wind is pausing. It was sent by another Mundane, and maybe it's curious, because there can't be many Mundanes here."

"Another Mundane?" Winter asked, interested.

"Yes. A man. He wears a crown. He seemed nice."

"Maybe I should meet him. At least he would understand why I find this place so strange."

The wind divided, and one gust swept back up the path. "Just follow that wind," Forrest said. "It should lead you right to him."

"Thank you," Winter said, smiling so brilliantly that it seemed like sunrise. She followed the gust.

"Hey—I feel heavier," Forrest said, surprised.

"You just did someone a favor," Imbri said. "I think the wind did recognize her as a Mundane, and felt an affinity because Todd Loren was Mundane. They should like each other: he's mature and nice, and she's young and pretty."

"I guess so," he agreed.

The half gust of wind resumed its motion, and they followed it as the path wound around blue hills, across blue fields, through blue forests, past blue lakes, and under blue skies. Then it paused again, by what looked like a cemetery.

"This is just a field full of crosses," Forrest said. "They must be marking graves." Indeed, there were big crosses and little ones, each one carved from wood and slightly different from all the others. Some were fairly straight, but others were curvaceous. In fact they seemed to be about as individual for crosses as people were for people. Forrest had a vested appreciation for wood, and found it intriguing in its own right whatever form it might be carved into, but he didn't recognize this particular variety.

"But in Xanth graves aren't marked by crosses," Imbri said.

"This isn't Xanth. In fact, it isn't even Ptero. Who knows what the rules may be on Pyramid?" He was suspicious, because of the way the crosses had been used in Contrary Centaur's game on Ptero. If these were anything like that, he wanted no part of them.

"Maybe so," she agreed. "Let me send a dreamlet down to see whether there's a body."

"Dreamlets can explore?"

"Not exactly. But I can send them to anyone, including the dead." She concentrated, and he saw a dreamlet in a little cloud float down and disappear into the ground below a cross. In a moment it bobbed up again, its dream figure looking perplexed. "No, there's nothing there," Imbri said in a separate dreamlet to Forrest.

"So they are just stuck in the ground," Forrest said. "They aren't alive. I suppose Eve could tell us all about them, if she were here."

"Perhaps we should wait for the girls to catch up. I'd like to be sure they are all right, as long as the wind is willing to wait."

"All right. It does seem to be a smart gust." At that the swirling wind darkened, blushing; though it could not speak to them, it evidently understood what they said.

That gave him a notion. "While we wait, Gust—is there anything to eat around here?"

The gust swept across to a billboard on the far side of the field. It had a painting of a grand assortment of berries. All were in shades of blue, of course, but seemed to be of many varieties. They looked delicious.

"But this is just a picture," Forrest said.

The gust brushed up against the picture, and it almost seemed that some of the berries moved. So Forrest reached out to touch a berry— and it was round, not flat. He picked it and put it to his mouth. "A bill-berry!" he exclaimed. "I should have known."

Imbri trotted over. "Bill-berries? They are very good for you." She put her mouth to the billboard and took a bite of berries. But then she spat something out. "I got a billfold by accident," her dreamlet figure said, making a face.

Forrest saw the object on the ground. It was a wad of folded paper, gray on the front, green on the back. It did look inedible. Apparently the billboard wasn't perfect; there was some contamination.

Something tapped him on the shoulder. He jumped. There was a vague female shape smelling faintly of morning. "Oh—Dawn," he said, relieved. "I hadn't noticed you."

"Because of the blanket of obscurity," her voice breathed in his ear. "I can see you quite clearly."

"And so can I," Eve's voice murmured in his other ear. Then they both nibbled on the tips of his ears.

"Stop that!" he exclaimed.

Imbri looked around. "Did I swish you with my tail? I didn't mean to."

"No. The girls are here."

She squinted. "Why so they are. That obscurity is effective. Now that I know what to look for, I can see them."

So could Forrest. "Eve, would you check one of those crosses and learn what it's all about? The wind brought us here, so there must be some reason."

"I'll be glad to." Her vague form kissed his cheek and departed.

"That wind must like you," Dawn said, kissing his other cheek.

"I think it's just doing its job. Maybe it appreciates the way I cooperated with it to send Lady Winter to Todd. It has been very helpful."

"Eve is signaling. We had better go there."

Forrest looked, but no longer saw Eve. The blanket had covered her.

"I'll lead you," Dawn said. She took his hand in hers, squeezing his fingers in a way that reminded him exactly how female she was. These girls might be young, but they had learned a good deal already.

In a few steps they approached a gradually clarifying figure holding a cross. As Forrest concentrated, Eve became recognizable. "These crosses enable folk to cross things," she said. "Eyes, T's, mountains, rivers, people—anything."

"Then they could be useful," Forrest said, relieved. The function of Pyramid crosses *was* different from Ptero crosses.

"Indeed. They are put out here for anyone to take and use. But when one is used, their maker gains the benefit of a given favor, and the one who uses them loses mass. So we don't want to take too many."

"Can one cross enable more than one person to cross something?"

"A big one can. A small one is limited both in person and distance. Four small ones would enable four people to cross one mountain, while one big one might enable all four people to cross a whole range of mountains. But the big one will exact a greater amount of mass, so we don't want to use any of them more than we need to."

"Suppose we take several crosses, but don't use them?"

"Then there is no price. It doesn't matter where the crosses are, only how they are used."

"Then we should take a fair collection of them, and not use them unless we have to," he decided.

"How intelligent," Eve said.

"Are you trying to tease me again?"

"No, just to remind you."

He walked among the crosses. That was when he discovered that he was still holding Dawn's hand. She had not reminded him. He let go, embarrassed, and heard her obscure chuckle. "I think we should each carry two small ones and one big one. Can we do that? I mean, I have room in my knapsack, but do the rest of you have a way to carry things?"

"Sure," Dawn said. "In our purses."

"And I have a pack," Imbri said.

Forrest leaned down to take a cross, but now Eve's hand stayed him. "I wouldn't," she murmured.

"Why not?"

"Because that particular one is made of petrified wood."

Forrest froze. Then he moved his hand very slowly down, barely touching the cross. Fear coursed through him. It was true; this cross made anyone who touched it terrified.

"But I might be able to use this too," he said. "If I got caught by a monster I couldn't escape."

"But how can you take it with you, if it frightens you?" Imbri asked.

"It shouldn't frighten me once I'm not directly touching it." He reached into his knapsack and pulled out a handkerchief. He wrapped this around the cross so that he could pick it up without touching it. The handkerchief was thin, so his fright was there, but he was able to handle the cross until it dropped into his knapsack.

"That was a brave thing to do," Dawn said, taking his hand again."

"No it wasn't. I was scared, but I knew there was no danger."

"It's not handling danger, but handling fear that makes a person brave, isn't it?"

Forrest hadn't thought of it that way. "Maybe. But it had to be done, if I wanted that cross."

They each took two small crosses, which disappeared into their various packs and purses without trouble. But the large crosses were too big to fit. Finally Eve found one folding cross, and they fit that into Imbri's pack, which was larger than the others. That would have to do.

Now the wind, having dallied all this time, amusing itself by whirling up dry blue leaves and grass and making funnel-shapes of them, resumed its forward progress. They followed. The blanket of obscurity was fading, so that the girls remained fairly clear.

The path led past several huge blue bee hives. They had been constructed in the shape of wooden boats with closed tops, and these were arranged in a giant semi-circle. The bees were very large, and they were flying in with blue books.

Forrest paused to take in this scene. "I never knew that bees collected books," he said, surprised.

Eve went up cautiously to touch one of the fancy hives. It seemed that enough of the blanket of obscurity remained on her to keep the bees from being disturbed. Then she laughed. "These are Ark-hives," she explained. "Where the bees store books, so they won't be lost. That must be why these bees are so large; they are constantly doing good deeds for this region, by saving all these good references."

They went on, hurrying to catch up with the gust. But now they came to a wide blue lake, and the wind was moving right across it, toward a blue island.

Forrest considered the water. "Do you suppose we could swim?"

Eve touched the surface with a finger. "I think not. This water contains all manner of horrible blue monsters."

"Then this must be what we have the crosses for. We had better each use one small one, saving the other for the return trip."

They dug out their small crosses and held them up. "Uh, how do they work?" Forrest asked, belatedly.

"Just describe where you wish to cross, and say 'invoke,' " Eve said.

"To that island," Forrest said, looking at it. "Invoke."

Suddenly he was there, and the cross was gone. He felt lighter, though that might have been his imagination. He turned to look back—and the others arrived. They made streaks as they crossed the water in half an instant.

"That was fun," Dawn said.

"But we don't want to do it too many times," Eve said.

The wind was waiting for them. They followed it along a winding path to a blue ridge of mountains. On the ridge was a house built of blue stone. As they approached it, a woman emerged. "Aunt Ida!" Dawn cried, going up to hug her.

"You haven't changed at all," Eve said, doing the same.

Ida returned their hugs, then inquired, "You seem like such fine girls. Do I know you?"

10
TORUS

orrest approached. "I must explain. We are from the world of—of Ptero. Do you understand?"

"Oh, my, yes! But I have never had visitors from there before. How nice."

"I am Forrest Faun, and this is Mare Imbrium, and these are Dawn & Eve, the daughters of Prince Dolph and Electra."

"I am so glad to meet you."

"Do you have nieces here?" Dawn asked.

"I don't think I do. But this is not the same world as Ptero."

"Yes," Eve said. "We have been trying to get used to its rules. We have come to stop its Wizards from hurting our people on Ptero."

"Oh, are they doing that? I didn't know."

"I'm afraid they are," Forrest said. "We hoped that you would know how to stop them."

Ida shook her head. This caused her moon to wobble and careen into view. Apparently it had been hiding behind her head until now.

"Look at that!" Dawn exclaimed.

"A doughnut!" Eve said.

The moon zipped back into hiding.

"Please don't use that word," Ida said. "The correct term is Torus."

"Oh, we're sorry," Dawn said, blushing a modest blue.

"Extremely sorry," Eve agreed, blushing an immodest blue. "We're so ignorant."

Forrest knew that this was at least in part an act, similar to their flirtation with him, but it was nevertheless impressive. The twins were very good at manners.

"Well, I suppose you couldn't know," Ida said. "Being from another world."

"Yes, but we want so much to learn," Dawn said.

"And never to make the same mistake again," Eve said.

Ida glanced at Forrest in a way that indicated that she was not being much fooled. "At any rate, I was saying to my regret that I don't know the answer to your problem. The Blue Wizard has confined me to this island, to keep me, as he puts it, out of mischief. I am surprised that you were able to locate me so readily."

"We asked around," Forrest said. "We thought that since you have the Sorceress talent of the Idea, you might have an idea about how we might proceed."

"Why yes, of course."

"You mean you do know how to stop the Wizards?"

"No. But I do know how you should proceed."

They looked at her blankly.

"You see," Ida explained, "I know where the answer is to be found. I don't have it, because I can't go there." Her eyes fixed momentarily on her moon.

Oh, no! "On Torus?" Forrest asked weakly.

"Yes. I'm sure that the Ida who lives there has the answer. That's why the Wizard confined me: to be sure that no one had access to my moon. And no creature of this world is able to come here; a powerful spell repels them. But perhaps he didn't reckon on visitors from another world."

It was beginning to make sense. "We are certainly from other worlds," Forrest said. "The girls are from Ptero, but Imbri and I derive originally from Xanth."

"Xanth? What realm is that?"

Forrest exchanged half a glance with Imbri. Ida didn't know about Xanth? "It is a larger land," Imbri said in a dreamlet. "On it is Princess Ida, about whose head Ptero orbits."

"Fascinating! And what larger land does Xanth orbit on?"

"Larger land?" Forrest asked blankly.

"Since Pyramid orbits the Ida on Ptero, and Ptero orbits the Ida on Xanth, what land's Ida does Xanth orbit?"

Forrest found his jaw hanging as low as Imbri's jaw, which was surprising, because her mare's mouth was larger than his. "Why, we don't know," he said.

Ida smiled. "Maybe after your mission here is done, you can descend to that world and find out. I wonder whether it's an infinite progression?"

"I wonder too," Imbri said.

"But now you will want to visit Torus," Ida said. "You will have to leave much of yourselves here, however. Fortunately I have room in my house. But I am obliged by our nature to take some of your mass for the favor of facilitating your trip. Unless you can do me a return service."

"We hope to free you from this island, and free Pyramid from the tyranny of the Wizards," Dawn said.

Ida shook her head. "These are hopes rather than realities."

"We can tell you all about what we find on Torus," Eve said. "So that you will know it as well as if you had been there yourself."

Ida smiled. "Now that is a service no one else can do me, that I would very much value. So though I may gain some of your masses when you go, you won't miss it because your bodies will be asleep, here. And you will recover it when you tell me about Torus. Do come this way."

She led them into her blue stone house, which was neatly kept. There were two beds there, and a couch. The girls lay on the beds, and Forrest took the couch, and Imbri lay comfortably on the floor. Then Ida sat between them, in her chair.

Forrest brought out his bottle. He gave each girl a sniff, and lay back on the couch and sniffed it himself. One by one they dropped into unconsciousness, as their soul fragments drew free.

The process was becoming more familiar with experience. This was the third time for Forrest and Imbri, and the second time for the girls. Efficiently they wafted up, forming into floating shapes, making eyeballs and ears and mouths. Soon they looked reasonably like themselves. Then they flew toward Torus, condensing as they moved.

The world loomed larger, its doughnut shape becoming dramatic. Where should they land on it?

Imbri seemed to know, so they followed her horse form. She headed first for the center of the hole, then to the inner surface. The world was variegated, which was a relief; that meant that they would not be confined to shades of a single color.

"I am orienting on Ida's identity," Imbri said in a dreamlet. "It is an ability of night mares, to locate the sleepers who need their dreams. It's not very accurate when folk are awake, so it didn't help on Pyramid, but I think we'll be reasonably close to her when we land."

They were drifting toward a forest. In the forest was a glade, and in the center of the glade was a single large tree. That did seem like the best place to land, as their navigation was a bit unsteady and a clear spot was best.

Indeed, they came down somewhat hard, having misjudged the oddly contoured terrain of Torus, which curved away to east and west and upward to north and south. Imbri landed solidly on her four hoofs, but Forrest fell on his back, and the two girls tumbled in spread-limbed disarray that would have been embarrassing if they hadn't been in blue jeans.

As they got to their assorted feet, they discovered that the glade was not nearly as nice as it had seemed from afar. It was bare of grass, and littered with bones. "What kind of place is this?" Dawn asked nervously.

Eve touched a bone. "Uh-oh," she said. "This bone belonged to an animal that was eaten by a tangle tree."

"But that means—" Dawn said, looking quickly around.

Now they all saw it: the single tree in the center was the largest, awfullest tangle tree Forrest had ever seen. It had an enormous number of tentacles, and these were now quivering as the tree realized that prey was near.

"We have about half an instant to get out of here," Forrest said, starting to run.

But a tentacle lashed out and struck his knapsack. There was a dragon claw on the end that hooked right in. In only a quarter of an instant Forrest was hauled into the air.

Imbri galloped over. "I'll rescue you," she cried in a dreamlet. "I'll bite through the vine before it hauls you into the maw."

"You can't!" Dawn cried. "That tentacle is armored with dragon scales!"

She was correct. Imbri reared up on her hind feet and clamped her teeth on the tentacle just over Forrest's head. There was a clang as enamel ground against metal. Then Imbri dropped down, unsuccessful.

"Get away from here, the rest of you!" Forrest cried.

"Not while you're in trouble," Eve said. "We'll stop it somehow."

"You can't stop an armored tangle tree!"

But the two girls, heedless of their own safety, drew two sharp little knives he hadn't known they carried, and reached up to stab at the tentacle from either side. One must have gotten a point past the armor, because suddenly the tree squealed in pain or outrage, and the tentacle hauled Forrest up twice as high. Then two more tentacles whipped out and wrapped around the girls. They screamed as they too were hauled into the air.

"Oooh, this is worse than I thought," Eve cried, as she reached up to touch a metal scale. "The tree has eaten many dragons, and saved their scales to make it impervious."

Dawn reached up similarly. "And it has healing elixir in its sap, so that it heals as fast as it is injured."

"Look at that trunk!" Eve cried. "It has mirrors to make it almost invisible."

"And it has the strength of a sphinx," Dawn said, gleaning more information from the living part of the tentacle she touched.

"If the trunk is also protected by dragon scales," Eve said, "then it can't be burned, even by salamander fire."

"And it has a voice, and can talk," Dawn said.

"For sure," the tree said. **"Now which of you delectable creatures shall I chomp first?"**

"None of them!" Imbri cried in a dreamlet. "I'll kick your bark in!"

"Oh, sure." Three more tentacles whipped out and wrapped around the mare. Soon she was dangling in air too.

"I'll send you Torus's worst dream," Imbri threatened.

"I *am* Torus's worst dream!"

Then Forrest got halfway smart. He reached into his pack and brought out the canned blanket of obscurity spell. "Invoke!" he cried.

The blanket wafted out and covered him and part of the tentacle that held him. The tree forgot about both. The tentacle went limp, letting Forrest drop to the ground.

"Ha ha—the faun got away!" Dawn cried gleefully.

"What faun?" the tree demanded.

"The one you caught," Eve said. "Now you can't eat him."

"I'll find him!" And the tree wrenched its roots from the ground and began writhing across the glade, searching for its missing prey. It shot tentacles out to circle the edge of the glade, so that no one could escape, even if unseen.

All four of them stared, astonished. "This truly *is* the worst tangle tree ever," Imbri said.

Now a tentacle reached into the tree's central foliage and brought out a sword. **"Where are you, faun?"** the voice rasped. **"Come taste this steel I liberated from a human fool who attacked me. He didn't taste very good, but I love his sword."**

That sword was whipping around so swiftly that Forrest had to stay well back to avoid it. Even if the tree couldn't locate him directly, it knew there was a faun somewhere, and was bound to get him eventually. He could feel the merest tingle of the blanket covering him, and realized that he could move it about if he handled it carefully. That explained Cathryn Centaur's throwing motions; she really did have hold of her blankets.

Then Dawn tried a new tack. "I know all about you, tangler," she called. "You lied. You're not Torus's worst dream. What about the Golem King?"

The whole tree shuddered. **"I will eat you first, you impertinent creature,"** it said. **"You look delicious."** The tentacle started to swing toward the trunk.

"I *am* delicious," Dawn retorted. "But you don't deserve me, because the Golem King is worse than you, and he should get me."

The tentacle hesitated. **"You're bluffing,"** the tree said. **"You don't know anything about the Golem King."**

Forrest made his way toward her. If he could throw the blanket over her before she got eaten, the tree would lose track of her too.

"Yes I do!" Dawn said. The tree didn't know that she was reading all this information from its own partly living wooden flesh. "The Golem King can make golems in a second. He can make golems like people, and like tangle trees, and like dragons, and he can make them life size or gnat size. He's a golem himself—and so are you, you big fake!"

"Aieeee!" the tree screamed.

"And if he ever got hold of a pretty living girl like me, he wouldn't eat me, he'd marry me," Dawn concluded triumphantly. "Because he's lonely down in the earth region where he lives, because nobody else will go there. He's cunning and can change his form instantly, but he has no company, and that's what he wants most of all. So when he finds out that you caught me and ate me, instead of turning me over to him, he'll destroy you with one flick of his finger. Or maybe turn you into a golem privy potty."

"Or a golem sphinx dropping," Eve added, tittering.

It almost worked. The tree shuddered, and the three captives were lowered toward the ground. But then it recovered some of its wooden cunning. "But I'll make sure he never finds out. I'll gobble all of you down immediately and bury your bones where they'll never be found." The tentacle started moving again.

Forrest leaped the last few steps toward Dawn, and flung the blanket over her head. He couldn't see it, and hoped it didn't hang up on the tentacle-vine holding her.

Then she dropped slowly to the ground. It had worked! The tangler had forgotten about her.

"Oooo, thank you!" she exclaimed, kissing him firmly on the right eye. "I was afraid you wouldn't be in time."

"You were great," he said. "You made it pause long enough."

She kissed him again. "Say, I have an idea—"

"Not now!" he cried, realizing that her contact with him was affecting her in the usual way. "We have to save the others."

"Oh, yes," she agreed, remembering. "I'll help."

They ran after Eve as the tangler hesitated, realizing that it had been about to do something but not remembering quite what. Forrest realized that the blanket of obscurity must work as much on the mind of any person or creature who might notice, as on the folk being covered. It was an excellent spell.

They held two ends of the blanket, and tossed it over Eve. In a moment she dropped to the ground, joining them in their coverage. "Get Imbri," she said urgently.

Indeed, it was time, for Imbri had been carried almost to the gaping wooden maw in the trunk of the tree. The mirrors had been moved aside so that its complete horror was evident.

The several tentacles holding Imbri swung her back and forth, getting ready to heave her into the maw. Forrest and the girls ran close and heaved the blanket with all their force.

It sailed over the mare and into the maw. Oh, no!

The maw creaked closed. There was a crunching sound. The blanket had been consumed.

Now they were exposed. The tree became aware of all of them. "There you are!" it creaked. "Now I'll—I'll—"

"Has it been an hour?" Imbri asked.

"I don't think so." For it took an hour for the canned blanket spell to recharge. They had to find their own way out, if they were going to.

"It seems to be in doubt," Imbri remarked. "Let me see if I can peek into its vegetable brain."

They waited, while the tentacles flailed. "Why isn't it attacking us?" Dawn asked, shuddering.

"Maybe the blanket tastes funny," Eve said.

Then Imbri had it. "It's forgotten its mouth!" her dreamlet exclaimed. "It can't eat us because it has lost track of how!"

"The blanket saved us after all," Forrest said, relieved.

They walked slowly out, and the tree ignored them, obsessed with its own problem. It knew it wanted to do something, but couldn't figure out what it was. Its wooden mind wasn't very sharp, and it couldn't focus well on more than one thing at a time. So they were escaping. But it was no sure thing.

They made it to the edge of the glade. The tree was still distracted. They breathed a collective sigh of relief.

"And let's stay clear of the Golem King, too," Dawn murmured.

Forrest looked around. The glade was surrounded by thickly meshed thorny brambles, except for several paths. Above loomed the vast shape of the other side of Torus, curving around and downward north and south like a massive rainbow. It made him feel dizzy, as if he were about to fall upward toward it, so he pulled his eyes back to the ground. The girls, following his gaze, looked similarly giddy.

"Just out of curiosity," Dawn began.

"Why didn't you use the petrified wood cross to scare the tree off?" Eve finished.

Ouch! He had a ready answer: "I never thought of it."

"Neither did the rest of us," Imbri pointed out.

They followed a path out. It was intended to bring prey into the tangler's glade, but it was a two way track. It led, in due course, to a village.

"Do we want to meet any people?" Forrest asked the others.

"Has it been an hour yet?" Dawn asked.

"Almost, I think."

"Then maybe we can use it if we get into more trouble. Let's talk with the people. I can learn a lot if I can touch one of them."

That seemed good, because though Ida should be reasonably nearby, they had no idea in which direction. The villagers might know.

They walked on in. There was a banner flying in the center. It said HOLLOWDAY.

"A holiday?" Imbri asked. "They don't seem to be celebrating."

Eve approached a wan villager. "Excuse me sir," she said prettily. "What are you celebrating?"

He glowered at her. "Nothing!"

"But you have the big banner up."

"It's Hollow Day. It's empty. We have nothing to do on it. We hate it."

"Then maybe you should find something good to do," Eve suggested. "That would brighten the day."

"Like what?" the man demanded grumpily.

"Like helping a group of strangers to find Ida, the lady with a moon."

He considered. "Very well. Take that path." He pointed out one they wouldn't otherwise have noticed.

"Thank you so kindly," Dawn said, flashing him a smile and a bit more as she bowed slightly.

"So very very kindly," Eve added, doing much the same.

"It doesn't matter," the man said. "We exchanged." He faced away from them. "Hey villagers! We have something to celebrate!"

There was a cheer.

Forrest and the others moved on along the path. "Do you think this is really the way?" Forrest asked. "I don't want to be unduly suspicious, but—"

"He was telling the truth," Imbri said in a dreamlet. "I can tell, when a person isn't guarded. They really were looking for something to celebrate."

"And couldn't think of it themselves," Dawn said, shaking her head.

"This is a very small world," Eve said. "Maybe they don't have much sense."

"Which is our good fortune," Forrest said.

Soon the path brought them to a large lake or small sea. It curved up at the end and down at the sides, in the manner of this world. They stood at the bank and gazed across it. Barely in sight was an island. "On Pyramid she was on an island," Imbri remarked. "Do you suppose it's the same here?"

"It could be," Dawn said brightly.

"Or it might not be," Eve said darkly.

Forrest sent a grizzled glance at them. "You girls are not being really helpful."

They exchanged one of their own glances. Forrest wasn't sure why, as they pretty well knew what was on each other's minds before they spoke.

"Should we be helpful?" Dawn inquired.

"Maybe in exchange for a kiss," Eve answered.

"No physical contact!" Forrest cried.

"Awwww," they said together.

"We do have a mission," Imbri reminded them with just the merest hint of annoyance suggested by the background image of her dreamlet: a horse kicking two girls in the rear so hard that they went flying through the air to land with a double splash in the lake.

"I think that means no kiss," Dawn said with faintly feigned regret.

"We'll have to help without repayment," Eve agreed with mock irritation.

"It's your turn."

"It's my turn." Eve walked to the edge of the water and poked her finger in. "This is the Sarah Sea, containing the Isle of Niffen, which is a large island with white beaches and lush, colorful foliage. Sparkling streams run in all directions, and there is one huge flat rock right smack dab in the middle of the island. It's inhabited by unicorns, dragons, Pegasus, griffins, mermaids, elves, winged goblins, harpies, genies, and assorted crossbreeds, all living in harmony. Especially Niffy Gliff, who is half dragon, half Pegasus, with a unicorn horn from somewhere in her ancestry. They don't much trust strangers, because once hunters came in an ugly little boat, wanting to capture and kill the people and animals and build a squat commercial tourist hotel instead. Fortunately Niffy and his friend Cliffy put on their scariest costumes, snuck up on the hunters, cried, 'Neeeiiiggg-hhhooooooouuuuu!!!' and scared them out of their skins, saving the isle." She stood and came to take Forrest's hand.

Forrest was impressed. "You can tell all that, just from sticking your finger in the water?"

"It's my talent," Eve said. "Just as my sister could tell all about every nymph you ever chased and caught, just from touching one of your fingers. Including the one who turned out to be a harpy. But of course she wouldn't tell anybody about that, or about the way the leaves of the neglected tree got disgustingly soiled with—"

"Thank you," Forrest said tightly. "Your talents are indeed impressive. So is Ida on that isle?"

"Oops, I didn't check for that." Eve let his hand go, knelt, and stuck her finger back in the water. "Yes, she lives on the flat rock, and goes each day to fetch water from the nearest sparkling stream." She stood again, and took his hand again. What was she up to now?

"How do you know about the living creatures on the Isle?" Imbri inquired. "Isn't that Dawn's talent?"

"Not exactly," Dawn said. "Our talents overlap somewhat. So when I tell everything about some living thing, I also know what it is wearing, where it lives, and what the weather around it is, even though these are inanimate, because they relate to the creature I'm examining. Similarly Dawn knows about the living things that relate to the inanimate thing she is examining. So if I touched a pool, and she touched a fish in the pool, we would both learn most of the same things."

"That does make sense," Imbri agreed.

Forrest didn't comment. He was embarrassed because of the discovery of just how much the girls had fathomed of his past history. He had thought of them as provocative but essentially innocent creatures; now he knew that they knew everything they wanted to know, of whatever nature. Probably the dread Adult Conspiracy of Silence had never had much effect on them, though they would have been careful to seem properly innocent.

"So what should we do now, adviser dear?" Dawn asked brightly.

"Now that we know where Ida is, Forrest darling," Eve added darkly, giving his hand a tweak.

"We go see her," he said gruffly. "We'll have to use our other small crosses."

"Oooh, suppose we get trapped on the Isle of Niffen," Dawn said.

"And there's nothing to do but live there forever and raise our children," Eve said.

"Which we will no doubt have to signal the stork for many times."

"Somehow coaxing the cooperation of a reluctant faun."

Imbri sent a dreamlet of two lovely nymphs, one fair and one dark, tugging a reluctant faun toward a love spring. His hoofs were leaving drag-marks in the soil. The mare was evidently enjoying the way the twins constantly put him on the defensive. Both girls laughed, appreciating the apt image.

"We won't get trapped," Forrest said, trying to sound neither intrigued nor grumpy. "We'll have the one big cross left, and anyway, once we talk with Ida, we can return directly to Pyramid to pursue our mission."

The two girls exchanged yet another unnecessary glance. "Are we losing our teasing skill?" Dawn inquired of no one in particular.

"Or is he losing his teasability?" Eve asked of the same person. Once more she squeezed his hand.

"He just wants to get the job done," Forrest said, finally freeing his hand and taking his small cross from his knapsack.

The girls dug theirs out of their purses. Forrest was never sure what happened to those purses when they weren't in use; they just seemed to disappear. Imbri used her teeth to get hers. Then they invoked them, almost together, and zoomed across the lake to the Isle of Niffen.

It was exactly as described. The beach was white, and the foliage was lush and colorful. And there, gliding in, was Niffy Gliff, the combination griffin Pegasus with the horn. He looked threatening.

"We aren't hunters!" Imbri cried in a dreamlet. "We are visitors from another world who must talk with Ida."

"Neigh?" Niffy inquired.

"Well, we're not exactly friends of hers," Imbri said in the dreamlet. "But we know her—her cousin on the other world, and she sent us to talk with Ida. So I'm sure we'll be friends the moment we meet."

Niffy considered, and decided that that was good enough. "Neigh," he said, and led the way.

They followed him along a nice path that wound through the lush foliage to a sparkling steam. The lushes looked a bit tipsy, but the sparkles were beautiful. They came to the huge flat rock, which had steps at one edge, so they could climb to the flattop. And there was a nice little house with a pleasant little garden.

Ida came out to meet them. She looked just the same, except that her moon was in the shape of a cone. "I am told you know my cousin," she said. "What cousin would that be?"

A number of creatures had gathered around the house. Evidently news of the visitors had spread rapidly across the Isle. They seemed to be in a state of readiness. Forrest realized that if the creatures thought the visitors were not on the level, they would be quickly leveled.

"Cousin may not be exactly the right word," Forrest said. "She is your analog on the world of Pyramid, about whose head this world of Torus orbits. She thought you could help us learn what we must know to save Pyramid from cruel exploitation by the colorful Wizards.''

"Why I suppose I could," Ida said. "I don't know the answer myself, but I believe it's on Cone."

Forrest quailed. "We have to go to another moon? We're already on the moon of a moon of a moon."

Ida smiled. "I suppose that would get confusing. No, I can take a conic section and get the information. Let me concentrate."

She concentrated. The moon took note, as its point pointed straight up for a full orbit. "Yes, I have your information," Ida said. "But there is a complication you may not have considered."

"There always is," Imbri muttered in a dreamlet sent to Forrest alone.

"What complication is that?" he asked Ida.

"It is that here on Torus, anyone who does another a favor or a service incurs a burden of emotion. The greater the service, the greater the emotion. So we are rather careful about the services we render, and to whom."

"Emotion," Forrest said. "As in happiness or sadness?"

"Not exactly. As in liking or loving."

"Uh-oh," Dawn murmured.

"Mischief," Eve agreed.

Forrest agreed. "Does this mean that if you do me the service of telling me what I need to know, you will—that is—"

"Exactly. Considering the importance of the information to your mission, I will be in love with you. And without meaning any affront to you, I must say that I do not care to be in love with a creature who will immediately leave me forever."

"I would not care to have that happen either," Forrest said. "Even if I were staying here, I am not at all sure it would be proper. You surely have some prince who will seek you out at some time."

"That would be nice," Ida agreed.

"Is there any way to counter or nullify the effect?" Imbri asked in a general dreamlet.

"Yes there is. People can exchange equivalent favors, so that the effect cancels out. These must occur at about the same time. If one favor is done at one time, and the other at another time, both will incur the penalties. In fact this is the way marriages are made: by the exchange of favors on consecutive days. So if you have some favor you can do me in return, that is as valuable to me as my information is to you, we shall be all right.''

"Oh, wow," Dawn said. "We were all doing each other favors, trying to escape that tangle tree."

"So they canceled out," Eve agreed. "But then I got a favor from that villager.''

"No, you did him the favor of showing him how to have a good day," Imbri said in a dreamlet. "It was a fair exchange."

"Oooo, that's what he meant!" Dawn exclaimed, clapping her hands. "When we thanked him, and gave him something to see."

"He said, 'It doesn't matter—we exchanged,' and we didn't understand," Eve agreed. "He meant that we didn't love him, and he didn't love us, so there was no point in showing him anything interesting.''

"But he *was* interested, or he wouldn't have said that."

"Yes. It's nice to know that our stuff works here, too."

"You girls seem to enjoy impressing men," Ida remarked.

They both smiled, acknowledging it.

"But then you did a service for Forrest," Dawn said. "Telling him all about the lake and Isle."

Which had enhanced her feeling for him, Forrest realized ruefully. That explained some things. But there seemed to be no point in discussing that now.

At least they could balance things, with Ida. This was looking better. "What information do you want, that is this valuable?"

"Unfortunately, what I most desire is knowledge of something I fear you would be even less in a position to know than I. As you may have noticed, the Isle of Niffen is on a small sea. I would like to know all about this sea, from its name to its deepest creatures. I already know all about the Isle, but the water has eluded me.''

"I can—" Eve started, but Forrest cut her off with a sharp glance. Her sister wiped the cut off her face; the glance had been too sharp.

"You don't want to do that," Forrest said. "Because then you would love Ida.''

"Then Eve would love Ida, and Ida would love Forrest," Dawn said. "That's no good."

"But suppose Eve gave Forrest the information?" Imbri asked. "And then he gave it to Ida in exchange?"

"Then Eve would love Forrest," Dawn protested.

"Doesn't she already?"

Eve's mouth formed a pretty round O. "I do!"

"We both do," Dawn said. "But wouldn't she love him more than I do?"

"I think I already do," Eve said. "Because it was for him I got the information on the lake and Isle. I didn't realize the effect it would have on me."

"Oh, my," Dawn said, dismayed. "That's why you were holding his hand."

"Was I? I suppose I was. I didn't realize."

"You could do him a favor some other time, Dawn," Imbri suggested.

"Maybe so," Dawn agreed thoughtfully. "I will keep it in mind."

Forrest wished he had known of this complication before asking Eve for the information on the lake. He had wondered about the hand holding, because up until that time the two girls had done things evenly. But he hadn't understood, so had done her no return favor.

But that complication would have to wait. Forrest faced Ida. "Eve can tell anything about anything inanimate. She will learn all about the lake, and tell me, and I will exchange that information with you. Does this seem fair?"

"Yes, remarkably fair," Ida agreed.

"Then Eve and I will go to the water and learn what we need. Meanwhile Dawn and Mare Imbri can chat with you, if you like. I'm sure there are incidental things you could exchange, keeping them in balance." Even as he spoke, he wondered why he had set it up that way. Surely he didn't want to be alone with Eve at this time! Or *did* he?

"Yes, surely," Ida agreed.

So Forrest and Eve followed the path back to the water. The assorted animals of the Isle let them be, knowing that they were not hunters. Eve insisted on holding his hand again. "If I am going to be

even more in love with you, I want to grab every moment I can,''
she explained.

"But such contact with me will only increase your desire to—to
do what we should not."

"It can't," she said dreamily.

Forrest decided not to argue, though he was not entirely at ease
with this. For one thing, this was the first time he had been really
alone with either girl, so the inhibition of numbers was gone. Eve
was evidently working up to more than just information. And he was
evidently facilitating it, though he knew he should not. The complications of relationships with non-nymphly women were both confusing and tantalizing.

They reached the water, and she knelt down, ready to stick her
finger in. Then she stood. "No, I have a better notion," she said,
approaching him.

"What is that?" he asked warily.

"This." She lurched suddenly, and pushed him into the water.
When he tried to catch his balance, she flung her arms around him
and hauled him down. They both made a great splash as they fell in.

"But there may be water monsters!" he cried, trying to scramble
back out.

She just clung more tightly. "No there aren't. Not at this beach.
Now let me tell you all about it."

"But you don't have to hold me while you tell me," he protested.

"Yes I do," she said firmly. Very firmly, for she was plastered
against him, and she had dissolved all her clothing.

"You are taking advantage of the situation," he informed her. And
he was letting her, he realized.

"I certainly am. This is almost as good as a love spring."

"But what's the point? You know I'm not going to—not until the
mission is done."

"I know. But you will be sorely tempted, and you will remember
what I feel like, this close, and when the time comes, you will not
try to find a pretext to avoid it."

She was eerily accurate. Already it took most of his willpower to
maintain his nominal diffidence. "How do you know so much about

me, when it's Dawn's talent to know all about living creatures, not yours?'' He was trying to distract her; they had already explained about the overlapping of their talents.

''She told me.''

''But doesn't she have a—an equal interest? Why should she tell you how to—''

''When her chance comes, she'll do the same. My chance just happened to come first. So she didn't interfere, and I won't interfere during her turn.''

''But how does she know you won't—''

''Our agreement is up to, but not including, the stork. We must be together for that. So I'll give her the chance to do you an equivalent favor before then, so we'll be even again. And we'll both give you opportunity to do us favors, on other days, so your interest will match ours. We will keep you quite busy, for a while.''

''You girls are almost frightening in your cooperation.''

''Never trust a Sorceress,'' she agreed. ''Let alone two of us.''

Forrest resigned himself. These girls had his number, and knew it. He really didn't need to do them any favors, to find them dangerously appealing. ''Tell me all about this lake.''

She started talking, punctuating her sentences with kisses on his ears. It took some time.

At last they emerged from the water. Forrest was shaky, not from the information, but from Eve's kisses. There might not be magic in them, but they nevertheless had extraordinary force. She was right: he would be dreaming of her during whatever off moments were available, and when the time came, he would not make any excuses. She had captured his desire. The irony was that his weakness of the moment gave her the pretext to put her arm around him and help support him. She hadn't bothered to form clothing, and her touch remained electric.

''If you had been a nymph, all this would have been abated in seconds,'' he muttered. ''With no emotional complications. Instead you have chained me.''

''I know,'' she said smugly. ''You're not used to dealing with women with minds. We're dangerous. We are aware of consequences, and we know how to make a temporary interest permanent.'' She nudged him without using an elbow. "But somehow this session hasn't changed my feeling for you."

"It couldn't increase what was already complete," he said glumly.

"Maybe."

He decided not to inquire what she meant. She surely understood further aspects that would only alarm him worse. He had anticipated problems with terrain, monsters, magic, and people, but never with emotions. He had hardly known what emotions were, before all this began. Now he knew that they were the most formidable of the lot.

They returned to the central plateau. Along the way Forrest recovered his steadiness, and his fur dried, and Eve shifted to dry clothing. Their immersion in the water was not obvious. She released his hand, so that even that aspect disappeared. He was struggling to keep his face and manner straight, and was privately amazed at how readily Eve made herself look cool, as if nothing of any kind had even been thought of. Obviously girls were better at this than men. Or fauns, at least.

"That was one close call," Imbri said in a dreamlet. "If she had kissed you on the mouth instead of the ears—"

Dawn also looked knowingly at them, without comment.

Forrest approached Ida. "The name of the lake is the Sarah Sea," he began. He went on to describe its depths in meticulous detail. As he spoke, he found himself becoming increasingly interested in Ida. She was an attractive woman, with a remarkable talent, and now he was in a position to know how special her moon was. Eve had tempted him wickedly, but he knew it was desire rather than love. Ida did not tempt him in that manner, but his feeling for her was becoming encompassing. He wanted to stay with her forever, and bask in the delight of her mere presence. This, he realized, was love, an emotion he had never before experienced. It was different from desire, though there were connections between the two. Should Ida express any interest at all in desire, he realized it would spring fully formed from the broad base of the larger emotion. Fortunately she gave no such indication, though her moon angled to observe him better.

"Now it is my turn," Ida said when he finished. "You have delivered in full measure, and satisfied my lifelong curiosity. Do not be concerned about your present emotion; it will shortly pass. Here is the information you need. You have to talk to the margins, and explain to them that they have been deceived. That they are not giving favors, they are stealing them, and will be diminished thereby.''

"Margins?'' Forrest asked. "The lines?''

"The creatures who generate the lines,'' Ida said. "They are kept in the cellars, and not told much of anything that is true.''

A bulb flashed over Forrest's head. "So if they learn the truth, they'll stop generating the lines, and the power of the Wizards will collapse!''

Ida smiled. "I'm glad that this information is useful to you.''

"It certainly is!''

"But how can we get into the castles, to tell the margins?'' Imbri asked.

Forrest relayed the question.

"You have merely to locate Ghina, whose talent is to put people to sleep,'' Ida said. "She is somewhere on Pyramid's red face, and will help if you ask her. Also Jfraya, whose talent is to draw a door that opens.''

"But how do we find Gina and Jeffrey?''

"Ghina, the daughter of Graeboe Giant and Gloha Goblin-Harpy, I believe. A large invisible winged goblin girl. And Jfraya, of uncertain origin, on Pyramid's green face. I fear you will have to accept some favors there, and be accordingly diminished.''

"I can do that,'' Imbri said.

"So we have it,'' Forrest said. "Thank you so much.''

"No thanks necessary; it is a fair exchange.''

Then he realized something. "My emotion—it has faded. I don't love you any more. Not that you are unworthy. It's just that—''

"Yes. It abated when I returned the favor. But I trust you can appreciate why I demurred, before.''

"Yes! It's a great emotion, but it must be invoked suitably.''

"That is correct. I am glad we were able to arrange our exchange of information, for we both profit handsomely thereby.''

"So am I,'' he said, much relieved. If only Eve could be similarly turned off. But he knew of no favor he could do her at the moment.

"Now we must return to Pyramid. Do you have any objection if we go directly from here?"

"None. I have not before observed travel between worlds. It should be interesting."

"Maybe so." He looked at the others. "Are we ready?"

"No," Dawn said. "I haven't had the chance to do you a favor to match Eve's."

"Better yet," Forrest suggested, "why don't I do Eve an equivalent favor, so that her emotion abates? I can't think of one, but maybe you can."

"Maybe I can," Dawn said.

"Nuh-uh!" Eve protested. "I like it this way."

"But we have to be even," Dawn said.

"How long has it been since Eve did her favor for Forrest?" Ida asked.

"An hour," Dawn said.

"Then it's too late. Favors have to be exchanged soon, before the emotion sets in place."

"Then I'll just have to do Forrest some favor," Dawn said. "Forrest, what do you really, truly, most want to know about some living thing?"

"Where to find a faun for my neighboring tree. That's my whole mission here."

"But I have to touch a living thing to know about it. I can't find your faun from a distance, unless I can touch someone who knows where he is."

"I wish you could do me that favor," Forrest said. "But it is evident that you can't."

"Maybe one of us knows," Dawn said. "Without knowing she knows, I mean. So I could find out."

"I do not," Ida said. "I would have to query Cone again, and that would mean—"

"Don't do that!" Forrest said. "It's Dawn's favor I must have."

Ida smiled. "I understand."

"Let's hold hands," Dawn said desperately. "If the information is among us, I can get it."

"I can't hold hands," Imbri said in a dreamlet.

"But you can touch us," Eve pointed out.

So they formed another circle, with the two girls holding Forrest's hands, and touching Imbri on the other side. There was a pause.

"There is something," Dawn said. "Not the faun. Something—something better, I think. Oh!" She let go.

"What happened?" Eve asked. "Is something wrong?"

Dawn looked awed. "I—I don't think so. But I don't know what to do. It's all—all mixed up."

Forrest was getting impatient. "Do you have the answer or don't you?"

Dawn turned to Ida. "Aunt Ida—where I come from, that's what you are—you always had good advice for us. I really need it now. Is there any way—without complicating things—"

Ida nodded. "There may be, dear. If you care to tell me what is on your mind, I would be free to offer an opinion, which you would be free to ignore. So there would be no actual service. Would that do?"

"Yes!"

"Then we shall do that. Let's take a little walk into my house."

The two went into the house. The remaining three looped a glance around. "What do you think she saw?" Eve asked.

"It must have been something that one of us knows, or maybe has seen and not realized its significance," Imbri said.

"She knows just about everything I know," Eve said. "So I don't think it's me."

"I have seen too many things to remember," Imbri said. "In the course of my delivery of bad dreams. So one of them could relate. But why wouldn't she tell us, or at least Forrest?"

"All I know I learned in the vicinity of my tree," Forrest said. "This adventure has shown me more new things than I ever saw before. So unless I saw a faun in passing and didn't realize it—and why wouldn't Dawn tell me that?"

"She said it wasn't a faun, but maybe better," Eve said. "But that still doesn't explain why she's so confused."

Dawn and Ida emerged from the house. Dawn looked radiant. She marched right up to Forrest. "I love you as much as Eve does, now," she said, embracing him and kissing him ardently on the mouth. He realized that it must be so, for her passion was heating him, making him desire her as much as he desired Eve. Her body was pressing him in all the places Eve's body had, just as urgently. "So we're even, again." She gave him a final squeeze, and turned him loose.

He reeled, and would have fallen, had not Imbri alertly intercepted him and supported him with her solid shoulder. "We had better complete this mission soon," Imbri said in a dreamlet. "Those girls are too much for you."

True words! He put his arm across her shoulder, gradually regaining his equilibrium. "I'm just not used to this sort of thing," he said.

"But what favor did you do him?" Eve was asking Dawn.

"Sister, I can't tell you. And I can't tell you why I can't tell you. But believe me, you would do the same, in my situation."

"I don't understand!"

"I know. I'm sorry. But so it must be, for now."

Eve looked at Ida. "So it seems it must be," Ida agreed. "And now I think you are ready to return to Pyramid and complete your mission."

"But how can she have done me a favor, and I not know it?" Forrest asked, as perplexed as Eve.

"In time you will understand."

Forrest exchanged a glance of mottled frustration with Eve. "Don't you hate it when someone says that?" Eve asked.

"Yes. It makes me feel like a teenager."

"Exactly," she agreed. Then she came across and kissed him on the mouth. "If Dawn can do it, so can I."

"But I didn't get to press my bare body against him in the water," Dawn retorted.

"How do you know about that?" Eve demanded.

"When we held hands, I fathomed everything."

"Including what you're not telling us."

"Yes," Dawn said smugly.

"It's time to go," Forrest said, before it could erupt into a sisterly fight.

"Yes," Imbri agreed, her dreamlet figure sounding no more pleased than Forrest or Eve. "Time to go."

"Let's hold hands," Eve suggested.

"Just to be sure no one gets lost," Dawn said.

At another time Forrest might have objected. But at the moment his main concern was that they make a safe return to Pyramid before anything else happened to confuse the issue. So he didn't argue.

Eve took hold of his left hand, and Dawn took his right hand, and the two of them caught Imbri's mane on either side with their other hands. Each of the girls squeezed his fingers with knowing implication. They were even, all right—but what of him? Then all of them diluted their bodies.

"This is impressive," Ida remarked as they expanded and thinned. "I wish all of you the very best. Give my regards to Ida of Pyramid." Then they became too diffuse to hear her. They were drifting up into the sky, which was the hole in the center of Torus. They had to move out of it, so as not to collide with the world again as they continued to expand.

The lakes, forests, fields, and mountains spread out below and around them as they went. Forrest peered at the inner side of the doughnut, until he located the Sarah Sea, with its island in the center. He hoped Ida wasn't lonely. It would not have been a bad place to reside.

They moved well clear of Torus, growing impossibly large. Then Forrest saw a far larger shape beyond, and realized that it was Ida's head. Ida of Pyramid. They would have some interesting things to tell her, too!

It became easier as they oriented on the larger world. They were too diffuse to continue holding hands; their substances passed right through each other. But now there was no danger of getting lost. Still, one nebulous figure clung to his left extremity. That would be Eve. Or was it? What was he to do about her, whichever one it was? When the two girls had been equally interested, it had been awkward, and worse when Eve was more interested, but now it was worse yet. Because now he was wishing that the mission could be finished, so that he and they could do whatever they had in mind. He would have to play no favorites, but that would be a lie; Eve had become his favorite. She had aroused emotions of a scope and complexity he had not before experienced. Yet Dawn had the capacity to even it up, as her last embrace had shown. Just what *had* she done, to increase her emotion?

When their own monstrous bodies came into view, they separated, each descending toward his or her own. Even Eve's empty body intrigued him now; it looked lovely in its dark perfection. He would have to dissipate that feeling, if he could.

Mare Imbri was the first to reach her body. She landed on it with her hoofs and sank in. So that was how it was done! Forrest moved his own feet toward that landing. But he hung back somewhat, wanting to make sure that the others docked successfully before he did. He didn't know what he would do if anything went wrong, but he felt it was his responsibility.

He saw Dawn reach her body. She elected to swan-dive into it, her soul-self assuming the form of the bird just before it disappeared into the flesh. Actually her whole body was condensed soul, but that didn't seem to matter in this circumstance. Her head faced him at the last instant, and winked. What did she know?

Then Eve reached her body. She assumed the form of a perfect image of herself, only without the clothing, and sank down on her back. She glanced lingeringly at him as she disappeared, and smiled. Oh, yes, she remained aware of him!

Then it was his turn. He dropped in feet first, trusting Imbri's technique, and felt his feet and legs encounter slow resistance. He arranged himself and lay down across his body, sinking in.

Then it became stifling. He was suffocating. He wanted to pull out, to escape, to win free, but couldn't. The body had hold of him, and was sucking him into itself, in all its solid parts and aspects. But he reminded himself that this really was his body, in this world, and that he would like it as soon as he truly got back into it. It merely felt a bit corroded from disuse at the moment.

Then the melding was complete. He opened his eyes. Around him the others were stirring. "What an experience!" Dawn said. She looked at Forrest as if pondering experience of another kind.

"Yes indeed," Eve agreed. Then she sent a sultry glance in Forrest's direction. "In more respects than one."

For sure.

11
WIZARDS

I da helped them reorient. "Are all of you all right?" she
asked. "You were gone for several hours."
Forrest looked at the tiny Torus orbiting her head. So
much had happened there! "Yes, I think we are, physically," he said.

Both girls laughed. "Emotionally, we changed," Dawn said. "The
two of us fell in love with him, and he became fascinated with us."

"But we learned what we need to know," Eve said. "Your persona
there was very nice."

"And now we will share it with you," Forrest said. "We will tell
you all about Torus."

"I'm so glad," Ida said, bringing a plate of cookies.

And for the next two hours they told her everything they could
remember that they deemed important or interesting. Ida was fascinated, especially with the revised rules of services and emotions there,
and with the information about the other Ida's conic moon. "How I
wish I could meet her!" she said.

"That, I fear, is impossible," Imbri said. "How could you take
your moon along—when going *to* that moon?"

"How, indeed," Ida agreed sadly. "But this detailed knowledge
of it is the next best thing. I'm glad she has a nice residence."

"She sent her regards to you," Forrest said, remembering.

"Oh! How nice."

"She's a nice person," Dawn said.

"Just like you," Eve said.

"Oh!" Ida blushed.

Then it was time to resume their mission. "We must locate Ghina on the red face, and Jfraya on the green face," Forrest said. "With their help, we can nullify the Wizards. Then you will be free."

"That will be nice," Ida agreed. "But do be careful, because the Wizards may not take kindly to your effort."

"As long as nobody tells them what we are up to, we should be all right," Imbri said in a dreamlet.

"I will certainly never tell," Ida said. "Farewell, good visitors."

Dawn & Eve hugged her. Then the four of them left her blue stone house, and walked off the blue ridge to the blue lake. There Forrest took the large cross from Imbri's pack. They clustered together, and shot across the water in a bundle.

They landed tumbled together on the far shore. Dawn was plastered across Forrest's front, and Eve across his back, all of them on top of Imbri. But no one was hurt. He wondered to what extent the girls had arranged things that way. Did it matter?

They disentangled, and resumed their trek. The red face was in the direction they thought of as west, though such a designation was meaningless here. A straight march in that direction would get them there. Forrest invoked the blanket of obscurity so that they would not be bothered by natives.

But night was coming. They needed a place to spend the night. They were in deep woods, and weren't sure how safe it would be, because the blanket would wear off long before the night ended. Already they heard the howling of the hunting wolf spiders. They didn't want to blunder into a wolf web.

Dawn went from tree to tree, touching their trunks. "This is a tea tree," she said of one. "It grows all kinds of teas: Mediocri, subversi, adversi, propensi, versatili, priori, superiori, monstrosi—"

"We get the point," Eve said. "We won't be drinking any of those."

Dawn circled around it. "And on this side it's a Tree Tea," she announced. "When enemies meet here, they can make a peace agreement."

"There's a house," Eve said. "Maybe we can stay there."

"How long has the blanket been invoked?" Imbri asked.

"Over an hour," Forrest said. "But what we want is friendly accommodation. So if we find that, we won't need the blanket."

"So who inquires at that house?"

"I will. We all have our own value, so none of us are more at risk than the others."

"But we love you," Dawn said. "We don't want anything to happen to you."

"And I don't want anything to happen to any of you." He glanced at Imbri. "If an ogre or something answers the door, throw a bad dreamlet at him to distract him until I can get away."

The others nodded, realizing that this was probably sufficient protection.

He went up to the blue house and knocked on the door. A young woman with blue hair answered. She reminded him of someone. "Hello," he said. "I am Forrest Faun, from another world, and I and my friends need a place to stay the night. We wondered if you—"

"Another world?" she asked. "Do you mean Ptero?"

"Yes, as a matter of fact. We are on our way to the red face, and—"

"You are welcome. We haven't had visitors from there for a long time. In fact, we've never had them. I am Ilene, and this is my brother Gerrod." She indicated the man who came up behind her. He looked familiar too.

"Don't you want to meet my companions, to be sure—"

"Certainly. Bring them in."

Forrest turned and beckoned the others. They came to the house.

"You look familiar," Ilene said, looking at the twins.

"I am Dawn."

"I am Eve."

"We are the twin daughters of Prince Dolph and Princess Electra."

"That's it!" Ilene cried. "You are our cousins! We are the children of Grey and Ivy."

"Oh, more cousins," Dawn said. "How nice."

"Do you have Magician caliber talents?" Eve asked.

"Of course. I control storms, and Gerrod communicates with water."

"Fascinating," Dawn said. "I know about living things."

"And I know about inanimate things."

"Let's compare notes," Ilene said.

Soon Gerrod and Eve were telling each other about all manner of aspects of a cup of water, and it was clear that their talents were genuine. Similarly Ilene and Dawn were demonstrating storm clouds and information about living things. Then they all settled down inside, including Imbri, for a nice supper and more talking. Forrest realized that on these worlds, where the might-be's resided, it was easy for them to accept alternate folk. Dawn & Eve knew all their cousins on Ptero, and Ilene and Gerrod knew all their cousins on Pyramid. They considered it a fair exchange of information, and no one gained or lost size. Imbri paid her way by demonstrating her ability to project dreamlets, and Forrest brought out his panpipes and played a merry melody for their hosts. So it was a good night.

In the morning, refreshed, they set off again. Ilene and Gerrod did not know what was to be found on the red face; it seemed that the folk on one face kept pretty much to their own color, and those who tried to cross over stood out like sore big toes. But Gerrod gave them several packaged storms to use in case of need. Imbri accepted them, and did lose some mass, but it seemed worth it.

As they progressed, the ground tilted. It didn't bother them, since they tilted with it, but they were aware that they were getting near the edge of the blue triangle.

When they reached it, the demarcation was striking. The border was like the ridge of a mountain range, blue on one side, red on the other.

"We'll have to change color," Forrest said.

"Maybe not," Imbri said. "With the blanket of obscurity, we may not be noticed."

He hadn't thought of that. "Then let's go ahead. You can ask directions with dreamlets that show the correct color."

They crossed the ridge—and abruptly their tilt was wrong. It was geared to the blue face, which was sharply different from the red face. They were now at a steep angle to the terrain. In fact their heads wanted to collide with the ground at a slight angle, while their bodies wanted to point slightly into the air.

"We are oriented ninety degrees to the blue face," Imbri said.

"The red face differs from the blue face by a hundred and twenty degrees. We shall have to crawl on our hands. I don't feel comfortable with that." Indeed, she was lying on her side with two feet in the air.

"Maybe I can figure it out," Eve said. She touched a finger to the red rock. "Aha! There's a colony of lings near the edge. We can make a deal with them."

That was a relief. They crossed back to the blue face and walked along the edge until they were near the lings. This happened to be by the shore of a blue lake that went right up to the boundary, bent around the corner, and became a red lake at the new angle. Then they waited for the obscurity to wear off, so that Forrest could crawl to the lings' camp. But as the spell faded, a large canine creature loped toward them from the blue side.

"What is it?" Eve asked, concerned.

"That looks like a dire wolf," Dawn said. "Get well away from it!"

"Maybe I had better invoke the blanket of obscurity again," Forrest said, taking it out of his knapsack.

"No, just cross to the red side," Dawn said urgently. She and Eve were already doing so, while Imbri stood warily by.

A deep bass note sounded from the lake, almost under Forrest's elbow. He jumped—and the can flew out of his hand. It splashed into the water, where a big fish swallowed it.

"Oh, no!" Dawn cried. "That's a largemouth bass. It swallowed the can."

Meanwhile the dire wolf was coming close. Forrest quickly brought out a storm package and opened it. Dark clouds swirled out, making sheets of rain and peals of thunder. The wolf got a blast of spray in the snoot, reconsidered, passed close by them, and ran on, not attacking. "Of all the bad luck," Forrest said.

"That's the thing about a dire wolf," Dawn said. "Wherever it goes, disaster follows. That's why we had to get away from it."

And he hadn't done so, not realizing what she meant. Now their main protection from hostile interest, the blanket of obscurity, was gone. If only he had understood in time!

There was nothing to do but dry off and proceed with their mission, hoping they could get along without the obscurity. Forrest crossed to the red and crawled to the place where the lings were. They were easy to deal with; they flocked to the edge, and treated each person as she crossed. Imbri was the one who made the actual deals, so she lost several more bits of her substance and became a smaller horse. But now they were able to walk at the correct angle. They were also red; they had had to deal for that too. Things were looking better, but they were paying a price. If only they hadn't lost their main protection! Maybe they were blundering because of the prior loss of the Good Magician's list of words.

Dawn touched the plants, and Eve touched the objects, and soon they had a notion where a sleep-talented woman had been. They followed her trail, being watchful for any dangers, and in due course located her.

Except that when they found her, they couldn't see her. There was her nice little red brick house, but no woman. They had not wanted to be sneaky, but their awareness of danger made them careful, so they peeked in a window first. And saw nothing.

"But she's there," Imbri insisted. "I can feel her fleeting dreams."

Then Forrest made a connection. "She's the daughter of Graeboe Giant. Is he an invisible giant?"

"Not any more," Imbri said. "He's a winged goblin now."

"But he has the invisible heritage. She's invisible!"

Eve touched the house. "Why so she is! This is the house of an invisible woman."

"So maybe we should just knock on the door and introduce ourselves," Forrest said. "Instead of generating our own complications."

The others, abashed, agreed. So Forrest knocked—and in a moment a red-cloaked woman answered. "Yes?" she inquired from the depths of her cowl.

"I am Forrest Faun. I have come to ask a favor from Ghina."

"I am she. I am glad to give favors, for they increase my stature. What is your wish?"

"My friends and I need your help to nullify the four Wizards of Pyramid."

"Oh, my!" she exclaimed. "That is a very dangerous undertaking."

"Yes. But if we succeed, the tyranny of the Wizards will be ended, and you will be free."

"Free? We're free now. The Wizards have done a great many favors for us."

Oops. He had forgotten that though the Wizards were oppressing the folk of Ptero, it was the opposite for the folk of Pyramid. Ghina might not want to cooperate.

He pondered as swiftly as he could, and decided that the truth was best, though it was dangerous to utter. "We are from another world. The Wizards are harming that world, in order to do favors here."

She considered. "Are any of my friends being harmed?"

"They could be. There are many might-be folk there, and surely some of them are relatives of yours." He wasn't quite sure what system there was, as there seemed to be might-be's on all the worlds, but it seemed a safe assumption that there were invisible giants, goblins, and harpies on Ptero. So her ancestry was surely well represented.

"Well, then, I suppose I had better help. And if I am helping my relatives, it isn't really a favor to you."

"It's a fair exchange of favors," he said, relieved.

"Very well. I'll help." She stepped out the door.

"But don't you have to close up your house, or anything?"

"It will keep until Mom and Dad fly home. Or until my brother Geddy walks home; he's out charming the ladies with his songs. Where are your friends?"

"Here they are." The three others were stepping forward. "This is Mare Imbri, who speaks in dreamlets."

Imbri sent a dreamlet of a winged goblin girl. "Hello."

"And these are Dawn & Eve Human, whose talents are to know all about living and inanimate things." The twins in red jeans nodded. Forrest noticed, irrelevantly, that Dawn's hair color had returned to its natural flame hue, while Eve's hair was now midnight red. Both girls remained infernally attractive.

Ghina's cowl looked thoughtful. "Are you related to Magician Trent?"

"He's our great grandfather," Dawn said.

"Now rejuvenated to his twenties," Eve said. "So he's not much older than we are."

"That's the one! Mother knew him." The cowl looked down, as if blushing. "In fact, Mother rather liked him. If he had been willing, she would have ordered me from the Stork Works with him, instead of with Graeboe, and I might have been visible. Not that I have any objection to Graeboe; he's a fine father. It's just that sometimes I wonder what I might have looked like."

"Like this," Imbri said. In the dreamlet, her human figure conjured a bucket of red paint and flung it at the cowled Ghina figure. The paint splashed all over, washing off the cowl and leaving a red winged goblin girl.

"Oh!" Ghina cried, delighted. "I'm pretty!"

"Just like your mother," Imbri agreed.

They started off. "I suppose we should do the Red Wizard first, since we're here," Forrest said. "Do you know where his castle is?"

"In the center of the red triangle," Ghina said. "But I don't know the best way there. I'll ask the chess nut."

"Chestnuts talk?" Forrest asked.

She must have smiled. "You're funny." She led the way through the forest to a glade wherein stood assorted life sized redwood figures of men, women, horses, towers, and children. The floor of the glade was marked in squares: light red and dark red. As they approached, a figure of a light red man with a pointed hat slid across a diagonal and grabbed a dark red child figure. It tossed the child to the edge of the glade, where it joined a tumbled collection of figures.

"Uncle Kerby!" Ghina called.

There was a stirring. "Yes, Niece Ghina," a voice came from the air.

"Oh—an invisible giant, of course," Dawn murmured.

"From her father's side of the family," Eve agreed.

Imbri made a dreamlet showing the glade with its wooden figures, and the outline of an invisible giant standing over them, ready to move another piece. The giant seemed to be of about average size for his type, with unruly brown hair and green eyes. Apparently his invisibility allowed him to be normal colors, instead of shades of red.

"Where is the center of the triangle?" Ghina asked.

"All paths lead to it," Kerby replied, moving another chess piece. "Thank you, Uncle!"

"But we're forgetting something," Dawn said.

"That's right: Jfraya," Eve agreed.

So they were. They needed both people to do the job. "We'll have to go to the green face first," Forrest said with regret.

Kerby overheard him. "That will be a harder trip."

"Uncle, could you help us?" Ghina asked.

"I could, but I don't want to take any mass from you, sweet thing."

"I will trade you this smile," she said, turning her invisible face in Kerby's direction.

Forrest couldn't see the smile, but the glade brightened. The giant must have seen it, being also invisible.

"Climb on," he said.

Imbri's dreamlet showed a huge hand being laid on the ground before them. They climbed on and took hold of the fingers, and Imbri lay in the palm. Then the hand lifted above the trees, and the red terrain whizzed by below.

It didn't take long. Kerby lowered them at the corner between the red and the green faces. "Actually I could reach across, if you know where your friend is," the giant offered.

"Let me touch a tree," Dawn said. "Maybe she walked past it once."

"Let me touch the ground," Eve said. "Maybe a path leads to her home."

They scrambled off the invisible hand. They had the usual trouble with the changed angle of the green face, but crawled to a green tree and green stone.

Soon they returned. "Someone once opened a door near here," Dawn reported. "The trees were astonished, for it was a door into the ground."

"And the ground knows of other doors that opened in it, in that direction," Eve said, pointing.

"I will reach as far as I can in that direction," Kerby said.

The girls scrambled back onto his hand. Then they rode way out across the green terrain, until the giant's reach reached its farthest reaches, and he lowered them to the greensward.

"Thank you, Uncle!" Ghina called, flashing another glade-brightening invisible smile as they slid to the ground.

"Welcome, Niece," he called back, as he started back toward his chess game, his voice sounding lower because of the special magic of Doppler. It occurred to Forrest that Doppler must have been an interesting Magician, though it wasn't clear why he wanted to fool with sounds.

Now they had to struggle with the terrain. It was possible for them to walk erect, if they clung to trees and other features of the green-scape, but not easy. There seemed to be no lings in the vicinity. So they were stuck in the greenery, being both red and grounded.

"Maybe we can brace each other," Dawn gasped. "So we can walk more or less upright."

"Or tie ourselves together," Eve added. "So we can be braced without using our hands."

They found some greenbriar vines, but they were too thorny to use. Then they saw a green rope leaping around. Forrest managed to snag it as it jumped over him. The rope struggled, wanting to be free to leap some more, but the girls grabbed hold of its ends and subdued it. "It's a jump rope," Eve gasped. They wound it around, and tied themselves into a clumsy mass. It worked, not well, but better than nothing, and the rope's natural inclination to jump helped. Imbri was the center, and the other four clustered around her, their feet bracing outward. It was uncomfortable, but feasible, for now.

Forrest was wedged against Ghina, because there needed to be two people to a side and the twins couldn't agree which one of them would get to press against the faun. Ghina was invisible within her cloak and cowl, and quickly shed those so as to be entirely invisible and less noticeable. But her body was solid. Forrest felt her wings brushing him every so often, and he was aware of other parts of her. He realized that he was in close contact with yet another healthy young woman. How did he keep getting into these situations?

"She's that way," Eve said, after touching the ground for information. "Not far."

So they trundled along in that direction. Forrest had no idea what they would do if something unfriendly spied them. They weren't in any condition to fend anything off. Maybe another storm package would drive it away, but maybe not.

"Say, I never realized that fauns were so interesting," Ghina murmured. "Do you suppose we could—?"

"Unfeasible," he said. Was there any point trying to explain about the effect faunish contact had on females?

"Oh," she said regretfully.

They half dragged, half jumped onward until they came to the greenhouse residence that Eve indicated was the one. Rather than knock on the glass door, and possibly freak someone out, they decided to let Imbri contact the woman with a dreamlet.

"Jfraya!" Imbri's joint dreamlet called, showing Imbri's human form in a green dress, properly upright. "May we speak with you?"

A woman appeared in the dreamlet. She was of course green, especially her thumbs, and carried a green watering can. "Who are you?"

"I am Mare Imbri, from another world. My friends and I need your help to stop the Wizards."

"But the Wizards haven't done us any harm," Jfraya protested.

"But they are doing others harm, by stealing from another world," Imbri responded. "We have in our group two people from that world, whose people are sorely suffering."

"What makes you think I can help?"

"Ida of the world of Torus said you could."

"Ida? But she's confined to an island on the blue face."

"Yes. She's Ida of Pyramid. The Ida I mean is on the world of Torus, which orbits her head." Imbri made an image of blue Ida and her doughnut shaped moon.

"This is too complicated to argue," Jfraya said. "So I suppose I'd better help you."

"Very good. I think your world will be better off without raiding other worlds. After all, you wouldn't want other worlds raiding yours."

"I suppose."

Then Imbri introduced the others of their party, in the dreamlet.

"But why are they all tied together? Are they prisoners?"

Imbri explained about the difficulty of walking on this face.

"Oh, I can fix that," Jfraya said. "Where do you want to go?"

"To the Green Wizard's castle, first."

Jfraya stepped outside her greenhouse. "Open this door," she said. She brought out a large pen and drew a crude door on the ground, with hinges on one side and a handle on the other. Then she went back into her house to finish watering her plants.

The group trundled up. Forrest reached down for the drawn handle. To his half surprise, he caught hold of it. He hauled on it, and the door opened, folding out of the ground. Below was a passage slanting down. It had a floor, a ceiling, and two sides. There was a faint green glow, so that it did not become dark deeper in. "You know, we could walk on one of the walls," Forrest said.

They untied themselves, one by one, and climbed down into the passage. Dawn went first, and stood on the slanting wall, which was about right for her orientation. Then Eve joined her. Their upper bodies were pointing slightly downward, so the wall was close to right angles to them. Their four dainty feet were aimed almost directly at Forrest.

"Say, we'd look good in skirts," Dawn said.

"Yes, considering the angle," Eve agreed.

Their red jeans fuzzed and became flaring red skirts. Forrest quickly clapped a hand to his eyes before he saw very far beyond their four nice knees. "Stop it!" he cried.

"Awww," they said together, laughing.

"I wish I could do that," Ghina murmured.

That intrigued him, though he knew it shouldn't. "Couldn't you, if you put on stockings and panties?"

"No. They're too close to my body. They turn invisible. Only the thicker material can retain its opacity."

"I'm sure it's for the best," he said insincerely.

"Their jeans are back," she informed him.

He ventured a look. Sure enough, it was safe. And probably the mischievous girls had not really let anything show. They knew that the mission wouldn't get far if they freaked him out in the middle of it.

Now he and Ghina climbed down into the hole and stood on the wall. Finally Imbri rolled over and in, and they were all there. Fortunately it was a large passage, with room, though there wasn't much clearance for their heads.

Then Jfraya emerged. "I think my greens have enough water for a few days," she said. She entered the passage, standing in its floor. This was awkward, because she was about at right angles to them, and their upper bodies were at cross purposes. But they would just have to give her space and make do.

They walked along the passage, giving each other sufficient room. "This goes to the Wizard's castle?" Forrest asked.

"It should. But I should warn you that one never can be quite certain what one will find along the way."

"But if you made this passage, there shouldn't be anything else along it, should there?"

"I made the door, not the passage. I made a door into a passage that goes to the Wizard's castle."

"Oh." That meant that they might not be safe, after all. "Are there likely to be dangers?"

"There could be. But I could make another door, to escape the passage."

Eve touched the floor, which was her wall. "This is a goblin tunnel!" she exclaimed.

"Why yes, so it is," Ghina said. "I should have recognized it, from my goblin heritage."

"But it is deserted," Dawn said.

"Good," Jfraya said. "I tried to pick an empty one."

They proceeded onward with greater confidence. In due course the passage opened into a series of galleries. In one some metallic green plants grew, with fierce straight spikes. "A steel plant!" Eve exclaimed. "They make swords from these." She touched one of the spikes. "Too bad we delicate girls don't know how to use swords."

They knew how to use whatever else they had, though, Forrest thought darkly.

The next chamber was encrusted with green gems. "Now these we might use," Eve said, touching one. "They are strata-gems, from the strato-sphere. They help folk devise plans."

Forrest agreed. "Let's harvest some and keep them for use when we need them."

So they pried several of the gems free, and each person put one in purse or pack.

The next chamber was filled with bouncing orange-green balls. "Basketballs," Eve said after checking. "For storage."

"Storage?"

She caught a ball and pulled at its binding. It opened out into a basket. "Put whatever it is inside, then close it up and let it bounce. It will keep until you open the basket ball again."

"Too bad we don't need to store anything," Ghina said. She had recovered her red cloak from somewhere and was wearing it, so they could see her general form.

They moved on. Before long they approached the surface. "No passages actually enter the castle," Jfraya said. "The Wizard saw to that. But they should exit in sight of it, and I can make a door through the wall. But it won't be safe; I understand that the Wizard has monsters and things guarding his premises."

"Leave them to me," Ghina said. "My talent is making folk sleep. When I was young, I thought I was just boring, but then I learned it was magic."

"And you will be able to approach them, because they can't see you," Jfraya said. "That's nice."

"Actually, they can smell me. But I'll put them to sleep before they can do us any harm."

"Still," Forrest said, "they could give the alarm. So we had better approach carefully."

"Let's wait until night," Dawn suggested. "Then we'll all be halfway invisible."

He nodded. "We might as well rest. We don't know exactly what we'll face inside the castle."

They foraged for something to eat. The first plant they found had berries like big green toes. "Well, maybe," Dawn said, touching it. "These fruits make a special kind of jam." She paused. "Toe jam."

"Ugh," Eve said, wrinkling her nose.

Then they found a sweetie Pi tree, with 3.14 sweetie pies, and feasted on them. After that they settled down in a chamber to which

Jfraya opened a door, and found a number of nice pillows therein. It was wonderful to relax for a while.

Forrest woke to find himself extraordinarily comfortable. Dawn was stroking his hair, Eve was polishing his hoofs, and Ghina and Jfraya were buffing his fingernails. He couldn't actually see Ghina, for she had evidently doffed her red cloak, but he felt her touch on his right hand.

"Uh—" he said, intelligently.

"Oh, you're awake," Dawn said.

"Then we had better get on with our mission," Eve said.

"Which is to get into the Green Wizard's castle," Ghina said.

"And inform the margins," Jfraya concluded.

Then they all laughed. They had had their little joke, making like quadruplets.

"I didn't mean to sleep," he said, embarrassed. "Just to rest."

Ghina squeezed his hand. "You forget my talent."

"We didn't want a male overhearing our Girl Talk," Jfraya said.

Oh. Well, at least that demonstrated that her talent was effective. It also left him curious about what they had talked about.

"The magic of fauns," Dawn said, answering his thought, to his further embarrassment.

"How they may not look like much, but their touch makes a girl think of long-legged birds."

"It's similar to the magic of nymphs," he said. "Just the sight of them running makes a male think of the same birds."

"But the magic of fauns also works on other females," Ghina said.

"So does the sight of other women running also work on fauns?" Jfraya asked.

"Yes," he said. "As does their soft touch, and their pretty speech. So if you girls don't mind—"

They laughed again, and let go of his extremities. Their Girl Talk must have established that this one faun was harmless.

"Yes," Imbri said, in a private dreamlet. "But they do like you, Forrest."

And he liked them. But they all had business to accomplish.

They organized themselves, then quietly exited the chamber. It was dark outside, but the green castle was illuminated from within, the pale green light spilling out through the green glass of the windows at each story. Several large, ugly, grotesque, and generally unpleasant green monsters patrolled the premises.

Unfortunately, they still could not stand on the green surface. Their feet wanted to be just slightly higher than their heads. In the ease of walking along the tunnel wall, they had forgotten the problem. Only Jfraya was properly upright.

"We will just have to crawl," Forrest decided. "It won't be comfortable, but it will get us there."

"Maybe I can fly," Ghina said. She tried it—and promptly flew sideways, almost colliding with a tree. They couldn't see her, but saw the disturbance in the air.

"Try flying up at a steep angle, or diving down," Forrest suggested.

Ghina experimented, and after a while managed to get the right orientation. "I think I'm flying almost straight up, but I'm really flying more or less level," she said. "I have room to make mistakes, if I stay high enough."

"I don't think I can crawl well enough," Imbri said. "But I think I can project my dreamlets as far as the castle. Why don't I remain here, and be with you in dreams?"

"Then we are ready," Forrest said. He started crawling mostly on his hands, pulling a foot down frequently to give a push. He was getting the clumsy hang of it. The others did similar maneuvers. The twins made intriguing outlines, with their jeans mostly in the air. He noticed that their hair fell to the side, instead of toward the ground. It was clearer than ever why few creatures crossed to faces of Pyramid not their own.

Ghina went first, spreading her invisible red wings and flying toward the nearest monster, which resembled a corpulent tangle tree with tentacle rot. In a moment that monster lay down to sleep; Ghina had exercised her talent.

In two and a half more moments, another monster lay down. That one was a cross between a huge green slug and a crushed caterpillar. Then the third and fourth, which were too ill-favored to describe. Now the six of them could approach the castle without being challenged.

But they were careful, because the folk inside the castle were not asleep, and if any of them looked out and saw the sleeping monsters, they might give the alarm. So there was no hurry, so that they would not stumble in the darkness, and no talking; they knew what they were doing. Any communication between them was to be handled by joint dreamlet.

There was no moat; apparently the Green Wizard believed that the monsters and wall sufficed. They reached the wall, and Forrest put his sensitive ear to it, instead of to the ground where it had been dragging, and listened. There was a faint sound to the side. That should be the margins. Eve touched the wall, and verified it; the little creatures were working inside. They went to the portion of the wall closest to that sound, and Jfraya drew a door. They opened it and stepped inside.

There were perhaps a dozen little green pyramids with triangular faces, sitting on the stone floor. From several of them green lines projected upward.

"Are these the margins?" Forrest asked mentally, his thought taking the form of a dreamlet that Imbri shared with the others. "Are they alive?"

"They are alive," Dawn replied in her own dreamlet as she touched the nearest pyramid. "But clothed in green stone. They live in the fissures of the stone. They can't move of their own accord, but can be moved by others. The Green Wizard brought them here."

"Can you establish contact with them?" he asked Imbri.

"I think so." Imbri formed a picture of a green pyramid. "Hello. I am a visitor from another world."

"Hello!" several pyramids chorused.

"Would you tell me what you are doing?"

"We are marginalizing a segment of Ptero, so as to improve it, and thus gain mass."

Dawn & Eve put their hands over their mouths, so as not to exclaim in maidenly indignation.

"How does marginalizing it improve it?" Imbri asked.

"There are bad folk there. Marginalizing captures them, and takes away their magic, so they can't do any more harm."

Dawn opened her mouth to protest, but Eve stifled her.

"Who told you this?"

"The Green Wizard."

"Let me show you how it really is," Imbri said. In the dreamlet, the world of Ptero appeared and expanded. There were happy people all across the human section. Then colored lines appeared, cutting people off, making the others afraid and unhappy. "Those are not bad folk," Imbri said. "They are good folk. They are being harmed by your margins."

"But how can this be so? The Green Wizard said we were doing great favors, and would grow greatly in size."

"And have you grown in size?"

"Not yet. We were wondering—"

"Yet you know you have captured many folk on Ptero. The change occurs instantly. So you must see that you are not doing favors. It is the Green Wizard who is growing in size—by giving away those stolen talents."

"It is true. He has become enormous."

"While you have not. So wouldn't it be better to stop helping him?"

The pyramids consulted. It seemed that however strong their magic might be, they were not phenomenally smart. "Yes," they decided. "We'll stop."

"Wait!" Forrest cried in his share of the dreamlet. "If the Green Wizard is stopped now, the other Wizards will be warned, and will be on guard. We need to delay it."

"It would be better if you waited three days," Imbri said. "Could you stop then?"

"Yes."

"Thank you." Then Imbri thought of something. "What will happen to you, if the Wizard is mad at you?"

"Nothing. If he bothers us, we'll marginalize him."

"Very good," Imbri said. "We thank you, and the world of Ptero will surely thank you, in due course."

They left the dungeon, well satisfied. The four monsters were beginning to twitch. Ghina didn't bother to put them to sleep again; it was better to have them wake and resume their guard duty, with the Green Wizard none the wiser. They were able to crawl fast enough to get clear before any monster actually woke.

"Well, that part of the mission went well," Forrest said. "But now we have three days to do the other three Wizards. I hope you can open doors to passages that go there, Jfraya."

"Oh, yes."

"Then let's do the Red Wizard next; I think that's the closest one."

"Actually they are all the same distance from each other," Eve said. "Because each is in the center of its triangle."

"But since we're red, we might as well do that one," Dawn said.

Jfraya opened a door to a passage slanting to the center of the red face, and they walked along its wall. That was a relief, after their struggle on the surface. This one was unused, like the other, but not perfect. They passed a gallery supported by pillars that resembled feline creatures: cat-I-pillars. There was what appeared to be a prison cell there, wherein was a comely young woman. "Look," Ghina said. "The goblins left a prisoner behind. We should rescue her."

"I don't trust this," Forrest said. "We had better first find out why they imprisoned her and left her, and why she seems healthy despite this neglect."

Eve touched a pillar, learning what it had seen. "That is a geis-a girl," she said, pronouncing it GAYSH-A. "Anyone who gets close to her may be caught by her geis, and have to do whatever she says."

They paused, reconsidering. "That's dangerous," Forrest said. "We don't know what she might demand. The goblins must have isolated her here deliberately, so she couldn't do them any mischief."

"Pretty girls are mischief," Dawn said.

"Especially those with strong magic," Eve added.

"I think we had better just leave her there," Forrest said regretfully. "We can't risk being diverted from our mission."

The others reluctantly agreed. "Uncle Grey Murphy could take away her magic, as punishment, if she did anything wrong on Ptero," Dawn said.

"But Uncle Grey is trapped in the margins," Eve said. "Caught before he could nullify their magic."

"Then maybe Mother Electra could use an Outlet to free her when no one else was near," Dawn suggested.

"Which is a secret passage only Mother Electra can open," Eve explained.

"That's interesting," Jfraya said. "I'd like to meet your mother."

"I don't know if that's possible," Forrest said. "We of larger worlds can travel to smaller ones by leaving most of our mass behind, but I think it would be more difficult for those of the smaller worlds to go to the larger ones. They would probably be insubstantial, and seem like ghosts."

"Maybe someone with the talent of blessing could reverse the curse of the geis-a girl's compulsion," Ghina said as they moved on.

Another chamber was filled with snakes. "I wish we had the blanket of obscurity now," Forrest said. "Those look poisonous."

Indeed, in a moment they were surrounded by very poisonous looking snakes. The snakes were on the floor, while most of the people were on a wall, but in the confines of the passage they were close enough. "There are too many for me to put to sleep," Ghina said.

"And they could follow if I made another door," Jfraya said.

Forrest couldn't think of anything intelligent to do, so he tried something stupid: "Take us to your leader!"

The snakes made a path through their number toward a special cave. Forrest and his party walked the nearest wall in that direction. Here lay a large snake wearing a crown. "It's the King Cobra," Dawn whispered.

Forrest had another idea, not nearly as stupid as the last one. "O King Cobra, we crave a favor," he said. "We need to proceed quickly to the Red Wizard's castle."

The king nodded. Several monstrous snakes slithered up. The travelers, including Imbri, climbed onto these snakes, and were carried swiftly onward. They rode at a considerable angle, but the snakes seemed to understand.

Forrest looked back. Sure enough, the King Cobra looked a size larger.

Soon they were at the end of the tunnel. They slid off the snakes, who seemed even larger than before, and moved back out onto the red surface. Now they were correctly oriented, except for Jfraya. She had to lie on Imbri's back, because she couldn't stand on the ground.

It was still night. They proceeded directly to the Red Castle, and Ghina put its guardian monsters to sleep. Except for one. This was an animated angle.

"I recognize that," Eve said. "It's a guardian angle. It protects folk against math courses."

"But we aren't math courses," Forrest said.

"Right." She approached the guardian. "Please don't let any math courses get us," she beseeched it.

The angle nodded its acute point graciously. It would protect them from that threat.

They entered the castle in the same manner as they had the other, and explained things to the red margins inside. The margins agreed to cease operations in two and a half days.

They emerged, and passed through a door to a passage leading directly to the blue face. This one, however, was not completely deserted. "But there aren't any really bad folk on it," Eve said, after touching its wall. "Except maybe the cuss today."

"A toad that swears?" Forrest asked.

"Not exactly. It is found in the grounds for divorce. If we avoid the chamber where those grounds are, it shouldn't bother us."

They avoided that chamber by taking a detour. On the alternate passage they encountered a man of many colors. His skin was not blue, red, green, or gray, which explained why he wasn't walking the surface of Pyramid. Instead it was rainbow colored.

"Hello," the man said. "I am Hue Man."

The six of them introduced themselves, then moved on. It wasn't that there seemed to be anything wrong with Hue Man, who seemed completely human, but that they were in a hurry to complete their mission, and didn't care to advertise it, lest word get to the Wizards.

It was a long trip to the blue face, and by the time they reached it the night was done. They had to remain in the passage. Forrest still had some food in his knapsack, and Ghina had some invisible sandwiches, so they ate lightly and relaxed.

When night arrived, they went out onto another face where they couldn't walk. This time they tilted the opposite way, but it hardly mattered; their feet still wanted to be slightly above their heads. Jfraya's feet went the opposite direction from theirs. But again Ghina was able to adjust her flying, and she put the monsters to sleep so that the group could crawl in and alert the margins.

This time they learned something new. The blue margins mentioned that they were able to communicate along their lines. That was how they identified people trapped within the enclosures formed by the lines. So if anyone got in the line of sight of a line, between the margin and the world of Ptero, he or she would be able to talk to the margin generating it. The lines did not become solid barriers until they were close to the surface of Ptero, because there was no sense wasting magic. Actually, the whole of Pyramid was close to the surface of Ptero, but Forrest understood what they meant. The lines went up to the top of Castle Roogna, then bent at right angles, and came down after another bend to intercept the ground. Only with that last bend did they become actual walls.

"So if we climbed to the top of the Wizard's castle, we could intercept the lines and talk to you," Forrest said, getting it straight.

"Yes. That is how the Blue Wizard does it."

However, it seemed enough of a challenge just to crawl into the dungeon from the ground. Trying to get to the top of the castle seemed pointless.

They got the margins to agree to stop in a day and a half, and crawled back out. One Wizard to go!

Outside, Jfraya cast about uncertainly. "I can't find a suitable passage to open a door to," she complained. "There just don't seem to be passages to the bottom face."

"It wasn't a place the goblins wanted to go to," Ghina said. "Mother commented about that. It's all stormy and cold."

"That's right," Jfraya agreed, remembering. "Because it never gets any direct sunlight, and is always in shadow. By most accounts, it's this world's dullest face."

"But trying to trek all across this face to the edge, and then all across the gray face, would take days," Forrest said. "We have to move faster than that."

"It will have to be on the surface," Jfraya said. "There aren't any safe passages."

"Maybe we could get rides," Dawn suggested.

"On cooperative centaurs," Eve added.

"Can you locate such centaurs, quickly?" Forrest asked, feeling halfway desperate.

"I think so," Dawn said, touching a tree. "They pass by here often enough."

"And their prints form paths," Eve said, touching the ground.

"So let's go and ask them a favor," Forrest said.

"Is that wise?" Imbri asked. "We are all smaller than we were."

"If we don't accomplish the mission, our size won't much matter," he pointed out.

The others nodded. "I'm sorry I couldn't find a suitable door to make," Jfraya said. "This seems to be the best alternative."

"They are said to live in the Atlas Mountains," Dawn said, reading her tree.

"Which are beyond the tropical depression," Eve said, reading her ground.

"Are they within ready crawling distance?"

"Yes, if we go straight there," Dawn said.

"Which means going through the depression, which isn't fun," Eve said.

"We aren't here for fun," Forrest said.

They started crawling in the indicated direction. Imbri, who just couldn't crawl well, decided to wait where she was; they would arrange to pick her up later.

Soon the ground sank lower as they entered the depression. Exotic warm weather plants grew in it. But Forrest started feeling extremely sad. Was any of this worthwhile? Or would it be better just to quit trying?

"Oh, I'm depressed!" Jfraya complained.

"That's because of the tropical depression," Eve said. "Just crawl on through it."

Forrest was glad he hadn't spoken. He had assumed that it was just a warm low place. Now he knew better.

Beyond the depression rose the peaks of mountains, shown outlined against the dimly illuminated sky. Then they reached the base of the first mountain—and discovered that it consisted of piled books. Atlases. What else had he expected?

"Watch out for the bookworm," Eve warned.

They paused in their crawling as a large worm crawled across their route. Its segments consisted of books.

At last they reached the centaur village. Centaurs came bearing torches. "Don't you folk of the red face know you can't travel red-ily here?" one demanded. "You're just not red-dy for the blue."

Forrest dispensed with explanations. "We need to be carried to the gray face," he said. "There is also a mare who will require several to carry her."

"Are you asking for favors?"

"Yes."

"And you know the consequence?"

"Yes."

"Then we are glad to help. I am Chaz Centaur." He looked around. "Chalice—you take the faun."

An earthy brown-blue mare trotted up. She was as well endowed as the usual centaur filly, which was impressive by the standards of lesser females. Forrest tried to mount her back, but couldn't; his angle was wrong. Finally she picked him up with her arms, pressed him to her ample bare bosom, twisted him around, and plopped him on her back. Once firmly set there, he was able to hang on and maintain his position.

"Chafe and Chide—take the girls."

Two sneering young stallions trotted up. The sneers faded when they got two good looks at the girls. Then they became very helpful. One picked up Dawn and set her on the other's back; then the other picked up Eve and set her on the first one's back. The girls, quickly zeroing in on the situation, were very appreciative and flattering. Two males who might have been annoying were quickly being tamed.

"Checkers—take the green lady."

A dappled stallion trotted up, and managed to get Jfraya on his back.

Chaz looked around. "Is that all?"

"No," Ghina called. She donned her red cloak so as to become partly visible. "I am a winged goblin girl from the red face."

"Chenille—take her."

A centaur filly trotted up, and managed to get Ghina aboard.

"Now where is this mare?"

"Across the tropical depression, toward the Blue Wizard's castle," Forrest said.

"We'll go around that." The centaurs got moving, while their passengers hung on. Soon they reached Imbri. "Chicory, Chiffon, Chime, Chip," Chaz said, and four more centaurs trotted up. "Chenille, sew a sling."

Ghina's filly brought out cloth, and with magical speed formed a sling suitable for a horse. The four other centaurs lifted Imbri onto it, then picked up the four corners, which had been fashioned into harnesses. These harnesses went over their heads and around their human torsos, so that they did not need to use their hands to hold on. They took up their positions and stretched the harness taut. Imbri was hauled into the air.

"To the Gray border: march," Chaz said. All ten centaurs set off in perfect step.

They were on their way. But Forrest felt lighter; he and the others were paying a price for this invaluable assistance.

"How is it that a red faun is traveling here?" Chalice asked him.

"My companions and I are trying to carry out an important mission," he explained. "Several of us are actually from another world." Then, to divert her attention, he asked about her. "Where I come from, not all centaurs have magic talents. Do—"

"Certainly. My talent is with pottery. I can fashion blue-brown clay into excellent utensils. The other centaurs have talent too. You saw Chenille's ability as a seamstress. Checkers has great ability with board games. Chicory is a herbalist. Chiffon can make things transparent. Chime is an excellent minstrel. And Chip can shatter objects. He's my foal," she added proudly. "We discovered his talent at the expense of a vase."

Thus the time passed amicably enough. Soon they came to the edge. "You know, it's cold around the corner," Chaz said. "Would you like warm garments?"

Forrest looked at the bleak landscape beyond. "Yes, I think we had better have that favor too," he agreed with resignation.

In moments Chenille had made warm caps and jackets and trousers for all of them, including Imbri. The six members of their party were surely slightly smaller, because of this favor, and Chenille became the largest of the centaurs. "Thank you," Forrest said.

"You are all welcome," Chaz replied. Then he produced a horn from his pack. "Here is a bull horn. If you return this way and need more favors, blow it."

"A bull horn summons centaurs?"

"No. It summons bulls, of course. They graze at the bull market. But we will hear the stampede of their hoofs, and come to investigate. You would not want to ask favors of the bulls."

"Are bulls bad folk?"

"No worse than the bears, generally. But these ones can be. Edi and Para Bull are all right, with their food and stories, but Stum is clumsy, Trem is fearful, and you wouldn't want to encounter Trou or Terri. You wouldn't believe Incredi Bull."

"Surely not," Forrest agreed.

They bid parting to the centaurs, and crawled over the edge onto the gray face. Immediately a chill wind rose, stirred by their presence, and blew snow in their faces. They were at a different angle here, but it was no better than the other angles; they were unable to walk. They could slide somewhat on the snow, which facilitated things, but this promised to be a difficult journey.

"Do you think we could get more help traveling?" Forrest asked. "I fear we'll never make it, at this rate."

"I'm checking the snow," Eve said. "But it's freshly fallen, and doesn't have much experience of this region."

"And there don't seem to be any living creatures or plants here," Dawn said.

So they slogged on. They found that they could slide Imbri across the snow, especially if they braced each other so as to get good temporary footholds. So progress improved. But it was still too slow.

At last, as the day faded, worn out with the struggle, they had Jfraya open a door into an isolated cave. It was blessedly warm, and they were able to stand comfortably on the walls, but Dawn and Eve were doubtful. "There are mites," Dawn said. "Stalag mites."

"And they stop anyone from using this cave," Eve added.

"Too bad," Forrest said. "We need to rest here. We're protected by our clothing." For all of them were wearing closely fitting jackets and pants that kept them warm despite the weather. They did not remove them right away, preferring to be sure the cave was safe.

Forrest looked at the stone spikes hanging from the cave ceiling, and rising from the floor. "What are these called?"

"Stalactites and stalagmites," Eve said, touching them. "The first descend from the ceiling, and the second rise from the floor."

"How can we keep that straight?" Jfraya asked. "They sound so much alike."

Suddenly Forrest jumped. "Something bit my leg!" he said, trying to scratch at it through the tight trousers. It was not a problem he had had before, because he normally did not wear clothing on his furred lower half.

Then the twins jumped. "Ooo!" Dawn cried. "Something bit my calf."

"And something bit my thigh," Eve said. "It's the mites. They are crawling up under our tights."

Then all of them were jumping and trying to scratch.

"We have to get them off," Jfraya said, yanking down her own pants.

Forrest turned away from her, as a matter of courtesy, but that turned him toward the twins, who were yanking down theirs. Their bare legs were astonishingly nice, but he tried not to notice. In any event he was busy pulling down his own, so as to be able to get at the biting mites.

In two thirds of a moment all of them were bare-legged and scratching off the mites. Then Ghina managed to fill the cave with her sleep spell, and the remaining mites fell asleep and dropped off. However, the spell also affected the rest of them, though more slowly because they were more massive. So they lay down to sleep.

The last thing Forrest remembered was Imbri's dreamlet. "Now we know how to remember the stone columns," she said. "when the mites go up, the tites come down." He groaned and tried to forget it.

After some time, he woke, and so did the others. The mites seemed to have given up, or maybe they remained stunned by the sleep spell. But it was time to resume travel. So they pulled their leggings back on, tightened their jackets, and braved the snow above.

It wasn't as bad as they remembered it. It was worse. The snow had piled up until it was chest high on Forrest, and it was dense and hard. This promised to be absolutely awful.

"Say," Imbri said in a joint dreamlet. "Why can't we use the snow the same way as we do the cave walls?"

The others turned to her, not understanding. But then she made a dreamlet picture, showing a path being trampled into the snow—sidewise. So that five of them could walk on it, sidewise, and the sixth, Jfraya, could walk on the other side of it.

Suddenly it made sense. Jfraya and Dawn held each other, their heads going in opposite directions, and used their feet to stomp banks of snow to either side. When they tired, Eve and Forrest tried it, she using her feet to stomp while using her hands to hold him in place so he could use his own hands to beat the snow into shape on the other side.

It worked, to a degree: Imbri was able to walk on the sideways path, her body scraping the snow of the center. But it was too slow. They needed not merely to use the path quickly, but to make it quickly. So they simplified it. Since only Jfraya faced the other way, her path was for her alone, and she hardly needed it once she had made it. So she became a brace instead, stabilizing the others without wearing herself out. That allowed the others to take turns, with one tramping out the path while the others followed, walking normally.

So their progress improved. Still, they had a long way to go, and the terrain was rough, and their time was limited. They needed to reach the Gray Wizard's castle by dusk, to be sure of their success. When they encountered steep hills, they were able to tramp their sidewise path more readily. When they came to a frozen lake, they slid rapidly across it. But as the day passed, it slowly became clear that they were not going to make it in time.

Worse, Jfraya slipped and injured one foot. Now she had to hop, following the path at the rear, and leaning on Imbri for support.

"So do we plow on through the night, hoping the Wizard has not gotten the word about the other Wizards?" Forrest asked. "Or do we take our time, recover our strength, and hope we can handle him anyway?"

The others exchanged a circular glance. "We plow on," Jfraya said. Since she was the injured one, that was enough.

They plowed on, and in the night they finally spied the gray light of the Wizard's castle. It was surrounded by snow-covered trees and looked peaceful. "Maybe he doesn't know," Eve breathed.

But as they made their way to the castle's outer wall, passing the ring of trees, Eve stiffened. She signaled Dawn, who brushed by the tree Eve had just touched. Then came a joint dreamlet: "Those are orc trees."

Forrest felt a chill not of the landscape. Orc trees were actually huge vicious animals that resembled trees only when in repose. They were the most dangerous of guardians. They might be snoozing now, but if they came alert, they might pounce too suddenly for Ghina to put to sleep. It would be impossible for them to flee these monsters at any speed, because of their sidewise orientation. The party had to hope that the orcs were not alert. So far that seemed to be the case.

They fetched up against the castle wall, at last able to stand almost normally. What a relief that was!

Eve touched the stone with a finger. "There is no disturbance within," she announced via dreamlet. "A number of living creatures are on the other side."

Forrest nodded. Jfraya drew a door on the base of the castle wall, and opened it. They entered the dark chamber. It looked as if they were going to win after all. They found an inner wall to stand on, Jfraya still leaning on Imbri.

Suddenly lights came on. They were surrounded by creatures, and none of them looked friendly. It was a trap.

"So you come at last, my pets," a huge dark woman said. "But where is your last member?"

This must be the Wizard—or Wizardess. It hadn't occurred to Forrest that the Wizard could be female, but of course it was possible. More than possible. It hardly mattered; they had walked into a trap, with the orcs outside and the Wizard's guards inside. All the Wizard had had to do was wait.

"Last member?" Forrest asked blankly.

"It was reported that there were six in your party. Where is the last one hiding?"

"No one is hiding," Forrest said. "We are all here." For Ghina was visible, in her heavy winter clothing.

The huge woman frowned. "So you think to deceive me. We shall see about that. Cerci!"

Two servants pushed forward a large tank of water. In it was a mermaid, her tail in the water, her head above the surface. "Yes, mistress," the mermaid said.

"Change—" The Wizard looked around. "That one." She pointed to Ghina.

The mermaid reached her arm toward Ghina. "Oink!" she said.

And Ghina became a visible pig.

Forrest was appalled. So was Ghina. She squealed as her clothing dropped off. She ran around the floor. She was clearly horrified.

Guards circled the pig and prodded it into a cage. It looked out, tears welling from its eyes, understanding its plight.

The Wizard turned back to Forrest. "Now I ask you again, faun: where is your sixth member? Where is she hiding?"

"But no one is hiding," Forrest said.

The Wizard pointed to Jfraya. "That one."

The mermaid gestured again. "Oink."

And Jfraya became another pig. She was just as chagrined as Ghina.

"It will be kinder if you tell me," the Wizard said. "Otherwise, after all of you are swine, we shall just have to hunt her down and kill her. Now where is she?"

Suddenly Dawn caught on. "She thinks Imbri's an animal!" she said in a dreamlet.

"So one person is missing," Eve added.

And the Wizard was going to turn them all into pigs, trying to find that missing member of their party. She was really taking this matter seriously.

But that gave him the key to victory. "Imbri!" he said in the dreamlet. "Locate the margins, with your dreamlets. Tell them. Now."

Then he spoke aloud to the Wizard. "She is hidden where you will never think to look. She will destroy your power. You can turn us all into pigs, but she will get you."

"So now you are ready to deal," the Wizard said, satisfied. "Turn her over to me, and I will let all of you live."

"As prisoners?" he asked. Actually he knew she would kill them, thus effectively banning them from this region. But he was stalling for time.

"Perhaps," the Wizard said. "Unless you agree to use your talents on my behalf, so I can take over the provinces of the three lost Wizards."

So that was why she even bothered to negotiate! She wanted to increase her power yet more.

"We won't do anything as pigs," he said. He glanced at Jfraya's cage—and saw that she had opened a door in it and was escaping. Neither the Wizard nor the guard monsters had noticed.

That gave him another notion. "Ghina," he said in a dreamlet. "Put the mermaid to sleep."

The Wizard considered. "It will be double or nothing. If you serve me, you can have your natural forms back. If you don't, you can be fed to my hungry orcs."

"How do I know you won't feed us to the orcs anyway?"

"You're stalling. Cerci! That one." The Wizard pointed to Dawn.

There was no response. The mermaid had fallen asleep.

The Wizard glanced at her. **"Cerci!"** she snapped.

The mermaid was jolted awake. She looked surprised.

The Wizard squinted. "So one of you has the ability to induce sleep. Then we shall delay no more. Polly!"

Another young woman approached, coming from the far chamber.

"Polly Graph, tell me the truth," the Wizard said. She faced Forrest again. "Where is your sixth member?"

Polly's talent had to be to know when a person lied. So Forrest was careful. "She is here."

The Wizard looked at Polly. "It's true," Polly said.

But Polly couldn't read the whole truth in the subject's mind. So as long as he told part of the truth, while evading what the Wizard wanted to know, he could get away with it. Still stalling for time.

"*Where* is she here?"

Oops. The Wizard was too sharp. What could he say? He said nothing.

"Cerci. That one."

This time the mermaid did it, and Dawn became a very pretty light colored pig.

"The answer," the Wizard said. "Now."

Could Imbri still communicate with the margins, if she were changed into a pig? Probably so. The Wizard didn't realize that animals had intelligence. But if he identified Imbri, the Wizard might have her immediately killed. He couldn't risk it. "I won't tell you," he said.

"That one." And Eve was a lovely dark pig.

Now there was only Forrest and Imbri. And only very limited time before they were finished. If the Wizard had them all killed now, she would win. Maybe it was time to tell the truth. He hoped that would give Imbri the time she needed.

"She is here," he said. "She is this one." He indicated the mare.

"Impossible! That's just a beast of burden."

"It's true, mistress," Polly said.

The Wizard stared at her. "This beast?"

"Yes, mistress. He is speaking the truth."

"So I have them all. None are still out there."

"You have us all," Forrest said.

"Good. Now I need to know how you destroyed the other Wizards."

So she knew only the fact, not the detail. "We stopped the margins."

"True," Polly said.

"Idiot! Of course they stopped the margins! But *how*?"

"We talked to them," Forrest said. "We told them the truth."

The Wizard nodded. "So I think I know enough. Guards, take all these creatures out to the orcs."

The guards closed in. But then a strange look crossed the Wizard's face. Something was happening to her. "Oh, I'm shrinking! I'm shrinking!" she wailed. "You horrible faun! Look what you've done!"

In half a moment the Wizard was the size of an elf. Imbri had gotten through, and the margins had cut off their lines. All the Wizard's stolen favors had been canceled, and she had reverted to her original size.

"You've destroyed the Wizard's power!" Polly said, amazed.

"True," Forrest said. "She will never again be able to exert such magic."

"Hey, that's great!" Cerci said. "But who will rule in her place?"

"All of you who served her are now free." He hoped they wanted to be free.

"Gee. Do you want your friends depigmented?"

"Yes, if you please. Then we shall have to go home—as I hope the rest of you will do." Actually, once they left this world, they would be able to form their natural shapes. But Ghina and Jfraya wouldn't. So it was better to get them changed back now.

They had won. And it was time to return to Ptero.

12
SPIRIT

J ust a moment." It was the former Gray Wizard, who was now a gray elf. Polly had grabbed her before she could escape.

Forrest looked at her. "You are hoping for better treatment than you accorded us?"

"Yes. Because you are kinder people than I was."

"True," Polly said.

"Why shouldn't we just have you changed into a piglet and put outside with the orcs?"

"Because you are too soft hearted, and I can be useful to you."

Forrest looked around. Cerci had changed all his companions back to their original forms. So no permanent damage had been done. "How can you be useful?"

"I can tell the orcs to obey the new mistress of the castle, so you won't have any trouble."

"Mistress?"

"Your green door opener. She would like the cushy lifestyle available as mistress of the Gray Castle."

"True," Polly said.

"But I never—" Jfraya protested.

"The folk here are a unit," the Gray Elf said. "They like working here. They just don't like me. If you treat them well, they will serve you well."

"True," Polly said.

"But I assumed they were all captives," Forrest said.

"True," Polly said. "You did so assume, but it is false. We were better off serving the Gray Wizard than we would have been out in the snow."

Jfraya remained bemused. "You, Cerci—you don't want to go home to the sea?"

"Well, maybe for visits," the mermaid said. "To see my parents, Cyrus and Merci. But the truth is that the water out there is cold, and I am more comfortable here in the heated pool."

Forrest realized that the elf was performing a useful service. She had gotten huge by doing services for many people, so was good at it, even if she had stolen what she gave away. "How about Ghina?" he asked.

"I know where there is a winged male goblin of relatively sweet disposition, on the blue face, where she never would have found him."

Ghina's outfit stood up straight. "How does he feel about appearance?"

"It is a matter of indifference to him. He is blind. This has severely restricted his flight and his social life. However, if he had a companion willing to guide him, he would be most grateful."

The elf was scoring. "What do you want in return?" Forrest asked. "Because we are not going to let you do too many favors and regain your size."

"Only to be returned to my home elf village, where they have no idea of my career after departing."

Forrest looked at the two women. "Are you amenable?"

"Yes," they agreed, almost together.

"Then I leave the premises in your charge, Jfraya, provided you will see to Ghina's trip to the blue face, the Gray Elf's safe return to her village, and any visits elsewhere that other members of this household desire."

"Gladly," Jfraya said.

"True," Polly said.

He looked at the twins and Imbri, who were standing on the wall. "Then let's return to Pyramid."

"But will you visit?" Jfraya asked. "I haven't known you long, but it has been thrilling."

The twins exchanged a glance. "We'll try," Dawn said.

"Now that we know how to do it."

"But that requires the Good Magician's bottle of soul dissolving elixir," Forrest said.

"We didn't need it to return from Torus," Imbri reminded him.

She was right; he had never thought of using the bottle. They had just expanded. So it seemed it was needed only for the "up" loading, not the "down" loading.

"I'll leave the bottle with you," Forrest said. "Since it seems that Imbri and I don't need it to return to Xanth."

Then they held hands and touched Imbri, and expanded their substance, diffusing into vapor and thence into spirituality. The castle shrank around them, and they drifted out through its substance.

The world of Ptero was below them, or rather, around them, shrouded in night. They headed for it, expanding as they went. Pyramid became a triangle-faceted world behind them, and the monstrous outline of Ida's head became apparent before them. They were more experienced at this than they had been, and quickly zeroed in on the star-like candle that Princess Ida had set out to guide them. There were their bodies, in repose. He was surprised to see that Imbri's was in girl form, until he remembered that this was all that she had mass for, here.

They went through the somewhat unpleasant business of re-entering their bodies. Forrest wondered briefly what would happen if anyone tried to enter the wrong body by mistake. Would he find himself in Dawn's body, or would Eve be in Imbri's? He hoped not. Surely there was some magical safeguard against it.

He opened his eyes and sat up. The others were doing the same. He glanced at the Tapestry, and saw that no lines were marked on it.

"Well, we're back," Dawn said.

"Which means the faun will soon be moving on," Eve agreed.

"Now that our mission with him is complete."

"So we had better get to our other business before he escapes."

The two of them stood, somewhat unsteadily, and converged on Forrest.

"But we don't yet know the outcome," he protested. It wasn't that he objected to the sort of dalliance the girls had in mind, but that this did not seem like the proper place for it. Fauns normally chased nymphs in pleasant glades, not castles.

"There is an outcome," Ida said. "Follow me." She stood and walked to the door.

They did so. They went down the stairs and through the hall to the main ballroom. Ida opened the door.

The room was packed with people. "Thank you!" they cried in one mighty voice.

Forrest, Imbri, and the twins stood amazed. Then the twins made twin shrieks of delight. "Everyone's back," Dawn said.

"Daddy!" Eve cried.

They ran to embrace their father, Prince Dolph.

"You see, your Service was for the Good Magician," Ida said. "So none of the incidental beneficiaries owe you exchange services. But they are nevertheless most grateful."

King Ivy approached. "The rescued folk wish to meet you and thank you. Perhaps we should form a receiving line. This way."

They followed her through the crowd to the stage section of the room. Forrest and Imbri stood there while the line formed. He still was having trouble getting used to her as a small dark woman, rather than a dark horse.

King Ivy snapped her fingers. There was immediate silence. "Forrest Faun and Mare Imbrium will meet each of you in turn. Please introduce yourselves as you approach, and do not dally unduly. They are surely tired from their unusual journey. There will be a banquet at—" She paused to look at her left wrist, where a collection of eyes resided. Then she looked at her right wrist, where a pack of tiny dogs were sitting. "At dawn, according to my watch band, and my watch dogs," she concluded.

The first in the line was a young woman. "I am Wigo, daughter of Hugo and Wira. My talent is draining magic, but I could not prevail against the margins. I am so grateful to you for doing it and rescuing us all!"

"Uh, sure, thank you," Forrest said, taken aback by such gratitude.

"We were glad to do it," Imbri said in a dreamlet.

The next one approached, a very small woman. "I am Glitter Golem, daughter of Grundy and Rapunzel. My talent is the sparkle." She illustrated by issuing a shower of sparkles. "Thank you so much for saving us!"

"Uh—" Forrest began.

"It was so nice meeting you," Imbri's dreamlet said.

Next were two young folk. One was a handsome young man in a gray suit. "I am Prince Grant, with the talent of reading minds," he said.

The other was a young woman with green eyes and brown hair, in a green dress. "I am Princess Isabella Emily Carolyn, with the talent of borrowing talents, for an hour," she said.

"We are children of Grey and Ivy," Grant added.

"But aren't there already—?" Forrest began.

"There are many of us, in this realm of might-be," Isabella explained. "And my friend Arien has a similar talent. Might-be covers a lot."

Oh. Of course Forrest knew that. How stupid he had been to forget.

"No, we understand about the difference in your world," Grant said.

"We would be similarly confused, there," Isabella agreed.

"Uh, you two remind me of—"

"Our cousins Dawn & Eve."

"So nice to meet both of you," Imbri's dreamlet cut in.

The two laughed and moved on. Forrest realized that Imbri had a much better notion of how to meet people than he did. She was preventing him from hopelessly embarrassing himself worse than he already was.

A child approached. "I am Nora Naga, daughter of Nina Naga and Briskil, son of Esk Ogre and Bria Brassie," she said. "I am twelve years old and my talent is to teleport folk or things anywhere. I wish I had someone to play with. Maybe now that everyone is back, I'll find someone."

The next one came up, a grown man. "I am Trenris, the son of Magician Trent and Sorceress Iris, following their rejuvenation."

"But they were rejuvenated only three or four years ago," Imbri said, this time speaking directly in her surprise. "How can you be full grown?"

"Well, of course I can be, on Ptero, where geography is time," he said. "But I take it that you mean I should be no more than about fourteen years old at this particular site. And the answer is that I *am* fourteen, but that I age rapidly, because they are both actually much older than they look. My talent is that of reversing the effect of other talents, thus making illusions literal or magical spots on the wall fade. But I wish someone could reverse my aging, before I become decrepit in my youth. However, that is neither here nor there; I came to congratulate you on the success of your mission, and to thank you for saving all of us from the dread marginalization."

"Wait," Imbri said. "Have you met Surprise?"

"I have been surprised by many things."

"No, I mean Surprise Golem, daughter of Grundy and Rapunzel. She has multiple talents, each of which she can use only once. Maybe she would change your rate of aging, if you helped her in some way."

"This sounds interesting. I will look for her."

"We met her sister Glitter," Forrest said. "She should know where to find Surprise."

"I do know Glitter," he said. "I will ask her. Thank you for something more."

"You're welcome," Imbri said.

A severe looking woman approached. "I am Misty Meanor, a curse fiend," she said. "I come to thank you not merely for myself, but for two who cannot be here directly: Gim and Gine giant, the children of Girard and Gina Giant. They are too big to enter the castle."

"But I thought the marginalization affected only the regular human section," Forrest said.

"The giants happened to be within it, and were caught. Now they are free, and hope to return a favor to you if they can."

Forrest looked at Imbri. "We will be traveling west, that is, To, tomorrow. If they could carry us some of the way—"

"I'm sure they would be glad to," Misty said, moving on.

A dusky youth stepped up. "I am Chaos, son of D. Metria after she discovered how to summon the stork effectively. I turn things transparent.''

The line continued, until Forrest lost track of all the names and talents. The folk were all duly grateful, but he wished that this could just end, so that they could go to the banquet, and then be on their way.

Then, suddenly, the end of the line came. There were two handsome young princes. ''We are Mourning & Knight,'' one said.

''The sons of Prince Naldo Naga and Mela Merwoman,'' the other added.

''We don't have talents as such, but we are extremely virile princes.''

Something jogged in Forrest's tired mind. ''Have you met the princesses Dawn & Eve?''

''We haven't had that pleasure, but we did catch a glimpse of them from across the room when the four of you entered. They look lovely.''

''I will send them a dreamlet,'' Imbri said.

It was effective. In a moment the two princesses came up.

''I thought you might want to meet Princes Mourning & Knight,'' Forrest said. ''The sons of—'' He broke off, because they were no longer paying him any attention.

The two princes were gazing at the two princesses, and steam was starting to rise from them. The two princesses were glancing at the two princes, and little hearts were floating out from them. In about three quarters of a moment, the four linked hands and walked away together.

''I think we won't be seeing them again,'' Imbri murmured.

''But we were going to—that is, the girls and I—''

''Did you really want to?''

''Yes! That is—''

''Do you really feel you should?''

''No.'' And he realized that along with his disappointment was a significant admixture of relief. After all, they were princesses, and he was just a faun. Their parents surely would Not Approve.

Imbri took his arm. ''It's time for the banquet.''

"I'll leave the bottle for them, so they can visit Pyramid again if they want to," he said.

"Princess Ida will surely keep it safe."

"Indeed I will," Ida said, taking the bottle.

The banquet was formidable, but Forrest was distracted. He remembered that all this was but a diversion from his main mission, which was to find a faun for his neighbor's tree. He wasn't sure how much time had passed in Xanth, but surely a fair amount. He needed to get on with it.

"Of course," Imbri murmured, understanding his concern. "The giants are waiting outside."

So they were. They were invisible, but Imbri located them by their minds. The two of them climbed into Gim or Gine's hand—it was a bit hard to tell the brother giants apart—and were lifted high.

"To the faun territory," Imbri told the giants in a dreamlet. "Or as close to it as you can go."

"Our territory borders theirs," a giant boomed. "But it will take a few hours, because we must step carefully in human territory, lest we squish somebody."

"That's all right," Forrest said. "I need some rest anyway." For after meeting all the people, and the banquet, he was quite tired.

"Sleep," Imbri told him, sitting down and taking his head into her lap. "I will send you sweet dreams." She stroked his hair.

Her dreams were very nice, and he reveled in them. This was the way to travel!

Then the trip ended. "We are too old to take you farther," a giant said. Indeed, his hand was wrinkled. "But immediately To is the faun section. We wish you success."

"Thank you," Forrest said, sitting up and sliding off the huge old hand. He felt much refreshed; Imbri's lap and dream had helped greatly. When his hoofs touched the ground, he turned and reached up to help Imbri down. Her slight girl form was pleasantly light.

They heard the shudder of the ground as the giants departed. Immediately west was a comic strip. Oh, no! If only the giants had been able to set them just beyond it.

There was nothing to do but plow through it. They braced themselves and did that. The first part of it was a paved section that looked deceptively innocent, but as soon as they stepped on it, there was a horrendous barking, as of dozens of fierce dogs. They jumped back, and the noise stopped.

"But I don't see any dogs," Forrest said.

Imbri explored with her dream mind. "There don't seem to be any."

So they tried again—and the barking resumed. No dogs, just the sounds.

"It's a barking lot!" Imbri cried, catching on.

Forrest groaned. "They should outlaw these zones."

"But then the puns would be infesting everything else, just as they do in Xanth."

That made him pause. "Maybe I can live with the comic strips after all."

As they came to the far edge of the lot, there was a deep dark pool. There was a narrow path around it. But the path was blocked by a many-toothed monster. "Can you guess my talent?" the monster enunciated precisely.

"Why should I?" Forrest asked.

"Because I won't let you use this path otherwise."

"Then maybe I'll just go around the other way, or swim across the pond," Forrest said.

"Suit yourself, if you can handle the rays."

They circled the pool in the other direction. But blocking that path was a squat box with a grill on the front. As they approached, it shot out rays of bad music. The closer they got, the worse the music got, until it was so utterly obnoxious that they had to fall back, with their hands over their ears.

"What is that thing?" Forrest demanded as the music faded to merely annoying.

"It's a Ray D O, stupid," the monster called. "The ray's letters stand for Deafening and Obnoxious. Only teenagers can approach it."

So it seemed. They returned to the monster. "What's your name?" Forrest inquired.

"Airy. Can you guess my talent?"

"Chomping folk?"

"One guess wrong. You evidently can't find the right words."

"Evidently not," Forrest agreed sourly.

He looked again at the pool. It seemed clear. He touched the surface with a hoof. Immediately a ray slanted up, almost catching his foot before he jerked it back. "What's that?"

"A ray," Airy said. "Can you guess my talent?"

"What kind of ray is it?"

"A ray of sunshine."

Forrest touched the water again. The ray shot out, and this time he saw that it came from a large, flat creature deep under the surface. Was it safe to swim there? He doubted it. Maybe the ray just liked to illuminate the depths—but maybe that light was so it could better see its prey.

"I think I know the monster's talent," Imbri said in a dreamlet. "Did you notice how clearly it speaks? Its talent must be diction."

"Diction, Airy," Forrest cried. "That's your talent! You pronounce words."

"Curses, foiled again," the monster said, and retreated.

They walked on around the pond. But they weren't yet out of the comic strip. There was a thicket ahead, and as they tried to make their way through it, two puny orange imps dropped onto their shoulders. They were invisible, but Imbri made a dreamlet that showed them.

"Who are you," Forrest demanded, trying to shake off his imp.

"We are pun-kins," the one on his shoulder replied. "We are pundits who live in the pun-k trees of the pun-kin patch and pun-ch out anyone who dasts try to cross it, until he groans from the pun-ishment. We are very pun-ctual."

It figured. At least the imps seemed reasonably harmless. They plowed on, ignoring the imps' comments, and finally lunged out of the comic strip. The imps jumped off, not caring to be carried out of their element. "But you'll never know when we may strike again!" they called.

Now at last they were in the region of the fauns. But was there a suitable faun for his purpose?

Forrest stared, for there, running up to meet them, was something he had never seen or even imagined before. It had goat's hoofs, a tail, and the upper section of a human being. But it was female.

"Hello," she said, bouncing to a stop. She had a huge head of blond hair that flared out and down, framing her upper torso to the waist without covering anything. "I am Deanna Fauna. How may I help you, visitor from afar?"

"Fauna?" he echoed numbly. Yet it made sense. Fauns were crosses between humans and goats. Why shouldn't there be any female crosses? He had never heard of any, but this was the world of might be's, and indeed, there might be such creatures.

"I—am Forrest Faun from Xanth. I came to ask—" he faltered, halfway mesmerized by her bare front as she breathed. A true female of his species! What a discovery!

"Yes?" Her eyes were big and blue.

"I—I need a faun—or maybe a fauna—to come to be the spirit of the tree next to mine. So it won't fade. Do you—would you consider—"

"To be with you?" she finished. "Why of course; that's what faunas do. You must have been horribly unhappy, with only nymphs to chase, instead of the real thing."

Forrest hadn't thought of it quite that way, but realized that the case could be made. This did seem to be the answer to his quest. "Well, then you can come to Xanth, and—" He paused, realizing that he wasn't sure how she could do that, since she didn't have a body already in Xanth.

"It is done by going back in time," Imbri said. "The Good Magician explained it to me. He gave me a spell to enable me to take my spirit back to the conjugation of a faun and nymph, to enable them to have their signal actually reach the Stork Works. Then the stork would deliver Deanna as a baby fauna, and in due course she would grow to her present age and appearance. So she would be there, waiting for Deanna's spirit to animate her, at the same time as you return to re-animate your own body."

"Then she can become a real person," Forrest said. "Bound to her tree, remembering her past, growing gracefully older."

"Ugh!" Deanna exclaimed. "I didn't know there would be such penalties."

"But this is the nature of life in Xanth," he said. "Fauns and nymphs who adopt trees lose their shallowness and become real people.''

''Yuck! I couldn't stand it.''

''But you would be real. You would have substance. Xanth has different rules than Ptero. For example, time is not geography; no one can change his or her age just by traveling.''

''I would be stuck at one age all the time? I couldn't get old and wise or young and sexy any time I wanted?''

''Not without youth elixir.''

''Gross!''

Forrest stared at her, this time seeing her nature rather than her front. She was so shallow that she *liked* shallowness. This was no fault in an ordinary faun or nymph, but he discovered that he no longer cared for that type of association. He had learned too much of full human ways to ever return to contented mindlessness.

''I guess it wouldn't work out,'' he said with real regret. ''Are there any other fauns or faunas here who might feel otherwise?''

Deanna considered. ''There's Faust Faun. He's a bit odd. He chases fauns and hates trees.'' She ran off, her limited attention span exhausted.

That wouldn't do either. ''Then I guess what I'm looking for isn't here,'' Forrest said with regret. He looked at Imbri. ''Is there any point in remaining here any longer?''

''I'm afraid not,'' she said. ''I'm really sorry, Forrest.''

''Yet the Good Magician said—'' He paused again. Humfrey hadn't actually said anything, because he had refused even to hear the Question. Had this entire adventure been for nothing?

''I'm sure he meant to help you,'' Imbri said consolingly.

''He has a funny way of doing it!'' he retorted bitterly. ''And he even made you assist me, wasting your time too.''

''He always knows what he is doing. Maybe he refused your Question because there was no Answer for you. But he accepted mine, and I'm sure he will deliver.''

''You want a new pasture to gallop in,'' he said, remembering. ''Maybe this is that pasture, and you should stay here.''

''But I don't have enough mass to gallop,'' she reminded him. ''That's why I'm in nymph form.''

"Well, maybe on Pyramid, where you can be a full mare."

"And leave most of my soul here on Ptero? I would be nervous about that, as a permanent thing."

He sighed. "I guess so. Well, I will be glad to have your company a while longer. I hope the Good Magician has the very best pasture for you."

"I hope so too," she said. But she seemed less than enthusiastic.

They dissolved their bodies, becoming large vague shapes, then clouds, then growing blobs of thinning souls. They drifted into the sky. Forrest saw the patchwork world of Ptero spreading out below, and felt nostalgia. It had been a remarkable adventure, and he had enjoyed much of it. Especially the interaction with Dawn & Eve. But he had known that that relationship wouldn't last, and maybe it had been best that it had ended as abruptly as it had, with their discovery of princes of their own world. Unfortunately they had left their mark on him, leaving him forever disappointed with mere nymphs, as the scene with Deanna Fauna had shown. So this adventure had spoiled him; he would never be satisfied with the type of existence he had known before. *Thank you, Good Magician!* he thought with irony.

Now he saw Princess Ida's huge face. He continued to expand, orienting on his reposing body in the Tapestry chamber of Castle Roogna. But he didn't see Imbri's body. What had happened to it?

Then he realized that she didn't have a body in Xanth. She had only her half soul. Imbri did not exist as a living person here. The wonderful, supportive guide who had traveled with him through three weird worlds could not truly do so in this one. That was a loss of another nature.

He landed on his body and spread into it, animating it. But it was no glad homecoming. What did he have to return to? A failed quest, and what promised to be an insoluble loneliness of intellect.

He opened his eyes and sat up. "Oh, you are back!" Princess Ida said. "Do you have your answer?"

"No."

"But how can that be? I'm sure there was something there for you. Humfrey would not have sent you there otherwise."

He was too weary of it all to argue. "Maybe not. I'd better get on home now."

They went downstairs. There was a commotion, and two six year old children dashed around a corner, spied them, and skidded to a stop. "Aunt Ida!" Dawn cried.

"Forrest Faun!" Eve echoed.

Then both girls looked intently at Forrest, and split a smile between them. They looked eerily knowing.

Could these children have any notion of their adult association with him on other worlds?

"Don't let them bother you," Ida murmured. "Dawn can't really tell what's in your mind unless she touches you, and Eve can't tell where you've been unless she touches some object that was with you."

That was a relief. And in a moment the two dashed off, each hurling back half of a "Bye-bye." So he was safe from a potentially embarrassing scene.

Ida saw him to the front door. "I'm sure you have your answer," she said. "Perhaps you just don't yet know it."

Forrest shrugged. "Thank you for the use of your worlds," he said.

"You must return and tell me all about it," she said. "I am really curious to know what happened on Ptero."

"I'll do that," he said. "Once I am sure that my tree is well."

Then he faced outward and headed for home, feeling desolate.

"May I accompany you?"

"Imbri!" he exclaimed. "I thought you were gone."

Her faint human form appeared beside him. "No, I prefer to see you safely to your tree. I don't know when my assignment ends, but I think it's all right to do that much."

"But don't you want to go to the Good Magician for your new pasture?"

"Somehow that pasture has lost its appeal."

"I know the feeling. Did the adventure on the little worlds spoil you for regular existence, as it did me?"

"I fear it did, Forrest."

"I'm sorry. I never meant to ruin your life too."

"I really don't have a life. Just half a soul. So there wasn't much to be ruined."

He turned to her. "Oh, Imbri, I wish it hadn't happened! I was satisfied, until this."

"I *wasn't* satisfied. So my loss is less than yours. I wish I could console you, Forrest."

"If I could go back to Ptero, I'd let you console me. In fact—" He hesitated, surprised. "I wish I had played Faun & Nymph with you, on Ptero, when you offered. Now I never can."

"But you wanted a real nymph."

"No. I wanted a real person. And you are that, Imbri."

"But I'm an animal."

"In the same sense I am. Somewhere in my ancestry the human and caprine stocks got together, so I am mostly human at the top and goat at the bottom. You are equine in body, but human in mind, as your nice animation of the nymph form showed."

"Thank you," she said sadly. "I would gladly have played with you, when I had solidity."

They encountered two folk going along the path, looking lost: a young man and a short haired, green eyed cat. In fact they looked about the way Forrest felt, so he paused to address them. "Are you looking for something?"

"The Region of Madness," the man said. "I'm Christopher 'Joker' Justino. I think I'm either coming from it or going to it, I'm not sure which. I thought Bluejay knew the way, but now I think she's lost."

"You're from Mundania!" Forrest said.

"I guess."

"Tell him to keep going the way they're going," Imbri said. "The Region of Madness is shrinking, but there's still plenty of it to the south."

Forrest remembered that others couldn't see or hear Imbri, unless she planted a dreamlet in their minds. So he relayed the message. Man and cat thanked him and moved on.

Then Forrest realized something. "They're like us!" he exclaimed. "Without bearings, depressed, not knowing or much caring where they're going."

"Because they can't go back to where they were, and wouldn't want to anyway," Imbri agreed. "Oh, Forrest, if it weren't for your obligation to your tree, I would truly wish we could go back to Ptero.''

''Maybe to keep company with Cathryn Centaur, or on Pyramid,'' he agreed.

''Or even on Torus, if Ida cared to share the Isle of Niffen,'' she said dreamily. As a day mare, she was very good at dreams.

''I remember how that odd beautiful woman Chlorine with the ugly dragon ass said that when I got back, I would be happier than I have ever been. Instead I am sadder.''

''You surely are,'' she agreed. ''At least I will be able to make Jenny Elf happier, when I deliver Vision Centaur's message about the gen-e-tic to fix her vision.''

''Oh, yes, I had forgotten about that. That's nice.''

Something swirled ahead of them. It coalesced into a familiar demoness. ''So you're back! But where is your fellow faun?''

''Please don't tease me, demoness,'' he said tiredly. ''I'm really not in the mood for it.''

''I'm sorry. I didn't mean to.''

He glanced sharply at her. ''You are apologizing?''

''I am the Demoness Metria. I have a quarter of a soul. So I do care somewhat.''

''But it was the Demoness Mentia I talked to before.''

''Yes, my worser half. She's baby-sitting Demon Ted while I stretch my substance. So I came to check on you, following her report. What happened?''

''My quest failed.''

''Oh, no! What then of the clog tree?''

''I don't know.''

''But didn't the Good Magician help you?''

''Not that I know of.''

''Well, I feel a quarter bad about this, so I'll help you slightly. I'll give you a lift back to your tree.''

''That isn't necessary.''

But she was already firming her hands under his elbows and lifting him up. In a moment he was flying above the trees, and then over the Gap Chasm. Actually this did help, because he would have had a problem crossing the Gap on his own. He did need to get back to his sandalwood tree promptly, because he wasn't sure how much time had passed. There was no sense losing two trees instead of one.

She set him down in the glade between the trees, where in the past he had celebrated with nymphs. "Bye," she said, and faded out.

"Wait!" he cried.

She faded back in. "Eyb?" she asked.

"I met your son Chaos. His talent is to make things transparent."

"But I don't have such a son."

"Not yet. But I think he's on the way. Did you signal the stork again?"

She toted up the count on her fingertips. "Seven hundred and fifty times in the past year."

"One of the signals must have gotten through."

"Fancy that," she said, pleased, and faded out again.

"That was nice of her, giving you the lift," Imbri said. "She's a different creature since she got that half soul. So am I, since I got mine."

Forrest ran to his tree. It was all right; the spell had maintained it. He hugged it, then nerved himself for the unpleasant chore.

"Where are you going?" Imbri asked.

"To tell the clog tree that I have failed. I hate this, but it wouldn't be right to let it fade without knowing."

"You're a nice person."

"No. I'm a failed person."

The clog tree, too, was in good order, thanks to the spell. But Forrest knew it wouldn't be, after he told it his bad news. So he dawdled, feeling ashamed, but unable to squeeze the unkind words out just yet.

Imbri walked up to the tree. "I like your clogs," she said.

Then something strange happened. Misty colors flitted through the foliage of the tree, forming into an image. It looked like a woodland scene, a lovely little glade in the morning. Flowers blossomed around its edges, and water flowed into a pool in its center. A lovely dark-haired nymph sat sunning herself on a slab of sandstone, running a crystal comb through her lustrous tresses.

A figure appeared behind her. It was a man, no, a faun. He put his hands over the nymph's eyes, then bent down and kissed her on the mouth.

Then he brought out his panpipes and played a merry melody; the little black notes rose up, scattering across the scene. Some of them turned white, assuming the form of little storks. As he played, he danced. In a moment she got up and danced with him. They moved around the glade, in a mock chase, kicking their feet high to the music. But his dance was faster than hers, and soon he caught up to her. The panpipes disappeared as they joyously embraced and celebrated.

Then they adjourned to the meal she had evidently prepared: lemon herbal tea, oatcakes, and an assortment of creamy goat cheeses. He teasingly offered her a horse nut, but she declined any more after the first bite. Tiny hummingbirds flew in to perch on the stones and on the faun and nymph. They were all colors, scintillating like gems: topaz, ruby, opal, and lapis lazuli.

Suddenly Forrest recognized the figures. They were himself and Imbri in her nymph form. But what were they doing in a picture in the foliage of the tree?

He tried to make sense of it. Imbri had gone to stand close to the tree, and then the scene had formed. With the two of them in it. Loving each other. As if the tree had somehow picked up Imbri's secret thoughts and animated them. The dreams of a night mare.

A glorious suspicion washed through him. He reached over his shoulder and plunged his hand into his knapsack. He found the dear horn and hauled it out. As he did so, a fragment of paper fluttered down. It must have been caught in the horn. He reached down to pick it up. Could it be the lost notes of the Good Magician?

No, it was a different piece, royally embossed. A single word was written on it, in a princessly script: *Imbri*.

Suddenly he remembered when Dawn had touched them, on Torus, and learned something she wouldn't tell. She had talked with Ida, and then hugged and kissed Forrest, her special favor done. But she had never said what it was. She must have slipped this note into his knapsack, under the cover of her embrace. Her answer about the identity of the creature he was looking for.

But why hadn't she just told him? Now that came clear too. If she had, his quest would have ended right there—and his mission with Dawn & Eve wasn't yet complete. It might have been out of his control; he and Imbri might have dissolved into soul substance and gone back to Xanth, unable to stop themselves. Leaving the human section of Ptero to its fate of marginalization. So Dawn couldn't tell him, until after that was done. But she wanted to tell him immediately, so that her love for him would be equal to Eve's. So she had done so, in her fashion, giving him a note that he would be sure to see eventually.

He lifted the dear horn and blew. The delightful sound went out, and echoed from Imbri, though she had no substance. She was indeed the one.

She had turned and was looking at him, not understanding. "Imbri—I saw your dream. Of you and me, together. The tree animated it."

"Oh!" she said, blushing.

"Are you willing to become the spirit of the tree, to share its fate until the end?"

"But I can't. I have no substance."

"Yes you can. And if you do, the tree will lend you enough substance to make a solid body. A nymph—or a mare, so you can gallop in new pastures. Spirits help trees; trees help spirits. They are bound together. And you and I can be together physically. As in your dream."

"But I never thought—"

"Why did you do so much more for me than was required by your Service to the Good Magician?"

"I wanted to be sure you succeeded."

"What about when the twin princesses were seducing me? You never interfered."

"I wanted you to be happy."

"But don't you see—that's true love! You were doing everything for me, with no thought for yourself."

She blushed again, unable to deny it.

"And why didn't you return to the Good Magician for your Answer, when your Service was done? Because it *was* done, even if my part of it seemed unsuccessful.''

''I just—didn't want to leave you,'' she said.

''And you thought there was no way that the two of us could be together in Xanth. You didn't know about what trees offer.''

''I didn't know,'' she agreed.

''But the tree knew. As soon as you came near, it knew. Its spirit interacted with yours. It was that interaction I saw.''

She nodded. ''But the Good Magician surely knew. Why didn't he tell me?''

''Because I wasn't ready. I thought that all I wanted was a faun for the tree. But in the course of the adventure I learned some of the human breadth and depth of mind and emotion. That left me forever unsatisfied with less. The Good Magician wouldn't take my Question because he knew it was the wrong one. He knew that I was your Answer—for you didn't know your real desire either. It wasn't for a new pasture, it was for true love. And I could be that love—once I learned how. And now I know that neither nymph nor human woman is what is right for me. What I need is a companion who has a similar length of life to my own. Who truly understands. Who I can love and be loved by. And that is you, Imbri. It was always you. It just wasn't always me.''

''This is so hard to believe.''

''Just adopt the clog tree. Then we will play out your dream scene. While you learn to believe, I will learn to love you. I am already falling.'' For he saw the little hearts forming, orbiting his head like tiny moons. They were shaping into gem-like hummingbirds. She was perfect for him, and not only because they had shared an experience like no other.

''Oh, you mustn't fall and crash,'' she said. She turned to the tree, stretching out her arms. As she did so, the foliage became brilliant, and her body became solid, in the form of a lovely nymph: small but perfect.

Then she turned back to Forrest, to catch him before he fell too far.

Author's Note

When I wrote this novel, I was reminded of the fifth Xanth novel, *Ogre, Ogre,* because that one introduced a wild new setting of Xanth: the world of dreams, inside the gourd. This twenty-first Xanth novel, *Faun & Games,* introduces the wild new settings of Ida's moons. I love them, and I hope that my readers do too. Whether there will be more adventures there I don't know; not immediately, as the next novel will relate to zombies.

When I started on this one in Jamboree 1996 I checked my list of reader sent notions, and discovered there were 300—and more were piling in. It wasn't possible to use them all. There are limits, even to Xanth, and the story comes first. Readers seem to be unable to stifle their urge to emit puns. But not all readers like puns. So I try to maintain a healthy, or at least tolerable, balance. The problem can be shown by this example, which occurred while I was writing *Faun*: a reader wrote to suggest that too many puns were degrading Xanth, so I should slow them down. Then he concluded his letter with a page and a half of more puns. Any questions?

Some readers send me multi-page notions for future Xanth stories. I consider these, but often they just don't fit in the framework I have. It's much easier to invent my own story than to work from notions suggested by others. The idea most often suggested is the talent of borrowing talents from others. I finally have reference to it in this novel, and do give a credit, but at the risk of alienating hundreds of readers who suggested it before and haven't been credited.

This time I used reader notions dating from 1993–96, trying to give preference to older ones, and managed to catch up on most of them through FeBlueberry 1995, and scattered ones thereafter. So there are over 100 waiting for the next novel. I'm still making notes of good ones, but this seems to be a losing race; each novel I am further behind. So for those of you who hoped to see your notions here, and didn't: maybe next time. I'm really in the business of writing novels, not publishing lists of names. It's not that your notions are bad, just that there are too many of them.

Meanwhile, my dull mundane life continued as I wrote this novel. I am not entirely sure why readers want to know about my personal existence, but they complain when I don't mention it, and on occasion I'll get a letter inquiring whether I have died. No, not that I know of. I gave a talk for the "Last Lecture" series at the University of South Florida, the theme of this series being that if you knew it was to be your last lecture ever, what would you say? I thought about it, and concluded that I would want to let others know what I had learned, in the course of my researches for my serious writing—the GE-ODYSSEY historical fiction series—about the nature of mankind. So I told of the evolution of our species from Australopithecus to the present, of the complications entailed by learning to walk two-footed, of the "triple ploy" women use to capture and hold men, and the true nature of dreams, which are actually the brain's "downtime" processing of the experiences of the day for cross-referencing and long-term memory. The following month I talked at the American Humanist convention in Florida, telling a love story adapted from the third GEODYSSEY novel, relating to the global crisis we face and the manner in which two communities, survivalist and pacifist, manage to work together to survive it, despite their opposite philosophies. No, not many laughs in these talks; both were deadly serious. For laughs, come to Xanth.

This was the first novel I wrote completely on Windows 95 and Word 7 on my new Pentium system. These are powerful programs, and slowly I am coming to like them, and especially the ergonomic keyboard, which looks like a Salvador Dali painting. The programs were the least user-friendly to learn, compared to CP/M and DOS and many applications thereon, but the most powerful. I remain irritated that I can no longer use the number-pad "Enter" key to do my Saves, and that the keyboard cursor, renamed the vaguely obscene "Insertion Point," is almost invisible and can't be made into a visible square as in DOS, and that there is no ongoing indication which files are Saved or Unsaved (you have to do a special check on each, which Unsaves it; only an idiot would set it up that way), but other features are beautiful, such as the Auto-Correct that fixes things as I type; True-Type that enables me to ensure that it will print exactly as it looks on-screen, with a wide variety of fonts; and the range of views and colors and sizes I can have on-screen for convenience. So now I have green Courier New 12 print on a brown background for my novel text, and yellow Times New Roman 10 print for related notes, so I know instantly what text I'm in. Revisions stand out in cyan, and deletions in purple. I made a 42 keystroke macro that splits the screen, puts postage stamp sized images of my pages in the upper pane, and 140% size type in the lower pane, so I can see the whole page format at the same time as reading the comfortable magnified print, with alternate views on tap when I want them. Ain't magic wonderful!

Some years back I had a problem with my tongue: it got sore when it touched one place in my mouth. A host of specialists could not fix the problem. I remember one: he listened carefully to my description, then checked it by pulling my tongue about a foot from my face and poking his finger two inches through the bottom of my mouth. Okay, so this is a subjective impression; still, it gives me a notion how a horse feels when the vet grabs its tongue. I think my dentist thought the problem was elsewhere in my head, but he made me a stint to protect my tongue from that place, and it works. I still use it. Once I was at a party, and it came out when I was eating, so I put it on the napkin; then my wife threw the napkin away. No, it was an accident; she went and fished through the garbage until she recovered it. And, yes, I did wash it before I put it back in my mouth. I do keep my mouth clean, whatever critics may think; I brush my teeth carefully three times a day, use a special little brush shaped like a Christmas tree once a day, and floss once a week. I also watch my diet, staying generally clear of sweets and alcohol, and of course I am a vegetarian. Yet still my gums recede, making my teeth sensitive and at risk for decay. During this novel it got worse; my gum was festering in one place and the tooth and bone structure were deteriorating. What was the matter? So my dentist sent me to a periodontist, who discovered that it was a specific problem in an otherwise healthy mouth: one root of a root canal job had gotten unsealed, and infection had weaseled in. So he in turn is sending me on to an endodontist, to see if it can be repaired. It seems it's easier to do a root canal than to repair a bad one. Thus my continuing adventures in dentistry, strictly of the mundane kind.

I also exercise. For over a decade I ran three miles cross country, three times a week, but finally the sand-spurs (Florida's version of curse-burrs), sugar sand, thorny blackberry bushes, biting flies, and vicissitudes of weather got to me, and I moved it indoors. I used a stationary cycle with connected handles to exercise the arms as well as the legs, and I read publications like *Liberal Opinion Week* and *New Scientist* and several health newsletters while doing so, so it didn't get dull. But those machines wear out or break down, and it happened again during this novel. This time we bought a self-powered treadmill with arm handles. But how could I read? So we bought a music stand to hold the magazines, but it was too short. So we set it up on a stool with a square of plywood on top, but then it was too far away. So my wife brought out her needlework stretcher frame stand, which is a weird multi-jointed wooden device, and clamped it below the top section of the music stand. It was unbalanced, so we put a small roll of fence wire on its feet to stabilize it. And it worked! Now I can read again while exercising. All it takes is a treadmill, stool, plywood, fence wire, needlework apparatus, music stand, and a magazine.

In other respects, life had some unusual aspects. The hottest year on record, 1995, was followed by our coldest winter in some time. As I finished the novel, the Comet Hyakutake passed; my wife and I went out at odd hours of the night to try to outsmart the ornery trees and clouds and moon so as to catch a glimpse of it. I mean, if the brightest comet in five centuries comes to celebrate the completion of my novel, the least I can do is look at it.

Folk also ask about Jenny, my paralyzed correspondent who had been hit at age twelve by a drunk driver, as described in *Letters to Jenny*. I still write to her every week. At this writing she's nineteen, and still mostly paralyzed, but she can say several words in one breath, can walk several steps when buttressed by leg braces and a wraparound walker, and uses a computer to facilitate communication. She hopes to go to college, if it can be arranged. But her life is complicated by continuing bouts of jaw surgery and the need for constant attendance. All because one drunk just couldn't wait for schoolchildren with the right of way to get out of *his* way.

At this time I also read a book, Robert A. Heinlein's *Grumbles from the Grave*. Heinlein was arguably the science fiction genre's greatest writer. It's a collection of his letters, mostly to his literary agent Lurton Blassingame, who was also my agent, describing his reactions to idiot editing, critics who pretended to know what was in his mind, the demands of fans who thought he should drop everything and give them his full time, requests for attendance at numerous functions, his travels, and thoughts on life. I relate to it very well, having encountered the same problems. It's as if other folk believe that a writer's novels spring full-blown from the head of Zeus, requiring no effort, so that the writer's time has no value. One reader angrily stopped reading my novels when he learned that I normally work from 9 A.M. to 8 P.M., seven days a week, catching up on reading during meals and exercise, always behind on the mail and whatever else is demanding my attention. I love writing, but it has been decades since I had actual free time; the mail has taken all of it away. I simply do the things I need to do, and try to catch up after.

But that mail has its rewards. I have been credited with saving a number of lives, simply by responding to those who are suicidally depressive, and with teaching a number of children the joys of reading, because they found my funny fantasy the first interesting books. I have grown because of what I have learned from my readers. It is also clear that I will never run out of ideas; my readers are eager to share theirs with me.

Here, at any rate, is the list of credits for this novel, roughly in order of appearance. One of them I am unable to credit, because it dates from a decade or so back and I no longer have the correspondence, but it still deserves a mention. It was a letter from a girl in the neighborhood of twelve who sent me a picture of her ideal planet for a fantasy setting: a triangle. I pointed out that probably it wasn't flat, but three dimensional, like a pyramid with four triangular faces, and she agreed. That was it; she has since disappeared into adulthood, I'm sure. But the notion remained, and finally I decided to use it. So if by chance that vanished girl is still reading Xanth, this is my credit for the notion. Thank you for Pyramid.

Shorter shrift to the others, though they are similarly deserving: Kara Oke—Sarah P. Bonnett. Gladiolas, horse radishes, Ray D O, Alpha Centauri, Attila the Pun—Katie Leonard. Com Passion—Gordon Johnson. Compatible female computer for Com Pewter; Cathyrn Centaur, with talent of blankets—Karla Sussman. Pewter chips— Dana Bates, Gregory Masseau, Andrew Graff. Cereal port for the mouse—Thomas-Dwight, Sawyer, Dorr. Demoness Sire, Deanna Fauna—Sarah Curran. Doughnut—Nicole R. Fuller. Psychologist shrinks folk—Rachel Gutin. Mer-dragon—Thomas Ferguson. Locomotive, Rave-on, talent of changing things to strawberry jam, talent of charisma, Ark-hives with books—K. Benjamin Perilstein. Dot, with spots on wall talent—Eugene Laubert. Talent of frightening folk—Danny Barton. LA as a name—Chris Seagrave. Air mattresses in the Nameless Castle—Adam Ross. Kero, winged unicorn—Vickie Roberts. Chemare, centaur night mare—Lizzy Prosser. Ilura, centaur filly—Ilura Windus. Imina and Imino Hurry—Rich Frazier. Dear horn, invisible ink pen—Jennie Metcalf. Vision Centaur, gen-e-tic— Patrick M. Burns. Gallop poll—Misty Zaebst. Half brother, Glitter Golem—Mandy Owston. Jelly fish; cat people—Nick Lawton. Sock that punches, jump rope—Lara Petredis and Amy Baniecki. Bay-bee—Robert Cobb. Polynomial plant with square roots, turtle recall—Kenneth Cain. Knuckleheads—Carl A Snodgrass. Venetian blinds—Thomas Sawyer Dorr. See weed—Erin Hoffman. See-an-enemy—Jake Watters. B's, tac-tic—Stephen Monteith. Punnsylvania punitentiary—Neil Ballou. R-tickle bush, head line— Ari S. Rapport. Spaghetti plant—Ken "Wirehead" Wronklewicz. Man-Age-Mint—Liz Driver. Fourteen crosses, and the "crossing" crosses; petrified wood—Robert Charles Pickthall. Revy—Jamie Mastros. Demos; Wigo, Hugo and Wira's daughter—Kenneth D. Hardy. Nigel—Star Nicholson. Talent of being the exception (Scintilla)—Sarah Gordon. Talent of entering books and changing their story lines (Hugh Mongus)—Brian J. Laughman. Miss Gnomer—Richard Vallence. Canary Island, C-gulls, night hawk, mockingbird—Malcolm Jones. Owl Tree—Patrick J. Hall. Waterfoul—Debby Enloe. Good Magician's castle on Ptero—Ray Koenig. A funeral procession in Xanth—Seth Poor. The stork's view—Nick Kiefel. Justin Case—Mike Weber, Meghan Jones, Laura Petredis, Amy Baniecki. Justin Time—Brandon Eller, Laura Petredis, Amy Baniecki. The play Raven, Sonata Socksorter. Miss Take, Out Take—Dale Saunders. Dawn & Eve description: Dawn Mynatt. Dawn & Eve go on a quest—Emily Ashcroft. Lings who do the impossible—Adam Williams. The seas: jealous, Indecen, Mer; sham rock—Wayne Gile. Sham rock makes you deceitful; Cat-I-pillar—Kirsten Slotter. Nightshade and sweetgum trees—Tyler Merchant. Assorted teas—served by June Bugg, a character in the fiction of Don Edward Davis. Spellcheck—Vicky Peterson. Talent: changing the color of the sky—Michael Ferreira. Throwing the voice, Hand gun—Kate McCrimmon. Ultra-Violent light bulb—Mat Powerman Powers. Jan Itor, A. Lert, talent of sending the wind—Matt Trost. Tooth-paste, Electra's outlet—Meghan Jones. De-odor-ant—Benny Irizarry. Mountain goat, Polly Morph, Ghina—Jennifer Gregory. All ears creature—Chris Higgins. Todd Loren—Lori Munion. Lady Winter—Mike Ferreira. The super tangle tree, the Golem King—Jay W. Harmon. Hollow Day—Dale Saunders, Saaun Kline. Isle of Niffen—Sarah Schmidt. Talent of putting folk to sleep—Chris Robinson. Geddy Goblin—Stacy Ksenzakovic. Jfraya—Cheryle Koch. Talent of drawing a door that opens—Johnny Fink. Wolf spider howling—Sasha Skinner. Tea tree, Tree Tea—Brandon Eller. More fancy teas, seven bulls—Samantha Parsons. Ilene, Gerrod—Angella Castellano. Dire wolf, King Cobra—Robin Tang. Largemouth bass—Kris Stroup. Chess nut, Hu Man—Gregory Masseau. Kerby—Robin Jeffreys. Steel plant, stratagems—Carl A. Snodgrass. Basketball—Katie Leonard, Daniel Chambers. Toe jam from toe berries—Caroline Wilson. Pi tree with 3.14 pies, Guardian angle, Polly Graph—Eric Steiger. Geis-a girl—Kirsten Slotter's dad. Grey Murphy taking away magic, as punishment—Veronica Frank. Talent of blessing—Trista Casey. Grounds for divorce; cuss toady—Sue DiCamillo. Tropical depression—Donovan Lee Beeson. Atlas Mountains—Daniel Chambers. Bookworm—Shelly Robichard. Ten centaurs (of thirty-five)—Christopher "Joker" Justino. Bluejay—Angela C. Moerschell. Bull horn—Larry Hornbaker. When mites go up, tites come down—Mr. Ferguson or Professor Martin, relayed by Sheryl Stewart, who isn't sure which man told it. Orc tree, Cerci—Jamie Malos. Watch band—Nathan Paquette. Watch dogs— Richard A. Medlin. Grant & Isabella, Grey & Ivy's children—Amy Whitacre and Brookie Butler. Emily Carolyn, with talent of borrowing talent for an hour—Carolyn Bernhard. Arien, talent of borrowing talents—Robyn Fitkin. Nora Naga—Katie Green. Son of Trent and Iris ages rapidly; talent of reversing talents—Zoë Marriott. Misty Meanor—Margaret Fitzgerald. Children of Girard & Gina Giant— (anonymous because I forgot to list the credit). Chaos, son of Metria—Devon Prewitt. Talent of making things transparent—Emily Waddy. Mourning & Knight Naga—Dwayne E. Favors. Barking lot, Airy with diction—Liz Homsy. Ray of sunshine—Ray Koenig. Punkins—Cliff Roberts. Faun & nymph glade scene—Barbara Hay Hummel.

I'll try to use up more of the pun backlog in the next one, *Zombie Lover,* a year hence, if they don't rot first.